A GOOD DAY
FOR A
MASSACRE

Look for these exciting Western series
from bestselling authors
William W. Johnstone and J.A. Johnstone

The Mountain Man

Preacher: The First Mountain Man

Luke Jensen: Bounty Hunter

Those Jensen Boys!

The Jensen Brand

Matt Jensen

MacCallister

The Red Ryan Westerns

Perley Gates

Have Brides, Will Travel

The Hank Fallon Westerns

Will Tanner, Deputy U.S. Marshal

Shotgun Johnny

The Chuckwagon Trail

The Jackals

The Slash and Pecos Westerns

The Texas Moonshiners

A GOOD DAY FOR A MASSACRE

WILLIAM W. JOHNSTONE
and
J.A. JOHNSTONE

KENSINGTON BOOKS
www.kensingtonbooks.com

KENSINGTON BOOKS are published by

Kensington Publishing Corp.
119 West 40th Street
New York, NY 10018

All Kensington titles, imprints, and distributed lines are available at special quantity discounts for bulk purchases for sales promotion, premiums, fund-raising, educational, or institutional use.

Special book excerpts or customized printings can also be created to fit specific needs. For details, write or phone the office of the Kensington Special Sales Manager: Attn. Special Sales Department. Kensington Publishing Corp., 119 West 40th Street, New York, NY 10018. Phone: 1-800-221-2647.

Kensington and the K logo Reg. U.S. Pat. & TM Off.

Library of Congress Card Catalogue Number: 2019951362

ISBN-13: 978-1-4967-2416-8
ISBN-10: 1-4967-2416-X
First Kensington Hardcover Edition: March 2020

10 9 8 7 6 5 4 3 2 1

Printed in the United States of America

CHAPTER 1

"You two old scalawags stop that wagon and throw your guns down, or we'll fill you so full of lead, they'll need an ore dray to haul you to Boot Hill!"

The shout had vaulted down from somewhere on the forested ridge jutting on the right side of the old wagon trail. The words echoed around the narrow canyon before dwindling beneath the crashing rattle of the freight wagon's stout, iron-shod wheels.

Jimmy "Slash" Braddock turned to his partner, Melvin Baker, aka the Pecos River Kid, sitting on the freight wagon's seat to his left, and said, "Whose callin' us old?"

Driving the wagon, handling the reins gently in his gloved hands, Pecos turned to Slash and scowled. "Who . . . *what?*"

"Someone just called us old."

Pecos lifted his head and looked around, blinking his lake-blue eyes beneath his snuff-brown Stetson's broad brim. "I didn't hear nothin'."

"You didn't hear someone call us old from up on that ridge yonder?"

"Hell, no—I didn't hear a damn thing. I think you're imaginin' things, Slash. It's probably old-timer's disease."

"Old-timer's disease, my butt." Slash's brown-eyed gaze

was perusing the stony ridge peppered with lodgepole pines and firs, all cloaked in sparkling, smoking gowns of high-mountain sunshine. "I heard someone insult us way out here on the devil's hindquarters."

A rifle cracked on the ridge. The bullet punched into the trail several feet ahead of the two lead mules and spanged shrilly off a rock. Instantly, the mules tensed, arching their tails and necks. The off leader loosed a shrill bray.

"Whoa!" Pecos said, hauling back on the reins. "Whoa there, you cayuses!"

As Pecos stopped the mules, Slash snapped up his Winchester '73, pumping a live round into the action. He'd started to raise the rifle, to aim up the ridge, when another rifle barked—this one on his and Pecos's left. The bullet cracked loudly into the wagon panel two feet behind Pecos. The sound evoked a low ringing in Slash's ears; it made his heart kick like a branded calf.

Pecos flinched.

As men who'd spent over half their lives riding the owlhoot trail, robbing trains and stagecoaches and evading posses and bounty hunters, they were accustomed to being shot at. That didn't mean they'd ever gotten comfortable with it.

"You were told to throw your weapons down, buckos!" said a man with a British accent from the pine-clad slope on the trail's left side, on the heels of the rifle crack's dwindling echoes. "You won't be told a third time. You'll just be blasted out of that wagon boot to bloody hell an' gone!"

Slash glanced at Pecos, who sat back on the hard wooden seat, holding the reins taut against his chest. Pecos returned Slash's dark look, then lifted one corner of his mouth, clad in a silver-blond goatee that matched the color of his long, stringy hair, in a woeful half-smile.

Slash cursed. He eased the Winchester's hammer down against the firing pin, then tossed the rifle into some soft-looking brush to his right. Pecos set the wagon's brake, wrapped the reins around the whipsock, then tossed away his Colt's revolving rifle, which had been leaning against the seat between him and Slash.

Crunching, scraping footsteps sounded to Slash's right. He turned to see a man descending the steep, talus-strewn ridge on the trail's right side, weaving through the scattered pines. He held a Spencer repeating rifle in one hand, aiming it out from his right hip while he used his free hand to grab tree trunks and branches to break his fall.

"Now, the hoglegs!" he shouted as he approached the bottom of the canyon.

He appeared to be a young man—whipcord lean and wearing a shabby black suit coat coppered with age over a ragged buckskin shirt unbuttoned halfway down his bony, hairless chest. A badly mistreated opera hat sat askew on his head, from which a tangled mess of lusterless, sandy hair hung straight down to his shoulders.

An old-model Colt jostled in a soft brown holster hanging loose on his right leg.

He stopped near the bottom of the trail, sidled up to a stout pine, and aimed the rifle straight out from his right shoulder, narrowing one coyote eye down the barrel at Slash's head. "Ain't gonna tell you old tinhorns again. Just gonna drill you a third eye. One you can't see out of!"

He gave a crow-like caw of laughter, obviously pleased with his own joke.

"More insults," Slash said, staring at the coyote-faced youngster. He couldn't have been much over twenty. The scars from a recent bout of pimples remained on his cheeks and forehead. "First we're old scalawags. Now we're tinhorns."

"You fellas are startin' to hurt our feelin's," said the Pecos River Kid, looking from the younker on the right side of the trail to the Brit now descending the slope on the trail's left side.

"We'll hurt more than that, old man," said the limey as he dropped down even with the kid, on the opposite side of the trail. He was older but not any better-looking. "If'n you don't shed those shootin' irons I can plainly see residin' in your belt sheaths, you're gonna be snugglin' with the diamondbacks. The knives, too. Nice bowies, they appear. Might have to confiscate those. I'm a knife man, myself. Had to be in the Four Point. I have quite a collection, and an ever-growin' one, I might add."

He smiled, showing large, horsey teeth the color of old ivory. "I keep 'em sharp enough to split hairs with, don't ya know." The smile grew more suggestive, menacing.

Slash exchanged another dark glance with Pecos. Slash carefully slid his two matched, stag-butted Colt .44s from their holsters—one positioned for the cross-draw on his left hip, the other thonged on his right thigh—and tossed them away, again aiming for a relatively soft landing. As a man who'd lived his life depending on his guns to stay alive, he didn't like mistreating them.

Pecos wore only one pistol—a big, top-break Russian .44—in a holster tied down on his right thigh. He pulled the big popper free of its holster with two fingers and heaved it into some brush on the trail's left side, near where the limey stood aiming his Winchester at him.

When he and Slash had both gotten shed of their bowie knives as well, the two ex-cutthroats and current freighters sat in uneasy silence, hands raised shoulder-high, palms out. Slash didn't like this position. He wasn't used to it. He was usually the one calling the shots and facing men staring back at him, warily, with their own hands raised shoulder-high.

He hadn't realized what an uneasy feeling it was, having guns held on you, your life almost literally in the hands of someone else. Someone who might just have an itchy trigger finger, like the scrawny kid in the opera hat, for instance. The kid not only looked like he had an itch to sling some lead, but the maniacal glint in his coyote eyes told Slash he had a fondness for killing.

Or at least for inflicting fear.

The kid and the limey continued on down the slope, keeping their rifles aimed at Slash and Pecos. As they did, two more men appeared, stepping out from behind boulders on either side of the trail, thirty and fifty yards beyond, respectively, where the trail doglegged to the left.

One was a big, beefy Mexican in a shabby suit that was two sizes too small for him. He'd probably stolen the garb off some hapless wayfarer now feeding buzzards in a deep mountain ravine. He wore a bowler hat and two sidearms, and was wielding a Winchester Yellowboy rifle. A thick, black mustache drooped down over the corners of his mouth.

The other man was almost as big as the Mexican, but he was older, maybe in his forties. He had red hair beneath a black slouch hat. He was dressed in a paisley vest and sleeve garters, like a pimp or a gambler, and he carried a double-barreled shotgun at port arms across his chest—a grim, angry-looking gent with a large, wide slab of a face outfitted with small, gray eyes set too far apart, giving him the look of a demented mongrel. All four were likely riding a bout of hard luck in these remote mountains, probably having followed gold veins to nowhere. They'd probably thrown in together to make do, which meant haunting lonely trails for pilgrims to plunder and send nestling with the diamondbacks.

The redheaded mongrel's thick lips were set in a hard line. His ratty string tie blew back over one shoulder as he caught up to the Mexican, and they stopped about ten feet out beyond the two lead mules, who shifted uneasily in their hames and traces.

"How much you carryin'?" asked the red-haired man, giving his chin a belligerent rise and shoving it forward.

"I'll do the askin', Cord," said the Brit.

"Get on with it then," Cord said, an angry flush blazing in his nose.

The Mexican grinned as though nothing thrilled him like dissention.

The limey turned to Slash and Pecos. "How much you carryin'?"

The kid squealed a little laugh. The Mexican's grin broadened.

Their demeanors told Slash that they weren't professionals, and that they hadn't been together long. Sure enough, they'd merely thrown in together to try their hands at highway robbery for a stake that would take them to the Southwest before the first winter snows. Their types were a dime a dozen on the western frontier.

"What're you talkin' about?" Slash said.

"Don't let's chase the nanny goat around the apple orchard," the kid said, canting his head and twisting his face angrily. "We seen you comin' up this trail two days ago. You had a good load on ya. You came up from Fort Collins. We followed you out of town. Now, your wagon bed is empty, and we're thinkin' you mighta made a tidy little sum for deliverin' them goods up to one o' the minin' camps in the higher reaches."

Pecos glanced at his partner and said, "Slash, I think they're fixin' to rob us of our hard-earned wages. What do you think of that?"

"I don't like it, Pecos. I don't like it one bit."

Pecos looked at the limey and then at the kid standing on the opposite side of the trail from him, aiming his rifle out from his right hip. "Why don't you four raggedy-heeled vermin get yourselves some honest jobs? Try workin' for a livin'!"

Given his and Slash's shared past, Slash glanced at him skeptically. Pecos caught the glance and shrugged it off.

"Wait, wait, wait," the kid said, scowling again, again canting his head to one side and staring at the two former cutthroats through skeptically narrowed eyes. "Did you say *Slash* an' *Pecos?*"

Slash winced.

Now that he and Pecos had given up their outlaw ways and had bought a freight company in Fort Collins and become honest, hard-working, and more or less upstanding citizens, he and his partner had tried to forget their old handles and call each other by their given names instead. Slash was now Jim or Jimmy, and Pecos was now Mel or Melvin.

Old habits died hard.

The kid grinned like the cat that ate the canary and slapped his thigh. "I'll be damned!"

"What?" asked the Mex.

The kid glanced at each of his long coulee-riding partners in turn and said, "You know who these two old coots are?"

"Who?" asked the limey.

"Why, they're Slash Braddock and the Pecos River Kid, that's who!" The kid threw his head back and laughed, showing that he was missing one of his eyeteeth.

"You mean," said the Brit, dubiously, "you think these two old men sitting here in this freight wagon are Slash an' Pecos?" He stared at the two freighters and shook his head. "No. No. Nonsense. You're gettin' soft in your thinker box, Donny boy."

"We ain't that old, fer chrissakes!" Slash said, scowling angrily at the younger men, all four of whom were now laughing at him and his partner. "We ain't but fifty or so . . ."

"Give 'er take," put in Pecos.

"Whatever," Slash said. "That hardly makes us old men. Besides, were you fellas raised by wolves? Don't you know you're supposed to respect your elders, not rob and belittle 'em?"

The limey shook his head again and stared in disbelief at the two middle-aged freighters. "Damn, you two sure have changed. I've seen pictures of you both in the illustrated newspapers, an', an', well . . ."

"Yeah, well, we all get older," Slash said, indignant. "Just wait—it'll happen to you, amigo."

"What's Slash Braddock an' the Pecos River Kid ridin' a freight wagon for?" Donny asked, keeping his rifle aimed at the two former cutthroats. "You mossyhorns get too stove up to sit a saddle? Your peepers dim so bad that you can't shoot?"

He smiled again, mockingly.

"As if it was any of your business," Pecos said, "which it ain't, we was both pardoned by none other than the president of the United States his ownself. So we got no more paper on our heads, and we're free to live honest lives workin' honest jobs, which is exactly what we're tryin' to do."

That wasn't the entire story. The agreement was that they'd be pardoned for their many sundry sins in exchange for working under the supervision of Chief Marshal Luther T. "Bleed-Em-So" Bledsoe unofficially from time to time as deputy U.S. marshals, hunting down the worst of the worst criminals on the western frontier. Between those man-hunting jobs, they were free to run their freight business, which they'd been doing now for six months, having bought the small outfit from an old man in Fort Collins who'd wanted to retire and live with his daughter in Denver.

"You're also free to get robbed by blokes like us," said the Brit, narrowing his eyes threateningly again, clicking back his rifle's hammer. "Now . . . back to how much money you're carryin', which, by the way, we'll be relievin' you of."

CHAPTER 2

Pecos turned to Slash and made a face. "Ah, hell. How much we got, Slash?"

Slash sighed as he reached inside his black wool suit coat, which he wore over a pinto vest and suspenders.

"Slow, now," the limey warned, steadying the aimed Spencer in his hand.

Slowly, Slash reached into the breast pocket of his chambray shirt and withdrew the manila envelope in which he'd collected his and Pecos's pay after delivering an organ to a canvas dance hall up in Boulder and sundry dry goods and whiskey to a mercantile in Estes Park.

He ran a thumb over the slender stack of bills, making soft, clicking sounds. "One hundred and fifty dollars."

"What?" the kid said, shocked.

"You heard me."

"You mean you two old cutthroats ran a load of freight all the way up there into them mountains and are only bringin' down *one hundred and fifty dollars* for your trouble?"

Slash felt the flush of embarrassment rise in his leathery but clean-shaven cheeks. Pecos glanced at him. He, too, looked sheepish. It used to be they'd done jobs for thousands of dollars. They never would have done a job—taken down a train or a stagecoach—unless they were sure they'd take home at least three times what they were carrying today for a whole lot more work.

Now, here they were busting their backs several days on the trail for a measly one hundred and fifty.

"That ain't so bad," Slash said, indignant.

"And it's honest," Pecos added, defensively.

"Jesus Christ!" said the limey, glancing at the kid. "From now on, I reckon we'd best keep our sights on whole freight trains instead of single wagons."

"And on younger men," said the redheaded mongrel, Cord, mockery flashing in his eyes.

Slash said, "You could try makin' an honest livin' your ownselves."

"We tried that," Donny said. "We been bustin' rocks for two summers. The winters damn near killed us. We found a little color, all right, but not enough for a stake. Hell, this is easier." He moved toward Slash's side of the wagon, keeping his rifle aimed straight out from his hip. "Throw it down."

"We need that money more than you do," Pecos said.

"You don't need it." The kid stopped and looked up darkly at the two former cutthroats, his mouth lengthening, though the corners did not rise. "You ain't gonna need a dime from here on in."

"What're you talkin' about?" Pecos said.

Quietly, the kid said, "Throw the money down, Slash Braddock. Just toss it down here by my right boot." The kid tapped the toe of his boot against the ground.

Slash glanced at Pecos. Pecos looked back at him, expressionless.

Slash glanced at the limey, then turned to the kid. "If you're gonna kill us anyway, why should I turn over the money we worked so hard for?"

"You never know," the kid said with quiet menace, dark amusement glinting in his cold eyes, "I might change my mind . . . once I see the money. It's enough to buy us all whiskey and girls for a coupla nights, anyway. We haven't had neither in several days now.

"Throw it down, Slash," the limey ordered.

Pecos turned to his partner, his eyes wide with fear. "Oh, hell—throw it down, Slash. Don't give 'em a reason to kill us." He glanced at Donny. "You wouldn't kill two old codgers in cold blood, would you, boy? Throw it down, Slash. Throw it down, an' let's go home!"

"Yeah," Cord said, moving slowly toward the wagon, stepping around the mules and striding toward Slash's side of the driver's box. The Mexican was sidling around toward Pecos. "Throw the money down, Slash . . . so you old cutthroats can go on home. Looks like one of you has lost his nerve in his old age."

He stopped and blinked once, smiling.

"Oh, lordy," Pecos said, throatily.

Slash glanced at him. "What is it, Pecos?"

"My ticker."

"What?"

"My ticker. It's . . . it's actin' up again." Sweat dribbled down the middle-aged cutthroat's cheeks.

"Ah, Jesus, Pecos—not now!"

"What the hell's happening?" Donny said.

"Ah, hell," Pecos said, leaning forward, dropping a knee onto the driver's boot's splintered wooden floor. "I can't . . . I can't breathe, Slash!"

"What the hell is going on?" asked the limey, striding down the slope, letting his rifle hang nearly straight down along his right leg.

"Can't you see the poor man's havin' ticker trouble?" Slash said, dropping to a knee beside his partner.

"He's fakin' it," said the kid. "He ain't havin' ticker trouble."

Slash shot an angry look at him. "Yes, he is. It started a couple months back. We were hefting heavy freight down from the wagon box, and his chest tightened up on him and his arm went numb. He said he felt like a mule kicked him." He turned back to Pecos, who was really sweating now, face mottled both red and gray. "Fight it, Pecos. Fight it off . . . just like last time!"

"I'll be damned," said the limey, leaning forward over the wagon's left front wheel and tipping his head to one side to stare up into Pecos's face. "I think he really is having ticker complaints." He chuckled and glanced at the kid. "I think we done made the Pecos River Kid so nervous, his heart is givin' out on him!"

They all had a good laugh at that.

Meanwhile, Slash patted his partner's back and said, "We need to get him down from here. We need to get him off the wagon and into some shade. Anybody got any whiskey? The sawbones told him he should have a few swigs of who-hit-John when he feels a spell comin' on."

"Yeah, I got whiskey," the limey said. "But I sure as hell ain't sharin' it with him."

They all had another good round of laughs.

"Just hand the money down, you old mossyhorn," the kid said, extending his hand up toward Slash, who'd stuffed the envelope into his coat pocket. "Then you can be on your way and get that poor old broken-down excuse for the Pecos River Kid to a pill roller . . . if he lives that long." He snapped his fingers impatiently. "Come on, hand it down, Slash. I ain't gonna ask you again!"

"Oh, hell!" Slash said, drawing the envelope out of his coat pocket. "Here, take the blasted money!" He threw the envelope down. In doing so, he revealed the small, silver-chased, pearl-gripped over-and-under Derringer he'd also pulled out of his pocket and that was residing in the palm of his right hand.

He flipped the gun upright. He closed his right index finger over one of the two eyelash triggers housed inside the brass guard. He shoved the pretty little popper down toward the kid, who blinked up at him, slow to comprehend what he'd just spied in Slash's hand, his mind still on the money beside his right boot.

There was a pop like a stout branch snapping under a heavy foot.

The kid flinched as though he'd been pestered by a fly. His eyes snapped wide. Instantly, the rifle tumbled from his hands as he lifted them toward the ragged hole in the right side of his slender, lightly freckled neck.

A half an eye wink after the Derringer spoke, Pecos, recovering miraculously from his near-death experience, shoved his right hand beneath the driver's seat just off his right shoulder. He closed his hand around the neck of the twelve-gauge sawed-off shotgun housed there in the strap-iron cage he'd rigged for it, constructed to resemble part of the seat's spring frame.

He pulled the short, savage-looking gut-shredder out from beneath the seat and swung it in a broad arc toward the limey, who'd just turned to stare in shock toward where the kid's precious bodily fluids were geysering out of the hole in his neck. As the Brit's eyes flicked toward Pecos, dropping his lower jaw in sudden exasperation as he began raising his rifle once more, Pecos tripped one of the double-bore's two triggers.

The limey's head turned tomato-red and bounded backward off the man's shoulders. Even as the limey was still raising the Spencer in his hands, his head bounced into the brush and rocks beside the trail.

As the head continued rolling and bouncing, like a child's bright-red rubber ball, Slash slid the smoking Derringer toward Cord, who shouted, "Hey!" and lunged forward, raising his Henry repeater. The gray-eyed Cord didn't quite get the butt plate snugged against his shoulder before Slash squeezed the pretty little popper's second eyelash trigger.

Having only one more round with which to save himself from St. Pete's bitter judgment, Slash decided to play the odds. He aimed for the redheaded mongrel's broad chest and curled his upper lip in satisfaction as the bullet nipped the end off the man's string tie as it plowed through his shirt into his breastbone and then probably into his heart.

"Oh!" the redhead said through a grunt, looking down at his chest in shock as he staggered backward, the Henry wilting in his arms.

At least, it appeared to Slash that "Oh!" is what the man said as the bullet shredded his ticker. He didn't know for sure, for the man's exclamation, whatever it was, was resolutely drowned out by the second, dynamite-like blast of Pecos's twelve-gauge on the other side of the wagon.

That fist-sized round of double-ought buck punched through the chest of the Mexican, who, just like his cohort on the other side of the mules from him, was bounding forward as he realized he and his brethren had just found themselves in dire straits. He didn't get his rifle raised even halfway before the buckshot picked him two feet off the ground and hurled him straight back into the brush already bloodied by the limey's disembodied head.

Meanwhile, Slash looked at the redheaded mongrel who'd stumbled backward to sit down against a boulder a few feet off the trail. He sat there against the rock, his chest rising and falling sharply as blood continued to well out of his chest and turn his shirt dark red.

He stared at Slash in slack-jawed, wide-eyed shock and said, "I'll be damned if you didn't kill me."

"If I hit your ticker, then you'd be correct," Slash said. "Do you think I hit your ticker? There's a chance it might have ricocheted off your brisket and missed your heart. If so, I'd better reload."

Cord shook his head once, his gray eyes glazed with deepening shock and exasperation. "No, no. You got my ticker,

all right." He paused, staring at Slash, then added simply, "Hell," because in his shock and mind-numbing realization that he was teetering on the lip of the cosmos, he couldn't think of anything else to say.

Slash couldn't blame him. He didn't know from personal experience, of course, but he was sure that the place where Cord was just now entering was hard for a mere mortal to wrap his mind around. Slash would know soon enough. Every day, he was a little closer and more and more aware of that bitter fact . . .

Slash looked at the kid, who was rolling around on the ground, squealing like a stuck pig and cursing like a gandy dancer, clamping his hands over his neck, for all the good it did him. He was losing blood fast.

Slash looked across the wagon to see the carnage Pecos's shotgun had left in the brush over there. He glanced at his partner, who was just then breaking open his twelve-gauge and plucking out the smoking, spent wads.

"How's your ticker?" Slashed asked him.

Pecos grinned. "Better."

Slash chuckled as he climbed down off the side of the high, stout wagon, a Pittsburg freighter he and Pecos had bought along with the business. He walked over to the brush where he'd tossed his weapons and picked up one of his .45s.

"I need help," the kid croaked out, sitting up against a rock, holding his hands over his neck.

"You're askin' the wrong jake, kid."

"Please don't kill me! Please don't kill me!"

"Kid, even if you weren't already a goner, I'd still kill you. Think I'd leave a little demon like you alive to sow your demon seed? What this world does *not* need is more of you."

The kid's eyes appeared ready to pop out of their sockets. "Please don't kill me! Please don't kill me!"

Slash killed him with a neat, round hole through the middle of the kid's forehead.

The demon spawn fell back against the ground and lay quivering.

"Kid," Slash said, flicking open his Colt's loading gate and shaking out the spent round, "I've come to know that what we want in this life and what we get are very rarely the same damn thing." He glanced at Pecos, who was staring down at him from the driver's boot. "Ain't that right, partner?"

Pecos laughed and shook his head as he shoved his shotgun back into its cage beneath the seat. "Partner, sometimes your wisdom astounds me. Purely, it does!"

CHAPTER 3

Slash and Pecos chinned for a time about what to do with the dead men.

Slash wanted to drag them off the trail and bury them under a few rocks. They weren't worth burying, but since they were men, albeit no-accounts to a man-jack of them, he supposed someone should make at least a little effort by way of laying them to rest.

Pecos, more tenderhearted than his lean, dark, and moody partner, wanted to deliver the dead men to the town marshal in Fort Collins. "I mean, they might have family in the area, Slash. Or family *somewhere*. If one of your kin met his demise, you'd want to know about it. You wouldn't just want to have to think about it all the rest of your life, would you? To be left to imagine all the various nasty ways they might have met their ends? I mean, even if said kin had gotten exactly what they deserved . . ."

Pecos usually won such arguments. He won this one, as well. As hard and cynical as Slash was, he knew his partner was the better man. Besides, he always felt guiltily wicked when he found himself trying to argue with Pecos's moral authority. He might have been a wicked man in other folks' eyes, but he didn't like feeling that way himself.

Also, he had an ulterior motive in caving in to his partner's wishes so easily. There was a chance there was a bounty on the heads of one or all of these men. Slash figured this wasn't their first holdup. If so, and if someone had put a reward on their heads—well, in this humbler life the two former cutthroats were now living on the right side of the law—he and Pecos could use all the extra cash they could get.

They loaded the dead men into the wagon, covered them with the canvas tarpaulin they'd used to cover their freight on the way into the mountains a couple of days ago, and vamoosed on up the trail. When they came to a broad, grassy area in some trees along Marmot Creek, they pulled off the trail and into the shade of the breeze-ruffled aspens and pines. They fed and watered the mules and built a fire over which they boiled coffee.

It was midday, after all. They had only a few hours of travel before they'd be home, and besides, they weren't as young as they used to be—a fact so wickedly emphasized by the men now lying belly-up in the wagon.

Slash Braddock and the Pecos River Kid needed a break.

"How in the hell did you do that, Pecos?" Slash asked after he'd taken a sip of his piping-hot, oily black mud.

Pecos glanced at him from where he sprawled against a grain sack on the other side of the fire. "How did I do what?"

"You know—make your face go so pale and cause that sweat to pop out on your forehead. For a few seconds there, you had me goin'. I was afraid you really were having a heart stroke!"

"Truth be told," Pecos said, taking a sip from his own, steaming cup, "for a few seconds there, I was worried I was, too!" He gave a sheepish chuckle, then took another sip of his coffee.

"What?"

"I wasn't fakin' it, Slash." Pecos looked at him directly over the low, crackling flames. "At least, not at first. For some reason, when I tossed away my weapons and it was just you and me sittin' up there, facin' them four cutthroats who looked so damn eager to snuff our wicks, a strange feelin' came over me. It was like I was suddenly runnin' a powerful fever. My heart started poundin' and bangin' against my ribs. I felt like someone had shoved a dull, rusty knife in my guts. My back got so damn stiff, I felt I couldn't move!"

He shook his head and stared off into space. "I can't figure it, partner. You an' me rode roughshod over thirty years. We faced lawmen an' bounty hunters—some o' the best on the whole damn frontier—an' nothin' like that ever happened to me before. Seems like . . . seems like lately . . . I been more aware of . . ."

He let his voice trail off, as though he were having trouble finding the right words. He turned to Slash and continued with, "I don't know . . . I guess lately I just been more aware of the sand in the ole hourglass. You know? Been . . . well, I been thinkin' about . . . you know . . . the end. Kinda scares me a little. You know?"

"Yeah." Slash nodded as he stared into the dancing flames. "I know."

"You, too?"

Slash looked at Pecos. "Yeah. Me, too." He sipped his coffee, sighed, and thumbed his hat back off his forehead. "That young juniper's crazy eyes sort o' got to me, as well. It was like death starin' right at me, an' I realized then and there that I wasn't ready for it."

"Hell's bells." Pecos raked a thumb down his bearded cheek and shook his head fatefully.

"You know what I think's causin' us both to get gloomy?"

"What's that?"

"Boredom."

Pecos scowled. "Huh?"

"You heard me. Neither of us had jobs like this—haulin' freight. Aside from what happened earlier, these long hauls have been nothin' but back-busting on each end and boring in between. Hell, sometimes I imagine we got a posse on our tails just to keep from falling asleep . . . or just to entertain myself, to keep my heart pumpin'!"

Pecos shrugged and recrossed his ankles, stretched out before him. "Oh, I don't know about that, Slash. I don't think I'm bored."

"You're bored, Pecos. You just don't wanna admit it."

"Okay, so say we are bored. Say we do have too much time to think about things. What're we gonna do about it?"

Slash shrugged. "Nothin'."

"Nothin', huh?"

"What else can we do? We're gettin' old. Our holdup days are over. Even if we wanted to go back to 'em, we couldn't. Old Bleed-Em-So would have us run down in a matter of days. His marshals would hang us right where they ran us down, and that would be the end of it."

Pecos took a bite of the jerky he was nibbling, along with his coffee. "Hell," he said, chewing, "maybe that wouldn't be so bad."

"Yeah . . . well, maybe."

They didn't say anything for a few minutes. They both just sat there, staring into the fire's small, orange flames that leaped around like ghostly yellow snakes in the brassy sunshine filtering through the forest canopy.

Finally, Pecos frowned across the fire at Slash. "What you got there?"

Slash glanced up at him, dark brows arched over his cinnamon eyes. "Huh?"

"What you foolin' with in your pocket there? You was foolin' with it earlier, before the stickup."

Slash pulled his hand out of his pocket and sat back with a sheepish air. "I don't know what you're talkin' about." He sipped his coffee and looked off through the trees.

"Ah, come on, Slash. What you got in your pocket? You

was fingerin' it on the way up, and you been fingerin' it on the way down."

"It's the Derringer."

"No, it isn't. You keep the Double-D in your right-hand pocket. Whatever you was fingerin' you got in your left pocket."

"Oh, never mind!"

"Ah, come on! Humor this old reprobate, Slash! I'm burnin' up with boredom!"

"It's Jimmy, damnit, Melvin. We gotta remember to use our given names. Slash an' Pecos are dead."

"Don't change the subject."

"I wasn't."

"Yes, you were."

"Ah, hell!" Slash brushed his hat off his head and ran a hand through his still-thick and mostly dark brown hair, give or take a few strands of gray, which hung down over his ears and his collar. He raked it up like a shaggy tumbleweed, then threw it straight back off his forehead. "It's . . . it's a, uh . . ."

"It's a what? Come on, Slash . . . er, I mean Jimmy . . . you can say it. Spit it out."

Slash drew a deep breath and stared up at the forest canopy, where a crow was doing battle with an angrily chittering squirrel. "It's a ring."

"Huh?"

"My mother's ring."

"Your mother's ring?"

"Weddin' ring."

"What you got your mother's weddin' ring for, Sla . . . I mean, Jimmy?"

"I wrote to my sister in Missouri, had her send it to me. Since I'm the only livin' boy in the family, she's been savin' it for me."

"Okay, well, let me ask you again—what you got your mama's weddin' ring for, Jimmy?" Pecos's eyes snapped wide, and he opened his mouth in sudden recognition. "Oh . . . *hell*!"

He grinned across the fire at his sheepish partner. "You . . . Jay . . . you're gonna pop the question—ain't ya, you old rattle-snake?"

Slash tried to snap a fly out of the air in front of him with his hand, and missed. "I don't know."

"What do you mean you don't know? If you went to the trouble of sending for your momma's ring, you must *know*!"

Slash cast him a fiery look, his cheeks reddening beneath his deep brown tan. "Ah, hell—I never shoulda told you a damn thing. Look at you—you're actin' like you got ants in your pants!"

Pecos dipped his chin demurely and held up his hands in supplication. "I'm sorry, partner. I apologize. I shouldn't make fun. It's just that—well, hell, you really caught me by surprise. I mean, I know you an' Jay got . . . well, got *somethin'* goin' on, though I can't rightly put my finger on just what it is. You take her out to breakfast a whole lot, an' she buys you more beers than what you pay for at her saloon, but . . . Well, you're pretty tight-lipped on the subject of women, Slash. You always have been."

Pecos studied his stoic partner, who was looking off through the trees again as though he were watching for Apaches. In fact, Pecos could tell that Slash would probably rather tussle with Apaches than continue the current conversation. James Braddock was not a man who could speak frankly on subjects of the heart.

"All right, all right," Pecos said, using a glove to grab the coffeepot from the iron spider over the fire. "You'll tell me when you're good an' ready. I won't prod you about it no more."

He refilled his coffee cup, then held the steaming pot up to Slash. "More mud? Pretty good pot, if I do say so my—"

"I think I'm gonna ask her." Slash was still staring off as though watching for those imaginary Apaches. He turned to Pecos again and said, "You think she'll have me?"

Pecos just stared back at him for a few seconds, still overcome with shock. Slash had never confided in him about women before. Pecos had confided plenty in Slash, but never the other way around. Mainly because Slash had never seemed interested in women. At least, none beyond the sporting variety. Oh, he'd made time with plenty of parlor girls, but Jimmy Braddock had always been a love 'em an' leave 'em kind of fella.

"Well," Pecos said, when he found his tongue. "I think she's too good for you, but, yes, I think she'll have you." He grinned, chuckled. "Yes, I do indeed think that Jaycee Breckenridge will accept your hand, James."

"Son of a buck! Do you really think so, or are you just sayin' that to humor me?"

It was Pecos's turn to cloud up and rain. "You dad-blasted fool! What does it take to convince you? Can't you see the way she looks at you? Why, as soon as we step into that saloon of hers, her eyes light up like a Christmas tree. Like a barn fire! And a flush always—always!—rises in her cheeks. And, believe me, it ain't me she's lookin' at. Why, that pretty li'l redhead is pure-dee gone for you, Slash!"

"Jimmy."

"I mean Jimmy!"

"Okay, okay," Slash said, running a sleeve across his nose. "If you say so."

"Can't you see it for yourself?"

Slash winced, shrugged. "I'm a little slow that way, I gotta admit. Besides . . . ."

"What?"

"I don't know, Pecos, but—"

"Melvin."

"Melvin, I mean. But it always feels like there's a hand inside me, holdin' me back." He punched the end of his fist against his chest.

"What is it?"

"I don't know." Slash raised a knee and hooked his arm over it. He picked up a stick with his other hand and poked it into the flames. "I've never been good with women. I've never really known how to talk to 'em. I reckon that's why I always preferred parlor girls to . . . well, you know, to real women. Real ladies like Jaycee."

"Well, that just don't make sense."

Slash frowned. "What don't?"

"Women fall all over you, Slash. I mean, Jimmy. They always have. Leastways, they always seem primed to. It's your looks. You're a square-jawed, handsome devil. I've always been jealous of that. I suppose we're so old now it don't matter if I go ahead and confess it."

"Pshaw." Slash flushed.

"No, no. You're a dark-eyed, handsome devil. Me? I'm too big an' lumbering. I'm an ole bulldog. And I got this stringy hair, an' the sun makes my face all splotchy instead of Injun-dark like yours. Oh, I've had me some women over the years. I don't deny that. Some I've loved. Some have even loved me back." He chuckled as he stared into his steaming coffee cup. "But I've always had to work for the ladies. You? Hell, all you gotta do is walk into a saloon or restaurant, and the eyes of every girl in the place just naturally shuttle to you like steel to a magnet."

"Well, I sure wish I knew how to talk to 'em."

"You gotta pretend like they're just people."

"Huh?"

"Like they're just like you an' me. 'Cause they are. Just start talkin' like you'd start talkin' to a man an' see where it goes from there. You'd be surprised. But, then, hell—you al-

ready got that figured out with Jaycee. I seen you two huddled over some long, serious conversations lately. You appeared to be givin' back as good as you was gettin'."

Slash nodded. "It's easier. Talkin' to her. Always was—
leastways, it was when Pistol Pete was still alive."

Jaycee Breckenridge had been married to Slash and Pecos's
outlaw partner, Pistol Pete Johnson, until Pete had met his
end by way of a posse rider's bullet late one night in a deep-
mountain box canyon. That had been five years ago now.
Slash had loved Jaycee before she'd married up with Pete, but
he hadn't known how to tell her. Or even how to just carry
on a casual conversation with her.

He'd gotten more comfortable with her, though, over the
years that she was married to Pete, and they—Jaycee, Pete,
Pecos, and Slash—had holed up together in Jay and Pete's remote shack high in the San Juan Mountains of southern Colorado, on the backside of jobs they'd sprung. He supposed
Jay's being married to Pete had taken some of the pressure
off his expectations, since she was already married and there
was room for a genuine friendship to grow.

Now, however, Pete was dead.

"Well, you go for it, then, you son of a devil!" Pecos spat
into the fire, then ran a sleeve across his eyes. His voice
pinched as he added, "Go ahead and leave me high an' dry!"

"Don't tell me you're cryin'!"

Pecos blinked as he stared guiltily into the fire. A few tears
dribbled down his cheeks and into his short blond beard.
"Yeah, I reckon a little. Not out of sadness. Just chokes me,
is all—hearin' about you an' Jay. Here, I figured you'd be the
one to die alone pinin' for some woman you never had. I figured I'd be the one with a woman keepin' my feet warm on
cold winter nights, feelin' guilty about you out in some desert
cabin—just you an' the scorpions an' centipedes."

"Well, let's not put the cart before the horse. I haven't

asked her yet, and just thinkin' about it is givin' me the fan-tods. I might still be shackin' up with the scorpions an' cen-tipedes."

"Oh, you'll do it. You'll ask her. She'll accept. And you two will be standin' up before some sky pilot grinnin' at each other all dewy-eyed, and you'll slip Mama Braddock's ring on Jay's purty finger, and you'll tie the damn knot!"

Slash shuddered as he stared across the fire at his teary-eyed partner. "Jesus, will ya shut up? You're startin' to give me cold feet all over again!"

"An' you'll leave ole Pecos—I mean Melvin—all high an' dry." Pecos sleeved more tears from his cheeks.

"Ah, hell," Slash said. "You might be uglier'n a five-legged goat, but you're a silver-tongued devil. That's what always made *me* jealous of *you, Melvin*! You may not have a woman right now, but you'll wrangle one soon enough with that gold-plated charm of yours. The trick for you is—can you keep her long enough to marry her before you tumble for an-other!"

They both had a good laugh over that.

Belly laughs, both. Until they thought their ribs were gonna bust and poke out of their bellies.

They sobered up right quick when one of the mules brayed a sharp warning.

strains of a fiddle, and smell the tobacco smoke and the mouth-watering aromas of beer and fine spirits wafting out through the main set of batwing doors mounted atop a broad front veranda that wrapped around three sides of the yellow-and-white-painted, wood-frame structure.

They delivered the dead men to the county sheriff and were glad that the sheriff himself, a portly, contrary man by the name of Wayne Decker, was not on duty. Decker always eyed Slash and Pecos with suspicion, as though he'd seen them somewhere before, which he probably had.

On wanted dodgers tacked up across the West.

Even though Slash and Pecos had been pardoned by the president at the request of Chief Marshal Luther T. Bledsoe, they knew that their likenesses no doubt still adorned the walls of many post offices, telegraph offices, and Wells Fargo stations all across the frontier. Decker probably even had one on his own bulletin board, and a vague, nettling memory caused him to try to match the poor pencil sketches to the faces of the two Fort Collins newcomers who'd come from seemingly nowhere to buy the local freighting outfit.

Even though Slash and Pecos were no longer wanted men, they didn't feel like trying to convince the sheriff of that and having to explain the circumstances surrounding their pardons, which were supposed to be secret—known to only them, a few politicians, including Rutherford B. Hayes, and Chief Marshal Luther T. Bledsoe. Bleed-Em-So was counting on them to keep their true identities secret and to forevermore go by only their given names of James "Jimmy" Braddock and Melvin Baker.

"I don't know," one of the three deputies on duty that night at the new courthouse said, shaking his head as he stared into the wagon box. The dead men's four sets of eyes glittered eerily in the light from a nearby saloon window. "Sheriff ain't gonna like this. No, he ain't gonna like this a bit. He's gonna want to talk to you fellas himself."

CHAPTER 4

"What the hell was that?"

"One of the mules!"

"I know it was one of the mules!" Pecos said, scrambling heavily to his feet as Slash did the same thing. "What's got its neck in a hump?"

"Reckon we'd best find out." Slash stood with both pistols in his hands, looking around, half-expecting to find more highwaymen on the prowl. These isolated canyons were notorious for all stripes of long-coulee riders. That's why Slash had taken to carrying the Derringer in his coat pocket and Pecos had rigged the cage for his shotgun beneath the wagon seat.

Curly wolves could very well be on the lurk for a load of freight to steal and sell themselves, or for the takeaway from such a sale, which of course was the mistake that the four men in the wagon had made, or for the stock to which the wagons might be hitched.

Or two of the three . . .

Pecos strode quickly over to the wagon and pulled his Colt's revolving rifle out from beneath the seat. Holding the rifle up high across his chest, his thumb on the revolver's hammer, he looked around.

"I hear somethin'," Slash said, ears pricked.

"What?"

"I don't know." Slash followed the sound he'd heard into the trees flanking the coffee fire.

He moved through the trees to where the creek chuckled over its shallow, rocky bed and peered across the cool, blue, mountain water toward where two riders were galloping their horses up the shoulder of a bald haystack butte. One man followed the other. The second man glanced back over his shoulder, staring toward where both Slash and Pecos now stood at the edge of the creek, scowling toward the two suspicious riders.

The second man turned his head forward and followed the lead rider up and around the curve of the mountain and out of sight.

"You recognize 'em?" Pecos asked.

"Too far away."

"Who do you suppose they were? And what'd they want?"

"Your guess is as good as mine. They wanted somethin', all right. And they hadn't wanted to be spotted. They weren't just a couple of innocent saddle tramps—you can bet your boots on that."

"Damn," Pecos said. "Maybe this new line of work we're in ain't gonna be so boring, after all."

Slash looked around again, cautiously. "I was kind of starting to like the boredom, myself."

"Yeah, I reckon I was, too, now that you mention it."

Slash holstered his pistols. "Come on. Let's kick dirt on that fire and get a move on. I got the chilly-willies, and I'd as soon get back to Fort Collins before the sun goes down."

"I hear that." Pecos followed Slash back through the trees toward the fire. "Besides, you got you a weddin' ring burnin' a hole in your pocket."

Slash glowered at him over his shoulder.

Pecos grinned.

* * *

The two former cutthroats didn't run into any more trouble on the trail back to Fort Collins. They did not, however, make it to town before the sun had dropped down behind the towering crags of Long's Peak and Mount Rosalie and the purple blackness of good darkness had stretched out from the Front Range over the vast, fawn-colored, gently undulating prairie to the east.

It was over this prairie, having left the Front Range near Johnstown, that the freighters negotiated their wagon, heading north, the mountains on their left. They could hear the clashing piano chords issuing from several saloons in the town ahead as they passed the old army outpost of Fort Collins, which had been decommissioned several years earlier, on their right, along the bank of the Cache la Poudre River, and followed a sharp dogleg in the trail and on into the town proper.

Fort Collins was booming here, between the southwestern bank of the Cache la Poudre and the rocky cliffs and slanting sandstone ridges that were the first cuts and rises of the Front Range to the west. Miners, ranchers, and farmers in the surrounding area used the town as a supply hub as well as a center of entertainment.

That's why the saloon and bordello Jaycee Breckenridge had bought with the stake Pistol Pete had left her was doing so well. Tonight, as most nights, every window in all three stories was lit, and jostling shadows moved behind them.

The House of a Thousand Delights occupied a prominent corner on Main Street and sprawled across several lots. Except for a nearby opera house, the Thousand Delights was the largest business establishment in town. In nearly the whole county, in fact.

Now as Slash and Pecos rattled along the dusty street, clattering past the rollicking, bustling bordello, they could hear the hum of conversations and laughter and the raucous

"County coroner might wanna seat a jury," opined one of the others, also staring moodily into the bed of the freight wagon. "You're gonna have to write out an affidavit. There might even be a . . . a whatdoyacallit . . . ?"

"A coroner's *inquest*," said the third deputy from inside a halo of aromatic cigar smoke.

"A *what*?" both Slash and Pecos said at the same time, flabbergasted by the ever-growing complexity of these modern times.

"I told you we should have buried those boys under rocks," Slash told Pecos, when the coroner, unhappy at having been roused from his smoking parlor, had come to collect the dead men and the three deputies had returned to their courthouse office, smoking, shaking their heads, and casting suspicious glances over their shoulders at the two freighters. "Now we're gonna have to have a talk with Decker and the coroner, and you know how that fat badge-toter is always givin' us the woolly eyeball."

"What's right is right, Slash. I mean Jimmy, damnit!"

"Dammit, how are we gonna get out of the habit of usin' the old handles?" Slash said, rocking back on the seat as Pecos pulled the mules up to the small compound of their freighting office, which was flanked by a stable and a barn. "Maybe we oughta get ourselves hypnotized."

"Ah, hell," Pecos said, "we'll remember when the chips are down. Besides, we don't overly socialize in town all that much. Hell, this job has us toolin' around the mountains most days of the week. Breaking our butts for pennies and pisswater," he added with a surly grumble.

"Yeah, well, I reckon it's better than what most range hands make in a whole month."

"Yeah, but most range hands are young," Pecos said. "We're gettin' old, Slash. We gotta start savin' up for our retirement."

"Jesus," Slash growled, leaping down off the wagon when Pecos had drawn it up in front of the main corral. "You are one dark and depressing cuss tonight, Pec—I mean, Melvin. Galldangit, anyway!"

He kicked a front wheel.

"Yeah, well, I don't got a woman to go see. Nor one to marry, neither. Hell, you won't need to work once you marry Jaycee." Pecos looked around. "Now, where do you suppose Todd's at? He's supposed to be out here takin' care of this team."

Todd Elwood was the young wrangler they'd hired about a month ago to help out around the barn. He had a history of drunkenness and general sloth, Elwood did, but he'd promised he'd lay off the Taos lightning if Slash and Pecos would give him the job. He'd been plumb tired of bouncing around from one ranch spread to another.

Slash looked around, fists on his hips. He called for Elwood but was met with only silence from the darkest corners of the freight yard. No lamps appeared to be burning anywhere.

"I'd say he's on a tear," Slash said with a sigh.

"Damn his drunken hide!" Pecos cursed again. "That's what we get for giving a firebrand a second chance."

"I had a bad feelin' about him, and I told you so," Slash said. "He had layabout written all over him. Your problem is you got too big a heart."

"Oh, shut up!"

"Don't tell me to shut up!"

"Shut up!" Pecos walked around the front of the wagon to help Slash unhitch the team. He cast a glance back toward the giant, glittering jewel of the House of a Thousand Delights, from which they could still hear the fiddle music, albeit faintly. "As I was sayin' about Jay . . . if she ain't by now, she's soon gonna be one of the most money-eyed women in the whole damn county if not all of eastern Colorado Territory!"

That gave Slash pause. As he worked on snaps and buckles and removed hames and harnesses, he too glanced toward the Thousand Delights. He hadn't thought of Jay's money.

Could he suck his pride down deep enough to marry a woman who would for all intents and purposes be supporting him?

"Me?" Pecos said, taking a bridle strap in his teeth. "They'll likely be digging a shallow grave for me out in potter's field."

"Oh, shut up, will ya?"

Pecos looked at him, his eyes sharply indignant even in the relative darkness of the unlit freight yard. "Now, what the hell's got into you?"

"Oh, just stitch your mouth closed, will you?"

Slash cursed and began leading the team through the open corral gate.

Pecos yelled behind him that he should do something physically impossible to himself.

Slash's mood improved later, after he and Pecos had taken whores' baths in their respective rooms in their cabin flanking the freight yard office.

He and Pecos had silently agreed, as they always did after one of their frequent dustups, to bury the hatchet. They might argue bitterly from time to time but never for long. They brushed their clothes, rolled cigarettes, took a few pulls from a bottle, then tramped off side by side toward the Thousand Delights for drinks and supper—and, of course, so Slash could see Jaycee.

He wasn't planning on asking the woman to marry him tonight. In fact, he still hadn't decided whether he ever would pop the Big Question. While the whiskey had sanded the rough edges off the day, he was still wrestling with the idea of marriage. He shoved his hand in his coat pocket just to make sure the ring was still there, on the off chance his heart would overrule his mind and his pride and he'd blurt out a proposal.

It was still there, inside the small maple ring box, the box's top adorned with an antique gold metal flower with a rose crystal in the center. The inside of the box was lined with white burlap. Slash had to chuckle, thinking of his crusty old man, dead now these thirty years, buying such a feminine bauble for his mother, oh so many years ago.

But, then, the boy his father had been must have been as gone for Slash's mother as Slash now found himself gone for Jaycee Breckenridge . . .

"Stop thinkin'."

Slash glanced at Pecos as they both walked up the broad wooden steps fronting the Thousand Delights. "What?"

"Stop thinkin' about it."

"Stop thinkin' about *what?*"

"You know what. Just follow your heart, or you'll work yourself up so bad you'll turn tail and run all the way back to Missouri, yippin' like a butt-shot coyote." Pecos chuckled as he paused to toss his quirley into the dirt of the street behind them.

"Oh, shut up!" Slash snarled, and pushed through the batwings.

The main saloon hall was filled to near bursting. Slash and Pecos had to sidestep their way through the men as well as Jay's painted, scantily clad girls. The potpourri of male and female aromas was nearly overwhelming after several days of sniffing only the pure, high-country air.

Tobacco smoke hovered in a thick fog, skeining like ghostly snakes in the lights of the crystal chandeliers and gas lamps that lit up the well-appointed saloon, which resembled the tony set of some stage play or a mine magnate's ballroom.

Varnished oak, velvet draperies, expensive wall hangings, shining brass spittoons, and glistening leaded-glass mirrors shone every which way. Some of the floor was carpeted. Some was hard maple. The fiddle music, now accompanied by a horn or two as well as a guitar, was issuing from a side room given over to dancing. Slash could hear the cowboys letting their hair down, yipping and laughing and stomping their boots.

When Slash and Pecos finally made it to the bar, squeezing in between two drummers who didn't look happy about being crowded, one of the barmen, Vance Taylor, saw them and said, "Hey, Slash!"

"Set us up—will you, Vance? And, uh . . . where's Jay?" He'd been looking around but so far hadn't spotted her.

Taylor, flushed and harried, glanced at the ceiling. "She asked me to have you two head on up to her suite."

Slash and Pecos cut befuddled looks at each other. "Her suite?" Pecos said. "*Both* of us?"

Taylor just shrugged and then waltzed off to fill shouted drink orders with the two other aprons, all dolled up in pinstriped shirts, celluloid collars, foulard ties, and sleeve garters, working behind the broad, horseshoe bar.

Slash and Pecos again worked their way through the crowd and up the broad, carpeted stairs. As they headed down the third-floor hall toward Jay's suite of rooms, Pecos said, "What do you suppose she wants to see both of us about?"

"Your guess is as good as mine."

"That kind of cramps your style a little, don't it, partner?" Again, Pecos gave a mocking grin. "I mean, you probably don't want me around when you drop to a knee."

"If you don't shut up, you're gonna find out it's true that the bigger they are, the harder they fall."

Pecos snorted a devious laugh.

They stopped at Jay's door.

Slash tapped lightly three times. "Jay? It's Slash an'—I mean, it's Jimmy and Melvin!"

He cursed under his breath. Their given names sounded so foreign as to be comical.

He frowned at the door. Behind it was only silence.

He was about to tap again when a strangling, gagging sound rose from inside.

"*Slash! Pecos!*" Jay screamed. "*Hit the deck—it's a trap!*"

CHAPTER 5

You didn't have to tell the former Slash Braddock and the former Pecos River Kid more than once that they'd walked into a trap. They'd moseyed into several over their long and storied outlaw careers, barely escaping with their lives at times.

They both hit the deck so fast that any onlooker would have thought their old legs had suddenly turned to wet mud. No sooner had their chests hit the nicely carpeted hall floor than an explosion sounded from behind Jay's door. A round of what could only have been double-ought buckshot blew a pumpkin-sized hole through the door's top panel.

Chunks of wood peppered both Slash and Pecos, lying prone in the hall. Chunks and slivers flew against the opposite wall.

"Die, you cutthroat bastards—*die!*" bellowed a man on the heels of the first blast and on the nose end of the next.

Ka-boom!

The second blast was every bit as loud as the first, if not louder. It seemed to make the hall floor buck up hard beneath Slash and Pecos.

A second hole joined the first hole, slightly lower down than the first one and connecting the two, so that now there was a single, hourglass-shaped hole in the middle of the door roughly the size of a rain barrel's mouth. More wood chunks littered the two prone cutthroats and the floor around them.

Silence.

Slash lifted his head and turned to Pecos. Pecos looked back at him. Wood slivers peppered his hair, his beard, and his clothes. His blue eyes were bright with apprehension as, gritting his teeth, he reached down for the big Russian holstered on his right thigh.

As Slash reached for one of his Colts, a man inside the room said in a low, tense voice, "You think we got 'em?"

"Let's make sure," said another voice.

"No!" Jay screamed.

"You shut up, woman!" bellowed the last man who'd spoken.

As Slash and Pecos scrambled to their feet, what sounded like six-shooters began popping inside the room. The bullets screeched through the hole the two-bore had punched through the door and made new, smaller holes of their own. A couple even punched through the wall.

Slash rose to a crouch and pressed his left shoulder against the wall to the left of the door. Pecos rose and pressed his thick right shoulder against the wall to the door's right, wincing as the bullets continued to punch through the door and through the walls to either side of him and Pecos, a couple coming within a cat's whisker of hitting pay dirt.

They didn't have time to wait around and keep hoping the men inside the room would continue to miss their marks until they emptied their pistols.

Slash turned to Pecos and yelled above the din, "Whatever you do—don't hit Jay!"

He and Pecos glanced around the sides of the door to peer through the large hole the two-bore had carved. They swung their pistols up and shoved them through the hole and went to work, hurling lead at their targets inside the room, evoking indignant wails and curses and silencing the guns of the three men who were standing about seven feet back from the door, hurling lead through it.

Or had been hurling lead through it, blindly. Like fools.

Until Slash and Pecos had taken steady aim at their targets and sent the three gutless bushwhackers breaking into bizarre death dances and wailing and shooting their pistols into the floor and ceiling. When Slash, peering through the hole and into the smoky room beyond, saw that all three men were down, he pushed through the door, breaking out a remaining chunk of it and stepping into the room, keeping his six-gun aimed straight out in front of him.

Pecos followed him in, breaking out what was left of the door.

The two cutthroats stood side by side, peering through the smoke at the two shooters lying twisted on the carpeted floor before them. The third man was crawling away toward their right, toward an open window above Jay's pink brocade fainting couch. Trying to gain his feet, holding a smoking six-shooter in one hand and clamping his other hand over his chest, the man glanced over his shoulder at Slash and Pecos.

"Don't shoot me! Oh, god—please don't shoot me!"

At the same time, Slash and Pecos's pistols roared.

The man dropped to the floor near the fainting couch and lay quivering as he died.

Slash turned to his left, toward Jay's large, canopied, four-poster bed. Through the thick, wafting smoke he saw Jay lying on her side, hog-tied, bound wrists tied to her bound ankles behind her back. She lay diagonally across the bed with its thick red silk, down-filled comforter, and she was staring in wide-eyed terror toward Slash and Pecos.

"Oh, god!" Jay cried, her thick copper tresses lying in tangles across her shoulders and down her back, the top of which was exposed by her low-cut velveteen gown. "Oh, god—I thought for sure they were gonna kill my boys. I just knew they were gonna kill you!"

She lifted her chin, sobbing.

"Oh, fer chrissakes!"

Slash hurried over to her. He saw a thick, wadded stocking on the bed near her head. They must have gagged her with the sock, but she'd managed to spit it out when Slash had knocked on the door. If she hadn't warned them, "her boys," as she called Slash and Pecos in her typically endearing way, would indeed be wolf bait.

"Jay, are you all right?" Slash asked, sliding a lock of copper hair back from her left cheek with his hand, raking his gaze up and down her body, looking for injuries. "Did they hurt you?"

Jay stifled another sob and shook her head, tears rolling down her lovely, finely sculpted cheeks. "I'm all right, Slash!"

Slash dropped to a knee beside the bed and slid his face up close to hers, keeping his hand on her cheek. "What the hell happened? Who were they?"

Pecos answered for her. "Jack Penny."

Slash turned to him. "What?"

Pecos stood over one of the men sprawled in death on the floor several feet from the foot of Jay's bed. He glanced over his shoulder at Slash. "Our old friend Jack Penny. Remember him?"

"How could I forget?" Slash straightened and walked over to stare down at the bounty hunter, who lay on his back, slack in death. Jack Penny was a tall, long-limbed, bearded man with one unmoored blue eye, which had rolled to the outside of its socket while the other one stared straight up as though back at the two living men staring down. Penny wore a mismatched suit, badly worn, and his long, brown-gray hair stood out in patches around his hatless head. His brown Stetson lay on the floor beside him.

He stank of stale whiskey and tobacco smoke.

Blood oozed from two bullet holes in his chest.

Slash said, "How do you suppose he found us here? And . . .

why? Since he was in cahoots with ole Bleed-Em-So, he must've known those bounties on our heads aren't good anymore."

"Uh, fellas?"

Slash and Pecos turned to Jay, who still lay hog-tied on the bed. "I hate to interrupt your serious discussion, but do you suppose . . . ?" With a taut smile, she jerked her eyes to indicate the ropes binding her wrists and ankles behind her.

"Ah, Jesus—sorry about that, darlin'!" Slash hurried over to the bed.

By now, thunder rose from the hall as men ran up from downstairs to see what all the shooting had been about. As Slash pulled his bowie knife from his sheath and cut the ropes binding Jay, a big, mustached gent poked his head through the ruined door, looking around.

This was Charlie Lattimore, one of the three bouncers, all the size of small mountains, Jay had hired to keep peace about the Thousand Delights. The beefy gent with thick, curly, dark-brown hair beneath his crisp bowler was holding a sawed-off, double-barrel shotgun in both his ham-sized hands.

Lattimore was a street tough from back east. He spoke with a thick Boston brogue. He wasn't very smart, nor much to look at—his face was badly scarred, and one ear was cauliflowered almost beyond recognition—but his very presence alone usually served to keep the clientele on their best behavior.

Usually.

"Bloody hell!" he cried, hardening his jaws as he looked at the dead men, at Slash and Pecos, and then at Jay on the bed. He glanced at the loud, milling crowd that had gathered behind him, said, "Stay back, you men!" then pushed through the door and into the room. "What in the name of Jesus, Joseph, an' me dear sweet Mary happened here, Miss Breck—"

"Long story," Jay said, sitting up now and rubbing the circulation back into her hands. "All is well now, Charlie. Just please send someone for the marshal, will you?"

"Will do, ma'am!" Lattimore retreated through the door, admonished the crowd once more, and then stomped off to fetch the local law.

Slash sat on the edge of the bed beside Jay. "You sure you're all right? They didn't hit you or anything?" He looked her over carefully, again finding no obvious sign of injury. Her body was just how Slash remembered—splendid in every curve and plane. Even in her forties, Jaycee Breckenridge was still a head-banger and a heartbreaker.

"I'm all right, Slash," Jay said, smiling sweetly up at him, her jade eyes glowing in the light of a nearby lamp. "Really." The smile disappeared, replaced by a deep frown as she glanced from Slash to Pecos and back again. "It's you boys I was worried about. I thought for sure he was going to make good on his promise and turn you under with that ugly shotgun of his."

"How did he get in here, Jay?" Pecos asked, standing off the end of the bed and wrapping a hand around a canopy post.

"He must have picked the lock." Jay drew her left leg under her right one and massaged the ankle over the high top of her stylish, lace-up, doeskin shoe. "I came up to get ready for the night, and Penny jumped me." She glanced at the other two dead men. "Those two are . . . were . . . Willie and Clyde. Don't know their last names or where they came from, but they must have thrown in with Penny somewhere down the line. They weren't here until about a half hour ago."

"Those were the two we seen back along the creek, Slash," Pecos said. "My hearin' might not be too good anymore, but my peepers are still those of a young man."

"Well, it's good one last thing on you is," Slash dryly quipped. He raked a thumbnail down his jawline, in bad need of a shave, frowning thoughtfully. "Penny must have sent those two out to scout for us, to give him some idea when we'd be back to town. He must have been around Fort Collins awhile, scopin' out our habits. He knew that soon after we got back to town, we'd head this way."

"To pay a visit to the purtiest gal in the Territory," Pecos said, smiling down at Jay with several insinuating glances at Slash.

Slash flushed.

Jay shook her head darkly. "Yeah, well, this time your visit was almost your last."

"It would've been if you hadn't warned us." Slash gave her forearm an affectionate squeeze. "What was Penny's beef with us, anyway?"

"Oh, you know what it is."

"Hell, he had us outnumbered!" Slash said. "The odds were in his favor that day!"

He was talking about the ambush Penny had affected, with the help of a dozen other bounty hunters, on Jay's hideout cabin in the San Juan Mountains. Around a year ago, Slash and Pecos had holed up there with Pistol Pete's widow, in the cabin Jay and Pete had shared for many years up in the high and rocky.

None other than Chief Marshal Luther T. Bledsoe had sicced those bounty hunters on Slash and Pecos, intending to assassinate them. When Slash, Pecos, and Jay got the better of the dozen, after they'd used an escape tunnel to work their way around the ragged group of killers, and killed them all save Penny and one other man, Bledsoe was so impressed by Slash and Pecos's gun work, even at the pair's advanced age, that he put the two cutthroats on his payroll and gave Penny the shaft.

"Still, I can see how he was a might chafed," Pecos put in, glancing down at the dead bounty hunter with the roaming eye. "He was known to hold a grudge, Jack was. A prideful man. I'm sure Bledsoe givin' us the job instead of him burned him good, put him on our trail. He's probably been stokin' that fire in his belly for a whole year."

"Yeah, well, there he lies for his trouble."

Footsteps sounded in the hall. Most of the crowd outside the door had dispersed, and it sounded like there was only one man out there now, heading this way.

"Here comes the law," Pecos said, dreadfully.

"Just what we need," Slash complained. "More law."

"It's all right, fellas," Jay said. "The marshal here in Fort Collins is a good, fair man. He's new, and I know him personally." A slight flush rose into her cheeks. Slash didn't like seeing that flush there at all. Not at all.

He arched a brow at her. "You know him, do you?"

"Knock-knock," said a man's deep, resonant voice.

Slash, Pecos, and Jaycee swung their heads around to see a tall, handsome man poke his head through the remains of the door, then smile and wink when his eyes landed on Jay.

CHAPTER 6

The handsome gent looked around the room, frowning, then turned to Jaycee again with concern. "You all right, Jay?" He stepped into the room, doffing his hat, the look of concern deepening the frown lines cutting into his broad forehead.

He was a tall, handsome man in a handsome three-piece suit. A suit that didn't look like it was long from the tailor's dummy. A dark-brown suit of fine tweed and broadcloth, with a white silk shirt matched with a paisley vest and string tie. A gold-washed chain dangled from a gilt-edged pocket of the vest.

The man wearing the suit had been in turn tailored to wear such a finely sewn piece of duds. He was tall, broad-shouldered, slim-waisted, and long-legged. He appeared to be in his early forties. Thick, curly, cinnamon hair was combed into neat waves upon his regal head, just touching his ears and the back of his collar. His face was finely structured, handsome, even if the eyes were a tad on the oily side, the beard and mustache a little too finely and too regularly trimmed.

Slash could see this gent folding himself into a barber's

chair every morning of the week, as though he fancied himself some frontier version of Jay Gould, likely right at eight a.m., as soon as the barber had finished sweeping off his boardwalk, tossed his cigar stub into the street, and turned the placard in his window to OPEN.

No man should be that intimate with a barber's chair. No real man, anyway.

This one wore a well-polished, brightly nickeled town marshal's badge on his vest, positioned so that it subtly showed itself peeking out from beneath the fancy Dan's left coat lapel. A big, black Colt .44, with ivory grips in which a horse's head was carved, adorned a black leather holster residing high on his right hip. The holster bore the initials CW.

"Oh, hello, Cisco. Yes, yes, I'm fine," Jay said. Slash didn't like how a soft, feminine flush rose into the nubs of Jay's cheeks, nor how her green eyes seemed to at once soften and brighten as she stared up at the tall newcomer.

Cisco? Slash thought. She knows the badge-toter by his first name?

He tried to ignore the slight, uneasy churning of his innards, but there it was.

Slash rose from the bed. "You, uh . . . you two know each other, do you?"

"Jay an' me?" the marshal she'd called Cisco said, showing a full set of marble white teeth in a charming grin. "Sure, sure. Miss Breckenridge and I go back a ways—don't we, Miss Breckenridge?"

"Cisco . . . er, Marshal Walsh and I," Jay corrected with a smile and an ironic dip of her chin, "met in Dodge City some time ago. Before I tumbled for that old hornswoggler Pistol Pete."

The marshal and Jaycee shared a warm smile, which made Slash's guts churn and grow a little warmer, as though he'd eaten something he shouldn't have. The lawman turned to the business at hand, frowning at the dead men. "Trouble, I

see." He glanced at the door. "Three dead men and a ruined door."

"As well as a good bit of blood on my rug," Jay added, sourly. "Rest assured, however, Cisco, that the three dead men had it coming. They held me here to set a trap for Slash an' Pe—"

"Uh, that's Jimmy and Melvin," Pecos corrected with a toothy, sheepish grin.

"Oh, don't worry about that nonsense," Jay said. "Cisco here knows all about Slash Braddock and the Pecos River Kid. Cisco himself once rode the wrong side of the straight an' narrow." She beamed again at the tall, handsome marshal, adding, "Didn't you, Cisco?"

"That I did, that I did." The lawman slid his gaze from Slash to Pecos. "Until I, just like I've heard you fellas have done, mended my ways."

Slash turned to Jay. "You told him?"

She nodded. "I saw no reason to keep your past a secret from Cisco. I'm sure he'd have figured out who you were sooner or later. He's not as soft in his thinker box as Sheriff Decker or the man's cork-headed deputies."

"Not to worry, fellas," Marshal Walsh said, raising his hands, palms out. "Your secret is safe with me. Especially since you're making good on the sundry sins of your past by riding for—"

"Oh, my gosh!" Jay slapped a hand to her mouth, lowering her jaw and widening her eyes in shock. "In all the commotion, I forgot that Bledsoe sent word earlier."

"Bledsoe did?" both Slash and Pecos said at the same time.

"Yes, yes. One of his deputies came in to speak to me earlier. The chief marshal wants you boys to ride out to the old Cormorant Saloon. For a powwow, as the deputy put it. I assume Bledsoe has some trouble he needs his former cutthroats to iron out for him. I told the deputy when you two were due back, so he's likely been waiting for you."

Slash cursed and looked at Pecos, who glowered and shrugged. "So much for lettin' our hair down." He glanced from Slash to Jay, adding, "And for . . ." He let his voice trail off, dropping his sheepish gaze to the floor.

"For what?" Jay asked, frowning at Slash.

Slash's cheeks burned with both embarrassment and anger. The anger was directed at his partner. Pecos always seemed to get a bad case of hoof-in-mouth disease at the most inopportune time.

"Nothin'," Slash said quickly, absently brushing his hand across his coat pocket—the one in which his mother's ring resided. "We was just hopin' to have a few drinks and a slow, leisurely supper, is all. But, now, I reckon we'd best . . ."

Jay turned to the town marshal, who was walking around, staring down at each of the dead men in turn. "They can go—can't they, Cisco? I'll tell you the whole story and sign whatever needs signing. I assure you Slash and Pecos were acting in self-defense."

"That's all I need, then." The handsome town marshal glanced over his shoulder at Slash and Pecos. "I'm sure Chief Marshal Bledsoe needs you more than I do. If there are any holes left in the affidavit after I've talked with Jay about what happened here, I'm sure we can fill them in when you return. Good luck, gentlemen." Walsh smiled his broad, handsome smile once more, turning to face the two cutthroats, adding, "It was nice to meet you both. Don't worry about Jay."

He switched his warm smile to the copper-haired beauty standing beside Slash, flushed more than ever. "I'll take very good care of her while you're away. Rest assured."

Slash could almost feel the electricity popping around inside of Jay as she stood beside him, exchanging nauseating grins with the badge-toting fancy Dan. Slash just stood there, silently fuming, clenching his fists at his sides, until Pecos reached out and grabbed his arm, gave it a tug.

"Come on, Slash. You heard the lady. Ole Bleed-Em-So's waitin' on us. If we don't want him *bleedin'* us, we'd best hightail it."

Slash had been in a trance of sorts. When Pecos gave him another nudge, pulling him out of it, he said, "Yeah, yeah. Right. I reckon we'll be on our way."

As he glanced at Jay once more and stepped around the tall, handsome Cisco Walsh, the marshal glanced at him again with that infernal, charming smile and said, "Again, it was nice to meet you fellas. See you around."

"Good luck, boys," Jay called.

"Good luck, boys," Slash growled to himself as he picked his hat up off the hall floor, where it had tumbled when he'd first hit the carpet. "See you around . . . my ass!" Setting his hat on his head, he added, keeping his voice low, "Not if I see you first, you starch-drawered hooplehead!"

Pecos had retrieved his own hat and, donning it, caught up to Slash. He walked along beside him, scowling at him. "What the hell's got into you?"

Slash tried to respond, but only a growl bubbled up out of his throat.

"What is it?" Pecos prodded as they started down the stairs. "You think Jay's got somethin' goin' with the marshal?"

"Ain't it obvious?"

Pecos frowned, shrugged. "No. I mean, they're obviously friends. Like Jay said, they met back in Dodge. Before Pistol Pete. But old friends—that's all they are."

As they gained the bottom of the stairs and began sidling through the swarming crowd, heading for the front door, Slash said, "How do you know they were just friends? How do you know they're *still* just friends?"

Pecos threw his head back and laughed.

"What's funny?"

"You."

"How am I funny?"

Pecos snarled when they stepped through the batwings and started across the Thousand Delights' broad front veranda.

"You're jealous. Why, you stiffened up like a conquistador's suit of armor as soon as that big rake walked into the room. It was obvious as the nose on your face."

"Well, of course I'm jealous. Did you see that tailor's dummy? Some women like 'em . . . you know . . ."

"Tall and handsome as a freshly minted penny? Men who know how to dress an' comb their hair? I'll be damned if he don't bathe at least once a week, too. Oh, yeah—women are all over that!" Pecos chuckled as they headed for the freighting compound and the corral in which they kept their horses.

"Wears a badge, too." Slash shook his head and added through gritted teeth, "Big fancy pistol . . ."

"I bet he rides a big black Thoroughbred, too," Pecos teased his friend. "A stallion, no doubt. With fire in its eyes. Hah!"

"Oh, stop makin' fun of my misery," Slash railed as they approached the barn and corral to the left of their business's main office. "Can't you see she's gone for that . . . that badge-totin' fancy Dan?"

Pecos stopped in front of the barn door. "Oh, she is not."

"She is, too!"

"No, she's not."

"Is too!"

Pecos placed a hand on Slash's shoulder. "I seen the way she looked at that fancy Dan, as you call the jake. But I've seen the way she looks at you, too, and, believe me—because if I've learned one solid thing in this life, it's the hearts of the ladies—when Jay's eyes fall on your rancid countenance, for some reason or another they light up even brighter than they did for Cisco Walsh."

Slash frowned, canted his head to one side, skeptically. "Really?"

"And she gets an even pinker flush in those pretty cheeks of hers."

"Ah, hell—you're just sayin' that so I'll get the hump out of my neck."

"No, I'm not. She's gone for you, Slash. Pure and simple. You keep that ring in a safe place till you're ready to put it on her finger." Pecos paused. "Take one more word of advice?"

"Go ahead—you're on a roll!"

"Ask her soon. She's not gettin' no younger. You can't expect her to wait around forever, wonderin' if you're ever gonna pull the trigger."

He lifted the wire loop from the corral gate and drew the gate open. "Come on. Let's see what kind of nastiness ole Bleed-Em-So's got in store for us now."

CHAPTER 7

Chief Marshal Bledsoe thought it prudent that he and the two former cutthroats keep their arrangement as secret as possible. The marshal didn't think it would reflect well on the federal government if folks knew it had amnestied two career criminals in return for their service, that is, running down owlhoots every bit as bad as Slash and Pecos once were—and worse—and killing them.

The eastern newspapers would have an ink-fest if they found out that Uncle Sam had amnestied two career criminals and turned them into paid assassins.

Apparently, Bledsoe and even the president of the United States thought it made sense, though, given the nasty cut of the outlaws who currently ran off their leashes on the still relatively lawless western frontier. Who but two cutthroats would be better qualified for running down and bringing to justice—or flat-out killing—their own?

Bledsoe's sending Jack Penny and a whole pack of nasty bounty hunters to kill them, and then Slash and Pecos in turn killing the bounty hunters, with Penny now included, had been a pretty good test of their abilities. Even at their advanced ages, though neither Slash nor Pecos saw their mid-fifties as being all that advanced. Of course, Bledsoe hadn't intended Penny's ambush to be a test. He'd genuinely wanted Slash and Pecos dead.

Who could blame the man?

Slash himself had crippled Bledsoe many years ago. He hadn't intended to, but the lawman—a deputy U.S. marshal at the time—had caught one of Slash's ricochets. It had shattered Bledsoe's spine, confining him to a pushchair.

Slash knew that, given their history, Bledsoe wasn't going to pull any punches when handing out job assignments to the two former cutthroats. Slash and Pecos were always going to be going after the worst of the worst.

Until their tickets were punched.

Luther T. "Bleed-Em-So" Bledsoe would not shed any tears at their funerals. If they received funerals. Which they almost certainly wouldn't.

Bledsoe kept an office of sorts in the little, near-ghost town of Cedar City, which sat amongst rocks and cedars in a broad horseshoe of the Cache la Poudre River. The town had never been a city, despite its obvious aspirations, and had ceased even to be a town when the army pulled out of Camp Collins, which was the original name for Fort Collins. Now it wasn't even a fort anymore, and all that remained of Cedar City were a few abandoned mud-brick dwellings, an abandoned livery barn and stock corral, and a single saloon, the Cormorant, which mostly served the rare drifter and local cow puncher and acted as a home to the old gentleman who owned the place—a stove-up former Texas Ranger, Tex Willey.

Tex and the chief marshal had been friends for a couple of generations, having worked together in chasing curly wolves in their heydays.

These days, Bledsoe came out here to get work done when he found himself drowning in red tape in his bona fide digs in the Federal Building in Denver. It was a handy location, given its close proximity to the railroad line. An old freighting trail, still in good repair, offered access from the rail line to Cedar City.

Now as Slash and Pecos rode into the ghost town from the west, they saw the old Concord mud wagon that Bledsoe had customized for himself, nattied up a bit with brass fittings and gas lamps, softer seats and velvet drapes offering privacy, and brackets on the side for housing his pushchair. The horses milling in the corral flanking the mud wagon were likely the two that had pulled Bledsoe out here from the train.

The other two would be those of the two deputies who always escorted and ran interference against possible assassins. The wily old reprobate had locked up his share of owlhoots over his long years of service to Uncle Sam, and he had a poisonous personality, to boot. There were likely plenty of gunslingers who would love to add the crippled old devil's notch to their pistol grips.

The two deputies sat on the corral's top slat, to the right of the gate, smoking. Slash could see only their silhouettes in the darkness, but he could clearly see the badges pinned to their coats and the coals of their cigarettes, when they took drags, the gray smoke wafting around their high-crowned, broad-brimmed Stetsons.

Slash and Pecos didn't say anything to the two federals. The two federals said nothing to them. They just sat there atop the corral, smoking and staring dubiously toward the newcomers in the night, the darkness relieved by a low half-moon, stars, and the lamplight ebbing from the saloon's front windows.

Two saddle horses were tied to the hitchrack fronting the low, mud-brick, brush-roofed saloon. The cutthroats and old Bledsoe likely wouldn't have total privacy, but out here, men knew not to shoot their mouths off without getting something else shot off for their indiscretion. Also, very few who visited the saloon these days were from around here. Most were just passing through, keeping to the back roads and shaggy ravine trails. As travelers, they knew to keep their noses out of other men's business.

Slash and Pecos put their own mounts up to the hitchrack. The strains of a fiddle pushed through the batwings atop the narrow, rickety-looking front stoop. In one of the dimly lit windows fronting the place, two shadows moved close together, as though a couple were dancing.

Slash glanced at Pecos. Pecos shrugged.

The two cutthroats tossed their reins over the rail, worn down to a mere stick in places by the reins of many a soldier's horse, then negotiated the untrustworthy three steps to the porch and pushed through the batwings. Slash and Pecos stood side by side just inside the doors, hearing the batwings clatter back into place behind them.

The saloon was twice as wide as it was deep. The bar, comprised of pine boards stretched over three stout beer kegs and flanked by dusty shelves housing maybe a dozen or so dusty bottles, occupied the rear of the place directly beyond the batwings. An old man with snow-white hair hanging down his back in a tight braid and a crow's dark-eyed face with a sun-seasoned, liver-spotted beak of a nose sat in a chair in front of the bar, sawing away on an old fiddle. Tex Willey wore old denims held up on his skinny frame by snakeskin galluses, a grimy calico shirt, and a badly sun-faded red bandanna knotted around his red turkey neck.

To the right of the old man, in a place clear of tables in which soldiers used to dance with the parlor girls who'd worked here at one time, two middle-aged men in dusty trail garb were now dancing just like a young man and a young woman would have danced back in the day. Only, these two were men. One tall, one short. Both outfitted like cow punchers.

Unshaven. Battered hats on their heads. Old pistols in cracked leather holsters sagged on their thighs, above their mule-eared boots.

Just then the taller gent raised his hand and gave the short man a twirl, and the short man's batwing chaps buffeted out around his legs, whang strings flying. He closed his eyes, smiling dreamily as the old man continued to saw away on his scarred, ancient fiddle. Slash thought he recognized the song, even so poorly played, as "The Gal I Left Behind."

Slash and Pecos shared another look and a shrug.

By now, Tex Willey had spied the newcomers.

The old man paused in his fiddling—though the dancers did not stop dancing—to look at Slash and Pecos and nod toward the door at the back of the room, to the right of the bar.

"Thanks, Tex," Slash said as he began wending his way through the dozen or so dusty tables and around the two dancers, who appeared so absorbed in their two-step that they did not take note of the newcomers, even as they did a swing and an almost-graceful pirouette that nearly rammed the short one into Pecos as he stepped around them.

Slash rapped his knuckles on the door of the old storeroom that Bledsoe now used as a part-time office.

The knock was answered by a raspy man's voice saying, "If you're anyone but my two raggedy-heeled, over-the-hill cutthroats, stay out. I got work to do!"

Slash glanced at Pecos and gave a crooked smile.

Pecos shrugged.

Slash tripped the latch and stepped into the roomy office that owned the molasses aroma of liquor and malty ale. "*Your* cutthroats?"

"Oh, you're mine, all right." Luther T. Bledsoe was sitting at a big walnut desk he must have had hauled all the way out here from Denver. The chief marshal looked especially small and insignificant, sitting with his pushchair drawn up to the giant, cluttered desk on which a Tiffany lamp burned.

"Bought and paid for!" added the chief marshal with a delighted, mocking flourish, dropping the pen he'd been scribbling on a legal pad with to lean back in his chair. He ran his two bone-white, long-fingered hands through the cottony down of his unkempt, silver hair after thumbing his little, round, steel-framed spectacles up his long nose.

As Pecos closed the office door and stepped up beside Slash, Slash saw his tall partner's head swing toward where Bledsoe's comely female assistant, Miss Abigail Langdon, sat at another desk abutting the wall to the right of the chief marshal. Her desk was every bit as large as Bledsoe's, and just as cluttered. A pink lamp burned on her desk, illuminating her cool, remote, severely Nordic beauty in the flickering light's shifting planes and shadows.

Miss Langdon flipped a heavy curling lock of her red-gold hair back behind her shoulder, revealing wide cheekbones that tapered severely down to a fine chin and regal jaw. Her crystalline, lake-green eyes, long and slanted like a cat's eyes, lingered on Pecos's tall, broad-shouldered frame, raking him up and down. A dark cloak was pulled around her shoulders, over the purple velvet gown she wore so well. She reached for a shot glass on the desk before her, amidst the clutter of open files and dossiers and bound books on federal law, and took a sip.

Her eyes stayed on Pecos as she said, almost too quietly to be heard above the small fire crackling in the small sheet-iron stove flanking her boss, "Hello."

Pecos seemed to be breathing hard. He cleared his throat thickly and said, "H-hello, there, Miss . . ." He remembered his hat, quickly doffed it, and held it before him. "Hello, there, Miss Langdon."

Slash squelched a chuckle. Pecos had reacted to the remote beauty—whom Slash judged to be in her middle twenties, though with a decidedly more mature air about herself—the first time they'd met. Abigail Langdon had reacted similarly to Pecos. It was almost as though the two were giving off invisible sparks of attraction—a primitive reach for each other.

Bledsoe seemed to sense it now, too. Sitting back in his chair, hands behind his head, he studied the two with an amused half-smile, his eyes dubious.

He slid his gaze to Slash, his eyes vaguely curious. Bledsoe gave a dry chuckle, then leaned forward slightly and beckoned to the two cutthroats impatiently. "Come in, come in. We're burnin' moonlight. I have to get back to that consarned, infernal hellhole, Denver, for a meeting at nine o'clock tomorrow morning. I came out here to try to get a little work done in the peace and quiet of the bucolic countryside, and because I got a fresh job for my two over-the-hill cutthroats."

He smiled at that, again mockingly. He enjoyed ringing men's bells and watching for a reaction that might amuse him. Slash and Pecos had learned that the first time they'd met the man.

"If you really thought we was over-the-hill," Pecos pointed out, indignantly, his voice rising angrily, "we wouldn't have turned Jack Penny into a human sieve tonight, just like we done to the rest of his gang last year. And you wouldn't have called us here, *Chief Marshal*. So why don't you stop tryin' to rub our fur in the wrong direction just 'cause you're hip deep in bureaucratic sheep dip, and bored, and get down to brass tacks."

Slash turned to his partner, brows arched in surprise. Even Miss Langdon turned to look over her shoulder in shock at the tall, silver-blond cutthroat who had just shoveled it right back to old Bleed-Em-So. Pecos rarely got riled or spoke out even when he was. It took a lot to get his dander up. It appeared, however, that the chief marshal's riding him and Slash about their ages—in front of Miss Langdon, especially—had done just that.

Slash covered a chuckle by brushing his fist across his nose and clearing his throat.

her desk, Miss Langdon's eyes met Pecos's once more, and held.

Slash wasn't sure, but he thought the beautiful Scandinavian quirked her mouth corners ever so slightly, appreciatively, before completing her turn toward her desk and sinking back into her chair, once again moving the air touched with the aromas of a springtime desert.

Bledsoe flipped through the file before him, holding one hand on his glasses as he skimmed the typed words.

"Yes, yes, all right," the chief marshal said, closing the folder and tossing it aside. "Just needed to refresh my memory. As I said, don't let the simplicity of this job spoil you. I thought of you for it since you're in the freighting business and, after a year, seemed to be fairly handy at it."

"Did I just hear a compliment?" Slash asked Pecos.

"Nah, couldn't have been."

Ignoring the cutthroats' banter, Bledsoe leaned forward, elbows on his desk, hands steepled before him. "I want you to drive one of your freight wagons up to the mountain mining town of Tin Cup in the Sawatch Range, and haul a lode of gold bars from a mine up there, the Cloud Tickler, as it's called—due to the high altitude in those parts—to Union Station in Denver. There the gold will be placed on a train to the federal mint in San Francisco."

"Doesn't the mine company usually have Wells Fargo haul the ore out of the mountains, Chief?" Slash asked, frowning.

"Of course, they do. Most mines up in that neck of the high-and-rocky ship their gold out by stagecoach. But there's been a problem."

"Robberies," Pecos said.

"The Front Range Stage Company has been robbed so often that Wells Fargo refuses to haul gold for them anymore. Determined to catch the robbers but not wanting to risk losing another strongbox filled with gold, the mining company has instead hired undercover Pinkerton agents to

Bledsoe stared across his cluttered desk at Pecos, tapping his fingers on his blotter. "Well, well, it is possible to get his neck in a hump, after all."

"Oh, you can do it, all right," Slash said. "Always best not to, though. It takes some doin', indeed, but once Pecos has got a mad on, it takes a good long time to cool him off. Sometimes several days, and only after he's turned a whole row of saloons to little more than matchsticks and jackstraws." Slash chuckled dryly, switched positions in his chair. "That's a bonded fact. I'm an eyewitness!"

He chuckled again.

"Duly noted," Bledsoe said, impressed. He sipped from the shot glass on his desk. A tequila bottle stood near his right elbow, uncorked. He did not, however, invite the two cutthroats to imbibe with him and his assistant. It was one thing to employ two men he'd been, for most of his career, trying to run down and jail or execute, one of whom had crippled him, however inadvertently. But old Bleed-Em-So was not going to sink so low as to invite them to *drink* with him.

That would be like telling them he didn't hold a grudge, which of course he did. Anyone would.

Smacking his lips, he set the glass back down on his desk and brushed two fingers across his lips. "All right, all right. What's this about Jack Penny?"

"Gone to his reward," Pecos said. "Which means he's likely wielding a coal shovel about now."

"Hmmm." Bledsoe tapped his fingers on the blotter again. "Self-defense, I'm sure . . ."

"He bushwhacked us in the Thousand Delights. Baited us in with Jay."

"I do hope the lovely Miss Breckenridge is unharmed," Bledsoe said, sounding as though he meant it, though he was well aware that she'd once run with Pistol Pete and that Slash and Pecos had often holed up in her San Juan Mountain cabin between outlaw jobs. Still, it was hard for anyone to dislike Jay. Even old Bleed-Em-So.

"Fit as a fiddle," Slash said. "A little shaken up is all."

Bledsoe looked pointedly across his desk at "his" two cut-throats. "I hope I'm not going to read about this in the newspapers, gentlemen."

Slash and Pecos shared another look.

"Jay'll keep it out of the papers," Slash said, adding with a definite edge in his voice and a burn in his belly, "She an' the new marshal at Fort Collins are old pals, don't ya know."

Pecos glanced at him. Slash did not meet his gaze.

"Good, good," Bledsoe said, leaning forward and entwining his hands on his desk. "All right, then, let us get down to pay dirt."

CHAPTER 8

The willowy old chief marshal sagged back in his chair, thumbing his spectacles up his nose and entwining his hands once more behind his woolly head. "I got a job for you. Don't let its simplicity spoil you."

"A simple job," Pecos said, smiling. "I like that."

Bledsoe glanced at his assistant, who sat hunched over her desk, her back to the men. She appeared to be writing in one of the several legal pads surrounding her and her shot glass. Slash could hear the quick, unceasing sounds of her nib and the frequent clink as she dipped the pen into an inkwell.

"Do you have the file over there, Miss Langdon?" the chief marshal asked.

"Right here, Chief." The gorgeous young woman plucked a manila folder off her desk and rose from her chair. She was a tall, big-boned young lady, a creature of the rocky fjords, yet she moved with the grace of a forest sprite. The air she displaced smelled of cherries and sage—just the right combination of sweet and spicy.

Slash heard Pecos draw a sharp breath as Miss Langdon leaned over the chief marshal's desk to hand him the folder. Pecos squirmed a little in his chair. Slash elbowed him. Pecos glanced at him, scowling and flushing. Turning back toward

ride the stage, guarding a dummy strongbox in hopes to catch the robbers red-handed once and for all, and get them out of their hair."

Pecos was raking his thumb across the heel of his boot, which he had propped on his left knee. "Dummy strongbox, Chief?"

"You'll be carryin' the real one. You see, the Cloud Tickler isn't taking any chances. They can't afford to lose one more ounce of gold. So, while they're gonna fill that stagecoach full of Pinkertons—there'll even be a couple of Pinkertons in the driver's boot, acting as driver and shotgun messenger—they're not going to risk shipping the gold on that run. You'll be shipping it in your freight wagon, in a hidden strongbox, taking a separate trail."

"Just us?" Pecos asked, canting his head toward his partner. "Just me an' Slash?"

"Just you two. If all goes as planned, no one will suspect that you two are anything but what you'll be pretending to be—two freighters who drove a full load up to Tin Cup, picked up their pay, and are heading back out of the mountains to home sweet home." Bledsoe paused, blinked, snapped his mouth slightly, adjusting his false teeth. His eyes shifted quickly between the pair. "Think you can handle that, boys?"

"I don't know," Slash said. "Somethin' about this makes me a little uneasy. How much gold will we be hauling in our humble freighter?"

"Pretty damn close to a hundred thousand dollars' worth."

Slash and Pecos whistled at that.

Bledsoe said, "Gold prices are on the rise just now, and the Cloud Tickler is extracting some of the highest-grade ore in the Rockies at the moment. How long that will last is anyone's guess, but right now it's imperative they get their gold ingots out of those mountains and down to the train station in Denver."

"Why don't you throw a few guards in with us?" Pecos

said. "If the company is mining that kind of color, surely they could afford it."

Bledsoe took another sip of his tequila, extending one beringed pinky. He made sure the cutthroats knew it was right tasty stuff, smacking his lips and sighing as he returned the glass to his desk.

Again, he leaned forward and steepled his fingers before him. "Even the richest companies are tighter than the bark on a tree. The way they see it, that's how they stay rich. They're paying enough money for the Pinkertons they've hired to corral the stage robbers. They don't see the need to waste any more on your run, which should go without a hitch if you both play it right and don't go getting drunk and shooting your mouths off in the various and sundry bordellos up thataway!"

Now it was Slash's turn to cloud up and rain. "You know we didn't stay two steps ahead of you and the other federals as well as bounty hunters all those years by getting drunk and shooting our mouths off about our holdup plans in hurdy-gurdy houses, Chief Bleed-Em-So!"

Bledsoe sat back in his chair, chuckling delightedly at the reaction he'd evoked. "No, no, you're right there, Slash. That's partly why I've chosen you boys for the job. And why there's no need to throw Pinkertons at you. Besides, if anyone were to see more than you two within several hundred yards of your freighter, they might get wise to the ploy. No, it's better this way—just you two and a seemingly empty freight wagon. Only . . ." Bledsoe raised his brows to convey the gravity of the operation. "Only, you'll be hauling around one hundred thousand dollars of high-grade gold."

"Damn," Pecos said.

"Yeah," Slash said. "Damn!"

Bledsoe furled his brows and carved deep lines of castigation across his high, weathered, liver-spotted forehead.

"Don't you two old cutthroats go gettin' any ideas, now, you hear?"

"Ideas?" Slash said. "About what?"

"About what?" Bledsoe mocked, widening his eyes.

"Ah, hell, Chief," Pecos said. "You know we done mended our ways. Why, neither me nor Slash would ever consider runnin' off with that gold."

"No?" Bledsoe asked.

"Of course not!" Pecos cried.

The chief marshal jerked a crooked finger toward Slash. "Then why is he sweating?"

"What?" Pecos said.

"Look at him. He's sweating."

This nudged Miss Langdon's mind out of the paperwork before her. She turned her head to frown over her shoulder toward Slash sitting on the other side of Pecos from her.

"I am not!" Slash said. He brushed his hand across his left cheek and looked at it. He'd be damned if he wasn't sweating, after all. "Well, if I am, it's because you got a fire goin' on a warm night. Good lord, man, who lights a fire out here in August?"

"This is a chilly night for August," Miss Langdon said in her quiet, sonorous voice.

Bledsoe narrowed his eyes at Pecos. "You are, too."

"I'm what?"

"Sweatin'!" Bledsoe pounded his fist on his desk. "Look at ya, both of ya sittin' there sweatin', fairly salivating at the thought of high-tailing it all the way to Mexico with a hundred thousand dollars in high-grade gold!"

"Oh, hell!" Pecos said, quickly turning his head to Bledsoe's pretty assistant and saying, "Uh . . . pardon my farm talk, Miss Langdon."

She lowered her eyes and half-smiled, flushing in the flickering lamplight.

Turning to Bledsoe again, Pecos said, "You can't make a dog not lick his chops at the smell of fresh beef. That don't mean he's gonna rise up on his hind feet and snag a T-bone off the cookin' range."

"My partner's right for once in his life," Slash said. "You can't keep us from droolin' over the thought of that much gold. Lord knows we tried for that much a time or two, but never even got close. But we're not stupid enough to actually run off with the Cloud Ticker's ingots. Of course, you'd run us down before we even got to Denver, and we'd be hangin' from the gallows outside the Federal Building faster'n a judge could hammer his gavel. We know that. We're not stupid despite how Pecos might look."

Pecos gave him a frosty smile. "Thank you for so nobly rushing to my defense, partner."

"Don't mention it."

Miss Langdon snorted, then turned around quickly and dug back into her paperwork, scribbling away with her ink pen.

"Rest assured you'd be run down, all right," Bledsoe assured the cutthroats. "You wouldn't get far. And, believe me, the deputy marshals who ran you down would have marching orders not to waste time taking you back to Denver, where you'd only waste more taxpayers' dollars on a worthless court trial. They'd be under orders to hang you from the nearest tree and to leave you there, a feast for the buzzards and crows!"

Bledsoe pounded his desk once more. "Now get out of here. Miss Langdon and I still got a pile of work to plow through before we head back to the oversized stockyard perdition of Denver."

"When are we due in Tin Cup?" Slash asked.

"As soon as you get there. The Pinkertons are en route even as we palaver. Here—take this." Bledsoe tossed the manila folder over to Slash's side of the desk. "That's the file on the operation. The name of your contact in Tin Cup is in

there. It's a Pink—you know, one of Pinkerton's female operatives. Make sure—let me repeat—make damn good and
sure that file doesn't leave your side. Once you know everything that's in there, burn it." He frowned suddenly, cutting
his gaze between the two men. "Say . . . you two can read,
can't you?"

"Of course, we can read!" Slash said, chuckling his exasperation at the question as he flipped open the file. "Leastways, I can. I don't know about—"

"I can read just fine!" Pecos growled, rising from his chair.

"Say, Chief?" Slash said, also gaining his feet. "You said
we was supposed to haul a load of freight up to Tin Cup. To
make us look genuine, I assume. What freight did you have
in mind?"

Bledsoe shrugged and looked up impatiently. "I don't know.
Why don't you just fill the back of your freight wagon with
firewood or something like that? Tie a tarp over it so no one's
the wiser. Unload it once you get up there. And make sure no
one sees what it really is, or your goose is cooked!"

Slash and Pecos shared a glance, shrugged.

"Nice palaverin' with ya, Chief," Slash said, donning his
hat as he headed for the door.

Bledsoe only grumbled and muttered something incoher-
ent as he picked up his own ink pen and began scribbling,
holding his spectacles on his nose with one hand.

Pecos headed for the door behind Slash, turning toward
Bledsoe's pretty assistant and saying, "Just wanted to mention you look especially fine this evening, Miss Langdon."

Miss Langdon looked up quickly, arching her brows over
her lovely eyes in surprise. "Oh . . . well, uh . . . thank you,
Mister Bak—"

Backing toward the door and holding his hat over his
heart, Pecos said, "No, no—please, call me Melvin."

"Oh . . . well, then, uh . . . thank you for that nice compliment, Melvin."

"Be seein' you now," Pecos said.

"Good-bye," Abigail Langdon said, giving a little wave.

Pecos backed out the door. Slash grabbed a chair and thrust it behind him, turning it sideways. Pecos backed into it, ramming it over on its side, then giving an indignant cry as he twisted around, tripping over it and falling to the floor with a booming thud.

Chuckling, Slash ran to the batwings.

Pecos rolled up on his side. He saw Miss Langdon standing in the open door to Bledsoe's office, holding a hand over her mouth in deep dismay.

Pecos's cheeks turned as hot as a branding iron. He swung his head toward where Slash was just then running through the batwings, and yelled, "Come back fer your whippin', you black-hearted son of Satan!"

CHAPTER 9

"Slash, you know what I think?" Pecos said later that night as the two former cutthroats lay in their respective cots, on opposite ends of their small, crude cabin behind their just-as-small and crude freighting office.

"Forget it."

"Huh?"

"If you're thinkin' I should help you use the privy after all that steak an' beans you had for supper—not to mention beer and whiskey—forget it. You're too damn big an' drunk, and I drank too much whiskey my ownself to stay on my own two feet. You'd fall and kill us both."

It was true. After they'd gotten back to Fort Collins, they'd headed for the Bon-Ton Café on Larimer Avenue, where they'd proceeded to pad out their empty bellies with liberal portions of red meat, beans, and sourdough bread. They followed that up with whiskey in a little cantina on the other side of the street. They'd decided that after the dustup earlier in Jay's room, they'd probably best not show their faces in the Thousand Delights for a while. Someone might recognize them for who they really were and complicate their lives.

Pecos's wrath over Slash's high jinks out at the Cormorant had dissipated quickly. The big cutthroat could blaze as hot as a pistol in mid-fire, but the smoke and flames usually cleared just as quickly as they had erupted. Especially when his ire was directed at Slash. They could get into all-out brawls, the cutthroats could, but they were the brawls of brothers, not true-blue enemies.

Pecos's wrath would burn down quickly, even when Slash did something as boyishly devilish as what he'd done to his partner out in Cedar City, in front of the gal for whom he had, inexplicably, developed a mutual, animal-like attraction. Pecos knew Slash had merely been out to amuse himself as well as to distract himself from one Miss Jaycee Breckenridge. Pecos knew Jay was on Slash's mind. Her and the fancy-Dan town marshal, that was. Pecos always knew what Slash was thinking, just as Slash could read his partner's mind as well.

"That ain't what I'm thinkin' about," Pecos said. "I'm too drunk to even think about usin' the privy even with help. I was layin' here thinkin', waiting for this cabin to stop turnin' circles around me, that one reason Bledsoe selected us for that job up in Tin Cup is because he's wanting to get our goats."

"Oh, yeah."

"Ain't I right?"

"You're right, all right. One of the rare times."

"He's probably just chucklin' to himself right now, as he's rollin' back toward Denver, about how that gold is going to affect us. And there's not gonna be a damn thing we can do about it, 'cause we both know we'd never make a clean break with it."

"Oh, yeah," Slash said, keeping one bare foot on the floor as he tried to steady the cabin that was swirling around him, as well. "He's a devil, all right." He chuckled. "He'll ram the knife into each of us whenever he can, gettin' us back for past history. He can't jail us or hang us anymore, but he can do what he can to ride roughshod on us. Give us all the toughest, most dangerous jobs, likely half-hopin' in the back of his mind that we'll eventually get fed a pill we can't digest."

"He's takin' his revenge on us, ain't he?"

"Oh, yeah." Slash chuckled again as he stared up at the ceiling. Or tried to. It was hard to stare straight at something that was moving. "He knows us too well, don't he?"

"All too well." Slash turned his head to stare at his partner, whose lumpy silhouette was all he could see over there on the other end of the cabin. "You know what I was layin' here thinkin' about?"

"Jay."

"No." Slash drew a deep breath, let it out slowly. "I was thinkin' about that damn gold just the way I know Bleed-Em-So wants us thinkin' about it. Dreamin' about it."

"I know. I was, too."

Slash chuckled, shook his head, and resumed staring up at the ceiling. "That old catamount!"

"One hundred thousand dollars." Pecos whistled. "That'd take us a long way, Slash. We could go down to Mexico, all the way down to South America. Buy us a big ranch down there. Or our own mine. Oh, how the busthead would flow!"

"Not busthead," Slash corrected his partner. "Nothin' but the good stuff. The best tequila and pulque south of the border!"

"And the women . . ."

"Oh, lordy—the women." Slash had said that last sentence with little of the delight he'd intended. His own words had sounded flat to him. That's because he hadn't quite gotten the word "women" out of his mouth before Jay's face had floated up in his mind's eye. No sooner had he seen her face than he saw the face of Cisco Walsh, as well.

Walsh—that handsome face of his, and the fancy cut of his clothes.

Walsh with that smile on his face as he gazed appreciatively—all too appreciatively—at Jaycee Breckenridge . . .

"You could bring Jay," Pecos said. He had his head turned toward Slash, staring through the darkness at him. "She'd come along down to Mexico, if we were toting that much gold. She'd meet us down there . . . and you two . . . well, you could . . ."

"Forget it."

"Huh?"

"I don't want to talk about her tonight. I just want to lay here and torture myself with ideas about all the ways we could spend that gold down in Mexico, where we'd live like two Jay Goulds in golden castles."

"Best not do that no more."

"Why the hell not? We can at least dream about it, can't we?"

"Dreamin's one thing. Actin' on them dreams is another. I'm afraid if we keep layin' here thinkin' up all the ways we could spend that treasure we're gonna have in our possession for four or five nights—just you, me, an' a hundred thousand dollars in high-grade gold—we might start venturin' into dangerous territory. We might start plannin' on how we could really get away with it!"

Slash rolled onto a shoulder, facing Pecos. "Well, you know what, partner? I was just thinkin' . . ."

Slash let his voice trail off. Even in the darkness, he could see Pecos's two scolding eyes staring back at him.

Slash sighed and rolled back against his pillow. "All right, all right. Bad idea."

"Go to sleep, Slash."

"Yeah, yeah," Slash said, sheepish. "All right."

It took a while, but he finally did. But he dreamed of dusky-eyed Spanish queens and golden castles.

Slash woke earlier than he'd expected. Pecos was still asleep, and rather than wake him, Slash took a whore's bath, dressed, and headed out to fill his belly. He'd had a big steak and a platter of beans only a few hours ago, but the whiskey must have dissolved it and left a gaping hole in his innards.

He felt as hollow as a dead man's boot.

Since the dining room at the Thousand Delights boasted the best breakfast in town, maybe on the entire Front Range north of Denver, he headed that way. He wasn't much in the mood for seeing Jay, but he doubted he'd run into her at this early hour. Jay usually stayed up late, keeping an eye on the saloon and gambling parlor as well as overseeing the working girls on the third floor—she was as protective as an old mother hen to her doxies—and usually didn't roll out of her big, four-posted bed till mid-morning.

Not that Slash knew that from personal observation. He had not yet known the charms of the woman's boudoir. He was not a fast mover in that regard. Nor in matters of the heart. Sometimes he dragged his feet too long in the dust, and that's where he'd often gotten left. He feared he might be there right now, in fact.

Old Cisco Walsh was likely up there, sawing logs at this very moment, with a big, dung-eating grin on his handsome jaws, Jay curled up beside him.

The idea made Slash feel as though he'd just chugged a quart of sour milk. He almost decided against breakfast, but if he and Pecos were heading back into the mountains this morning, he'd need to fill his trough, so to speak. Neither he nor his partner were very handy with camp cooking, though they'd had plenty of opportunity. Usually, they just ate beans and jerky and baking powder biscuits, if they remembered to buy flour before leaving town. Occasionally they'd shoot or snare a rabbit and cook the meat on a makeshift spit, usually charring it beyond recognition.

Now, he needed some ham and eggs and a big helping of fried potatoes, and a half-dozen buttermilk pancakes with a big scoop of butter and a hearty helping of the real maple syrup they served in the Thousand Delights dining room.

The three steaming platters were set out before him in all their succulent glory, the scent of the warm maple syrup adding a pleasant sweetness to the smoky aroma of the slab of ham that resided half under four big, golden-yoked fried eggs fresh from the chickens of an old Norwegian woman who owned a little shotgun ranch at the edge of town, near Horsetooth Rock.

Slash was one of only four men in the dining room, which sat adjacent to a small, carpeted entrance hall from the saloon, and which was outfitted with a dozen round oak tables clad in fine white cloths and silverware wrapped in cloth napkins. Nothing but the best for Jaycee Breckenridge. Slash knew that she'd put down the stake Pistol Pete had left her as a down payment and taken out a bank loan for the rest, and already, only a year into the business, she'd paid the note down by half.

She was too good a woman for him. She had too much business savvy and plain old horse sense. She was a respected businesswoman in Fort Collins, and that reputation would do nothing but grow. It was just as well she'd taken up with the stylish town marshal, Cisco Walsh. They'd make a handsome couple. A pair of eights. A jack and a queen.

Slash Braddock had been a damn joker all his life, and he'd be buried in potter's field, a joker in death. It was what he deserved.

The livery-garbed waiter had just cleared Slash's table of everything except his coffee cup and the steaming silver server, when a familiar voice startled him from behind: "Good morning, Sla . . . I mean, Mister Braddock."

Slash looked up to see none other than Jaycee herself smiling down at him, one hand on the back of his chair. She was dressed in a beguiling gown, her hair was half up and half down, sprayed across her half-bare and beautifully freckled shoulders, and she looked ravishing already—here with the sun barely up.

"Jay!" Slash said, immediately chastising himself for sounding like an overeager schoolboy. "What're you . . . what're you . . . ?"

He'd started to rise, but Jay placed a hand on his shoulder and shoved him back down in his chair. "Please, sit. I know, I know—it's early for me. Believe me, I'd still be sawing logs, but I have a wedding reception at noon to prepare for. No rest for the wicked."

"Time for a cup of coffee?" Slash asked, nodding at the steaming server.

Jay glanced at a clock on the wall, then folded her long, well-formed body into the chair across from Slash. "Indeed, I can. I'm my own boss, aren't I?"

"There you go."

Slash glanced at the waiter, "Phil, a cup for the boss, will you?"

The waiter glanced at Jay, smiled, winked, then disappeared into the kitchen.

Slash sat back in his chair, holding his coffee cup, which he'd just refilled, in both hands. "Did you, uh . . . did you sleep well, Jay?" He felt a vein in his neck flutter.

She glanced across the table at him, then leaned forward, resting her elbows on the table before her and setting her chin atop the shelf of her entwined fingers. "I did. I was exhausted. Long day . . . as you well know."

"Yeah, sure was."

Jay smiled her sweet smile. "I took care of everything with Cisco. I mean, Marshal Walsh."

"Well, if you know him so well . . ."

Jay nodded. "I knew he wouldn't be a problem. He may, in fact, be a valuable friend to you two here in Fort Collins. I know I've found him a valuable friend over the years."

"You have, have you?"

"Indeed."

"Well, then . . ."

"He's agreed to make sure your real names stay out of the papers. I wrote out and signed an affidavit for him last night. Cisco . . . Marshal Walsh"—Jay amended with a coy smile— "thinks that's probably all we'll need. He'll let me know if you need to speak to a coroner's jury, but he's going to try and have my statement be the end of it. Jack Penny and the other two men were known outlaws with nasty reputations, so . . ."

"I didn't recognize the other two, but I know Penny had some money ridin' in his hat."

"Cisco said the other two were out-of-work, raggedy-heeled former railroad workers who'd been in and out of trouble along the Front Range for the past couple of years. One was wanted for cutting a doxie in Denver, and the other shot a gambler to death up in Leadville."

"Well, then't. . . you an' Cisco palavered it all out."

"Yes."

As the waiter delivered Jay's coffee cup, Slash sipped his own mud and gave a stiff half-smile. Again, he felt that vein in his neck flutter. "I reckon you was up mighty late . . . with ole Cisco. Uh . . . sorry about that." He dropped his gaze and took another sip of the coffee.

Jay lifted her cup and blew on her own steaming coffee. "Oh, it's all right. Cisco and I go way back."

"So you said."

Jay sipped her coffee, then, setting the cup back down on its saucer, frowned across the table at him. "Slash, is something on your mind?"

"What's that?" He cleared a constriction in his throat.

"You seem . . . well, odd."

"Odd?"

"Oh, I know," Jay said, lifting her cup again in her pale, elegant hands, the left one adorned with one simple ruby ring set in gold. "You met with Bleed-Em-So. That must be what's wrong with you. Can you tell me what he wanted? Some new job for you and Pecos? Whatever it is, I hope it's not too dangerous, Slash."

"Oh, nah, nah," Slash said. "Pretty simple, really. I won't bore you with the details. We'll be cuttin' out purty soon. In fact . . ." He took a large, quick sip of his coffee. "I prob'ly best be pullin' my picket pin. Pecos is prob—"

Jay reached across the table to place her hand on his. "Slash, what's wrong?"

He frowned over his cup at her. "What do you mean?"

Jay returned his puzzled frown, though he vaguely opined that hers probably looked more authentic. "You're wondering about Cisco Walsh and me, aren't you?" She probed him more intensely with her stony, dark pupils. "That's what's bothering you, isn't it?"

"Ah, hell!" Slash said a little too loudly. "No, you got me wrong, Jay. Cisco—he looks like a right nice fella. Big and tall and broad-shouldered. Handsome as all get-out, I'm sure. Wears a polished badge. Tailor-cut suit made special. Has him a good upstandin' badge pinned to his vest. I'm sure he's right enticin' to a purty woman like yourself. A good man all around."

Jay's expression changed from curiosity to incredulity. She set her coffee cup back down in its saucer, leaned back in her chair, and crossed her arms on the low-cut bodice of her dress. Her cheeks paled a little, and her lids hooded her eyes severely. "What if he did?"

"What's that?"

"What if he did look right *enticin'* to me?"

Jay paused, continuing to probe Slash with her gaze. He felt himself shrinking a little against it, his shoulders tightening, drawing closer together. That vein in his neck was writhing around like a rattler coming out of hibernation. He wished it would go back to sleep. He tried to say something, but the constriction had returned to his throat.

"Slash?"

He returned his gaze to her pointed one.

"How would you feel if I told you I fancied Cisco Walsh?" Keeping her eyes on his, Jay tucked her bottom lip under her top lip for a moment, then drew a shallow breath. "How would you feel if I told you that Cisco has told me that he fancies me, and that we've agreed to spend some time together. Some *romantic* time together. To see where it led us." Again, she paused, making Slash's heart flutter. He felt like a bug on a pin held up for close scrutiny. "How would you feel about that, Slash Braddock?"

CHAPTER 10

Slash stared back at Jay, sitting across the table from him. It was hard to hold her gaze. Her eyes were almost as hard and severe as that of an angry, challenging schoolmarm.

"How would I feel?" he croaked.

"Yes," Jay said, crisply. "How would you *feel?*"

"I'd, uh . . . I'd, uh . . ."

"Yes? Out with it, amigo!"

Slash's heartbeat increased. He sat up straight in his chair; then, crouching forward slightly, leaning toward Jay, he shoved his right hand into his right coat pocket. He wrapped his hand around the ring box. His heart was fairly racing now, and a hot wash of blood rose into his face. He started to pull the box out of his pocket.

Then he stopped.

He winced, grunted. He tried again to pull the ring out of his pocket.

Nothing doing. It was as though his right arm and hand had become paralyzed.

He tried again, but for the life of him, he could feel neither his hand nor the box he thought it was wrapped around. He grunted, winced. He looked at her staring back at him, one brow arched, waiting. She was opening and closing her hands around her arms, and he could hear her tapping the toe of one shoe on the floor beneath the table.

He tried again to pull the box from his pocket, but it was as though his entire body had returned to stone. His heart was pounding so fiercely that it ached. Sweat beaded his brows. That he could feel. It was not a good feeling at all.

Jay stared at him with those hard, cold eyes, waiting. "Well . . ."

Slash ran his tongue across the backside of his upper teeth and swallowed. It was as though another man were speaking, though he could feel his own mouth shaping the words and letting them slither out from between his lips, while yet another voice inside him—his true, authentic voice, the voice that spoke from his heart of hearts—bellowed, *"No, you damn fool! Tell her how you really feel, Slash Braddock! Ask the gal to marry you, because that's what you really want, you lame-brained post-head! It's all you've wanted for years, and it's all you're gonna continue to want for the rest of your silly days!"*

"Slash," Jay said, drawing another deep breath, "I'm going to ask you one more time . . ."

"How would I *f-feel*?" he said.

"Yes? How would you feel?"

The imposter inside him smiled winningly—oh, what a cunning, confident con artist he was, too!—and chuckled. "He's a helluva fella, Jay. I can tell. A right upstanding citizen with a bold future. You deserve the best of men. If you wanted to go ahead and let Cisco Walsh spark you, then I'd give you my blessing. I know Pecos would, too."

He pulled his hand out of his pocket, only vaguely amazed that he could feel it again, and glanced at the clock on the wall. "In the meantime, I reckon I'd best tramp on back to the salt mine before Pecos sends out a catch party for me. We have some ground to cover."

Chuckling again as though he didn't have a care in the

world—while his heart of hearts was tearing in two—he rose smoothly from his chair, tossed his napkin onto the table, and donned his hat. "Take care, Jay. See you when we get back. Say hi to the marshal for me!"

Jay sat back in her chair, half-slumped, as though all the air had gone out of her. She stared up at him, her face pale, a thin sheen of tears accumulating in her beautiful eyes. Slash winked, nodded, turned away, and tramped on out of the dining room and into the hotel's foyer.

He must have blacked out on his feet for a time, for he wasn't aware of anything for several minutes, until he found himself halfway across Main Street, heading for the freight yard, with a man's voice cussing him royally, "Get out of the road, you dunderhead! Watch where you're goin'! I damn near let ole Betty run you down!"

Slashed stopped abruptly and turned to see a big Percheron standing not six feet away from him, on his right. The big draft animal had her ears pinned back and was shaking her head incredulously, pawing at the dirt with one front hoof the size of a dinner plate.

"What the hell's the matter with you?" shouted the big man on the driver's seat of the wagon the Perch was pulling. "Are you drunk so early in the morning or soft in your thinker box?"

Slash realized with a shudder how close he'd come to being smashed as flat as an immigrant's hat. He held up a placating hand, palm out. "Sorry, friend."

"Damn dunderhead!" The big man, whom Slash recognized as a ramrod for one of the local ranches, shook the reins over the Percheron's back. As the horse and ranch supply wagon lumbered forward, the big man scowled down at Slash once more and said, "By god, you're lucky I wasn't asleep at the reins or you'd be no more than a grease spot in the street!"

Sheepish, Slash continued across the street and then turned

down a side street. He still felt numb, as though his body were not his own. He also felt a little sick to his stomach and imagined he looked a little green around the gills.

What had he just done?

He'd turned tail, that's what he'd done.

He started to feel a little better about things, to forget about the horrific scene he'd left behind at the Thousand Delights, when, walking into the freight yard, he saw a familiar figure standing on the freight office's wooden front porch with Pecos. A familiar horse—a calico mare—stood at one of the two hitchracks fronting the humble log building. Pecos and the young woman, dressed in a calico blouse, wool skirt, and worn boots, were facing each other on the porch, conversing, both smiling.

When Pecos saw Slash approaching on foot, he beckoned with one arm and said, "Slash, get your skinny ass over here and see who's come callin'!"

Slash quickened his pace. "Myra?"

Myra Thompson turned to Slash, and another broad smile split her young, pretty face, deeply tanned and owning a comely splash of freckles across her nose and her youthfully smooth cheeks. Myra was a pretty, brown-eyed girl of nineteen or twenty with a thick tussle of curly auburn hair spilling across her shoulders.

"Hi, Slash." Myra was turning a broad-brimmed felt hat in her hands, nervously pinching up the rawhide-stitched edges.

Slash laughed, happy to see the girl again, and leaped up to the veranda two steps at a time. He took her in his arms and squeezed her tight—this pretty, rustic young mountain woman, the daughter of a now-dead prospector; she'd once come very close to cleaning his and Pecos's clocks not all that long ago in the San Juan Mountains, near the mining camp of Silverton.

Jay had saved the two old cutthroats from that little whipsaw their own foolishness had led them into. Jay had knocked Myra out cold as the girl had been about to drill both Slash and Pecos where they'd lain reeling from the raw opium with which she'd spiked their whiskey, having feigned a twisted ankle and luring them into her camp. Both men had always been suckers for a comely female form, no matter what age. It had turned out that Myra had been riding with the very gang—Slash and Pecos's old gang, in fact—whom Bleed-Em-So had assigned Slash and Pecos to wipe out.

The Snake River Marauders had sent Myra to hornswoggle the old cutthroats with her youthful beauty and charm, and to snuff their wicks before Slash and Pecos could foil the gang's train-robbing plans. Myra had accepted the nasty assignment only because she'd been desperate for the gang's protection, her father being dead and her time as a pretty young woman alone in Silverton having turned out far darker than she'd expected. Slash, Pecos, and Jay had turned the girl back right, and Myra had helped them run the gang to final ground.

Now, here the pretty girl was—shy, beaming, and fresh as a May morning here on the porch of the freight office.

Slash held Myra away from him and smiled down at her. "Good to see you again, kid. But what brings you out here to this jerkwater town? I thought you were gonna throw in with your uncle in Denver? Didn't you say he ran a saloon up that way . . . ?"

"Yep, I sure did, Slash." The girl's smile turned stiff, and she glanced sheepishly up at Pecos. "I was just about to get to that with Pecos, in fact."

Slash assumed rightly that she'd just arrived.

"What's up, kid?" Pecos said. "Somethin' happen with your uncle?"

"It sure did." A bitterness entered Myra's voice, and a sour expression twisted her mouth. "He turned out to be little better than some of the saloon owners I'd known in Silverton."

Slash frowned. "You mean, he . . . ?"

"Wanted to put me to work. Upstairs. I went there to work for him. I certainly didn't expect him to put me up for free. But I didn't expect him, my own uncle, to expect me to work upstairs!" Tears rolled down the girl's cheeks, and she angrily swiped them away with the backs of her hands.

"Ah, hell," Pecos said, wrapping an arm around Myra's shoulders and drawing her taut against him. "What a rotten thing to do to a man's own niece."

"I didn't realize, but I guess my aunt died of some sickness nigh on a year ago."

"There, there, kid," Slash said, brushing another tear from her cheek with his thumb. "Everything's gonna be all right."

"What can we do to help? You need some money? It's not like we're loaded, but . . ."

"No." Myra shook her head and smiled up at the tall, blond cutthroat. "I didn't come here for a handout. I came here because you're the only two decent, honorable men I know in all the frontier. Not that I know that many."

She gave a rueful chuckle. "I came because I thought . . . well, I thought maybe that now, since you've been set up here almost a year, you could use a hand about the place. You know . . ." She glanced at the crude log cabin behind her, then looked from Pecos to Slash and back again. "A woman's touch. I can clean and cook for you, and over the long winters up in the San Juans, I got to know a schoolteacher who taught me to read an' cipher and even to keep accounts. I could keep your books for you, if you wanted," Myra added demurely.

Slash glanced at Pecos. Pecos looked at Slash, and then his gaze lifted to something or someone behind Slash, in the direction of the road that led to the freight yard. Slash heard the crunch and scuff of approaching footsteps. He turned to see their hired man, Todd Elwood, enter the yard through the gate. Elwood was a short-legged, round-bellied man with thin, straw-blond hair poking out from his battered felt hat. He wore a shabby red-and-white checked shirt under his usual suit coat, which was splitting at the seams and coppered from many hours in the sun.

Elwood managed to latch the gate, then, starting toward the office, he tripped over the torn front flap of his right, mule-eared boot. He stumbled forward and sideways and nearly went down before he got his boots beneath him once more.

"Whoa now," he said as though to an unruly team of mules. "Whoa . . . whoa, now . . ."

He continued forward, holding his arms, which appeared too long for the rest of his body, out to both sides as though for balance. The sunlight glinted on something poking up from the right, torn pocket of his coat.

Slash scowled.

A bottle.

Slash glanced at Pecos again. The two men shared a dark look, then Slash walked down the porch steps.

"Todd, where in the hell were you last night?"

The bedraggled man, in his late thirties and with a sun-seasoned face with a slender coyote nose bright red from drink, stopped ten feet from Slash and squinted his watery blue eyes, as though he were having trouble focusing. "What . . . what do ya mean, Mister Braddock?"

From the porch, Pecos said, "We pulled in last night late, and you weren't here to tend the mules. We had to tend 'em ourselves, as tired and in need of food an' drink as we was. That's what we hired you for, Todd—to wrangle and tend the mules and to swamp out the barn and to keep the corral clean."

"We got back to find the barn and the corral both a mess," Slash said, his voice sharp with anger.

Elwood looked around, vaguely sheepish, running his

hands nervously up and down on his ratty coat. "Well . . . I waited till five o'clock, an' . . . an' when you fellas didn't show, I, uh . . ."

"You headed off to a saloon and likely been there till a few minutes ago," Pecos said.

"Or some lowly doxie's canvas crib," Slash opined.

"We told you to stay here till we got back, Todd. We set you up in your own room in the lean-to off the barn. That's where you live. Right here. On the premises. So you can take care of the mules any time you're needed."

"You should've been here, Todd," Slash added. "That's what we pay you for."

Elwood's dark eyes flashed yellow bayonets of sudden, raw fury. He jerked an arm up and pointed a dirty finger at the two cutthroats. "I waited till five o'clock! I don't get paid to wait no later than that!"

Slash gave a dry chuff. "You waited till three at the latest. Then you lit out. We told you when we hired you that you're to tend the mules whenever we arrive from a haul—day or night. And no tipplin'!"

"I got me a feelin'," Pecos said, raking a pensive thumb down his unshaven jaw, "that Todd hasn't been here since we left. I got me a feelin' he thought that the days we were gone were a vacation for him. He looks a mite like he's been on a bender, Slash."

"I'll go you one better, partner," Slash said. "He smells like it, too."

"You've done this before, Todd," Pecos said in a stern, level voice. "We warned you before about cuttin' out an' goin' on a tear. I took a chance on you when, uh, Jimmy here warned me not to, and that makes him right, and I plumb hate it when he's right!"

"I can do what he does."

Slash and Pecos turned to Myra, still standing on the

porch, her hat in her hands, the morning breeze nudging the thick locks of her curly auburn hair.

"What's that, darlin'?" Pecos asked.

"I can tend the mules. I can muck out the barn and the corral. What's more, I can keep order in the office here and in your livin' quarters. I can cook and I can clean and I can keep your accounts in order." Myra's voice had been rising steadily with resolve as she'd looked from Pecos to Slash, then back again. "And I can do it all for what you're payin' him."

"A dollar a day to do all that?" Slash asked, skeptically.

"A dollar a day," Myra said with a slow nod. "And room an' board."

Slash and Pecos shared a conferring look. The two men, reading each other's minds, shaped slow, broad smiles. "Well, hell, darlin'," Slash said, "you got yourself a place to hang your hat!"

"Now, just wait a minute!" Elwood stumbled forward, his face turning red with fury behind a thin coat of scraggly beard stubble. "That there is nothin' but a girl. Why, she can't do a man's work!"

"I say she can," Pecos said, drawing Myra against him again, smiling proudly. "I say she can do all your work—if we can call it work—and one hell of a lot more. And you know what?"

"What?" Slash and Myra said at the same time.

"We're gonna pay her a dollar plus fifty cents a day."

"We are?" Slash said, weakly.

"Now, just you wait here!" Elwood took one more shambling step forward, his eyes even brighter now with rage and moist with emotion. "I won't stand for bein' insulted like this. I waited till three o'clock. No, no, wait! I meant five o'clock! I waited till five o'clock, an' then I headed off for a drink and got lassoed into a poker game!"

"Three o'clock," Slash said, smiling knowingly. "I had me a feelin'."

"No, no!" Elwood yelled. "You just got me all confused is all!"

Pecos's own blue eyes bored invisible holes through the enraged scalawag. "Give him his time, Slash. Send him on his way."

"Love to." Reaching into his shirt pocket, Slash withdrew the envelope containing his and Pecos's take from their last run. He counted out a few bills and held them out to Elwood, who merely glared back at Slash, fists bunched at his sides.

"I won't stand for bein' treated this way." The drunk's voice was brittle with barely controlled rage.

"I'm gonna drop these bills," Slash warned. "And then I'll be payin' the wind and you'll take nothin'. Try to buy whiskey and even the cheapest parlor girl with nothin', Todd."

Quickly, Elwood reached up and snatched the bills out of Slash's hand. He cursed both men, and he cursed Myra for a lowly whore, and then he wheeled and stomped back in the direction from which he'd come. When he'd crawled through the Texas gate, he turned back and shouted, "You three haven't heard the last of Todd Elwood—I'll guarantee you that!"

"If I see you on the place again," Slash warned, "I'll shoot you on sight, Todd. Just like any other damn coyote!"

Elwood made a lewd gesture, then stumbled away, casting frequent enraged glances back over his shoulder.

Pecos turned to Myra. "You sure you're up for this?"

"Hell yes, I am!" The girl smiled broadly, looking purely giddy at the prospect of finally having a home again. "I can do twice or three times that man's work."

"There's a hell of a lot to do around here," Slash warned. "Maybe you better have a look around first, and think about it."

"I can handle anything you two old cutthroats can throw at me!" Myra smiled proudly, then turned to open the office's front door. She peered inside.

She froze, tensed, sniffed, then turned back to Pecos and Slash.

"My god," she croaked, covering her mouth and nose with her hand. "What on earth is that smell?"

Pecos sighed. "Slash shot a rat last week. It's in there somewhere, but on account o' the mess, we ain't been able to find the wretched thing!"

CHAPTER 11

"That girl's taken a shine to you," Slash said, glancing at Pecos sitting beside him on the driver's seat. "You know that, don't you?"

Pecos frowned at him. "Who?"

"Myra, ya dope!"

"Myra? Taken a shine to me? Why, she's young enough to be . . . well, she's young enough to be the oldest daughter of my oldest brother. Oldest brother by a long shot!" Pecos snorted to himself and ran a sleeve of his suit coat across his mouth.

"She's old enough to be your daughter, ya lout!"

"She's old enough to be my daughter if I fathered her when I was still a boy. Now, that's as far as I'm gonna go. You keep pushin' it, I'm gonna drag you down off this noisy contraption and kick your bony behind!"

"All right, all right. Don't get your bloomers in a twist. I'll let that part go. Fer now." Slash shook his head and gave a wry chuff. "Believe me, I'm even more confounded by the situation my ownself. Don't see how anyone could take a shine to an old scudder such as yourself, let alone a pretty young thing like Myra Thompson. But she has, all right. You maybe can't see it, but I can."

He turned to his partner, gesturing with his hands. "Every time she looks at you, she gets two little pink dots and one large pink dot right here on her cheeks."

"Oh, she don't, neither."

"Does, too."

They were riding along through the mountains, following a narrow, winding valley toward the Sawatch Range. This was their first day on the trail. They'd gotten a late start after the row with Todd Elwood and having to show Myra around the freight yard.

It was just after midday, and Slash was driving the team of four mules. They were leading their saddle horses—Slash's Appaloosa and Pecos's buckskin. Sometimes a man had to ride far wide of these well-traveled mountain trails to find game of a night, and it was best to have a good saddle horse along for that purpose.

The box behind the two former cutthroats was empty. Slash had thought it best just to cover it with a tarpaulin rather than fill it with wood. This way, the pull would be easier on the mules, and they'd make better time in climbing to Tin Cup.

Bleed-Em-So's advice about the wood be damned. He'd likely never driven a freight wagon before.

No one had any reason to believe the two freighters were not hauling freight in their freight wagon.

"She don't neither."

"She does, too!"

Pecos glanced at Slash, one brow arched over a lake blue eye beneath a thin blond brow. "You really think so?"

"I know so. All mornin', she was followin' you around like a long-lost stray that had finally found its owner. Only"—Slash grinned at the big blond freighter—"I heard violins sawing soft and low in her heart."

"I'll be damned." Pecos looked straight ahead over the mules' twitching ears and shook his head. "So I wasn't just imagining it."

"You sensed it, too?"

Pecos grimaced, nodded. "Yeah, I could kinda feel her eyes on me too long at a stretch. Then when I'd look at her, she'd look away right quick an' flush like you said, or she'd continue gazin' up at me, her eyes fairly glowin' like sunshine through rose petals."

"Like sunshine through rose petals. Damn! No wonder she's gone for you—you silver-tongued old devil!"

"I think I mighta stole that from somewhere," Pecos lied.

Slash dug a half-smoked cheroot out of his shirt pocket, inside his coat, and stuck it in his mouth. "What're you gonna do about it?"

He scratched a lucifer to life on his thumbnail.

"I don't know. It makes a fella feel like struttin' with his feathers out to know such a young, purty thing gets all fluttery-hearted over him, but you're right. I'm too damn old for her. She needs her a younger man." Pecos sighed. "Oh, well. She'll be alone there in Fort Collins a few days before we get back. The way she looks, she'll turn more than a few heads around town in that time. Hell, by the time we get back to the freight yard, there'll probably be a whole line of young men linin' up at her front door, waitin' to ask for her hand in holy matrimony."

"Maybe."

Pecos glanced at Slash. "Say, I forgot to ask. Speakin' of our love lives, how'd it go with Jay?"

Slash's belly twisted. "How'd what go?"

"I assume you seen her this mornin' in the Thousand Delights. I figured you went alone so you could talk to her—you know." Pecos grinned insinuatingly. "Private-like."

"No, I didn't."

"You mean you didn't see her?"

"No, I didn't go in alone to see her *private-like*." Slash paused, winced. "Or . . . maybe I did. I'm not sure."

"Slash, fer cryin' in Grant's whiskey, did you see her or not?"

you couldn't count on the sodden wood to keep your boots or skirts dry.

About all they really did was kept you from drowning.

Slash and Pecos put their wagon and mules up in the High Country Federated Livery and Feed Barn, telling the pipe-smoking liveryman, whose boots were surrounded by half-wild barn cats of every size and color, that they'd already off-loaded their freight and were looking to hole up for a day before starting back down out of the mountains to Denver. Fortunately, the man wasn't overly curious about the pair of strangers. Nor did he seem skeptical about their story. Smoking his corncob pipe, he began unhitching the team and humming "Sweet Betsy from Pike" to himself while the cats rubbed against his ankles and Slash and Pecos headed out into the mire that was Tin Cup.

Following the instructions provided by Bleed-Em-So's file, which they'd burned in their previous evening's campfire, they headed over to the Sportsman's Saloon—a large but crude log building resembling a military barrack and fronted by a large halve-logged veranda propped up from the mud by two-foot-high stone pylons and outfitted with unpeeled pine rails. Smoke from the saloon's stone chimney flattened out over the roof to swirl into the street like thick fog laced with the enticing aromas of a succulent stew.

Burly men in mud-splashed wool laughed with parlor girls on the front porch.

Inside was a good-sized crowd for so early in the after-noon.

Slash and Pecos strode casually up to the bar. When the barman had finished setting a bowl of steaming stew onto the bar beside a frothy beer schooner fronting a one-eyed, thick-set jake clad in stinky damp wool and a leather-billed immigrant hat, he turned to Slash and Pecos, arching both brows inquiringly.

Slash smiled at the man and said, "Hello, friend. My partner and I would each like a beer. A big one. We're teetotalers, don't ya know, but we decided to celebrate."

"Oh?" the barman said. He was tall and middle-aged, with short, black hair parted on one side, shiny with oil and showing the tracks from his comb. He rolled a lucifer match around between his thin lips. His eyes were as black as the mud in the street. "What're you fellas celebratin', if you don't mind me askin'?"

"It's my dear pappy's birthday, don't ya know," Pecos said.

"Your pappy's birthday, eh?" the barman said. "How old would your pappy be today, son?"

"If he were still alive, he'd be eighty-one. Thanks for askin'."

The barman probed Pecos with his eyes, then slid his inquiring, vaguely suspicious gaze to Slash and said, "Well, hell, then. I reckon the first ones are on me. Why don't you fellas go sit down, and I'll bring you a bowl of stew and some fresh bread? Looks like you've come a far piece."

"We have at that, we have at that," Slash said, smiling and slapping a hand down atop the bar in gratitude. "And we thank you mighty kindly."

He and Slash moseyed over to a table abutting the front window, left of the batwings. They hadn't been sitting for long when the barman came over with a tray.

He set two big mugs of dark ale on the table and followed them up with two steaming bowls of what appeared to be venison stew rife with carrots, potatoes, onions, and even a few peas. He set a plate with several thick slices of crusty brown bread on the table between the two cutthroats-turned-freighters.

"There ya be, boys!" the man said, straightening and grinning down at the customers, showing one silver eyetooth. "Can I get you anything else?"

"Here, let me pay for the stew," Slash said, reaching into a pocket.

Clamping the empty tray under one arm, the barman held up his other hand. "I won't hear of it." He glanced at Pecos. "It's the least I can do to help you celebrate your pappy's birthday. Besides"—he leaned forward and grinned like the cat that ate the canary—"I know that once you've partaken of my own personally brewed beer and stew, you'll be back many times for more!"

He winked, chuckled, and strode away.

Slash and Pecos looked at each other, frowning incredulously.

Slash looked around at the surface of the table, and then, as inconspicuously as possible, he peered under it. Still not seeing what he was looking for, he glanced at Pecos and shrugged. He rolled up his shirtsleeves, took a long slug of the malty ale, grabbed a spoon, and started digging into his stew.

Lifting the steaming spoonful of meat and gravy to his mouth, he glanced across the table and froze.

He cleared his throat just loudly enough for Pecos to hear. Pecos looked at him. Slash dropped his chin as he stared down at the slip of paper poking out from beneath Pecos's stew bowl.

Pecos followed Slash's gaze. His eyes widened. He glanced around the room before casually pinching up a corner of the paper and sliding it out from beneath the bowl. It was a lined leaf from a small notebook, folded once.

Again casually, Pecos brushed his thumb across the note, opening it. Pecos lowered his head, frowning down at the missive, silently moving his lips.

So as not to look like he was interested in anything except his stew, Slash chowed down with his spoon in one hand, a thick slice of bread in his other hand. As he dipped the bread into the stew, he whispered across the table between bites: "What's it say?"

Pecos's brows ridged over his eyes as he looked down at the paper, still silently moving his lips.

Slash gave a dry snort. He quickly shuttled his eyes around the room. No one in the watering hole appeared in the least bit interested in the newcomers, so he set his bread down, reached quickly across the table, and pulled the note over to his side.

"Dammit, Slash, I woulda sounded it out if you'd given me half a minute!" Pecos complained under his breath, indignant.

"Half the day, more like. I thought you sparked a literate woman a while back. One who read books."

"I did, but she read *to* me, an' she wasn't all high an' mighty about it, neither!"

Again, Slash snorted as he stared down at the note, written in a swirling feminine hand in blue-black ink. Quickly, he folded the note closed, slid it beneath his bowl, then took up his bread again.

"Well?" Pecos said, cutting a furtive glance around the room and then spooning stew into his mouth. "What's it, say, you smug bastard?"

"It says, 'Room fourteen, the Palace Hotel, eleven-thirty p.m. Do not draw attention to yourselves.'"

"That's it?"

"What more did you want it to say?"

"Well . . . I don't know . . ."

"Eat your stew and drink your beer, ya big dummy."

"Don't press your luck, you scrawny-assed cuss!" Pecos said, eyes blazing angrily. "You still got my blood up for mocking my readin' skills."

"Or lack of same," Slash said, chuckling and stuffing a chunk of stew-soaked bread into his mouth.

*   *   *

An eerie *ping!* sounded to Slash's left. Just off his left ear, in fact.

It was followed closely by a dull wooden *thud!* in the wall on the other side of his and Pecos's small room in the Palace Hotel.

Slash saw the nickel-sized hole in the opposite wall, just above a small oil painting of a scantily clad blond woman lounging dreamily on a fainting couch while a man in a dark suit and wearing a creepy smile crept up behind her through an open door. At the same time, the report from the gun that had fired the bullet reached Slash's ears—a sharp bark of thunder characteristic of a .45.

"What the hell?" Pecos said from where he lounged on the room's single, brass-framed bed, inside a cloud of his own cigarette smoke.

"Ambush!" Slash cried, and hit the floor.

Pecos blew out the oil lamp on a table beside him. Judging by the heavy thud in the darkness, he too had thrown himself to the floor. "How many?" he yelled softly, his voice pinched with anxiety. "You see 'em?"

"Not yet!"

Slash clawed one of his own stag-butted .45s from its cross-draw holster on his left hip and lifted his head to edge a careful look out the window, which, he could see in the light from the street's burning oil pots, sported a hole with web-like cracks spoking out around it.

"Harley Anders, you low-down, four-flushin', dirty dog!" a man cried on the street somewhere below the second-floor room.

There was another thundering boom. Slash saw the flash of the gun straight off down a street that was a maze of shadows and flickering light from the oil pots and occasional torches and trash or cook fires. Slash couldn't hear where that shot landed, but it didn't appear to have struck anywhere near his and Slash's room.

"What on earth . . . ?" Pecos had slid up to Slash's left and was also peering cautiously out the window, a few inches above the sill.

The two men watched a figure stagger into the light of two guttering oil pots. He was mostly in silhouette, but Slash could see that he was a short, pudgy gent with long, gray hair. He wore no hat, only a shirt with suspenders and sleeve garters, and dark trousers stuffed into the high tops of mule-eared boots. He was holding a pistol down low in his right hand.

Light from the fires on both sides of the street glinted on the .45's bluing.

That he was drunk there was no doubt. He was nearly dragging the toes of his boots, and his head was wobbling as though his neck were broke.

As he raised the .45 again, Slash started to raise his own Colt. He held fire when the drunk flashed off another shot, this one toward the street on his own left, to Slash's right.

"Christalmighty," Pecos said. "A nasty damn drunk with a bone to pick!"

"Looks that way." Slash raised the window a few inches, and cool night air as well as clearer sounds from the street issued into the room.

"Harley Anders, you hear me, you black-hearted son of a three-legged cur?" The drunk's .45 barked twice more, both bullets sailing into the front of a small saloon to his left and startling the six or seven horses tethered to the hitchrack there. One broke away from the rack, gave a shrill whinny, and ran off down the street and out of sight. "You owe me twenty-four dollars and twenty-six cents! I knowed you was markin' them cards . . . and the whore was in on it . . . givin' signals over my damn shoulder!"

The .45 flashed and barked again. There was the crashing sound of breaking glass and then the indignant yells and screams of men and women inside the saloon. There was also a shrill, agonized curse, telling Slash that the drunk's bullet had struck flesh and bone somewhere inside the watering hole.

A man ran out of the saloon, the batwings clattering into place behind him before another man followed him out onto the narrow stoop fronting the place. "Elwyn Muskey—is that you, you drunken fool?" Slash thought he saw the tell-tale glint of a lawman's star on the man's vest, which he wore behind a long duster. There was an oil pot nearby, so Slash could see him fairly clearly, even from this distance of fifty yards or so.

The drunk had turned toward the saloon and stopped. Or had tried to stop. Drink had made him all loose joints and wobbly-headed. He was swinging his arms around, as well as the gun in his hand, as though to help him maintain balance. "Stay out of this, Reeves, or you'll get what Harley's gonna get!"

"Put that gun away or I'm haulin' you in!"

"Haul this in, you scum-suckin', badge-totin' horns-woggler!" Muskey raised and aimed the .45, which flashed and popped.

The badge-toter on the saloon veranda cried and flew backward against the saloon wall to the right of the batwings. He crumpled and slid down the wall to the porch floor, cursing loudly.

The other man who'd barreled out of the saloon moved quickly down the veranda steps and into the street, sliding a pistol from a holster on his left thigh. "Now you've done it, Muskey!"

"This ain't about you, Merle!" Muskey cried, tossing away his empty .45 and pulling another gun he'd had stuffed down inside the waistband of his pants.

"You shoot up my saloon, it sure as hell is about me!" The gun in Merle's fist flashed and roared.

"Oh, you devil!" Muskey stumbled forward, extending his second gun and firing.

The two men walked toward each other, Muskey stumbling, Merle walking in a straight line, firing another round. The second round made Muskey flinch. He gave a grunt and staggered backward. He extended his pistol again.

It thundered, flames blossoming from the stout barrel.

Merle cursed as he triggered another round into Elwyn Muskey.

Muskey stumbled backward again, then dropped to his butt in the street.

Merle groaned and, clutching a hand to his belly, fell to his knees, his hat tumbling off a shoulder and into the dirt. He cursed again as he raised his revolver and fired another round into Muskey.

Muskey cursed again, maligning the saloon-owner's bloodline, as he lifted his own gun and triggered yet another round into Merle, who promptly returned the favor . . . until both men's gun hammers pinged benignly down onto firing pins and the two opponents lay in miserable heaps on the street, grunting and groaning and thrashing and cursing.

Meanwhile, a small crowd had pushed out onto the saloon's veranda. One man broke away from the crowd and stepped down off the porch. He was a tall, thin man in a frock coat and bowler hat. He walked past the cursing and groaning Merle to stand over Muskey, who lay on his back with his legs curled beneath him.

He was wailing shrilly, flopping his arms and lifting his head.

The tall newcomer stared down at Muskey and said, "That was Matt Sullivan who cheated you at stud poker, Elwyn. Not me! And it was nine years ago in Abilene, you green-livered, prune-brained barrel-boarder!"

Harley Anders shucked a revolver from one of his own two holsters and emptied it into Elwyn Muskey. The drunkard's body leaped violently with every round. By the time the sixth round had punched into Muskey's crumpled body, his wails had died.

The echoes of Harley Anders's hogleg chased each other around the eerily still mining camp until they dwindled away toward the stars. Silence fell, as dark and heavy as a burial shroud.

"Christ!" Anders holstered his empty pistol and stomped back into the saloon. "Now, where was I?"

Inside their dark room at the Palace Hotel, Slash and Pecos glanced at each other.

Shaking his head, Pecos whistled and said, "Well, now—wasn't that a fine howdy-do?"

"There's a minin' camp for ya."

"Yeah."

Both men jerked as a soft knock sounded at their door.

CHAPTER 13

In the silence after the lead swap on the street, the soft knock had almost sounded like another .45 report.

Slash and Pecos jerked their heads toward the door, raising their pistols again and clicking back the hammers.

"What the hell?" Pecos grunted.

"Pinkertons, maybe." Slash rose, depressing his pistol's hammer but keeping the gun in his hand, barrel aimed at the door. "Light the lamp."

When Pecos had gotten the lamp lit, Slash walked over to the door and tilted his head toward the panel. "Who is it?"

Someone cleared his voice—or was it *her* voice?—in the hall.

Keeping his Colt aimed straight out from his right hip, Slash opened the door a few inches and peered through the crack. A tall man and a woman of average height stood before him. The man wore a clerical collar and was holding a Bible. The woman was dressed all in black. Her severe wool dress was buttoned clear to her throat. She wore a black bonnet that looked like crow wings. It was snugged securely to her chin by a black ribbon.

Slash glanced at Pecos. "Did you call a prayer meetin'?"

The woman hardened her jaws. They were pretty jaws.

Her eyes were pretty, too, despite how flinty they'd become. "Mister Broaderick?" she said, tightly, turning her head to glance both ways along the hall. "Let us in." She'd spaced the words out, enunciating each one angrily.

Slash shrugged and drew the door open. He stepped back as the pair walked into the room, moving softly. The man closed the door with care, latching it with a click that seemed to cause him pain.

"Um . . . that's Braddock," Slash told the woman.

He didn't know if she'd heard or not, for the instant the door latched, she and the tall man in the clerical collar started hustling around the room. They looked in corners where the lamplight didn't reach. While the woman dropped to her knees to look under the bed, the man opened a door to a small closet, peering around inside.

They scoured the walls with their gazes and sometimes their hands, running their fingers across the worn paper that was peeling at its seams in places. They took a good five or ten minutes, scouring the walls—apparently for peep holes, for Slash couldn't think of anything else they might be suspicious of—and then wandered around the room, staring up at the low, wainscoted ceiling that was badly smudged with soot from the coal burner in the corner.

Finally, the woman turned to Slash and crossed her arms on her chest. "Mister Broaderick?"

"Braddock."

She turned to Pecos. "Baker?"

"If you say so." Pecos stood against the wall near the broken window, one stocking foot kicked back against the wall behind him, slowly building another quirley. His hat was off, and his thin hair hung down past his shoulders. His tweed suit coat hung over a chair back. He wore only his broadcloth trousers, white shirt, brown vest, and string tie. His pistol, of course, was thonged on his thigh. Both his and Slash's rifles, and Pecos's shotgun, leaned against the wall between him and Slash, who was dressed similarly to his partner only in dark whipcord trousers and a black leather vest over a red and black calico shirt with a black foulard tie. His low-crowned, broad-brimmed black hat was hooked over a bed-post. His black, square-toed boots stood against the wall by the door.

They'd been making themselves comfortable before the drunk had threatened their lives with the .45 slug through their window.

The woman wasn't in a joking mood. "I'm asking you, sir. Is it Baker or isn't it?"

"Don't get your bloomers in a knot, darlin'," Pecos said, poking the cigarette between his lips and scratching a match to life on his holster. "It is Baker, indeed. You can call me Melvin, if you want to." He touched the flame of his lucifer to his cigarette, and Slash snorted as he watched his partner give the comely young, dark-haired, dark-eyed young lady the twice-over with his lusty gaze.

"Baker is fine."

"And you are . . . ?" Slash asked her.

The tall man was about to speak, but the young woman cut him off with, "You don't need our real names. This is the only time you'll ever see us. Think of me, if you must think of me at all, as Operative One and him as Operative Two."

The tall man glanced at Slash and threw his arms out with a sigh.

Keeping her voice just above a whisper and sliding her serious brown-eyed gaze between Slash and Pecos, Operative One said, "We are here to give you instructions for picking up the gold tomorrow morning at nine a.m. Not a second sooner or later." Again, she slid her eyes between the two former cutthroats. "Understand?"

"Sure," Slash said.

Operative One looked at him, blinked, and then a frown began carving lines around her eyes.

"What is it, Operative One?" Slash said, growing self-conscious.

"I've . . . I've seen you somewhere . . . before."

"You have?" Slash and Pecos asked at the same time.

"Sure." The lines around Operative One's eyes grew even deeper. "Sure . . . I know . . . I have . . ."

"Where, Hattie?" asked Operative Two.

Operative One jerked a recriminating stare at her partner, and he wilted like a rose touched with frost. Turning quickly back to Slash, her eyes widening with recognition, Operative One, aka Hattie, said, "Oh, my god!" She clamped a hand over her wide-open mouth.

"What is it, Operative One?" Slash said. "Is my handsome mug givin' you the fantods. Don't feel bad. I do that to all the pretty women."

He shared a sly grin with Pecos.

Ignoring the remark, or possibly not having heard it against the vexation inside her head, Operative One slowly lowered her hand from her mouth, then swiveled her head to slide her gaze from Slash to Pecos. She backed up a step, as though shrinking from a possible assault.

Keeping her eyes on Pecos, Operative One reached up with her left hand and grabbed the sleeve of Operative Two's wool coat. "Oh, my god, Operative Two, do you know who these men are?"

"Braddock and Baker?"

Again, Operative One, or Hattie, clamped a hand over her astonished mouth. "This is Slash Braddock and the Pecos River Kid!" She was whispering, but her voice was so frantic that she gave the effect of shrieking.

Operative Two frowned skeptically as he looked at each man in turn. Then he laughed. "Oh, come on!" He gestured with his hand. "These two?"

"Hey!" Pecos said, indignant. "Why's that so damn hard to believe?"

"Easy, partner," Slash warned him.

"Why, Slash Braddock and the Pecos River Kid are young firebrands!" Operative Two laughed. "These men are . . . well, sorry, fellas . . . but they're *old*!"

"That tears it!" Pecos flipped his quirley out the open window, then lunged for Operative Two. "I'll show you how old I am!"

"Hold on!" Slash grabbed Pecos and shoved the taller man back against the wall. "Hold on, partner! Hold on!"

Pecos snarled and growled at the young Pinkerton like a stick-prodded wildcat.

Operative One was slowly shaking her pretty head. "It's them, all right. I recognize them from their descriptions. When I first entered the agency, I was assigned to gather as much information as I could on these two . . . these two . . . *cutthroats*!" She thrust out her hand to indicate the two men. "Slippery, they were. Very slippery. And, because some folks saw them as likable, they'd give them shelter and make them even harder to run down."

"All right, all right," Slash said, holding up his hands palms out. "Guilty as charged, Operative One. Nevertheless, we ain't wanted no more. Now we work—unofficially, you understand—for Chief Marshal Bledsoe. That's why we're here."

"Killers!" Operative One raked out hoarsely between her plump, pink lips. "Killers—both!"

"Hey," Pecos intoned, thrusting an accusing finger at her, "we never killed a single man that wasn't out to kill us first!"

"Some of those men were merely doing their jobs!"

"So were we, sweetheart!" Pecos said, bending slightly forward at the waist and poking a thumb against his chest.

"All right, all right!" Operative Two stepped between Operative One and the two indignant cutthroats, holding up his arms in supplication. "I see we have a situation in need of defusing." He turned to Pecos and said with a gentlemanly dip of his chin, "I do apologize, sir. I did not mean to give offense. I, too, have followed your careers and must admit to tendering you both a great deal of admiration for your considerable wiles and dodges, if not for your greed and occasional savagery."

"There," Pecos said, drawing a calming breath and giving his waistcoat a tug from the bottom. "That's better."

Operative One continued wagging her head in astonishment. "I had no idea we would be turning the gold over . . . for safekeeping . . . to known cutthroats!"

"Take my word for it, honey," Slash said. "You're no more surprised than Pecos and I were when we heard the plan."

"So you gentlemen now work for Chief Marshal Bledsoe," Operative Two said.

"There you have it."

Operative Two fingered his clerical collar. "I did think it odd when you seemed to just disappear roughly a year ago. I'd thought you were probably living the good life in Mexico or perhaps Hawaii. Maybe South America . . ."

"Well, here we are," Pecos said, giving a dry chuckle. "An' I know Slash an' I . . . as well as old Bleed-Em-So hisself . . . would appreciate it no end if both you an' Number One there kept it all under your hats. It's supposed to be a secret, you understand."

"And I know how you two can appreciate a secret," Slash added with a wry grin.

"Boy, this really goes against the grain," Operative One told Operative Two, puffing out her cheeks with a long, fateful exhalation. "I mean—turning gold over to two known cutthroats! How can we be sure they won't abscond with it?"

"Age'll keep us from stealing your gold," Slash said. "Age and decrepitude."

"Yeah, even though we ain't all that old," Pecos interjected, favoring the young Pink with a severe look.

Number Two turned to Number One and said, "Obviously, the chief marshal trusts these men. That means we must trust them, as well, Hat . . . er, I mean, Number One! Besides, once the gold is in their freight wagon"—he turned to Slash and Pecos with a none-so-vague look of warning— "it becomes their responsibility. Their heads will be on the chopping block—unless of course, gentlemen, the gold arrives safely in Denver."

"That it will," Slash said. "I know it goes against your Pinkerton fiber, but you can trust me an' Pecos here. When we sign on to do a job, we see her through. Our word is bond, see?"

"Honor among thieves?" the haughty young woman asked, raising a skeptical brow.

"Yeah," Pecos said. "You could call it that."

"Tell me," Slash said, "how many Pinkertons ya'll have here in Tin Cup? I take it the barman's one?"

"He is, of course, and everyone riding the stage tomorrow will be a Pinkerton agent," said Number Two, fingering his collar again as though it were resting uncomfortably against his neck.

"Including the jehu and shotgun messenger," said Number One.

"In addition," added Number Two, "even the hostlers from the local relay station are our agents, in case the gang preying on the Cloud Tickler's gold shipments decides to strike before we've even left town."

"You see, this has been a very involved, carefully planned operation," said Number One. "We agents have been here for the past three months, making preparations as well as fitting into the community, to avoid suspicion."

"So you've been pretendin' to be a sky pilot," Pecos said.

"Indeed." Number Two chuckled self-effacingly, clutching his coat lapels. "I come by it naturally. My father was a Baptist preacher."

"I see, I see." Slash cut his gaze to Number One. "And you're his wife."

"Yes." She gave a brittle, uppity smile. "I come by such station quite naturally, as well, as I was raised in a good, God-fearing family who read the Good Book daily and had nothing, absolutely *nothing*, to do with the dishonest dregs of our society."

She gave both Slash and Pecos a brashly judgmental up and down, curling her upper lip and then lifting her nose so high in the air Slash thought she was in danger of breaking her neck.

"Hey, now," Pecos objected. "Just you listen here, little Miss Hoity-Toi—"

"There, there, now, gentlemen . . . and lady," Number Two said, holding up his hands again, with placating eyes and giving his condescending partner an admonishing glance. "Suppose we get down to brass tacks so we can all get a good night's sleep. We're going to need it, as we'll all have a very full day tomorrow."

He opened his Bible and held it out in the palm of his hand. "Here, now, we have a map . . ."

CHAPTER 14

Slash and Pecos were beat, but in spite of their need for a good night's rest, neither cutthroat-turned-freighter slept for more than a half hour at a time. Even during those rare half hours, their sleep was stitched by uneasy dreams and vague anxieties. Their hearts beat abnormally fast, they sweated, and their muscles twitched. It was as though they'd contracted an ague.

Neither would have admitted it under threat of being drawn, quartered, and spitted over a low fire, but the gold was preying on their brains. Neither dreamt of outright absconding with the goods, so to speak, but you can't have robbed banks, trains, and stagecoaches for thirty years and then be in charge—just you and your former partner in crime—of delivering nearly a hundred thousand dollars in gold without that gold lodging in your brain like a bone in your throat.

"How'd you sleep?" Slash asked his partner the next morning at dawn as he sat up and stretched, feeling tight in every joint.

"Great," Pecos sighed, raking a big hand down his pale, lined face. "You?"

"Wonderful," Slash grumbled. He smacked his lips and reached for his makin's. "Ready to hit the trail?"

"Reckon."

As Slash rolled a quirley, he said, "How 'bout if we forego breakfast and get us a few belts of some cheap busthead before we head out? You know—a libation for the road?"

"That sounds fine as frog hair split four ways, partner." Pecos tossed his covers back and rose with an agonized groan. "Just what the doctor ordered, in fact!"

After they'd consumed a little over a half a bottle between themselves, and one raw egg apiece cracked into the Taos lightning, they rumbled out of town behind their four hitched mules, their two saddle horses tied to steel rings in the freight wagon's tailgate. Adding to their misery, the clouds that had been threatening since they'd left the Palace finally made good on their warning. Rain hammered nearly straight down out of a sky the color of greasy rags.

Pecos stopped the wagon long enough for him and Slash to hustle into their yellow rain slickers. The freight trail they followed north out of Tin Cup became a veritable river, and the mules had trouble keeping their feet on the slick upgrades. The rain made it difficult for the men to follow the map that the Pinkertons had shown them last night, and that they'd been required to memorize, both operatives playing true to the suspicious and paranoid Pinkerton form.

Pecos finally turned the wagon off the main road and into a little side canyon that had become a roiling creek, then halted the big outfit near the giant, lightning-topped cedar that had been marked boldly on the map. Pecos hadn't even set the brake before four men, also dressed in rain slickers, moved out from behind a snag of rocks at the edge of a pine forest. They were carrying a strongbox mounted atop two long four-by-fours. Each man carried an end of the four-by-fours.

As the steadily, whitely pouring rain sluiced off the brims of their high-crowned, black hats, they splashed through the mud and set the strongbox in the wagon. The four men, appearing indifferent to the pummeling the rain was giving them, crawled into the wagon's bed. There was a good bit of pounding, chain jangling, and box jostling before the men, whom Slash assumed were mine detectives, leaped down out of the wagon. Slash saw the strongbox residing in the middle of the bed, attached to four chains, the end of each chain padlocked to the four steel rings that Slash and Pecos had outfitted the bed with, one in each corner, before leaving Fort Collins.

The box itself was a stout doozy. It appeared to be solid steel and was secured with two heavy steel padlocks that would likely take a couple of dynamite sticks apiece to blow to smithereens.

The detectives unrolled the cream tarpaulin over the bed, covering the strongbox, and strapped the fabric securely to the side panels and tailgate. Quickly and with as much grim purpose as when they'd appeared, all four men strode back into the rocks and trees from where they had come, and were gone.

Slash and Pecos gazed over their shoulders at the strongbox.

Slash looked at Pecos. Pecos looked at Slash.

Each man acquired a sheepish expression.

Pecos turned forward in his seat, released the brake, and shook the reins over the team, whose sodden backs glistened like cold metal. Slash saw a man standing in the relative shelter of a big tree to the right of the trail. Slash nudged his partner with his elbow and jerked his head in the man's direction.

"Whoa!" Pecos hauled back on the reins.

The man stared up at them. He wore a three-piece suit under a gray slicker. He wore a tall, pearl-gray Boss of the Plains Stetson, beneath which his face was set like a badly mistreated and burned cameo carved in granite. He had gray eyebrows and a thick gray mustache. He was smoking a long, black cheroot, which he just now drew on before lowering and blowing the smoke out into the rain through his mouth and nostrils.

More smoke issued from his mouth and nose as he spoke, as though he had so much smoke inside his small, compact, ramrod-straight body that it would continue to come out on each breath he exhaled forevermore.

"I'm L. G. Tunstall, superintendent of the Cloud Tickler," he said just loudly enough to be heard above the weather's roar.

"Braddock and Baker," Slash said.

"I know." Tunstall took another deep drag on the cheroot. Slash saw a horse standing ground-reined on the other side of the tree—a fine, big, long-legged bay. "We've taken every precaution. Now it's up to you two."

"I don't get it," Slash said, glancing toward where the four detectives had disappeared. "Why didn't you just send them?"

Tunstall shook his head. "Too conspicuous. Besides, they're four of the total of six mine and ore guards I have on my roll. I need them at the mine. There's always a threat of thievery up there—both in the mine, with the ore, and in the hot box."

The "hot box" was the colloquial term for the locked, usually stone building that housed the gold concentrate and the ingots that had been smelted into bars.

Tunstall continued. "The two fellas who own the mine, both Englishmen who live back East, won't put any more money into the mine than they already have. They're tighter'n the bark on a tree. Must have some Scotch in 'em. They either need to make a lot of money or no money at all. If they keep having trouble, they're going to close the Cloud Tickler. That means I, at sixty-eight and counting, will no longer have a job. Those men you just saw won't have jobs. Nor the other two detectives nor the twenty-six miners and five operators in my employ."

He took another deep drag and, blowing out the smoke,

said, "Them Eastern limeys have played all their cards, hiring the Pinkertons to come in and clean the rats out of the privy. That's as far as they'll go. If this operation fails, I end up in an Odd Fellows Home of Christian Charity, though there's damn little charity in these parts excepting a bullet to the head. That's why I'm going to take it very personally if you don't get this gold back to Union Station in Denver. Understand?"

Slash nodded. "We got ya, Mister Tunstall."

"We'll get 'er there, Mister Tunstall." Pecos pinched his hat brim to the man, who remained standing beneath the tree, expressionless.

Pecos hoorawed the team back on its way.

Just before they cleared the curve that would take them back to the main trail, Slash glanced behind to see the small, gray, stoic-appearing but anxious Tunstall standing there beneath the dripping tree, smoking and staring expressionlessly toward the wagon.

"We've stolen from men like that before, you know, Slash," Pecos said an hour later, after the storm had cleared out and they were following the twisting freight road through a shallow valley beside the Taylor River, rushing and occasionally thundering against boulders on the trail's right side. Craggy granite and pine-clad ridges jutted on both sides of the canyon. Side canyons opened, as well—creases in the ridge wall, dark and mysterious and also threatening.

Slash and Pecos knew from their own experience that curly wolves could be cooling their heels in there, waiting to strike as suddenly as a mountain lion leaping from a tree branch on an unsuspecting cottontail.

Towering pines and spruces and pale-stemmed aspens dripped from the recent rain, beneath a sky suddenly as blue and flawless as a high-country lake. The air smelled as sparkly fresh, like champagne infused with pine needles.

Pecos's words had roused Slash from his own thoughts. He glanced at his partner in annoyance. "What're you crowin' about?"

"That man back there—Tunstall. We've robbed from men like him before. We've ruined men like him before. Old men who couldn't afford it." Pecos turned to Slash. "Don't you ever think about that?"

Slash scowled at him skeptically, as though a big bird had just dropped a load of plop on his hat. "No." Slash shook his head, his vexed scowl in place. "I don't think about that. We were robbers. The way some men ride for the law or bounties or the way some men run mines. We were robbers. That's what we did. That's how we survived."

"On the backs of others, I reckon," Pecos said, turning his head forward. He rose with his elbows on his knees, crouched forward, holding the leather ribbons lightly in his gloved hands.

"On the backs of fools, mostly."

"Oh, really? What if everybody did it our way? Stole from everybody else to survive?"

"That's the way it is!" Slash said.

"Huh?"

"Everybody makes it on the backs of everybody else, you damn fool." Slash swatted his hat across his partner's stout right shoulder. "Don't you know that by now?"

Pecos blinked. "*Huh?*"

"It's dog eat dog. That's how it is an' how it's always been. We were just more obvious about it, that's all."

Pecos studied him, frowning, stretching his lips halfway back from his teeth. "You really think that's how it is?"

"Sure enough, I do."

Pecos stared at him, and then he shook his head and shuttled his gaze back forward, along the sun-and-shade-dappled trail beyond the mules' twitching ears. "Damn. That's down-

right depressing to think that's how everything works. Here I
thought we was runnin' against the grain of things."

"We were really the most honest of all men, Pecos."

"Do you really think so, Slash?"

"I sure as hell do. And you know what? I don't see no
damn reason for us to fall for ole Bledsoe's ploy now, so late
in life. He's only bedevilin' us, havin' us haul all this treasure.
He knows how it's killin' us. I say as soon as we're out of
these mountains, we swing down to the old Santa Fe Trail
and drift straight south."

Pecos snapped a surprised look at him. "You mean . . . to
Mexico?"

"Hell, yes, to *Mexico!* We can cool our heels there for the
winter, then hop a steamer for South America. Why, I heard
the women down there were—"

He raised his hands to trace a figure in the air before him,
but Pecos cut him off with, "Ah, hell, Slash—you're just all
down in the dumps because you think you lost Jay."

"No, I ain't. I'm bein' practical. Why deny who we are?
Why pass up an opportunity like this, Pecos?"

Pecos stared at him, studying him closely, as though he
were trying to decipher a complicated line of prose. Sweat
beads popped out on his forehead, just below the brim of his
snuff-brown Stetson. His pale cheeks flushed above the line
of his silver-blond beard. His chest began to rise and fall
sharply. He was breathing hard.

A sweat bead ran into the corner of his left eye. He winced
against the sting and brushed it away with his shirtsleeve.
"Don't do this to me, Slash."

"What—make you rich?" Slash grinned.

"No, no, no, no, no!" Pecos shook his head. They'd both
been so deep in thought that even though the storm had rolled
away over an hour ago, and the morning had heated up, neither
former cutthroat had removed his rain slicker and rolled it
around his soogan stowed beneath the seat, with their saddle-

bags and rifles. Now Pecos unbuttoned his oilskin hurriedly, shrugged out of it almost violently, and stuffed it down beneath him with the rest of their gear. "We can't do it, Slash!"

"Sure, we can." Slash was grinning so brightly, so uncharacteristically, that Pecos thought his jaws would crack. "Who'd stop us?"

"Bleed-Em-So!"

As he shrugged out of his own slicker now, as well, Slash laughed. "We know the back trails and dark coulees, my friend. We have friends all along the way to the border. Have you forgotten?"

"No, no, no, no, no! Stop talkin', Slash! What about our word bein' 'bond' and honor among thieves!"

Slash laughed. "Yeah, honor *among* thieves! Not among Pinkertons an' thieves! Hell, did you ever know a thief whose word was 'bond'?"

"Stop!"

"I ain't gonna stop, Pecos! You can feel the heat of that gold back there just as hot as I can. Why, it's burning a hole right through my spine and stitching my innards all together in one great big ball!"

"What about Myra? We just gave her a home . . . a job. We gonna just run out on her?"

"We've run out on folks before. That's what cutthroats do!" Slash thought about it. "Besides—hell, we'll send her some dust. Enough to make a fresh start. A good, proper, fresh start in Denver. Hell, we'll send her enough so she can buy into her own saloon, just like Jay did!"

"You gotta stop talkin' now, Slash. You're talkin' like you used to talk, all heated-up like, and it plum scares me!"

"You're sweatin' like you just crawled out of a creek, Pecos."

"Hell!" Scowling straight ahead along the trail, Pecos scrubbed his sleeve across his forehead. His cheeks were rose red, and his eyes were as bright as the morning winter sun through a pane of hoarfrost. "Hell! Hell! Hell!" He sliced his arm down past his right ear, as though to smash an annoying fly. "Stop it, Slash!"

Slash leaned over and spoke like a green-horned, yellow-fanged devil in his partner's ear, his voice soft and wickedly resonant. "A half-day's ride farther west and then we take the old Ute Trail south to the Sangre de Cristos. You remember the route, Pecos. At that crossroads by Owl Canyon was where we turned back that posse from Cheyenne. As soon as we started shootin', they caught a bad case of homesickness. Remember that?"

Pecos shook his head and squeezed his eyes closed. "I don't remember that, Slash! I plum forgot an' I don't wanna remember!"

"From the 'Cristos, we drop straight down to the Sacramentos, then over to the Black Range."

"Stop it, Slash! I'm beggin' ya now!"

"We spend a night or two in Silver City with Pete Alvarez. Remember him? He was always good for a night or two of carne asada and his own homemade tequila. Remember his daughter? What was her name?"

"Isabella."

"That's right!"

"Oh, stop it, Slash—damn your rancid old hide, anyway!"

"After a night of watchin' Isabella dance in that skimpy little red dress of hers—remember the one, so small that either one of us could tuck it into one cheek and still chew a full meal around it?—we'll scuttle over to the San Francisco Peaks, then over to the Pinaleños farther west. From there—"

"Oh, stop it, now, Slash! You're killin' me!"

"From the Pinaleños we shoot down to the Chiricahuas, or if Geronimo's braves are runnin' off their leashes again, we'll slide over to the Dragoons, have a few drinks in Tombstone, say hi to ole Doc Holliday if the poor soul's still on this side of the sod, then high-tail it down through the Mules and straight south to the border an' beyond!"

Slash frowned at his partner. "Hey, where you goin'?"

Pecos had stopped the team. Now he was scrambling down the side of the wagon, puffing his cheeks out.

"Pecos . . . ?"

Pecos wheeled, then scrambled off into the brush beside the trail. He dropped to his knees, and, judging by the violent heaving sounds emanating from the wild currant bushes, disgorged everything in his chest and belly, except maybe a lung.

"Damn," Slash said, scowling toward where Pecos hung his head as though digging for worms beneath a log. "I do apologize, pard. I didn't realize you were so sensiti—"

Slash stopped and lifted his head to the forested ridge rising steeply off the trail's left side, far beyond where Pecos continued to retch. He'd heard something up there.

Something that had pricked the short hairs on the back of his neck.

Then it occurred to him.

A Gatling gun!

CHAPTER 15

Slash was still staring toward the eerie hiccupping sounds rising from the ridge when Pecos stumbled back toward the wagon, looking like a drunk after a three-day bender.

"Slash," he said, spatting to one side, "I purely think you're out to kill—"

"Shhh!"

"Huh?"

"Shut up."

"Hey, don't you—"

Pecos must have heard it then, too. Stopping a few feet from the wagon, he turned back around and lifted his gaze to the ridge. The distance-muffled *rat-tat-tats* of a machine gun continued to hammer away up there, somewhere near the ridge but on the near side of the mountain.

Pecos turned to Slash. "What's up there?"

"The stage trail is up there. Comes up from the backside, then swings north toward Leadville. The freight trail follows the easier-to-negotiate valleys to the south and across the Arkansas toward Colorado Springs."

"You think it's . . . ?"

"What the hell else could it be?" Slash's heart was thud-

of a stout aspen. Slash eased the man over with one foot, and his grimace grew more pronounced.

He cursed.

Pecos had dismounted the buckskin and now moved up to stand beside Slash. "What is—" Following Slash's gaze, he cursed, too.

The dead man was middle-aged and stocky and had a big, rounded gut. He also wore a beard. He'd lost his hat. His head was nearly bald. He was dressed in rugged trail gear, including canvas pants and a canvas jacket over a wool shirt and suspenders, and gauntleted gloves. Staring skyward and with an expression of agonized astonishment still twisting his mouth, he was either the driver or the shotgun messenger, Slash silently opined.

The most startling thing about him was that he'd been shot at least six times. Possibly twice that many. It was hard to tell because of all the blood.

Looking up the slope, Pecos pointed. "There's another one." He climbed the slope a ways, jerking his chin to indicate the incline, and then glanced over his shoulder at Slash. "Ah, hell—look at that!"

Slash stepped up beside him and sucked a sharp breath.

The stagecoach lay on its side about a hundred feet up the slope. Apparently, it had either turned over on the trail and then slid down the slope, or had rolled down the slope to come to rest against a cabin-sized granite boulder. The team must have broken away from the wagon when the shooting had started, because there wasn't a horse in sight, only a tangle of leather ribbons.

The Concord was honeycombed with bullet holes, and it was liberally splashed with blood. Four men lay in bloody heaps along the slope between Slash and Pecos and the carriage, which lay up the slope and to the right. The dead men, all dressed in various costumes corresponding to whatever

ding. "The stage must've gotten a late start on account of the rain."

They both stared in stunned silence up the spruce-green forested slope. A shrill scream cut through the Gatling gun's menacing belching. The high-pitched cry hung out over the shoulder of the mountain, echoing for nearly twenty seconds before it finally dwindled to silence.

When the scream died, the Gatling gun's *rat-tat-tats* also died.

Pecos turned to his partner. "That was a woman, Slash."

Slash just stared. He was thinking of the pretty young Pink who'd entered his and Pecos's room the night before.

Could that have been her scream?

Again, Pecos turned to his partner. "What . . . what're we gonna do, Slash?"

Slash grimaced as he stared up the now bizarrely silent shoulder of the mountain toward the unseen spot where the gold thieves must have hit the stage. He ran a perplexed hand down his unshaven jaw.

He glanced at the tarpaulin-covered box. He couldn't see the strongbox underneath. But he *could* see it, all right. What's more—he could see right *into* the box as though it was made of mere glass.

He could see all those ingots of high-grade gold all laid out like baby pigs in a blanket, pure and glinting and shinier than new brass. He could also see the big pile of greenbacks they would bring. More money than he'd ever seen in one spot in his entire life.

Half his own. The other half his partner's.

Oh, what a life in Mexico and South America that money would make!

He turned back to the ridge.

Still, though . . . the girl.

Slash leaped down off the wagon, hitting the ground flatfooted, then reaching up under the seat for his Yellowboy.

"What're you doin'?" Pecos said.

"Get the wagon off the road. Hide it behind those rocks over there."

"What're you doin', dammit?" Pecos asked as he scrambled back aboard the freighter.

"What's it look like?" Slash was untying their horses' reins from the steel rings in the tailgate. "We're gonna check it out."

"That's what I thought you was thinkin'!" Pecos said as he hazed the mules on off the trail. "I just wanted to be clear. *Hy-yahhhh*—Millie! Step it up there, Clyde!"

Slash had pulled both sets of reins free of the tailgate as Pecos swung the wagon off the road. Slash was sitting his own fleet-footed Appaloosa, and holding the reins of Pecos's big buckskin when Pecos jogged back to the trail. The taller of the two cutthroats had draped his gut-shredder over his neck and right shoulder, and he was holding his Colt's revolving rifle in both gloved hands.

When he shoved his rifle into its scabbard, Slash threw him his reins, then gigged the Appaloosa off the trail and through the shrubs on the other side.

"Wait for me, dammit, Slash!" Pecos bellowed as the big man heaved himself into his saddle.

"There may not be any time to waste, pard!"

Slash hunkered low over his Appy's jostling mane as the horse lunged up the slope and began weaving through the forest, carefully avoiding low-hanging branches, just as Slash had trained it, so as not to dislodge its rider. The first seventy yards were a hard pull for even the Appy, but then they gained a gently sloping bench barren of trees but spotted with the bright, paint-like splashes of late-summer wildflowers. After the bench, they crossed a creek, beyond which was another hard climb up a second steep inclination through dense pines.

After a hundred yards, Slash reined the Appy to a stop on a slight shelf. The horse needed a breather, and so did Slash. Crashing brush and pounding hooves sounded from below.

Slash turned to see Pecos and his buckskin, appropriately if unimaginatively named Buck, hammering up the incline, Pecos hunkered low and giving the big, beefy, but deep-bottomed beast a gentle rein, letting the sure-footed, experienced Buck pick his own way.

"Damn!" Pecos said, breathing hard. He spat to one side.

The buckskin shook and blew, switching its tail. Its blood was up, as was the Appaloosa's, both horses likely remembering with some fondness the hell-for-leather, ground-thundering gallops from posses not all that long ago. Such dangerous excitement could get in a horse's blood as much as in a man's, and be hard to let go.

Pecos stopped the horse near Slash and the Appy and stared up the slope, obscured by more forest just as deep as that they'd just pushed through. "You hearin' anything?"

"Haven't for a while."

The Appy whickered, then pulled at some grass.

"You sure that was a Gatling gun?" Pecos asked.

"Yep."

"Maybe we're just imagining things. You know—old timer's disease."

"Let's find out."

Slash reined the Appy around and booted it up the slope, the horse pushing hard with its hind feet and digging deep with its front hooves, kicking large gouts of moist, fragrant forest duff up behind it. Pecos galloped just off the Appy's right hip, throwing one arm out for balance, while the big buckskin leaped over deadfalls and caromed around rocks and thick brush snags.

"Ahead," Slash said after another hard pull. "I see somethin'."

He checked the Appy down, swung out of the saddle, dropped the reins, and climbed a few feet farther ahead, pushing off his knees with each lunging step. He stopped and grimaced when he saw the dead man lying twisted on the slope before him, in front

part the Pinkertons were playing in their ill-fated charade, lay spread out across the mountainside, some higher up on the incline than the others.

They all appeared to have been shot as many times as the first man had.

"Yep," Pecos said, raking a gloved hand down his face. "You had it right, Slash. It was a Gatling gun, all right."

"Do you see the girl?"

"Huh?"

"The girl? Operative One. You see her?"

Slash and Pecos moved on up the slope, looking around. They continued past the dead men and the battered, blood-splashed Concord to the graded trail that curved around the shoulder of the mountain. They saw a large spruce lying across the trail about thirty yards ahead, effectively blocking it. The tree had been chopped down within the past couple of hours with an axe. Cursing, looking for the girl, they thrashed around in the brush on the trail's upslope side.

All Slash found was the Gatling gun perched in a nest of rocks and brush about twenty feet up the slope on the opposite side from where the Concord and the dead men lay.

"They left the machine gun," Slash said, running a hand down the brass barrel that still felt warm.

Pecos walked along the trail and stared up the slope at the Gatling gun still mounted on its tripod and looking like a giant steel and brass mosquito there in the rocks, partly hidden by the wild currant and chokecherry shrubs.

"Why in the hell do you suppose they left it?"

Slash shrugged. "It did the job. Why carry it?"

"But . . . they didn't get what they came for."

Something bothered Slash about that last statement, but he didn't have time to ponder it. Just then something moved down the slope behind Pecos.

No, not something. Some*one*!

A person stepped out from behind some rocks and brush about ten feet down the decline from the trail. At first, Slash had thought it was an animal of some kind. A badly injured animal, because of all the blood covering it. Or at least mostly covering it. But then he saw that it was the young woman, Operative Number One, swinging around to face the trail and raising a stubby little pistol in both her bloody hands.

Slash wanted to say something to Pecos, but his breath got stuck in his throat. Pecos must have seen the shocked look in his partner's gaze, and that Slash's jaw had dropped nearly to his chest, because he muttered incredulously, frowning, and turned around to face the young woman, clad in a torn and bloody dress, moving up the slope toward the trail, aiming the Derringer at him and Slash.

Her brown eyes looked like two animal eyes staring flatly out from behind the tangle of her blood-sodden hair that had fallen from what had likely been a very prim and stately bun arranged atop her head. The dark-green bonnet she'd been wearing hung down her shoulder. It was also soaked in blood.

"Whoa, now," Pecos said, slowly raising his hands, palms out. "Easy . . . easy, there, now . . . little lady."

"Put the gun down, Operative One," Slash said, suddenly finding his voice.

Raising his own hands shoulder high, he walked slowly down the slope, the brush and grass crackling beneath his boots. "Easy, Oper—" *What had the tall man called her. Hattie?* "Easy, Hattie. It's us—Slash an' Pec—"

She didn't let him finish. As Slash stepped down onto the trail, ten feet to Pecos's left, the young woman gained the far side of the trail and said, "Stop!" Her voice was deep and guttural. It was raked with so much emotion that she sounded like a badly abused piano chord down in the lower registers.

She stretched her lips back from her teeth, and her eyes

glinted savagely. "Stop right there or I'll blast you!" She drew a sharp breath through fluttering lips and gripped the Derringer tightly in both hands, lowering her chin to aim down the stubby barrel. "I'll blast you both!"

"Easy, darlin'," Slash said. "It's Slash 'n' Pecos. Your freighter friends."

"*Cutthroats*! You were in with those . . . those *butchers*!"

CHAPTER 16

"No, no, no!" Pecos said, shaking his head. "We didn't have no part in that."

"We were below," Slash said. "We heard the Gatling gun. Rode up here to check it out. Put the gun down now, darlin'. You got no reason to be afraid of us."

She continued to aim down the little peashooter for almost another minute, sliding her gaze between the two former cut-throats. Then, gradually, doubt shone like a shadow across her retinas. She frowned, removed one hand from the gun to wipe blood and sweat off her forehead, and said, "You . . . promise you weren't one o' them?"

Suddenly, her voice had lost its guile.

Slash walked over to her, extending his hand for the pistol. "Cross our hearts, Hattie."

Fire returned to her mouth as well as her gaze. "It's Operative Number One, damn you!"

"All right, give me the gun, Operative Number One." Slash reached out and closed his hand around the Derringer, gently pried it from her hand.

As he did, the young woman gazed up at him, a sheen of emotion washing across her eyes. Her upper lip trembled, and then she flung herself forward against Slash, roping her arms around his waist and sobbing.

"It was awful!" she said, trembling in Slash's arms. "They bushwhacked us, opened up on us with that machine gun! They blocked the trail with that tree, and Donnally hadn't even got the coach stopped before they started shooting. They didn't shake us down! They didn't threaten us! They didn't demand the gold! None of those things!"

She tipped her head back to stare up at Slash, the tears mingling with blood and streaming down her cheeks and down her neck. "They just opened up on us with that Gatling gun!"

Pecos walked toward them. "Easy, girl—where you hit?"

The girl turned to him. "They shot us like ducks on a millpond. I don't think any of us . . . any of the others . . . even had a chance to draw a pistol!"

Slash lowered one arm and, keeping the other arm wrapped around her waist, led her over to a tree in the shade along the trail. "Come on—you'd best sit down over here, Operative Number One. You look mighty beat up."

Slash eased her down against the tree and raked her blood-soaked body with his eyes. "Where you hit? We're gonna have to—"

She shook her head. "I'm not hit."

"Huh?"

"I'm not hit. This is not my blood." She gave another sob and then, lips trembling, said, "I was sitting on the opposite side of the coach from that savage gun, facing forward. When those cowardly ambushers opened up, I was shielded by the other four Pinkertons in the coach. Somehow . . ."

She looked down at herself, swept her bloody hands across her bloody thighs. "Somehow, I don't believe I even caught a burn. When the horses headed down the slope, the coach broke away from the hitch and rolled. The door on my side opened, and I was thrown clear. I must've been knocked out. I remember hitting the ground . . . hearing that awful din! . . . and then I regained consciousness in those shrubs over there . . . and . . . and I saw you two . . . up here on the trail . . ."

Pecos was on one knee beside Slash. He looked at his partner and said, "How do you fathom them not stopping the coach to rob it but just shooting it off the road?"

Slash scooped up a handful of dirt, let it sift slowly to the ground, pondering. "Maybe they . . ."

"Knew it wasn't on the coach," the young woman finished for him. Her voice rising, she said, "They must have known the gold wasn't on the coach! They must have known only Pinkertons were on that coach, and they were out to kill us! To keep us off their trail! They shot us so fast . . . so fast . . . we didn't even have time to *pray*!"

Slash and Pecos exchanged dark glances.

"How in the hell could they have figured out our plan?" Pecos said.

Sitting up straight, a flush rising into her cheeks behind the crusted blood, Operative One said, "Where's the gold?"

Slash and Pecos winced, sheepish. Neither one said anything for a few stretched seconds. Then Pecos cleared his throat. "It's, uh . . . it's, uh—"

"Back down in the valley," Pecos finished for him, looking sharply, dubiously, at Slash.

They both suspected what they knew the young woman suspected.

Slash rose quickly. "I reckon we'd best get down there, partner. An' check on the gold, an' hope like hell what we think might've happened ain't what happened!"

"Wait!" Pecos grabbed Slash's shirt. "How could they know *we're* carryin' the gold?"

"Your guess is as good as mine. Come on!"

"Hold on." Hattie rose heavily, grunting, breathing hard now, anxiously. She extended her hand. "You still have my Derringer. Give it back."

Slash looked down at the Derringer poking out from behind his cartridge belt. He'd forgotten about it. He pulled it out and set it in her hand. "Here you go, darlin'."

"I'll be riding with you."

"Oh, no," Slash said. "We just got two horses. We'll check out the wagon an' come back for you later."

Hattie raised her pistol in both hands and clicked the hammers back. "You either take me with you now or I blast you both right here and take your horses!"

Pecos scowled at his partner. "That was a real swift move, Slash."

"Oh, shut up."

"Both of you, shut up, and get me down to the wagon!" the girl yelled.

"All right, all right," Slash said. "Don't get your bloomers in a twist." As he and Pecos started walking down the slope toward their horses, the girl following, aiming her Derringer at them, Slash said, "What about your friends here?"

"What about 'em?"

"Don't you wanna bury 'em?"

"They're dead. They don't deserve burying. No more than I would if I were among them—dead. Not after the foolish stunt we pulled—letting ourselves ride into that ambush!"

As they approached the horses, Slash shook his head. "You're a tough one, Hattie."

"It's Operative Number One to you, cutthroat!" the girl bit out behind him.

"I'm not gonna keep choking on my tongue every time I address you, Miss Hattie," Slash said, wheeling and, catching her off-guard, snatching the Derringer out of her right hand.

"Ouch!" she cried, stumbling forward. "Oh, you—"

"And you ain't gonna keep that little popper aimed at my back," Slash continued. "I don't doubt you know how to use it, but it's a silly man who'd let a girl keep a gun aimed at him when he don't have to."

"How dare you! Why, you're nothing more than a—!" She lunged at him, bringing her open right hand up and around to slap him. He grabbed her around her narrow waist, and before her hand could hit its target, he'd tossed her up onto his Appy's back, behind his saddle. Her hand swatted only air.

"How dare you!" she cried again, deeply indignant.

Slash glanced at Pecos, who regarded him skeptically as the bigger man swung up onto his buckskin's back. Slash sighed as he boarded his own horse. He glanced back at the young woman, who sat glaring at him, gritting her teeth and firing miniature bayonets with her eyes. "Hold on tight, now, darlin'," he said, adding with an ironic snort, "I sure wouldn't want to lose you!"

He pointed the Appaloosa downhill and touched spurs to its flanks.

Hattie cursed him all the way back down to the valley.

"Where is it?" she yelled behind him when they hit level ground. "Oh, my god—where is it?"

"Keep your pantaloons on—we ain't there yet!"

"Oh, my god!" the girl cried. "They've taken it! I know they've taken it! Oh, the humiliation of this! The shame! Mister Pinkerton will send me packing, and rightly so!"

"Like I said, keep your pantaloons on, honey," Slash said. "See—there it is! Right where we left it!" He laughed in relief as he and Pecos put their horses up to the rear of the wagon, behind the rocks that hid it from the trail. "Look there, the cover's still on it. Why, I don't think it's been molested in the least bit!"

He laughed again, giddy in his liberation from the anxiety that had gnawed at his gut while Hattie had chewed his ears all the way down the mountain.

He stopped the Appy and swung his right leg over the horn, dropping straight down to the ground. Pecos dismounted the blowing, sweat-lathered buckskin and straightened his hat.

"Check it out, partner," Slash said.

"Here we go." Pecos released the tarpaulin from the steel rings in the tailgate and then from around the sides of the box. He whipped it forward against the box's front panel.

Slash let out the breath he hadn't realized he'd been holding. The strongbox was still there, unmolested.

He blinked. Blinked again, rubbed his eyes.

He'd only been half right. The box was still there, all right. In the middle of the wagon. The chains were still attached. Only—the locks had been sprung!

Pecos must have seen the same thing Slash had seen at the same time Slash had seen it. He'd been grinning in relief. Only, now his smile quickly vanished without a trace.

The two men shared a dark look.

Slash leaped into the bed of the wagon. He dropped to a knee for a closer look.

Sure enough, the jaws of the locks were open.

His gloved hands shaking, Slash lifted the box's lid.

"Ah, hell!" rattled out his lips, pitched with anguish.

All the box contained were a dozen or so pine cones arranged into a stick figure's face complete with mocking smile.

Behind Slash, someone gave a breathy groan.

He turned to see Hattie, who'd been standing off the end of the wagon, faint. She dropped like a sack of thrown grain.

Just after sunset, Pecos was making his way back through woods toward the campfire he could see flickering in the near darkness of this narrow mountain valley, when he heard something on his left. A strange sound. Not a natural sound.

Could some of the gang of thieving killers have turned back to scour Slash, Pecos, and the pretty Pink from their trail?

The sound had come from the stream, a tributary of the Taylor River, rushing through the rocks and boulders over there, about seventy or so yards from the small clearing in which, after a long, frustrating afternoon of tracking the half-dozen thieves, Slash, Pecos, and the young Pinkerton had finally made camp.

Taking his Colt revolving rifle in both hands, Pecos moved toward the stream. He didn't have to move too carefully, for the low rushing of the stream itself would cover his approach. He stopped where he could see the last pink, pearl, and green wash of late light reflecting off the water beyond three tall spruces, then bulled slowly between two of the pyramidal evergreens, and stopped suddenly.

Oh, my . . .

A figure stood before him, not ten feet away. It was none of the thieving killers. It was the pretty, young Pinkerton, whose first name, Hattie, was the only name Pecos knew her by. Aside from Operative Number One, that was.

She must have finally gotten tired enough of the blood that had crusted on nearly every inch of her and that she'd refused to waste time cleaning off, so desperately focused had she been on catching up to the murdering gold robbers. Now, however, after they'd finally stopped for the night, and Slash was tending the fire, she'd decided to come out to the creek for a bath.

And . . . here she was . . . in all her naked, ripe young glory, standing not ten feet away from Pecos, on the edge of the stream, half facing Pecos while she ran a towel across her chest and dabbed it under her right arm.

Pecos's throat was tight and dry.

His pulse throbbed in his temples.

Oh, my . . .

He needed to be on his way, but he was afraid that if he moved, she'd see him. She'd think he was spying on her. Ogling her. And that, by god, had not been his intention!

No, sir. Not by a long shot.

But Pecos had to admit that if there were any pretty young Pinkerton detectives anywhere on the planet that he would have wanted to ogle, this one standing butt-naked not ten feet away from him, her wet hair glinting in the last light, would likely be the one.

Tightening his jaws and stretching his lips back from his teeth, Pecos began to backtrack ever so slowly. He wanted to move faster, but for some reason, his feet felt like lead, and he could not remove his eyes, howsoever much he intended to—wanted to!—from the spectacular, mind-numbing, heart-wrenching scene before him.

Come on, dammit, move! he silently ordered himself.

But he could not get his feet to work. That damn towel kept moving across the nicely rounded body before him, making certain parts move in such damned beguiling ways, that—

As the girl lifted her left arm to dab beneath it with the towel, she turned her head in the same direction. She must have glimpsed Pecos standing behind her, because she froze for just a second.

No, no, no, no! Pecos silently shrieked at the girl. *Don't look over here! No need to look over here!*

She screamed.

Oh, hell!

She screamed again and whipped around to face Pecos, covering her well-formed bosoms with the towel and leaping backward, long wet hair dancing across her slender shoulders.

"No!" Pecos shouted, holding his rifle out to his side in one hand and thrusting his left hand forward, palm out. "No! I wasn't . . . I wasn't . . . !"

"What are you *doing*?" the girl screamed, then lunged to her left. The hazy, weakening light glinted off something on a rock over there.

Oh, no. That damned Derringer of hers!

CHAPTER 17

At the same time, but roughly a hundred and fifty miles to the northeast, Jaycee Breckenridge drew in a deep draught of fresh, northern Colorado air and said, "What a heavenly time of the day. Thank you so much, Cisco, for luring me out of the Thousand Delights for a badly needed stretch of my legs and a good lung clearing."

"Not at all, Jay. Glad I could help."

"I swear," Jay said as they stopped, arm in arm, at the west edge of town to stare toward Horsetooth Rock, beyond which the sun had just dropped, pulling the crimson bayonets of its last rays down along with it, "I inhale so much cigarette and cigar smoke all day, I forget what clean air really smells like. I go to bed feeling as though I've smoked a couple dozen quirleys rolled with cheap tobacco!"

"Yes, it can't be healthy," the tall, handsome marshal said, squeezing her hand in his. "But I have to admit that my motives for asking you out for a walk were farther reaching than just my concern for your health, Miss Breckenridge." He rose up on the toes of his polished black cavalry boots and gave his chin a cordial dip while lifting his dragoon-style mustache in a toothy smile.

Jay turned to him, giving both her copper brows a feigned

coy arch. "Oh? And what other motives might you have, pray tell? Careful now, Marshal, I do believe I'm within hailing distance of First Avenue. You wouldn't want a scandal on your hands—now, would you? To be arrested by your own deputies would be downright embarrassing, I would think!"

She chuckled throatily.

Marshal Walsh chuckled, as well, and patted her hand, which he held firmly in his own. "Never to worry, milady," he said through another oily grin. "I give you my word as a gentleman as well as an upholder of the law that your honor is safe in my hands."

He chuckled again, a tad nervously, self-consciously, Jay silently opined. Then he cleared his throat and, sobering somewhat, bounced up and down again on the toes of his boots and said, "All jokes aside, I must confess that I invited you out here because I've simply come to enjoy your company."

"Oh?"

"Isn't it obvious?"

"Obvious?" Jay frowned. "In what way?"

"Well, you must have seen me frequenting the Thousand Delights. Several times a day," he added with another charming smile.

"You're not the only man, Cisco, who enjoys our free lunch counter. Some of that summer sausage I ship up here from Denver, and the cheese—"

"It is not the sausage nor the cheese, dear Jay, that beckons me through your doors so often."

"It's not? Oh, well, then'. . ." Jay let her voice trail off as she returned her gaze toward the appropriately named Horsetooth Rock, now fully silhouetted against a lime green sky. "You have me at a disadvantage, then, Marshal Walsh. I do know you haven't called on any of my girls in several weeks . . ."

"No, I haven't."

"Do you find them, um . . . less than satisfactory? Let me assure you, I have Dr. Raskin examine each one every two weeks, just to make sure none of my customers can complain of unexpected surprises."

Walsh canted his head to one side and arranged a mock-admonishing expression on his broad, handsome face beneath the narrow brim of his crisp bowler. "Come now, Jay. Don't be coy. You know how I feel about you. You must have known how I've felt about you since we first met in Abilene."

"A hundred years ago," Jay said.

"It sure is funny."

"What's funny, Cisco?"

Walsh turned square to Jay and placed his hands on her shoulders, bare beneath a teal-green shawl that matched the green of her sparkling gown. His eyes dropped furtively—or with what he probably thought was furtiveness—to her freckled cleavage, revealed by the gown's low bodice cut to accentuate the handsome woman's rounded curves, before rising again to her eyes. "It feels like only yesterday to me. And you don't look a day older. In fact, I do believe you've become even more beautiful than when you were a bouncing young redhead singing and kicking your legs up high for those border roughs in the Armadillo!"

"Oh, well," Jay said, chuckling her surprise. "That's quite the compli—"

Before she could complete the sentence, Walsh leaned down to place his mouth on hers. Jay was startled by the man's sudden show of passion. She tried to return the kiss. She wanted to, in fact, but for some reason her lips wouldn't soften and yield to his the way he wanted her to.

Walsh pulled his head away, dropped his hands from her shoulders, and averted his gaze, vaguely sheepish. "I'm . . . I'm sorry if that was unwanted."

Jay smiled, flushed a little, and turned away to stare off toward the shelving stone dykes to the north of Horsetooth

Rock, which were turning a darker purple now as the light left the sky. "Oh, Cisco, it wasn't so much unwanted as . . . as it just sort of startled me a little. Caught me off guard. I'm sorry."

She truly was sorry. She welcomed this man's attentions. She was flattered by them, for she was attracted to him. And yet she felt a barrier between them, a hesitancy, an aloofness in her own demeanor when he was near, which she'd known even before he'd mentioned it that he very much wanted to be near.

A part of her wanted that, as well.

And yet . . .

"It's Braddock, isn't it?"

The name as well as the question drew her shoulders together slightly.

She turned around to face the tall man again, frowning at him. "What?"

"It's Jimmy Braddock. Slash. He stands between us—doesn't he, Jay?" Walsh paused. He removed his hat, swept a hand through his wavy, thick brown hair with a sigh, then took the hat in both hands, tossing it absently, turning it between his long fingers.

Jay pondered that, made a sour expression. "I don't know. Yes. I guess so." She turned away again, abruptly. She sighed, lifted her chin, and laughed dryly deep in her chest. "Yes, yes, yes. Indeed, he does, Cisco. I'm sorry. Honestly, I don't know what it is about that scruffy, owly, cold, and aloof, middle-aged cutthroat—but I do harbor a deep fondness for him, indeed." She gave a guttural groan of frustration through gritted teeth.

She turned back to the marshal, frowning up at him in deep consternation. "I have no idea why."

"Sometimes the heart doesn't always tell the brain."

Jay smiled and placed a hand on Walsh's cheek, caressing it a little with her thumb. "That's very wise."

"Oh, I've got all kinds of wise things to say, Jay. But I

guess I'll be needing to find another woman to tell them to."
Walsh gave a pained smile. "Won't I?"

"Oh, I don't know, Cisco."

"Yes, you do. The man is gone for you, Jay. I could tell it
in your room the other night. There was something between
you. It was in the air, like electricity after a lightning storm. I
was jealous. I'll be honest with you . . . as I so seldom am
with other women, for some damn crazy reason . . . but I was
jealous as hell!"

"Maybe you're so seldom jealous," Jay said, keeping her
hand on his cheek, then playfully poking her finger against
his broad, blunt-tipped, sun-seasoned nose. "Maybe, mostly,
other men are jealous of you. You're uncomfortable with
having the tables turned."

Walsh laughed at that, turned away. He was kneading his
hat brim as though it were a flour crust he was packing along
the lip of a pie pan. "You know me too well, Jay."

"That's not a hard thing to figure out." Jay sighed and fingered the edge of her shawl, staring at the dirt of the trail
they'd followed out from town. "What's hard to figure is a
person's own heart."

"I have a feeling you're a lot alike—you an' Slash," said
Walsh. "If that helps any."

"Oh?" She frowned up at him. "How so?"

Walsh shrugged. "I honestly don't know. It was just a
sense I got up in your room the other night."

"Hmmm." Jay nodded slowly. "Maybe you're right."

"Does he know how you feel?"

Jay continued to nod, and she smiled a little. "He knows."

"Has he told you how he feels about you?"

"No. But not for lack of trying."

Walsh frowned, curious. "Come again?"

She laughed again, but with more than a little irony. "Slash
has told me more about how he feels with his eyes, when he
didn't know I was looking, than he's ever said with his words.

Long ago, I thought we were going to get together—Slash an' me. Before Pete came along. But Slash could never find the words back then, just as he doesn't seem able to find them now. So I took up with Pete.

"Oh, I was in love with Pistol Pete—don't get me wrong. Such a big, handsome, commanding figure, with more than a little of the rascal in him" She hacked out a bawdy laugh and shook her head in wonder. "But I think I was always a little in love with Slash, too. There was just something about his lonesomeness and his grumpy demeanor. That anger he always tries to show is betrayed by the gentleness of his eyes. I know he has a romantic turn of mind. Maybe not as much as Pecos does. Lord, Pecos can fall in and out of head-over-heels love in a week and do the very same thing the next week, and end up howling like a gut-shot coyote when the next one leaves him. Hah!"

Jay toed a line in the dirt with the heel of her high-heeled leather boot. "Slash falls harder and deeper, I think. And he doesn't do himself any good by being unable to express his feelings. I think I know why he has trouble with people, though."

"Oh? Why's that?"

"He was an orphan, Slash was. He was raised along the river piers and warehouses in St. Louis. Back when that town was wide open. His mother was a prostitute. She died when he was very young. Slash was raised by other prostitutes, each one of whom ended up the same unfortunate way as his mother. Dying slowly of one disease or another. Pleurisy, consumption, black fever . . . syphilis. That kind of life does something to a boy, and the man that boy becomes. He never trusts anybody. Not fully. Not ever. Never feels a part of something larger than himself. Can never fully belong. Can never tell a woman he loves her, because—who knows?—she might not return the favor and leave him even lonelier than he was before."

Jay sighed and looked up at the sky, in which the first stars kindled brightly. "Pecos had a mother. In New Mexico. I don't think she was worth much, but he had her, just the same. And the men who came in and out of her life for a time. I know he loved his mother very much. He told me one time. Slash never told me peanuts about himself. I learned what I learned about him from the women I knew on the line. Those who'd known him . . . had known his situation at home—back before he killed a man who killed one of the prostitutes who had unofficially adopted him. Then he cut out for the Wild West, and he's been running off his leash out here ever since. Him an' Pecos, who is the light tempering Slash's darkness. They met down in Texas. In some bordello, of course. All these years ago now."

She stopped and just stared at the stars for a time. Walsh stood beside her, staring skyward, as well.

Finally, he glanced over at her. "What are you going to do, Jay? About Slash, I mean."

She thought about that as she stared at the stars growing brighter with each flicker. She glanced over at Walsh and said thoughtfully, firmly, "I'm going to give him some time. Not a lot. Because neither of us is getting any younger, and I'd as soon not die alone, with no one around to give my cheek one more kiss. No, I'm not going to wait on him forever. But I'm going to wait a little while longer."

She smiled wistfully. "I owe him that much."

Walsh drew a deep breath and gave a dubious half-smile. "Far be it from me to say this, but say it I will. I don't think you owe him that much. Or is that my envy speaking again?" He smiled, shook his head. "Whatever is doing my talking for me, just know this, Jaycee Breckenridge."

He closed his hands over her shoulder again, drew her toward him. "If that old cutthroat can't muster up the courage to make an honest woman out of you, I'll be waiting in the wings to do just that."

Jay looked up at him in surprise, deeply touched. "Really, Cisco? You'd do that for me?"

"That, darling woman, is testament to how deeply I feel for you. I for one am not afraid to say it. I am also not so proud that I'd let pride stand in my way of one day placing a ring on your finger, facing a judge, saying 'I do forevermore,' and lifting your veil and kissing your tender lips."

He gave a courtly bow and kissed her hand.

"My god, Cisco," Jay said, sucking back a powerful wave of emotion, "I think I might have just swooned!"

"Don't worry—I'm here to catch you when you fall."

Jay frowned. "You said 'when.' Are you so certain?"

Walsh gave a regretful half-smile. "Unfortunately, I am."

"Don't be offended that I do hope you're wrong."

"Not at all." Walsh smiled. "But only if you'll join me for one drink before you start the wild part of your night in the Thousand Delights."

"First one's on me!"

Cisco turned sideways to her and crooked his arm. Jay hooked hers through his. They started back to the bustling heart of Fort Collins in the northern Colorado gloaming.

CHAPTER 18

"No, no, no, no, no!" Pecos bellowed as he watched the girl scoop her Derringer off the rock. As she raised the gun and took aim, she lost the towel but she seemed more bent on blood now than modesty.

"You *animal*!" she shrieked, clicking the little popper's hammer back and aiming down the stubby barrels.

"Slash, help me out here!" Pecos cried, stumbling back through the spruce branches.

The Derringer's top barrel blossomed rose flames and made a sound like a branch snapping. It was a good thing that Pecos tripped over a spruce root humping out of the ground or the bullet he felt pass through the air where his head had been a half a wink before likely would have drilled him a third eye.

As he hit the ground, the Derringer cracked again. The second bullet drilled into the ground not three inches off his left ear.

"Hold your fire! Hold your fire!" Pecos shouted. "I can explain!"

As he pushed up onto his elbows, he widened his eyes in shock when he saw the girl running toward him, still as

naked as the day she was born but a whole lot better filled
out. She wasn't wielding the Derringer, however. She'd replaced the empty garter gun in her hands with a stout pine
branch.

"I'll show you what happens to lusty old dogs!"

She stopped before Pecos and swung the branch from behind her right shoulder. Before she could land the blow, Slash
ran up from behind her and wrapped one arm around her
chest. In the near darkness, he probably didn't realize she
was naked. But when he realized what he'd grabbed, a wide-
eyed look of shock rolled over his lean, weathered features beneath the brim of his low-crowned, flat-brimmed black hat.

Still, he jerked up her arm holding the branch. He snatched
the branch out of her hand, and tossed it away.

He lowered his other arm to her belly and lifted her up off
her feet.

"Stop it!" she cried. "Let me go, you licentious desperado!
You craven outlaw! You gutless coyote! You common cur!
Let me *goooo!*"

"You want me to let you go?" Slash asked, holding the girl
up off the ground while she writhed and kicked in his grasp.

"Let me go, or I'll . . . I'll . . ."

"All right," Slash said. "I'll let you go!"

He stepped back, swung around, and tossed her into the
stream. She hit the water with a scream and a thunderous
splash.

Slash turned back to Pecos, chuckling. "There. That'll
teach her how to treat licentious desperados!"

Pecos climbed heavily to his feet, wincing and grunting
against the various and sundry aches and pains that are naturally spawned when a man of his years and size hits the ground
so unceremoniously. "What in the holy hell does lic . . .
lic-en—"

"Licentious?" Slash asked, chuckling again. "Beats me.

Leastways, that's what I thought she said." He frowned at his partner. "Say, what were you doing over here when the poor girl was trying to have a little privacy, anyways?"

Before Pecos could answer, a gurgling sound rose from the stream. It was followed by the sound of thrashing and chaotic splashing. Both men turned toward where the water slid between the low, rocky banks, reflecting the last light of day slowly filtering out of the early-evening sky.

"Where is she?" Slash said, scowling at the river.

"H . . . help!" the girl cried in a watery gasp.

Both men saw the struggling figure at the same time, about twenty feet downstream on their right and ten feet out from the bank.

Pecos pointed. "There she is! Lord o' mercy—you're drowning her, Slash!"

"Help!" the girl wailed, splashing and thrashing and desperately trying to keep her head above water. "I can't. . . I can't . . . *swimmmm!*"

"Oh, fer cryin' in the parson's tea!"

Slash took off running downstream along the bank, while Pecos branched off toward the camp, yelling, "I'll fetch a rope!"

Slash ran, swiping his hat off his head and shucking out of his leather vest, keeping his eyes on the silhouette of the girl thrashing in water that was a murky brown and green color in the fading light. She twisted and turned, stabbing at the water with her hands, gasping and crying and calling for help.

"Ain't this just like you?" Slash berated himself, pausing at the edge of the bank to rip off his string tie so it wouldn't get caught up on anything in the river and strangle him—though strangling would be no more than what he deserved. "First, you cripple a U.S. marshal, and now you've gone an' drowned yourself a Pink!"

He whipped out of his shirt, kicked out of his boots, ran downstream a few more yards, then leaped off the bank and onto a tree angling partway into it, having fallen from his side of the water. He thrust his arms above his head and sprang off his heels, diving forward into the cold, dark stream.

He came up fast, shivering, and thrust his head above the water. The girl was twenty, maybe thirty feet away from him. She appeared to be caught in the strong current out toward the center of the river. It had her fast, and it was taking her quickly toward the tributary's meeting with the Taylor a mile or two beyond.

If she got that far, she'd be a goner, for this far up the canyon, the Taylor was a raging torrent.

Slash swam out toward the current. When he felt it grab him, he turned toward the girl and thrust his arms forward, swimming hard and fast, kicking his legs.

"Imagine that," he grunted, swimming. "A Pinkerton detective who can't swim. Hell, no one taught me how to swim. I learned by happenstance. Either you sink or you swim!" Louder, he yelled, "This ain't some Chicago lawn party out here, honey!"

The current picked up as the stream narrowed between banks, closing like the jaws of a steel trap, so that the river became half as wide as it had been where the girl had gone in. Or where Slash had thrown her in, he silently amended to himself, with some chagrin.

Here, the current was faster, taking both the girl and Slash more quickly downstream toward the Taylor.

Slash gritted his teeth against the cold and swam as though his life depended on it. Which it likely did. If the pretty Pink drowned, Bleed-Em-So would likely hang him, with both the chief marshal and Alan Pinkerton smoking cigars as they watched the festive event from a doxie's hotel balcony.

Slash swam until he thought his heart, frozen as it felt, would explode in his frozen chest. He narrowed the gap between him and the girl, the river glinting and gurgling around him. The Pink's pretty head went under for a few seconds, and when she started to come back up, Slash grabbed her from one side and, sidling behind her, wrapped his arm around her chest and drew her close against him.

She gave a startled scream.

"Easy, easy," Slash said. "It's me, darlin'! I'm here to save your worthless, albeit lovely hide!"

The stark fear in the girl's eyes turned momentarily to disdain as she yelled, "Stop pawing me, you brigand!"

"I'm tryin' to save your life, you silly thing!"

"You don't need to grab me there!"

Slash was on the verge of letting her go altogether. But then his mind flashed on the imagined image of Bledsoe and Pinkerton enjoying his necktie party while newsboys hawked the local rag and middle-aged women from some civic sobriety society sold glasses of bittersweet lemonade, and he renewed his grip on the girl's upper chest, trying to keep his male mind off what he was touching.

Hell, he was so cold he could barely feel anything, anyway.

What he did register was that she felt like an icicle. A lumpy, wet one.

As soon as he tightened his grip on her and drew her against him once more, the terror returned to her eyes, and she started fighting him. "Oh!" she cried. "Oh . . ." Her head went under briefly, and she bobbed up, spitting water. "Oh, I'm . . . I'm . . . I'm . . . drown—!"

"Stop fighting me, dammit!"

"Help! I'm—"

In her terror and raging panic, she rammed her elbow against Slash's left cheek. As cold as he was, the pain was like a javelin shoved through both jaws, dazing him for a few precious seconds. Thrashing crazily, she drew him under with her, kicking and clawing him, and when he got both their heads above the river again, he spat water from his lips and said, "Sorry for this, darlin'—but it's for your own damn good!"

Slash rammed his balled right fist into her left cheek.

Instantly, her eyes rolled up in their sockets, and she sagged back in the water.

Slash grabbed her and, holding her head above the water, began to stroke with his free arm toward shore.

"Slash—rope!" Pecos called.

It was too dark for Slash to see the rope until it hit the water. He saw the glint as it splashed, and then he saw its silhouette writhing like a snake just ahead of him. He let the current carry him and the unconscious girl forward, then reached out to grab the braided riata.

He twisted the wet leather in his fist and yelled, "Got 'er!"

The slack was taken up out of the rope, and Pecos began to pull Slash, with the girl's back pressed hard against him, her head tilted back beneath his chin, toward shore. Slash merely treaded water, letting his partner do the work, wincing at the taut pressure in his right hand, where the riata bit into his skin.

Finally, he saw Pecos's hatted silhouette against the dull, green-dark sky behind him, as he stood on the bank about four feet above the water. Pecos pulled with one hand and threw the slack leather out behind him. The river's sandy, weedy bottom clawed against Slash's feet, and with a relieved sigh, he regained his balance and walked up the shelving shoreline.

Pecos continued to pull the riata until Slash and the girl were snugged up against the mossy, brushy bank, the river now swirling around their knees.

"You all right, Slash?" Pecos said, hurrying over to the waterlogged pair.

"I . . . I think so." When Slash had caught his breath, he grabbed the girl, pulled her over his shoulder, and extended his hand to Pecos, who grabbed it and pulled him up onto the bank. Slash glared at him. "No thanks to you!"

"What do you mean—no thanks to me? You're the one who threw her in the river!"

With the girl slumped over his shoulder like a hundred-pound sack of potatoes, Slash walked in his soaked socks toward the fire flickering in the darkness, beyond a black fringe of screening trees. "I didn't know she couldn't swim. Doesn't Pinkerton teach his operatives to swim, fer chrissakes?"

He glanced over his shoulder at Pecos, who was taking long strides to keep up with his soaked and shivering partner. "Besides, you were the one ogling her from the bushes, you depraved cuss!"

"I wasn't ogling her! I was out scouting them thieves' trail, just like I said I was gonna do—'cause you couldn't track a hog across a muddy yard!—when I come back an' heard somethin' over by the river. I thought fer sure that gang must've sent a man or two back to turn us toe down an' get us off their trail."

Slash entered the camp and headed toward where the girl had piled her gear, which they'd retrieved from the area around the stage before they'd set out on the robbers' trail. If she was joining the two ex-cutthroats on their hunt for the killers, which it looked like she was bound and determined to do, whether they wanted her to or not, she'd need some clean clothes and blankets.

Slash hurried past the small, crackling fire, saying, "Yeah, well, since it wasn't *them* but *her*, you just decided to stand there and get you an eyeful while she bathed herself—that it?"

"That ain't it at all!"

"Spread her blankets out there so I can lay her down!"

Slash stood, shivering, as he held the girl over his shoulder, while Pecos dropped to his knees and spread the Pink's blankets out at the base of a fir tree roughly six feet from the fire. "When I seen it was her and not no bushwhackers," Pecos said, "I . . . well, I . . . I reckon I just couldn't . . . I couldn't turn away." He gave a sheepish scowl.

"See? What'd I tell you? You're a mighty depraved soul,

Pecos. When you get back to Fort Collins, I suggest you join a church. If any church will have you and risk getting struck by lightning the minute you walk through its doors, that is!"

"Ah, cut it out, Slash! You're ridin' me too hard for this. It was a human mistake! She's a pretty girl, fer leapin' hellcats!"

"Help me get her down there. As cold an' stiff as I am, I'm liable to drop her."

"Jesus, she ain't movin'," Pecos said, taking the girl by her shoulders and, with Slash holding her legs, easing her onto the spread blankets. "Are you sure you didn't kill her?"

Kneeling to each side of the naked young Pinkerton agent, both men stared down at her. "Holy moly," Slash said, raking a hand down his face in appreciation of the sight before him.

"See?" Pecos said. "What'd I tell you? Now you're doin' it, too!"

"She certainly is an eyeful."

"What'd I tell ya?"

"Stop starin' at her, you old dog!" Slash got ahold of himself and, seeing that her bosoms were rising and falling as she breathed, which meant she was still kicking, he drew one of the blankets over her body and began rubbing her violently. "Help me here," he ordered. "Grab that other blanket and let's dry her and rub some blood back into her limbs."

"All right, all right!"

"Don't you go enjoying it!"

"I ain't enjoying it one bit! I think you're the one who's enjoying it!"

"I am not!"

"You'd have gotten stuck there same as me, Slash! If it'd been you in my shoes."

"Yeah . . . well . . . maybe," Slash allowed, grudgingly, as he rubbed the girl's left leg, watching all her parts jostling around beneath the blankets. Then he couldn't help but chuckle in spite of his chagrin. "Boy, she sure caught you with your hand in the cookie jar, didn't she?"

Rubbing the girl's left arm brusquely, Pecos shook his head. "Boy, I'll say she did."

"Either one of them bullets hit home?"

"No, but not for her lack of tryin'!"

"Hey, look," Slash said, "I think she's comin' around."

CHAPTER 19

The girl moaned and shook her head. Her lips fluttered. She squeezed her eyes tightly closed, rolled onto her side, and coughed, spitting up water.

Slash and Pecos sat back, gazing down at her hopefully.

"How you doin', darlin'?" Slash asked her.

She coughed up a little more water, then turned to look at the two middle-aged cutthroats staring down at her. She ran the back of her hand across her mouth, frowning as though it was taking her brain some time to get all its marbles back into their rightful pockets. The young Pinkerton's brown eyes seemed to focus gradually, and then, gasping with a sudden realization, she cut her astonished, horrified gaze to each grinning man in turn. She lifted the blankets to stare down at her naked body.

"Oh, my god!"

"It ain't what ya think!" Pecos said.

"Rest assured," Slash said, holding up his hands, "your virtue is intact. As is ours. We was just gettin' the blood goin' again in all your purty parts."

"All my *purty parts*?"

"Real helpful, Slash!" Pecos castigated his partner.

"Well, hell, there's no denying she ain't hard to look at."

Slash chuckled dryly. "You know that most of all, ya shameless, peeping scalawag!"

"Get away from me!" the girl shrieked, holding the blankets down tautly against her chest and making sure nothing was showing down along the rest of her as she sat up and curled her legs beneath her. "Go on—get away. Shoo! Shoo!"

"Shoo? Shoo?" Slash said, indignant. "Listen, darlin'—we just saved your life. Hell, I risked my life to save yours!"

"You hit me!" She probed at her left cheek with a finger.

"It was for your own damn good, honey. I barely tapped you. You just got a bone china jaw, is all."

"First you throw me into the river and then you swim out and attack me!"

"*Attack?*"

The pretty, waterlogged Pink shuttled her incriminating gaze to Pecos. "And you were ogling me while I toweled off after bathing. That's what started this whole thing. I remember it all quite clearly!"

"Ah, hell!" Pecos said. "Believe what you wanna believe. I'm tired of this. I'm hungry and thirsty."

"Yes, I'm sure that ogling a lady as she enjoys her private ablutions will make a scalawag such as yourself quite hungry." She raised her knees and rested her forehead on them. "Oh, god—here I find myself ambushed and badly battered, splattered with the blood of my own colleagues. The gold we planned so hard to keep safe is stolen out from under the noses of the two doddering cutthroats that Chief Marshal Bledsoe, for some *ungodly* reason known only to *him*, assigned to protect it . . ."

"Hey!" Slash objected. "There ain't nothin' *doddering* about *this* cutthroat!"

"And then I'm ogled by the notorious varmint known as the Pecos River Kid, only to nearly be drowned and savagely attacked by the vile and infamous brigand Slash Braddock!"

"Infamous?" Slash said. "Yeah, I'll take infamous."

"After I am finally fished out of the river in which I nearly drowned, I wake up butt-naked with the same two criminals hovering over me like a couple of snarling ogres. Who knows what they did while I was at death's doorstep!"

"Well, I know what I did," Pecos said, pouring soaked beans into a pot. "And it wasn't nearly as much fun as what you're talkin' about."

The girl lifted her chin and stared in anguish at the stars. "God hates me!"

She put her head down against her knees again and sobbed.

Slash had swaddled himself in his wool soogan and was kneeling by the fire, letting its warmth wrap around him and begin to push out the chill that had penetrated his very marrow. He'd also produced a bottle from his bag. He glanced at Pecos, who was stirring the beans.

Pecos sighed. "Poor girl. Her heart's done been broken." To the girl, he said, "I do apologize for my part in it, honey. You're right, I am a varmint. A lusty old varmint. I'll be shoveling coal soon, no doubt." He tasted the beans, then continued stirring the pot. "I do cook a good pot of beans, though."

Slash went over, dropped to a knee beside the pretty Pinkerton, and offered his bottle. "Here—have you a coupla pulls of that. You're just cold, is all. Cold and hungry, most like. The whiskey'll work on the chill, and Pecos's beans—if they don't kill you—will satisfy your hunger."

"I cook better beans than you do, Slash. You don't put enough bacon in." To the girl, Pecos added, "Slash is tighter'n the bark on a tree. He don't add enough bacon. Bacon—and a whole fletch of the right *kind* of bacon—is the key to a good pot of beans."

He glanced at his partner and sealed his conviction with a resolute dip of his chin.

The Pink lifted her head from her knees. She wiped tears from her cheeks with the back of each hand in turn and looked at the bottle in Slash's hand. "I don't imbibe."

"No better time to start."

Shivering, she looked at the unlabeled bottle again. She grabbed the forty-rod, looked at it, made a little face, then tipped it back and swallowed. She jerked the bottle down and, eyes bulging and lips twisting, her cheeks becoming first stony pale then sunset red, she coughed, choked, and scowled at Slash. "My god!" She could barely speak. "That's just *awful!*"

"He buys cheap whiskey, Slash does," Pecos said. "Everything about him is cheap."

"It grows on you," Slash told the Pinkerton.

Slash took the bottle back and started to rise. He stopped when the girl grabbed the bottle out of his hand and threw back another couple of swallows. She gagged and coughed, and scrubbed her hand across her mouth. This time her cheeks didn't turn pale but stayed red with the flush of warm blood.

"Awful!" she croaked. "But . . . you're right. It does fight the cold."

"Here." Slash plucked a bullet-dented tin cup, charred from many remote fires in countless hidden coulees across the western frontier, and splashed a couple of fingers of the busthead into it. He held the cup out to the girl. "Have a cup of your own. That bullet crease is compliments of Bill Tilghman his ownself."

The girl glanced dubiously at the dent. "All right," she said. "If you insist."

"Oh, I do. Doctor Slash's orders."

Slash winked at her, then went back and hunkered down close to the fire. He threw back several more shots of the whiskey and knelt there, shivering. Pecos grabbed the bottle out of his hand and splashed whiskey into his own cup before thrusting the bottle back to Slash.

Pecos filled a bowl of beans for himself, set the pot on a rock beside the fire, then sat back against his saddle, his cup of whiskey on the ground beside him, the bowl of beans steaming in his gloved hands. "Beans are ready anytime you want 'em. Slash can get his own, but I'll serve yours to you personally, young lady, in grand style."

He winked at her. He'd be damned if he didn't think she blushed a little.

After a time, staring into her cup, she said, "What on earth are we gonna do about that gold?" She had wriggled over to sit back against the bole of the fir tree, the blankets wrapped tightly around her, not showing so much as a square half-inch of her flesh.

"What are we gonna do about the gold?" Slash said, taking another pull from the bottle and giving another spasming shiver as a fresh chill rolled through him. "We're gonna get it back. That's what we're gonna do about the gold."

"Got no choice," Pecos said, scooping beans into his mouth as though he wasn't likely to see more beans till the next harvest. "Me an' Slash can't go back to Denver without that gold. If we do, we'll likely be greeted by a necktie party complete with a four-piece band. Ole Bleed-Em-So will hang us fer sure, and cheer on our midair two-steps."

"This wouldn't have happened if you two old outlaws hadn't let the gold get stolen right out from under your noses!" the girl scolded, glaring at each man in turn.

That climbed Slash's hump. He rose and pointed the bottle at her, returning her fiery gaze. "Listen here, little sister—we didn't let that gold get stolen out from under our noses. We had to leave it to go rescue you from certain death on that mountain, since you and your Pinkerton pals all went singin' and dancin' into that forty-five caliber Gatling gun hell storm!"

"Sort of lucky we did, though, too, Slash," Pecos pointed out. "If we hadn't heard that machine gun and stayed with the wagon, we likely would have ended up like her colleagues."

After Slash, Pecos, and the pretty Pinkerton, Hattie, had unhitched and turned loose the mules of the wagon, intending to return for them later, and started out after the robbers, they'd come upon the place where part of the gang had been lying in ambush, waiting for the wagon. That spot had been only about two hundred yards farther down the trail that Slash and Pecos had been following.

The place had been marked by the number of man and horse tracks they'd spied around two nests of rocks, one on each side of the trail. Pecos had found a bullet one of the bushwhackers had dropped, and Slash had found a still-warm quirley stub.

"And you'd likely still be wandering around up there—a little girl lost and alone in the big, cruel world." Slash jerked his chin to indicate the mountain, now out of sight, on which she and the other operatives had been ambushed.

"Little girl lost and alone, my foot!" Hattie snorted a caustic laugh. "I haven't been lost since I was eight years old. I can take care of myself just fine. I always have and I always will. What I want to know"—she cast each man another accusatory glare—"is how in the world did those killers find out about our plan? They had to have found out about it from someone."

"What are you insinuatin', you little—"

"Slash!" Pecos scolded his fiery partner. He turned to Hattie and frowned. "Yeah, what are you insinuating, Miss Hattie?"

The girl crossed her arms on her chest and wrinkled one nostril. "Isn't it clear? I think you two old cutthroats might be in with that gang. I think maybe, just maybe, you're intending on meeting up with them somewhere farther on down the trail to cash in on your cut of that hundred thousand dollars."

"Why, you little—"

"Slash!"

Slash had started toward the girl, balling his left fist down low by his side. He was holding the bottle in his right hand. He stopped and glared down at her. "That's a rotten thing to say to two men who rescued your purty butt!"

"I will thank you to not comment on any of my body parts forevermore hereafter! That you saw them *all* horrifies me no end!" She gave a groaning air of deep frustration and embarrassment. "Go ahead and kill me right here and now. Go on—cut my throat and get it over with!"

"What are you talking about?" Pecos asked.

"Yeah, what's wrong with you?" Slash said. "Your time in the river freeze your brain?"

"I suspect that when you meet up with your cohorts, you'll kill me. Or at least try to kill me. Since I'll be badly outnumbered, I will no doubt have very little chance against you. Rest assured, I do not intend to abandon the trail, however. I don't care how many you are in number, I am going to do everything in my power to retrieve that gold for Mister Pinkerton!"

"Believe me, little sister," Slash said, laughing caustically as he sat on a rock near the fire and rearranged his blankets around his shoulders. "If we really were in with that bunch, we sure as holy sin and taxes wouldn't have kept you alive this long!"

"That's no way to talk to the girl, Slash. She's alone out here with us, and we got us reputations as cutthroats, for sure. I can understand her suspicions." Pecos turned to where she sat against the fir tree, her arms crossed defiantly on her chest. "While I can't convince you of our innocence, Miss Hattie, I can only try to assure you that you're safe with me an' Slash, and we're gonna do everything in our power to get back that gold. We got our pride, me an' Slash do."

"We also don't want Bledsoe to play cat's cradle with our heads."

"That, too," Pecos said. "Whatever you think of us, I think one thing all three of us should do is try to get along and work together. The robbers are at least a dozen in number, all told, and they're doin' a pretty good job of covering their trail. I don't know where they're goin'. I would have thought Mexico. Instead, they circled around to the north, and now here we're following the Taylor *west*, more or less—upstream toward the Gunnison." He shook his head. "Don't make sense. But there it is. It's going to take three pairs of eyes to keep trackin' 'em, an' like I said before, Slash can't track a hog across a stock pen."

"Oh, shut up about that!" Slash turned to the girl to explain himself. "I never *had* to track men before this. I was always runnin' *from* men like us—an' doin' a very good job of it, I might add!"

"Well, I can track," Hattie said. "I'm rather good at it, in fact. I grew up in Arizona, and my father and I often had to track Apaches or border rapscallions who rustled our horses. I'm also very savvy, and I am a *very* light sleeper. So if either one of you cutthroats decides he's going to sneak up on me in the night and *cut my throat*, you'll get a bullet for your trouble!"

With that, she reached into a carpetbag and pulled out a big, ivory-gripped horse pistol. The revolver was so big and long-barreled, it made the girl's hand look like a doll's hand.

"That's one hell of a big hogleg, honey," Slash chuckled, lifting the bottle to his lips once more. "Can you hit anything with it?"

"Just try me," the girl said, narrowing one eye and spinning the big popper on her finger. She set the big Remington down beside her and looked imperiously at Pecos. "Now, I'll be served some beans, I think."

Slash snorted.

CHAPTER 20

Slash's sleep was shattered by an ear-ringing cacophony the likes of which he couldn't remember being assaulted by before.

If he had ever encountered such a tooth-shattering din, he would have remembered the hullabaloo itself as well as his murdering of the culprit.

Opening his eyes and discovering the instigator, it took every ounce of willpower in his body and soul from clawing one of his pretty Colts from its holster and shooting the pretty Pinkerton who stood over him and Pecos, rapping a spoon against the underside of the empty bean pot.

"Up and at 'em," the girl said beneath her ceaseless hammering of the spoon against the pot. "We got owlhoots to chase, and the sun is on the rise!"

"Stop!" Pecos cried, clamping his arms over his ears. "Stop! Stop! Oh, god—*please stop that racket*!"

The girl continued to hammer away at the pot, an arrogant little smile quirking both corners of her plump, pink mouth.

"You heard him!" Slash bellowed, shoving up on his elbows and stretching his lips back from his teeth. "Stop that infernal noise or I'm going to shoot you, little girl, and feed you to the crows!"

The girl stopped, lowered both the spoon and the pot, and arched a cool brow. "Are you both good and awake?"

"We're awake!" Pecos bellowed. "Good lord, you little polecat—how could we not be?"

Slash chuckled. "Now, Pecos, that's downright ungentle-manly—callin' the young Pink names like that!"

"You had it right, Slash," Pecos said. "I think we shoulda left her in the river."

"The man's right touchy about his sleep," Slash told the Pink, who continued to stand between him and Pecos as though threatening a resumption of the assault.

Despite her arrogance and downright nastiness, Slash had to admit she was a sight to behold, standing there with her chestnut hair freshly brushed and spilling across her shoulders. She wore a cream blouse under a leather jacket, and a dark wool skirt with a wide brown belt behind which resided her big Remington. On her feet were high-heeled black riding boots. A wool hat hung down her back by a braided horse-hair thong.

She might be as wicked as an April witch, but she was a pretty girl with all the right curves in all the right places. He didn't know if she looked better naked or dressed. He decided the former, though the latter was a close second.

"You two owlhoots have had plenty of sleep." Hattie canted her head to the east. "The sun's on the rise."

Slash looked in that direction. Only a faint gray wash of very early dawn shone in a small V of eastern sky peeking up between craggy mountain ridges, beyond the darkly silhouet-ted forest shrouding the river. The water had made a steady, constant humming whisper all night long. There was nothing like the sound of running water, especially running mountain water, for some reason, that made for a deep, dreamless sleep.

That and the cold, high-altitude air and the shimmering stars that had appeared close enough to reach out and grab. Slash had stirred a couple of times during the night, only to tumble back into that clinging somnolence, wishing it would swallow him forever.

The night's slumber was slow to release the dark-haired former cutthroat, but he knew from the way the girl was staring at him, pot and spoon still in her hands, that if he rested his head back against his saddle again, he'd likely get better than what she'd given him before. His ears couldn't take it.

"Ah, hell!" Slash flung his covers aside and yowled as he started the slow climb to his feet, his old joints, assaulted by not only the cold ground but his time in the frigid river, popping like miniature dynamite sticks.

Twenty minutes later, after a breakfast of hot coffee and cold beans, the trio struck camp and saddled up, Hattie starting the day's ride with Pecos, sitting atop his bedroll and saddlebags behind him.

They picked up the killers' trail where Pecos had scouted it last night and rode almost straight west along another tributary of the Taylor River. By evening, they'd left the tributary and headed northwest up into the Elk Mountains, where it was cool and windy, and where rain and hail soaked and pummeled them late in the afternoon.

The brief but powerful storm effectively wiped out the ragged bits of the killers' trail they'd been following. It was a glum trio who camped that night in a nest of rocks along the side of a granite ridge, enduring a cold, wet sleep, then waking to frost on the ground and ice-glazed rain puddles the next morning.

There was only one trail out here, aside from game trails and the fading traces of old Indian hunting trails, and they followed this main trail for lack of anything else to follow. The gang had been following this trail the day before, so there was no reason to believe they hadn't continued following it toward wherever in hell they were going.

"I just can't figure it," Slash said the next afternoon as they crossed a barren pass under a blue, sunny sky, a cool wind battering him and his two trail pards. "Why wouldn't they head south to Mexico like reasonable men? Where in the hell are they going? If they're still headed where they were headed yesterday, and we're on their trail, they're headed only deeper into the Elk Range. All that's up here is mining camps and old Indian ruins and ridge after ridge after ridge. I just don't get it!"

"Maybe they're just extra cautious," Pecos opined as, astraddle his buckskin, he began dropping into the next valley. "Maybe they're worried someone's trailing 'em, and they're trying to make it look like they're headed north when they're really headed to Mexico—by one heckuva roundabout way."

"If they knew we were trailing them," Slash said, "we'd know they knew it."

"How so?" asked Hattie, riding behind him, her arms wrapped loosely around his waist. He could feel the hard bulge of her horse pistol snugged against the small of his back.

Dropping down through pines, following the meandering cart and horse trail, Pecos said, "They'd have stopped and set an ambush for us. They like ambushes too much for 'em not to have at least *tried* to ambush us by now."

"Yep, what Pecos said," Slash said to Hattie, grinning over his shoulder at the somber Pink. "He's smarter than he looks."

"Thanks, Slash."

"Don't mention it, partner. Say, I hope you're keepin' a good, careful watch up there. I know we been in the saddle for a while, but you remember our old saw?"

"Yeah, I remember," Pecos said. "Lazy eyes'll get you a cold, dead hide."

"How poetic," the Pinkerton said snidely behind Slash.

"Oh, he's a poet," Slash said. "He just don't know it. Let's hope he never does, or we'll never hear the end of it!"

"Shut up, now, Slash," Pecos said. "Remember our other old saw?"

"Yeah, I remember," Slash said with some chagrin. "Bein' a chatter box will get you the bullet pox."

"You two are a real joy to ride with." Hattie sighed deeply. "And I believe it's all for naught. They could have turned off this trail anywhere, and we wouldn't know because last night's storm would have wiped out their signs."

"You got a point, senorita." Slash shrugged. "But what else we gonna do? Me—I'd rather be ridin' through these here mountains than ridin' back to Denver with my tail between my legs and likely right into a hangman's noose."

Hattie sighed again. "Yeah, well—it would be little better for me. Mister Pinkerton would likely give me my time and send me on my way. I've done this so long, it's about all I know how to do anymore. I hate the smell of tobacco smoke too much to wait on saloon tables for the rest of my life."

"You don't like men enough, either," Slash said. "Er . . . unless it's just me an' Pecos you harbor such a grudge against."

"No, it's pretty much all men," the girl said in her cold, flat tone once more. "But notorious owlhoots, especially."

"What's your last name, if you don't mind me askin'?"

"Aren't we supposed to be quiet?"

"Just tell me your last name, and I'll go back to avoiding the bullet pox."

"Friendly."

Slash scowled over his shoulder at her. "Huh?"

"Friendly. It's Hattie Friendly."

"Pshaw!"

Hattie sighed. "You asked me and I told you. I don't care two cents if you believe me or not."

"Hey, Pecos—did you hear that?"

"Hear what?" Pecos said, still dropping down the winding trail into yet another deep, forested canyon, at the bottom of which they'd likely find another stream or river. Maybe some prospecting or wood-cutting cabins, which these mountains had so far been sporadically peppered with.

"Hattie's last name is Friendly."

Swaying easily in his saddle, Pecos shook his head and laughed softly.

"Yep," Hattie said with another sigh, "you two are a real joy to share the trail with."

Around the same time the next afternoon, they followed the trail along a canyon sheathed by two steep, rocky, pine-clad ridges, and right up into the yard of a dugout cabin built into the side of a small butte rising against the base of the northern ridge. A small corral and stable fronted the dugout, which had an age-silvered front log wall and a brush roof with a tin chimney poking up out of it, issuing thick, gray smoke.

A good dozen bear skulls, maybe more, were tacked to the logs. Two bear hides were tacked to the log wall as well, and a fresh cinnamon hide hung over the rail of the narrow boardwalk fronting the place.

Two goats were grazing the colorless brush growing up from the roof, near the chimney pipe. One goat was black, the other white.

Several horses stood still as statues inside the corral.

There were a few more cabins off the trail's left side, opposite from the dugout side of the canyon. These appeared to be prospectors' shacks, lined up side by side and also issuing smoke from their chimney pipes. Three or four men were out in the stream that ran along its rocky bed over there, at the base of the southern ridge.

The men were bearded, dressed in wool shirts, suspenders,

canvas breeches, and high-tipped, lace-up boots. They wielded gold pans and toiled over sluice boxes running into the stream from the near side of the valley. A collie dog milled in the water near the prospectors, apparently looking for fish.

One of the men sat on a rock in the middle of the stream. He'd taken his boots off; the boots sat beside him on the rock. He was puffing a pipe, tipping his head back to take the sun on his face.

Pecos glanced at Slash. The girl rode with Pecos now. "What do you think?" Pecos asked his partner.

"I think I'm hungry, and I'm tired of your beans."

"You can take over the cookin' chores whenever you want to, Slash. Be my guest."

"Oh, stop your caterwauling. Let's go see if we can get our bellies padded out. Besides, maybe we can find a horse for little miss. We'd make better time if all three of us had a horse."

As they rode toward the dugout, fronted by two hitchrails at which five saddled horses stood, the girl said, "Maybe we can find out if the killers stopped here, and where they might be headed."

"Maybe so," Slash said. "But you let us do the talkin', little Pink."

"Stop calling me little Pink. And stop ordering me around. You are not my boss, Mister Braddock."

Slash only sighed as he brought his Appy to a stop before one of the hitchracks.

Pecos dismounted the buckskin, then reached up to help Hattie Friendly down and received a none-too-friendly response.

"Hands off."

Pecos threw up his arms and lowered his head in defeat.

The young Pinkerton lithely swung her right boot up and over the cantle of Pecos's saddle. Turning to face him, she slid straight down to the ground, landing flat-footed and staring up at him smugly.

She straightened her dress and adjusted the big horse pistol behind her wide leather belt.

"Do you gotta wear that in there?" Slash asked.

"You're going to wear yours, aren't you?"

"Yeah, well, they look natural on us. That big hogleg doesn't look natural on you. It draws attention to you, in fact."

"As if she wouldn't do that even without the cannon," Pecos said.

"Yeah, but that don't help. It could attract trouble."

Hattie gestured toward the weathered wooden door propped open with a rock and beyond which was a cave-like darkness. "I will not waltz in there unarmed."

"How 'bout if you just *walk* in there unarmed?"

The girl hardened her jaws and gave another croaking wail of frustration.

"All right, all right," Slash said. "Have it your way. Just let us do the talkin'. We're liable to contract food poisonin' in a place like this, and addin' lead poisonin' would cloud up and rain all over my day!"

CHAPTER 21

Slash marched up the three steps to the raised boardwalk. Hattie followed him, then Pecos.

Slash saw a man sacked out on the boardwalk to his right. The sleeper was a grizzled, gray-bearded oldster lying prostrate, ankles crossed, hands entwined on his fat belly, head resting back against a feed sack. He raked soft snores out through fluttering lips.

A coonskin cap, an empty bottle, and several mashed quirley stubs lay nearby.

Slash glanced at Pecos, shrugged, then reached across his belly to release the keeper thong over the Colt holstered on his left hip, just in case. He stepped through the door and to his left, so the door wouldn't frame him against the outside light. As Hattie and Pecos walked in behind him, Pecos stepped to the right, for the same reason that Slash had stepped to the left.

Hattie stood in front of the open door, frowning curiously at each man in turn.

"Damn fool," Slash bit out quietly through stiff jaws. "Gonna get your purty self perforated, entering a place out here like that."

Deep lines of incredulity cut across her forehead. "Like *what?*"

Slash just shook his head and peered into the thick shadows before him. The darkness was relieved by two sunlit windows in the front wall to his right, beyond Pecos. The windows were small. They were also very dirty, so the light that mixed with the shadows was murky at best.

He could make out five figures in the place—two sitting at a table to his left, and three against the cabin's far wall on his right. There were three other tables, all open.

Pine planks nailed to beer kegs at the rear of the room served as a bar of sorts. A wide-shouldered man with thin hair and wearing a ratty blue apron stood back there, leaning against the bar, a loosely rolled quirley smoldering between his lips.

Flanking him were shelves of bottles, canned goods, dry goods, and even some groceries. Bins were spread out to the right of the bar, also housing goods, including denim trousers, leather boots, caps, gloves, snowshoes, and axes and shovels. Stacks of flour were piled in a corner. Sausages and cheeses hung from the ceiling all across the room. The smell of the smoked and cured meat and cheese made Slash's mouth water.

Yet more bear skulls were mounted on the walls and on ceiling support posts about the room. A bearskin served as a curtain for the doorway flanking the bar.

Behind the bar, a pot bubbled on an iron range.

All eyes in the room regarded the three newcomers stonily, including those of the broad-shouldered barman, who puffed the quirley and exhaled the smoke through his wedge-like nose without using his hands.

Since there appeared no immediate threat, Slash nodded cordially to the barman. Stepping forward, away from the front wall, he said, "You got beer? I could really go for a beer."

The man nodded, his stony expression in place. A fly

buzzed around his left ear, and he lifted that cheek in a wince of sorts. He appeared so big and tired that he didn't have the energy to swat at the pesky fly. "Ale."

"That's what I'll have," Slash said.

"Me, too," said Pecos.

"Tea for me," said the girl.

"No tea. I got some coffee I can heat up from this mornin'."

"Just water," the girl said, turning her mouth corners down in disdain.

Slash headed for a table in the middle of the room, between the two men sitting against the left wall and the three to the right. He didn't like sitting out in the middle of the room like this, but he didn't see that he had a choice. As he slid out a chair, he glanced at the barman, who was drawing a mug of dark beer from a keg behind the bar.

"What kind of stew you got bubbling away on the range there?" He glanced at the skulls that made the place look like a catacomb. "Wait—let me guess. Bear!" He chuckled.

The barman merely glanced over his shoulder at him, his face as expressionless as before. The other customers regarded him with the same dullness.

Slash's smile grew wooden. He glanced at Pecos, who regarded him with a skeptically arched brow as he dragged his own chair out from the table. "I reckon we'll each have us a bowl of whatever you got cookin', then," Slash told the barman, then muttered under his breath, "Sure smells like bear to me."

When the newcomers were seated at the small square table, under a too-short leg of which Pecos wedged a lucifer to steady it, Slash glanced around. His eyes had adjusted enough to see more clearly the three men now on his left as he faced Pecos sitting across from him. He also faced the front wall. The three to his left were a hard-looking, bearded bunch in dusty trail gear. All three wore at least two six-shooters apiece, and a sawed-off, double-bore shotgun, not unlike Pecos's own gut-shredder, rested across a corner of their table.

Empty stew bowls were piled to one side.

The three were playing poker and drinking ale. Two were smoking cigars, while the third, sitting with his back to the far wall, directly facing Slash's table, had a lump of chaw bulging out his lower lip. He didn't appear to be concentrating on the cards fanned out in his hands. He appeared far more interested in the three newcomers.

Why?

Was it the girl?

Or was there some other reason?

Slash turned to his right, to inspect the two men sitting against the wall on that side of the room. They were identical twins, one the mirror image of the other. If they weren't full-blood Indians, they were close—two big, dark-eyed, copper-skinned men with broad, flat, hairless features and beak-like noses. Long, coarse, coal-black hair hung straight down from their bullet-crowned black felt hats. The hats were identical twins, as well.

In fact, the two men appeared to be entirely identically outfitted—worn wool suit coats over wool shirts and sweaters, and broadcloth trousers stuffed into high-topped, mule-eared moccasins. Each man wore a red neckerchief, tightly knotted, the ends dangling down their broad chests.

Colt pistols were holstered for the cross-draw on their left hips. Bowie knives were sheathed on the other side. Even the Colts and knives appeared similar if not identical.

The two Indians appeared even bigger than Pecos.

They were so fascinating, these two identical Indian twins, that Slash found himself openly staring.

The two big Indians, facing each other across a small table, stared straight back at Slash, one holding a smoking tin cup up in front of his broad, full-lipped mouth. As far as Slash could make out, the only way you could tell these two apart was by the eyelash-shaped knife scar, knotted and white, that resided on a cheek of the twin on the left, facing the back of the room.

This twin had a Henry repeating rifle leaning against the wall to his left.

Slash smiled and pinched his hat brim to the two. The scar-faced one on the left showed no emotion. The other one gave a stiff, fleeting smile and opened and closed his right hand above the table. If that had been a wave, it hadn't been a warm one. In fact, there'd been something vaguely ominous about it.

Slash felt a boot toe ram his shin beneath the table. "Ouch!"

"Stop starin', ya damn fool!" Pecos admonished him under his breath.

"Ah, hell," Slash said, scowling against the pain in his shin, "they gotta be used to it by now."

Hattie, sitting to Slash's left, was also staring at the two big Indians, whose eyes had found her as well, Slash saw with an apprehensive tightening of his shoulders. The girl didn't look too happy about it, either. She lowered her gaze to the table and wrinkled the skin above the bridge of her nose.

The barman came over and set big mugs of ale before Slash and Pecos. He set steaming stew bowls before all three. Looking into his bowl, seeing the dark-brown chunks of organ meat floating in a thin broth spotted with what appeared to be bits of fat and carrots, Slash grinned up at the man and said, "See—I knew it was bear!"

The man started to turn away, but Slash stopped him with: "Say, amigo, do you have any idea where we could buy a horse around here?"

"A horse?" the man said, scowling as though Slash had said dinosaur or dragon. "Nah." He shook his head and walked away, limping slightly on one leg.

Slash glanced at Pecos, who shrugged and began spooning

stew into his mouth. Slash did likewise. Hattie was going at the food a little more tentatively, as though she had something against bear, when out of the corner of Slash's right eye he saw one of the Indian twins rise heavily from his chair. Slash winced, then spooned another bite of the stew into his mouth as he saw the twin, the one with the scar on his cheek, hitch his pants up higher on his broad hips and begin sauntering toward Slash, Pecos, and Hattie's table.

The man's boots thumped loudly on the worn, badly scarred wooden floor.

Slash and Pecos shared another glance, this time a dark one, then looked at the big twin standing over their table, to Slash's right and Pecos's left. The Indian grinned, his eyes on Hattie, who scowled up at him, indignant. The Indian leaned forward and rested his big fists on the edge of the table, glancing from Slash to Pecos, then back again.

"I will give you one horse for the girl." The twin's grin broadened, his dark eyes flashing in delight.

Hattie's own eyes blazed up at him. "I beg your pardon, sir."

The Indian stared back at her, showing his horsey, off-white teeth through that broad, eager smile. "One horse for the girl."

Hattie's eyes widened. Her lower jaw hung nearly to her chest. She sank back in her chair with a shocked gasp, and said, "Why, I have never been so insulted in all my days!"

"Easy now, girl," Slash said, chuckling nervously as he smiled up at the eager-eyed Indian. "It's just a little misunderstandin' is all. You see, amigo, the horse is *for* her, don't ya know. She herself is not for sale. Hah!"

Again, Slash chuckled, and Pecos joined in with his own wooden laugh.

A stone dropped in Slash's belly when Hattie gave another one of her groans of outrage, scraped her chair back from the table, and rose to her feet like a wildcat preparing to pounce. In a flash, her big horse pistol was in her hand, and Slash watched in silent horror as she cocked it loudly and thrust it up and over the table and planted the barrel against the Indian's nose, yelling, "How dare you—you smelly, rock-worshipping heathen—come over here and insult me with such a moronic proposal! Purchase *me* for a *horse*?"

Both Slash and Pecos stared, tongue-tied, at the big, cocked pistol that the girl held tightly in both hands against the Indian's nose. Slash thought for sure the man would explode in fury.

But, no. He didn't look frightened or angry at all. He looked genuinely even more delighted than when he'd first walked over here.

He crossed his eyes as he looked down at the big gun snugged against his nose and then slid his gaze in raw delight, in euphoric enchantment, at the girl beetling her brows and pursing her lips at him, holding the pistol rock steady in her small, strong hands.

Meanwhile, the big Indian's just-as-big twin was sagging back in his chair, leaning back against the wall and laughing and stomping his boots on the floor in spasms of joyful humor. He held one hand to his forehead and the other across his mouth, child-like, as he continued to stomp his feet and roar.

The other three customers looked on, grinning from beneath their hat brims, cigars smoldering in two of the men's hands, chaw streaming down the chin of the third one.

The Indian twin whom Hattie was bearing down on slid his flashing dark eyes to Slash and said, "All right—we give you *two* ponies for this little wildcat!"

Hattie's jaws grew even tauter, and she yelled, "Why, you—"

Slash reached out with both hands, grabbed the gun, and lifted it straight up as Hattie squeezed the trigger. The blast rocketed around inside the cabin, the bullet plunking into a ceiling beam directly over the table. Slash wrenched the big popper out of the girl's hands. She screamed and cursed him, her hat tumbling down her back, her hair falling over her face.

Slash shoved her brusquely into her chair, lowered the smoking Remington to his side, and held his left-hand palm out to the Indian in supplication. "Friend, I want to apologize for my . . . my . . . my *niece* there. Her blood tends to run a little hot when she's hungry."

"Yeah, she just needs to get a little somethin' down her gullet is all," Pecos added, turning his reproving glare on the girl and adding, "Maybe a rusty nail or two would be more to her liking."

"Three horses!" the big twin said through a beam at Slash, holding up that many fingers.

Sitting low in her chair, peering through the screen of her mussed hair, Hattie gave another enraged wail through gritted teeth. Pecos hurried around behind her and clamped a hand over her mouth, muffling the outcry.

Turning to the big Indian, Slash grinned and shook his head. "No, no." He chuckled. "You see, this polecat's . . . well, she's my niece, you see. An' she's not for sale. Not that I wouldn't sell her, *personally*, if I could, but, well, she just ain't mine to sell, ya see? If I were to accept such an offer, we'd likely have quite the family dustup, don't ya know. Besides, if you wanna hear it from the horse's mouth"—Slash leaned toward the big Indian twin and held his hand to his mouth as though conveying a secret—"she ain't worth one ewe-necked broomtail, let alone three mountain-bred mustangs!"

He laughed.

Hattie squirmed in her chair and cussed. At least, Slash assumed she was cussing again. He couldn't tell for sure, because Pecos held his hand taut against her mouth.

"You not sell wildcat girl even for *three horses?*" The big twin looked incredulous and more than a tad heartbroken.

"Nah, can't do it," Slash said. "Sorry, amigo. I'll buy you

a beer, though. Apron, outfit the twins with a fresh round of your delightful ale, will you?"

That seemed to appease the big twin. He muttered under his breath, eyed Hattie as though she were a tasty meal he was having to walk away from, then tromped back over to his table, where his twin was still chuckling over the whole affair, apparently having the time of his life.

Pecos kept his hand over the girl's mouth. She sat fuming, glaring up at him.

"I'll take my hand away, but only after you promise to behave yourself," said the big ex-cutthroat. "I didn't come here to get shot over no caterwauling Pinkerton."

She just stared up at him, her face pale with fury.

"Okay, here we go," Pecos said. He glanced at Slash, then removed his hand from over the girl's mouth.

They both thought for sure she'd explode like a keg of dynamite and were surprised when she remained in her chair, pale with rage, jaws hard, eyes like two chunks of brown flint, but as quiet as a church mouse.

Slash and Pecos sighed in relief.

"Now, then," Slash said, "maybe we can finish up our meal in peace and ride the hell out of here."

"What about the men we're tracking?" Hattie asked him.

"What about 'em?" Slash said, spooning stew into his mouth.

"We haven't inquired about—"

"More beer, gentlemen?" The barman had limped over to their table holding a stone jug. "Refills only a penny."

"Sure, sure, I'll take a refill," Slash said, holding up his half-empty glass.

"Me, too," said Pecos. "Damn good ale, sir."

The man had topped off Slash's mug and had just started to pour more ale into Pecos's mug when Hattie set her spoon down, cleared her throat, and looked up at the big man. "Excuse me, sir, but I have a question," she asked loudly enough for the entire room to hear. "Has a group of riders passed through here recently? Perhaps a beady-eyed group of border toughs leading a pack mule or two?"

The barman dropped Pecos's heavy glass onto the table. The glass struck the table with a sharp thud and fell over. The ale spilled across the table and onto the floor.

The barman looked at the young Pinkerton, wide-eyed, lower jaw hanging.

The room fell deathly quiet.

All eyes were on Hattie.

Slash glanced around the room, heart tattooing the backside of his breastbone. Pecos looked around, his own ticker turning somersaults. Every muscle of every man in the place was drawn taut as razor wire.

Slash looked at Pecos. Pecos looked back at him in hushed awe. "Oh . . . boy . . . ," he muttered.

The men to the cutthroats' left and right leaped to their feet, clawing iron.

"Get down!" Slash cried, and hurled himself to the floor as the guns started thundering.

CHAPTER 22

Slash hit the floor much too hard for his old bones, to which such a violent landing was a grave insult. They let him know how they felt.

Hattie screamed.

Slash looked up to see her still sitting in her chair, covering her head with her arms.

"I said get down, girl!" Slash grabbed two chair legs and pulled the chair out from under the Pink with both hands.

Hattie screamed again as she and the chair were thrown sideways to the floor.

Guns thundered around Slash, making his ears ring. Bullets screeched over his head, thumped into the floor around him. Several drilled the barman, who'd been even slower to duck than the girl had been. He screamed as he did a bizarre little two-step as the bullets turned him like a pinwheel, blood leaping from his wounds.

Lying flat against the floor, Slash clawed both his pistols from their holsters and aimed straight out in front of him. The three men who had been sitting to his left were all standing, crouching, mouths drawn wide and eyes pinched to slits, as their six-shooters roared, flames and smoke blossoming wickedly from their barrels.

Quickly, but sucking a calming breath to steady his aim despite the bullets buzzing around him like angry honeybees enraged by a hive-plundering bear, Slash centered his sights on the man on his far left and fired.

As his bullet punched into the center of that man's chest, Pecos just then rose from where he'd thrown himself to the floor to Slash's right and returned fire at the two big Indian twins, both of whom were throwing lead at him, snarling like angry wolves, their pistols bucking in their outstretched hands.

One bullet sawed a nasty trough across the outside of Pecos's left arm while another nipped his earlobe. His own Russian roared, flames lapping toward the big twin on the left, punching the man back against the wall with a startled look on his dark-eyed face.

To Pecos's right, beyond where Hattie lay flat on the floor beside her overturned chair, her head buried in her arms, Slash steadied his left-hand Colt, picked out the hombre who'd been sucking the tobacco quid and drilled the man through his right shoulder. The man cursed as he dropped one of the two pistols bucking in his hands and twisted backward toward the wall behind him.

Wasting no time, Slash triggered his right-hand hogleg and blew the man on the right, who'd dropped to one knee, firing and blaspheming Slash's lineage with shouted epithets, a third eye just above his right one. That lifted the man up off his knees and threw him out the window behind him in a nasty squeal of shattering glass.

"Dangit!" Pecos yowled, glancing down at the tear in his denims carved by a bullet newly flung by the surviving big Indian twin, who'd somehow managed to dodge two more of Pecos's slugs.

The bullet burn, just above Pecos's knee, felt like a scorpion's bite.

"Take that, you rock-worshippin' devil!" Pecos bellowed, aiming down the big Russian's barrel again and stabbing

flames as well as a .44-caliber round of solid lead in the surviving big Indian twin's direction.

That bullet made the surviving twin a survivor no more.
He'd thrown his and his brother's table over and was using it
as a shield, but he'd lifted his head up at just the wrong moment. Pecos's bullet had skimmed over the table's edge, carving a slight notch out of it just before punching into the big
twin's Adam's apple.

It took his brain a while to get the news that he'd been re-
united with his brother, however.

The big twin lurched to his feet, clawing with both his ham-
sized copper hands at the gaping hole in his throat, which was
oozing bright red blood down his chest. As he kicked the table
out of his way and lurched toward the door, Slash, to Pecos's
right, fired again at the hombre on the room's opposite side—
the one who'd been sucking the chaw. The bullet Slash had
assaulted the man's shoulder with had not finished the man.

Now, like the second big Indian twin, he'd pushed his and
his two dead amigos' table over and had dropped to a knee
behind it. He snaked his Colt around one side and fired
twice. One bullet curled the air off Slash's left ear, and the
other warmed the air off his right ear, there where he knelt on
one knee, aiming both his own Colts at his adversary.

When the chaw-chewer pulled his revolver and his head
back behind his table, Slash fired both his own Colts directly
at the table itself. He triggered them again, both weapons
bucking and roaring in his hands, until four jagged holes
made a vaguely serpentine line across the table, from left to
right.

Behind the table, Slash's foe screamed angrily and with no
little anguish. He rose to his feet, grimacing and still cursing,
his face and chest a bloody mess, raising his revolver once
more.

He didn't get off a single shot before Slash shot him again,
punching him out through the same window through which

one of his amigos had flown en route to his own reward, which would most likely be a coal shovel.

Meanwhile, the second big twin Indian didn't make it to the door

He dropped to his knees five feet in front of it. He was wheezing and making strangling sounds as blood continued to pump out of the hole in his throat. He was dying hard and slow.

"Amigo, I'm gonna do you a nice turn you don't deserve," Pecos said, raising his smoking Russian once more and punching a merciful bullet through the second big twin Indian's left ear and out the other one.

The big twin's head jerked violently sideways. It steadied again on the big man's shoulders. He gave one last ragged sigh, then fell face-first to the floor with a heavy, liquid thud.

Wincing from his three bullet burns, Pecos looked around, blinking against the peppery sting of wafting powder smoke. Slash did the same thing, only he wasn't enduring any nips from bullet wounds but only the indignant barking of his knees and shoulders and sundry other age-brittled bones and stiff muscles. Said parts hadn't enjoyed their sudden meeting with the floor.

When both men saw there was no more immediate threat, they slowly gained their feet with groaning grunts.

Slash looked down at the dead barman, who'd been hit at least four times, it appeared. One bullet had plundered his right eye. "Poor devil."

Pecos looked down at where Hattie still lay flat against the floor, her arms covering her head. Her hair was fanned out across her head and shoulders, like a silky chestnut tumbleweed. The Pink was as tense as a coiled rattlesnake, trembling.

Pecos prodded her gently with a boot toe and said sourly, "You can get up now."

Hattie jerked with a start, then lowered her arms and glanced up at Slash and Pecos.

Slash cursed as he glared down at her. "What do you got to say for yourself, you crazy polecat?"

Hattie looked around, vaguely sheepish. She cleared her throat, then heaved herself to her feet with a sigh. Color quickly returned to her ashen cheeks. She looked around again, tossed her hair back, then grinned in unabashed pride and delight, rising up and down on the toes of her boots. "Do I know how to haze a rat out of its hole, or don't I?"

"I'd like to know what rats we're talkin' about!" Pecos said in exasperation, fingering his bullet-nipped ear. "Besides that—you almost got all three of us greased for the pan!"

Slash lunged toward her, gritting his teeth. "I oughta take you over my knee an' . . ."

He let his voice trail off when he heard something out on the raised boardwalk. Pecos had heard it, too—the squawk of a loose board. Both men raised their pistols, clicking the hammers back. The old man who'd been sleeping out there stepped into the open doorway, blinking sleepily into the saloon's smoky shadows.

When he saw the three revolvers leveled at him, he said, "Easy, now . . . easy, now, fellas." He held up one age-gnarled hand, palm out, and tugged at his tangled, gray bib beard with the other hand. "I ain't no threat. Years ago, maybe." He wagged his head. "Not no more. Even if I had me a hogleg, I couldn't shoot it straight."

He peered around the room, his eyes growing slowly wider as he took in the carnage. "Boy," he said, whistling, "you fellas sure clean a place up. Say, you ain't gonna kill me, now, too—are ya?"

He raised both hands now quickly, his washed-out blue eyes glinting fearfully.

"That depends," Pecos said. "You need killin'?"

"Hell, no!" The graybeard cleared his throat. "One of my ex-wives might say differ'nt, but what do they know? They're old and even uglier'n me. I didn't have no part o' this bunch, if that's what you're thinkin'."

Hattie strode toward the old man, her chin in the air. "What bunch are you a part of, old man?"

Keeping his hands raised, the graybeard grinned at the girl, his lusty eyes raking her up and down. "Say, now, you're right purty."

"What I look like has nothing to do with anything."

"I'd argue the point," the old man said, still grinning, still feasting his eyes on the saucy little Pink.

"What's your name?" she asked him.

"Jupiter Dodge. What's your name?"

"None of your business."

"Well, hell—I told you my name. Why can't you tell me yours?"

"Because I don't like the way you're undressing me with your eyes, old man!"

"Stop callin' me old! And I can do any damn thing with my eyes as I want at my age!"

Jupiter Dodge glanced around the girl toward Slash and Pecos. "If you ain't gonna kill me just yet, I think I'll mosey on over to the bar and have one on ole Earl Kinney." He glanced at the barman lying, belly down on the floor, in a pool of his own thick blood. "Since he ain't around no more to bust my chops over it . . . nor to keep my account," he added with a cackling laugh.

Slash and Pecos followed the man with their eyes as he walked around behind the bar and looked at the shelves flanking it, tapping a finger against his lower lip as he contemplated the bottles.

"Who are you, Dodge?" Slash asked him. "And who are these men we killed?"

"In self-defense," Pecos added.

Dodge glanced over his shoulder at the two former cut-throats. "Me? Why I'm just an old man. I live in a shack down the creek yonder. I still do a little prospectin' when my chilblains ain't actin' up, but mostly I sleep an' drink and fish some, fight the bears off my stoop. Valley's thick with bears. Used to hunt and trap before I took to prospectin'. I been in these mountains longer than I ain't."

He turned to the shelves flanking the bar again. "Ah . . . there we go. I knew he had a bottle of Spanish brandy up here somewhere . . . waitin' just for me all these years!"

Dodge cackled as he reached up to pull a bottle off a shelf. He blew the dust and cobwebs from the bottle and set it on the bar planks.

"What about them?" Slash asked the old-timer, glancing at the dead men strewn around the edges of the room. "Who're they? Why did they get iron-grabby when Hattie asked about a certain gang who might've passed this way?"

The old man grimaced as he pulled the cork out of the brandy bottle with a loud pop.

"Who are they?" Dodge asked, scowling, face still red from the exertion of popping the cork. "Well, hell—don't *you* know who they are?"

"If we knew who they were, Mister Dodge," Hattie said, "we wouldn't be asking you—now, would we?"

"All right, all right—don't get snippity, young lady. They're, uh . . ." Dodge glanced around the room, as though suspecting one of the dead men might be listening. He looked out the dirty front windows flanking Slash, Pecos, and Hattie, and then he said, keeping his voice low enough to be heard only in the saloon, "Why, they're owlhoots, of course. Thieves of some sort."

Slash started walking slowly toward the man, frowning with keen interest. His heart was beginning to quicken. "What sort of owlhoots, Dodge?"

CHAPTER 23

"Beats me what sort of owlhoots they were." Dodge had set a shot glass on the bar. He held up the bottle and glanced at Slash and Pecos, brows raised. "Splash of the good stuff? I hear this is damn near twelve dollars a bottle. Earl's had it fer—"

"Enough about the brandy," Slash said, walking up to the bar and resting his fists on top of it, leaning slightly forward toward the old-timer standing behind it. "Finish tellin' about these dead owlhoots."

"Yeah," Pecos said, walking up to the bar now as well. "Tell us what you know about these dead fellas, old-timer."

"All right, all right." Dodge carefully filled his glass, then set the bottle down beside it. "All I know is they come through this way once every couple of months. They pass my cabin on their way here. Been comin' an' goin' nearly two years now. Always the same bunch."

"Just these five?" Slash asked.

"No, not just these five. A whole bunch."

"How many?" Hattie said, stepping up between Slash and Pecos, giving each man a haughty shove with the backs of her gloved hands so she could stand between them, facing Dodge. "A dozen?"

"A dozen or more," Dodge said, carefully lifting the glass to his lips and taking a delicate sip, careful not to let any of the precious liquid dribble down the side of the glass. "How'd you know?"

"Holy cow," Pecos said, softly, glancing at Slash.

"I'll say 'holy cow'," Hattie said, placing her hands atop the bar, pressing her fingers into the scarred, liquor-stained wood. She pressed her fingers down so hard the tips turned white. "They wouldn't happen to be carrying gold, would they—these dozen cutthroats. *Stolen gold?*"

"I don't know what it is they're carryin'. All I know is they usually got 'em a big beefy pack mule, an' whatever they're carryin' in the pack frame is covered up good and tight with a tarpaulin, an' they don't let it out of their sight. They always stop here for drinks and food, and they always leave five men behind. Not always these five. Just five. Them five stay here for a couple of days, drinkin' an' playin' poker an' whatnot, and then they ride on—in the same direction the others went."

Hattie glanced at Pecos, then turned to Slash, her eyes wide and round. "It's them."

"Who?" asked Dodge.

"Holy cow," Pecos said to Slash. "They must leave five behind to make sure they're not bein' followed."

"Right careful," Slash said, his breath coming faster now as he looked around at the dead men.

"Well, that explains why they were so touchy," Hattie said.

Pecos wrinkled his nose at her. "I hope that learns you a lesson about not runnin' your mouth off so much. You might just run it off at the wrong folks again, like you done here."

"What are you talking about?" Hattie laughed with glee. "My sound detective work gave us the information we were so desperately seeking."

Pecos gave her the woolly eyeball, snarling.

"All right, all right," Slash said. "What's done is done. The Pink's right. At least now we know we're on the right trail." He glanced at the dead men strewn around the room. "And we even culled the herd."

Pecos turned to Dodge. "Where did the others go? They took the gold, I'm assumin'."

"All I know is they usually head north along Silvertip Creek."

"How long ago did they leave here?"

"Early yesterday mornin'. They pulled in last night, slept out in the barn. I know 'cause I was up in the loft. Earl lets me sleep up there when I've had too much to find my way home."

"You were up in the loft when they were down below in the barn?" Slash asked with renewed interest.

"That's right." Dodge threw back the rest of his brandy, then carefully refilled the glass. "I was quiet as a church mouse. Didn't want 'em to know I was up there. They frighten me—those fellas. A hard-lookin' lot."

"You must have overheard them talking," Hattie said. "Did they say anything about where they were headed with the gold?"

"Not that I recall," Dodge said. "Of course, I was three sheets to the wind, so . . ." He gave a self-deprecating chuckle.

"Come on, Dodge," Slash prodded the old-timer. "You must have some idea where they headed."

"You must have overheard *something*," Hattie added.

Dodge held the refilled shot glass up close to his face and stared off, squinting, pondering. He shook his head and pursed his lips. "Nope. Sorry. All I remember is hearin' what men usually say to one another. Mostly about cards an' . . . well"—he glanced at Hattie with a sheepish half-grin—"women."

"What a surprise."

"Did they mention any names?" Pecos asked the man.

"None that I can recall. Sorry, fellas. Young lady." Dodge scowled at the three standing before him. "Say, who are you, anyways? Bounty hunters?"

"Just call us concerned citizens," Slash said, grabbing a shot glass from the pyramid on the bar to his right and pouring some of the old man's brandy into it.

"Right good stuff," Dodge said. "It comes all the way from . . ." He let his voice trail off and acquired another thoughtful expression. "Say, now . . ."

"What?" Pecos said, pouring some of the brandy into the glass that Slash had slid over to him.

"Spanish."

"The brandy?" Slash said, throwing back half of his shot. "Them Spanish make damn good lightnin'—I'll give 'em—"

"No," Dodge said. "I heard one o' them say somethin' about *Spanish*. In the barn. When I was up in the loft."

"Spanish what?" Pecos asked.

"I don't know. Like I said, I'd imbibed a wee more than I should have, as I make a point of doing too often these days. But a fella gets bored, you see, with most of his life behind him." Dodge raked a thoughtful hand down his tangled beard. "I remember it caught in my craw, though. That one word. But I don't remember why."

"Spanish?" Hattie said, incredulous.

"Just Spanish," Slash said. "Nothing else?"

"As far as I can recall." Dodge thought about it some more. "Seems to me it might have been another word with it, but I can't recall, doggone it." He raked a hand down his face. "You get to be my age, everything gives out on ya, gall-blastit!"

"What's north of here?" Pecos asked. Having polished off his shot of the brandy, he refilled his glass. "Any towns of any size?"

"Hell, no. Still wild up thataway. Oh, there's a few minin'

camps, wood-cuttin' camps. There's a minin' camp called Aspen up near the Maroon Bells—but that's a far piece to the way north. Of course, there's a trail that cuts west over to Utah and Salt Lake City."

"Salt Lake City," Hattie said. "Maybe that's where they're headed."

Slash shook his head. "Too far away. If they come and go through here pretty often, they gotta be based somewhere near here. I'm guessin' maybe a day's, two days' ride at the most." He sipped his brandy, set the glass back down on the bar. "I reckon we just gotta keep ridin'. Maybe we can pick up their trail again north of here."

"Doubt that," said the old-timer. "It rains every afternoon up in these parts. Hell, we even had a little snow last night. Of course, it melted right off."

"I need a horse," Hattie said. "I reckon I'll go pick out one of these dead men's mounts."

She turned away from the bar and strode toward the front of the room, pausing to look, grimacing, at the big dead Indian twin whose head Slash had cored like an apple. "Disgusting," the girl said.

Pecos leaned forward on the bar, doffed his hat, and raked his hand back through his long hair. "Well, like you said, at least we whittled 'em a down a piece. By five, anyways. And we know we're headed in the right direction."

"Yeah." Slash dug his makings sack out of his shirt pocket and tossed it down on the bar. "That's something, anyway."

"Spanish," Jupiter Dodge said, glowering down at the bottle of Spanish brandy on the bar before him, trying to jog his memory. "Spanish, Spanish, Spanish . . ."

"Shut up, old man!"

Dodge jerked his startled gaze toward the door.

Slash and Pecos did as well, for that's the direction from which the harsh order had come. Whipping around, Slash dropped his hands to his two holstered Colts but stayed the motion when he saw the man standing in the saloon's open doorway.

Not just the man, but Hattie Friendly as well. He'd obviously grabbed the girl when she'd stepped out of the saloon, and he held her now, one hand wrapped around her waist while he held a cocked six-shooter to her right temple.

The girl was as white as a sheet, her brown eyes wide and round.

"Hey, Slash!" the man cried. "Hey, Pecos! Fancy meetin' you two way out here!"

Slash's lower jaw loosened in shock when he recognized the round-faced man, a little taller than Hattie, holding the gun to her head. He wore a funnel-brimmed, tan Stetson, a collarless shirt, and snakeskin suspenders, which held his green whipcord trousers, patched at the knees, up on his lean hips. Two holsters hung low on his thighs from the criss-crossed cartridge belts buckled around his waist; one of the holsters was empty.

An exaggerated grin made his eyes bulge and flash, stretched his thin, chapped lips back from his brown-edged teeth.

"Well, now," Pecos said. "Lookee there, Slash, it's our old pal Otis Pettypiece."

"What you up to, Otis?" Slash said, keeping his hands on his guns but leaving both Colts in their holsters.

"Can't you see what I'm up to, Slash?" Otis said through his lunatic grin, keeping the barrel of his Colt Thunderer snugged taut against Hattie's temple. "I'm about to sink a bullet into your purty little girl's brain. An' that's what I'm gonna do, too, if'n you don't toss both those purty hoglegs of yours over here toward the door. You, too, Pecos. Give up the Russian nice an' easy, or she's gonna join my dead friends you bloodied the place up with."

"Your friends, eh?" Slash said, trying to keep his voice calm but hearing the strain in it. "Why don't we have us a friendly talk, Otis?"

"Oh, we'll talk, all right. I don't know how friendly it's gonna be, but we'll talk, all right. After you've lightened your loads a little. Come on—throw 'em over here!"

"You ridin' with this bunch, Otis?" Pecos asked, frowning at the dead men strewn around the room.

Both he and Slash had forgotten how long ago Otis Pettypiece had ridden with their own gang, the Snake River Marauders. As was typical of outlaw gangs, members came and went. As Pecos remembered, Otis had decided to drift off to California when most of the gang had headed for Kansas and Missouri after a robbery up in Dakota. Obviously, Otis hadn't stayed on the coast.

Now here he was, threatening the life of the pretty Pink.

"Yeah, I'm ridin' with 'em. Makin' a damn better livin' than I was makin' with you an' the Marauders. I was sacked out in the barn when I heard the shootin'."

"Damn," said Jupiter Dodge. "I *thought* they left behind six this time. I was wonderin' where the other one was. I reckon I shoulda mentioned it," he added with chagrin.

"You sure are gettin' squishy in your thinker box, old man," Slash growled, keeping his anxious gaze on his old friend, Otis Pettypiece.

"Yeah, well, you'll be where I'm at someday," Dodge fired back. "See how you like bein' prodded about it by younkers like yourself!"

"Younker, hah!" Pettypiece chuckled, mockingly. "These two old dinosaurs might not be quite as old as you, old man, but they're about to head over the divide if they don't throw down them hoglegs right now!"

Slash glanced over Pettypiece's right shoulder, as though spying someone moving up behind him. "Oh . . . is that so?" he said and nudged Pecos with his elbow.

Pecos glanced at him.

Pecos jerked his chin to indicate the yard behind Pettypiece and the Pink.

Pecos turned to the outlaw and grinned.

"What?" The outlaw kept his eyes on Slash and Pecos, but his smile grew brittle, then faded altogether. "What's goin' on? No, no! You're up to your old tricks!"

"Just the same, Otis, I'd lower that Colt if I was you. Then our old pal Jack might spare your life instead of shootin' you in the back of the head." Slash raised his voice. "Ain't that right, Jack?"

Pettypiece winced. Unable to help himself, he cast a quick look over his left shoulder. It was no more than a jerking movement of his head, but it gave Slash just enough time to whip up his right-hand Colt, aim, and fire just as Otis turned his head back forward. The .44-caliber round bored a hole through Pettypiece's left eye, turning it to cherry jelly.

Pettypiece's head snapped back. He fired his cocked Colt into the ceiling.

Hattie screamed and dropped to her knees, covering her head with her arms again.

Pettypiece fell straight back out the door and onto the raised boardwalk with a heavy thud. He lay shivering as though deeply chilled.

CHAPTER 24

"You okay, darlin'?" Slash asked Hattie.

She was staring back over her shoulder at the dead man on the boardwalk.

Slowly, she turned toward where Slash was lowering his smoking Colt, the blood starting to return to her cheeks, but her eyes still wide and glassy with shock. "Yes," she said, drawing a breath. "Yes . . . I think so."

Slash walked over and extended his hand to her. "You'd best sit down for a spell."

"Yes," Hattie said, placing her hand in Slash's. "Yes, I think I'd better."

When Slash had helped the girl into a nearby chair, Jupiter Dodge said from his station behind the bar, "Say, that was one helluva shot." He frowned again, curiously. "Who in the hell are you two, anyway? I'm beginnin' to wonder if you two might be Slash Braddock an' the Pecos River Kid!"

"Us?" said Slash, feigning bemused incredulity. He looked at Pecos, and they both laughed.

The two former cutthroats stepped out onto the board-walk and stared down at the dead man, who stared up at them through his one remaining eye, which remained wide open in death as though he were perusing the cloudless sky for the angel that would take him to heaven.

"Nice shootin', Slash," Pecos said. "But you should've left him alive so's we coulda found out where the rest of his new gang headed with the gold."

"What'd you want me to do? Nick his ear so he could still drill a hole through Hattie's head?"

"That girl's trouble," Pecos said, staring down at the dead Otis Pettypiece.

He'd said it quietly enough that he'd thought only Slash had heard. He was wrong. Hattie had stepped quietly up behind him and Slash, and now she said, crisply and with no little air of offense, "Excuse me. I'm going to go and pick out that horse now."

"Ah, hell," Pecos said. "Why don't you stay inside and rest up? I'll saddle a hoss for you."

Hattie strode quickly and stiffly across the yard toward the corral straight out from the cabin, swinging her arms, her hair winging out behind her. She turned her head and said in the same crisply offended tone as before, "I wouldn't want to be any more trouble!"

She turned her head forward, continued toward the corral, and plucked a rope off a gate post.

Pecos turned toward Slash. "I didn't mean to hurt her feelings."

"She almost got more than her feelings hurt in there." Slash jerked his head toward the saloon behind him. "She came damn close to saddling a cloud instead one of those gold-robber's horses."

"She's just young," Pecos said, staring toward where the girl was moving around the corral, inspecting the horses that sidled apprehensively away from her. As she moved, she swung the loop at the rope's end, gradually enlarging it.

"She's green. She shouldn't be out here. I'm surprised

Pinkerton sent her. Or one of his field lieutenants. She may not have gotten herself killed today . . . or *someone else* killed today . . . but the day ain't over."

"Don't you start on her now, Slash. I feel bad about what I said. An' her hearin'."

"That's the trouble with you, partner," Slash said. "Your heart's too damn big."

"Oh, come on. She's just a kid!"

"You look out for her from now on, then, if she's just a kid. Me, I'm gonna go in an' have some more bear stew before we hit the trail. And another tug or two off Dodge's brandy."

"What the hell's climbin' your hump all of a sudden?" Pecos said as Slash stepped over the dead Indian twin and headed for the bar, where Jupiter remained, drinking the Spanish brandy. "You can't be feelin' bad about layin' out ole Otis. You know what a copper-riveted peckerwood he always was. No one shed a tear when he lit out for California."

"Shut up," Slash said as he ladled up a fresh bowl of bear stew from the pot on the range behind the bar. "You're interruptin' my dinner!"

Dodge grinned. He stretched out an arm and pointed a finger at Slash, looking between him and Pecos standing in the doorway. "I was right, wasn't I? Slash Braddock an' the Pecos River Kid! In my very presence! I'll be ding-dong-damned!"

Dodge lifted his leg and slapped his thigh.

Slash scowled at him, then kicked out a chair and sat down at a table. "Shut up, old-timer, or Slash Braddock an' the Pecos River Kid are gonna make you dance!"

Dodge suddenly looked stricken.

"Don't mind him," Pecos said from the doorway. "He's as moody as a pregnant puma!"

*   *   *

The former cutthroats and the pretty Pinkerton found scattered bits of the gold-robbers' sign north of the roadhouse. The killers appeared to have followed a relatively recently carved wagon trail, faint in places and likely cut by the supply and ore wagons of area prospectors.

Pecos found the sign, rather, while Slash and Hattie sat their horses, purposefully not talking to each other.

In fact, the girl didn't say anything all the rest of the day from where she rode, last in their Indian-file line as they followed the gold thieves' trail deeper and deeper into the Elk Range.

Slash thought he was seeing about as pretty a country as he'd ever seen in his life, as they rode generally northwest. He couldn't remember ever traversing this terrain before. He'd covered a lot of the frontier over his nearly forty years out here, but he knew if he'd ever been out here before, he'd remember.

He, Pecos, and Hattie followed a broad valley filled with tall grass and wildflowers lining the banks of a crystalline stream meandering through beaver meadows and aspen groves on the trail's left side. Beyond the stream, forest rose, cladding the apron slopes jutting as severely as a ship's prow to craggy gray peaks that must have stood two thousand feet above the valley floor.

More forest—both coniferous and deciduous—rose on the group's right, the aspens touched with the first bright yellows of autumn. Several times the trio spied elk cropping grass along the stream's far side, and once they heard the distant wail of what Slash identified as a grizzly bear likely marking his territory.

Deer were everywhere grazing like cattle. Mountain bluebirds flitted amongst the stirrup-high grass and pine branches. Beavers and muskrats played in the stream's deepest side pools, and both golden and bald eagles rode the air currents over the steep, rocky slopes on both sides of the canyon, occasionally giving ratcheting cries that echoed eerily in the clean-scoured, high-mountain air.

For most of the afternoon, the sun blazed down from a sky as clear as the pristine snowmelt stream that had carved the valley. Just after three, though, at the usual time, clouds rolled in, thunder rumbled, and lightning began dancing along the high ridges, flickering between peaks like inebriated witches on burning brooms.

"Head for cover!" Slash shouted, nudging the Appy with his spurs.

They made it to the cover of a jumble of massive boulders that had probably tumbled down from the high western ridge an eon or two in the past, just as the storm really unleashed its venom. Holding their horses by their bridle reins under the cover of the massive rocks, they watched the storm in all its varied manifestations, starting with rain that turned to hail, which, as the air cooled, turned to snow for about six minutes before the snow dwindled to sleet, then became slashing rain again.

The rain stopped abruptly, as though a lever had been thrown. Even before the last drops had landed, the clouds parted dramatically, as though swept from the sky by a large invisible feather duster from on high, and the sun shone, nearly as clear and warm as before. The last raindrops fell like large grains of pure gold sprinkled from heaven. It glinted on the marble-sized hail now melting together and crusting with a soggy, icy layer of wet snow.

Since there were still a couple of hours of good light left, the trio mounted their horses and set off once more.

They'd traveled a few more miles, following the trail around a bend in the west-angling canyon before the sun dropped behind the western peaks. They stopped to camp in a clearing in an aspen forest. Night as dark as the inside of a glove fell quickly. Good thing they managed to find some wood that hadn't been soaked by the storm, for the night was not only dark but cool.

Slash and Hattie tended the horses, while Pecos tended the fire and made supper, which would be a meager meal of only biscuits and beans tonight, as they'd run out of bacon.

Slash and Pecos cast each other conferring glances over the crackling fire as they spooned beans from their tin bowls. Hattie still hadn't said a word to either man. By her sullen expression, she was in one hell of a sour mood. She just sat there, a good ten feet from Slash and Pecos, silently eating her beans, keeping her own counsel. The firelight played in her rich brown hair, glinted in her brooding eyes.

Pecos looked at Slash again, scowling his dislike for the sour mood the girl was in. Being around an angry woman was hard on a fella's nerves.

Slash merely shrugged and swabbed his bowl with a chunk of stale baking powder biscuit. His sparse associations with women—associations that had lasted more than an hour or two, that was—had taught him that the best antidote to their sour moods was to let them stew in their feelings until they tired of them. Not even a woman could stay in a permanent snit.

Or so went his theory.

Finally, when they'd all finished supper, Hattie spoke. But it was nothing more than, "Toss your bowls over here. I'll take them to the creek." She looked at neither man.

When she returned from the creek ten minutes later, she dropped to her knees and set the wet bowls, cups, and wooden-handled, three-tined forks on a flat rock where they could dry by the fire and be handy for breakfast.

She sat back on her rump near the saddle she'd appropriated at the dugout saloon, along with a sleek sorrel gelding, and spoke her third sentence in the past eight hours: "I have something to say."

"Glad to hear it," Pecos grunted out. "I ain't used to bein' around a quiet woman. It's downright spooky."

"Shut up and let her talk!"

"Don't tell me to shut up, you—" He stopped abruptly and turned to Hattie. "See what happens when a woman don't talk?"

"I would like to apologize," Hattie said, casting her gaze between the two ex-cutthroats. A thin sheen of emotion coated her eyes. "I have not been an equal partner. I have been a burden. Not only a burden, but I have jeopardized our mission. I have said and done some very foolish things. I have endangered both your lives as well as my own."

She paused, looked down. Two tears rolled quickly down her right cheek, in the trough running along beside her nose. Her hair hung down along both sides of her face, somewhat concealing her expression.

She lifted her head and flung her hair back with one hand, and turned to Slash and Pecos again. "In the saloon, I was showing off. I was trying to prove to you both what a wonderful detective I was. I wanted very desperately to earn your respect. Instead, I proved myself nothing but a silly, silly girl."

She rose quickly, unsteadily, and turned her teary gaze to Slash. "I don't blame you for hating me. I will take my leave tomorrow. I will ride to Denver and tender my resignation to the Pinkerton field office, and you will never see me again."

She swung around and ran off into the trees, heading in the direction of the stream. Both cutthroats could hear her strangled sobs amidst the crackling brush, beneath the stream's quiet murmur.

Slash and Pecos shared a vaguely sheepish glance across the fire. Slash sipped his cup of post-supper coffee.

"What you got to say for yourself, you mean son of a buck?" Pecos asked him.

"Be nice to be shed of her," Slash said, taking another sip of the hot mud. He swallowed and added, "Never did cotton to riding with a female. They do their best work in parlor houses, where a man can get shed of 'em when they start gettin' harpie."

Pecos choked out a caustic laugh as he set his own coffee aside and gained his feet. "Good thing Jaycee found her a new beau. If she let the likes of you, you old scurvy dog, put your mother's ring on her finger, she'd see no end of misery!"

Pecos headed off in the direction of the girl.

"Oh, leave her alone," Slash told him. "She needs to cry out the nonsense."

"I didn't ask you for your sage advice," Pecos returned, drifting off into the darkness, sounding like a bear moving through the brush.

Slash gave a dry snort and took another sip of the mud.

Meanwhile, Pecos approached the stream, stepping over a deadfall that looked like a long, black witch's finger stretched before him in the darkness. The stream itself looked like a giant black snake, its skin glinting dully in the light of the myriad stars blazing in the black arch of the sky.

Hattie sat on a log facing the stream, only a few feet away from the water. Pecos could see only her silhouette as she sat there, leaning forward, elbows on her knees, head in her hands.

She sobbed wetly.

As Pecos walked up to her, she said in a strangled voice, "I want to be alone."

"No, you don't." He stepped over the log and sat down beside her.

CHAPTER 25

Pecos dug a handkerchief out of his back pocket and offered it to Hattie. "Need one of these? It's clean, more or less."

She plucked the hanky out of his hand and mopped her eyes with it, blew her nose. "I'm such a fool. I thought I was a real professional. But I'm only a fool. A silly little Pink."

"Ah, no, you're not."

"That's how you two see me."

"No, it ain't."

"Well, it's how Slash sees me." She blew her nose again, dabbed at her eyes.

"It ain't how he sees you, either."

"I should have stayed in Denver. I volunteered for this job because my boss, Mister Carter, needed a woman. I haven't worked in the country before. Only in towns. Chicago and Denver."

"Oh?"

"Believe it or not, I've helped ferret out murderers and corrupt politicians."

"I believe it."

"Mister Pinkerton . . . and then Mister Carter in Denver . . . saw me as a master of disguises. I've worked my way into

rich men's homes as housekeepers and private nurses and sec-
retaries. I once uncovered a counterfeiting scheme that way. I
pretended to be a fortune teller once, and even an actress,
helping bring down an opera house manager who was hiring
assassins to have his rival businessmen killed. I once worked
in a gambling parlor as a dancer. While the men ogled my
legs, my male counterparts uncovered rigged gambling tables
and shifty blackjack dealers."

Pecos chuckled at that. "I bet you sure could keep the men
distracted."

"I guess I'm better working in town. I've made a fool of
myself out here in this roughhewn country. I've made a series
of mistakes, one after the other. I took myself too seriously,
and you and Slash exposed me as the fool I am!"

She sobbed again, blew her nose. "I'll leave in the morning."

"No, you won't."

"Yes, I will. That last stupid thing I did was the final straw.
Letting myself get grabbed by that scoundrel Pettypiece on
the boardwalk of that dugout saloon! Slash had to shoot the
man when, if he'd been able to take him alive, we could have
learned where the gold was headed. The case could have
been solved right then and there!"

"Oh, hell, Hattie, you didn't do nothin' any more stupid
than Slash an' me have done countless times before. Livin'
out here . . . runnin' off your leash amongst others doin' the
same . . . is not an easy way to live. You've made mistakes.
We've made mistakes. We'll keep making them until we've
made one too many, that's all."

"Throwing in with me might have been one too many. I
don't want to get you two killed." Hattie pursed her lips and
gave him a begrudging look of admiration. "I sort of admire
you two old cutthroats, truth be told."

"We admire you, too, Hattie."

"Slash hates me."

"That ain't true."

"It is so true!"

"Slash has taken a shine to you, truth be known, Hattie."

"Ha!"

"If he hadn't, he wouldn't have taken such care to blow ole Otis's eye out!" Pecos chuckled. "You gotta understand one thing about Slash. He don't act like most people act. You can't really tell how he feels about anything or anyone until you've learned how to read him. Me? I may not be able to read three or four words strung together in a book, but I can read Slash better than an old sky pilot can read the Bible."

Hattie laughed in spite of herself.

Pecos chuckled. It felt good to see her smile again. She was a pretty girl even when she was in a sour mood, but she was downright beautiful when a smile dimpled her cheeks. "The secret about Slash, you see," he continued, "is that he has a great big ole heart. He says I got the big heart. But mine's the size of a frog's heart compared to his great big swollen ticker. Slash has a heart the size of a rain barrel. You see, he's just desperate to make sure nobody finds out."

Hattie stared at him, pensive. She smiled, nodded, glanced down at the hanky in her lap. "Thanks for tellin' me, Pecos."

"And with that," he said, climbing to his feet, "I'm gonna mosey back over to the fire before that old cutthroat drinks all the whiskey."

Hattie held up the soaked hanky. "I'll wash this out and give it back to you tomorrow."

"All right, honey." Pecos placed a hand on her shoulder and turned to start back to the camp.

"Hold on." Hattie grabbed his hand and pulled him down to her.

She placed a kiss on his cheek.

"You're all right, Pecos. Despite all your depredations, I mean." She gave him a mock scolding look.

Pecos grinned at her. "Why, thank you, Miss Hattie. You just made my day!"

Hattie sat there on the log, kicking her feet slowly as she stared out at the star-dappled water. She listened to Pecos tramping back toward the fire. His voice rose, deep and raspy, echoing hollowly in the quiet night. "Give me that bottle before you empty it, you cussed old fart!"

Hattie smiled.

Slash had settled back against his saddle for the night and drawn his blankets up to his chin, when he heard Hattie move through the brush toward the camp. Pecos was already asleep on the other side of the fire, snoring softly.

Slash looked out from beneath his down-canted hat brim to see the girl step into the firelight. She poured some water from a canteen into a tin cup and took a drink. She wrapped a blanket around her shoulders, sat on a log, and spent nearly fifteen minutes slowly brushing out her long, thick hair.

Slash drifted off to sleep, listening to the soft, regular raking of the girl's brush.

He didn't know how much time had passed when a deep, guttural growl sounded from somewhere off in the heavy mountain darkness.

Closer by, Slash heard a shrill gasp and a clipped cry. He poked his hat up onto his forehead and blinked groggily. To his left, the fire had burned down to a few low, snapping flames, but he could see Hattie sitting up about seven feet away from him, staring off into the darkness.

"Nothin' to worry about," Slash assured her quietly so as not to awaken Pecos, who continued snoring on the other side of the fire. "Just a bruin likely rousin' another bruin from his hidey-hole."

"Will it come over here?"

"Nah."

"Won't it attack the horses? Don't they eat horses?"

"There's plenty of deer in this valley. What would it want with a stringy ole hoss?"

Slash pulled his hat down over his eyes again.

Vaguely, as he started drifting back to sleep, he heard the rustling sounds of the girl moving around. Soft footsteps drew near. He looked up again to see Hattie drop down beside him, shrouded in her blankets. She slid up close to him, snuggled up against him, and threw an arm around his waist. She clung to him tightly, shivering.

"Whoa!" Slash raked out.

"I'm scared."

"Like I said—"

"Hush."

"Why don't you go over and pester Pecos? He likes you more than I do."

"No, he doesn't." She snuggled closer against him, tightening her arm around his waist.

Slash pulled his hat down over his eyes again. He placed his hand on hers, squeezed it gently, and smiled.

Just after noon of the following day, Slash stopped his Appy and sniffed the air. "You smell that?"

Pecos and Hattie, who'd stopped their own mounts behind Slash, also raised their noses to sniff the air.

"I don't smell anything," Hattie said, frowning. "Should I?"

"I don't smell nothin' neither," Pecos said.

Slash took a deep breath, sitting up high in his saddle. He coughed a little, chokingly, then grimaced and shook his head. "If I didn't know better, I'd say there's a town ahead. You can always smell a town before you see it. The privies and junk piles. No mistakin' a town."

"There's Slash's one gift," Pecos told Hattie, twisting his mouth into a wry grin. "He can't follow signs for beans, and a Mojave green rattlesnake has him beat all to hell for personality. But he's got a sniffer on him, all right." He looked at Slash, who was still sitting up high, staring up this side canyon they were now following nearly straight west, since the gold robbers' trail appeared to lead this way. "How do you know you *didn't* smell a town?"

"A town way out here?" Slash gave his head a single, doubtful shake. "What would a town be doing way out here? We haven't even passed a mining camp today. I don't recollect even spying a single prospector's cabin."

"Well, then we're due," Pecos said, booting his big buckskin, Buck, past Slash and continuing on up the canyon. "Come on. I'm thirsty, an' you drank all the tangleleg. Besides, maybe we've finally come to the gold thieves' hidey-hole."

As the trail widened, Slash booted his Appy up beside Pecos. They climbed a low rise, and there ahead, maybe a hundred yards away, several buildings appeared on the trio's side of the stream. As they continued toward the buildings, more buildings appeared beyond them and then up the slope behind them.

"You were right, Slash," Hattie said, putting her sorrel up between the two men. "It's a town, all right. A small one, looks like, but a town just the same."

As they continued toward the settlement, entering it where it abruptly began with a general merchandise store on the trail's right side and a blacksmith shop on its left side, the stream flanking it, a sign tacked to a cedar post announced HONEYSUCKLE in sloppily painted letters. A big man in a leather apron stood hammering what appeared to be an andiron on an anvil just outside the long, low shack's double open doors.

Hearing the horses, he turned abruptly, raking a thick arm across his forehead and scowling curiously at the newcomers, turning his head slowly to follow them as they continued on into the town.

Slash saw that Hattie had been right. The town was small, all right. Beyond the general store, on the trail's right side, sat a small livery and feed barn. Beyond that was a barbershop and bathhouse. A little man in small, round spectacles and armbands was sweeping the raised boardwalk fronting the barbershop. He glanced up over his sagging spectacles as the newcomers passed.

Beyond the barbershop was a harness shop and feed store. Across the street lay a butcher shop/grocery store, with a stock pen and chicken coop flanking it, and a gunsmith's shop. The only other buildings were two saloons, sitting catty-corner across the street from each other, Alma May's Café, a small hotel that doubled as a post office, a town marshal's office, which was little more than a small stone shack, and an assayer's office.

That was it. Ten business buildings total, with a few log and canvas dwellings flanking them in no particular order, as though they'd been built where the boulders and large pines and cedars scattered along that southern ridge would allow. There also appeared to be a half-dozen shacks along both sides of the stream on the town's north side, likely belonging to gold-panners.

The only folks visible anywhere in town were the blacksmith, the barber, and a tall, elderly gent wearing a five-pointed tin star and thick, red muttonchop whiskers. He was parked in a hide-bottom chair in front of the marshal's office. He held a double-bore shotgun across his bony knees.

He wore a pair of rectangular, gold-framed spectacles on his long, thick nose, which bore what appeared to be a knife scar just beneath the bridge. He was fanning his angular face with his brown slouch hat and giving the three newcomers the same once- and twice-over that the blacksmith and barber had given them.

No, there were two others, Slash saw as he and his trail pards reined up in the middle of town, on the broad main street. On a second-floor balcony of one of the town's two saloons, two scantily clad women stood smoking—and giving the three strangers the woolly eyeball.

Given their skimpy, garish attire, they were no doubt doxies, both well past their prime. One was short and fat, with jet-black hair likely from a bottle. The other was skinny, pale, and freckled, her own copper-red hair also from a bottle. The doxie's red hair, which hung long about her shoulders, reminded Slash a little unpleasantly, given the circumstances under which they'd last parted, of Jay.

Keeping his voice low, Pecos turned to Slash and said, "They musta come through here, them killers. Where do you suppose they are?"

Slash poked a back tooth with his tongue, looking up and down the street. "Hard to say. Looks like the end of the line, though." He couldn't imagine there being any more towns beyond Honeysuckle. The trail to the west, opposite the direction from which they'd ridden in, appeared to narrow down to a single-track horse trail dwindling past an old, mossy-roofed log cabin into thick forest.

"Reckon it's time to do some detective work?" Pecos asked.

"I reckon it is," Hattie said.

Both men looked at her. She was studying the front of the saloon, below where the two doxies gazed down at the three strangers in the street. A sign stretched beneath the second-floor balcony announced the name of the place as the Honeysuckle Saloon and Dance Hall. Honeysuckle blossoms were painted on each end of the sign. Or a crude artist's depiction of such blossoms, anyway. One of the blossoms had been chewed by a bullet.

"What you got in mind?" Slash asked her.

"A job."

"A *what*?" Pecos said, stretching his lips back from his teeth in disdain for the three-letter word.

Hattie dipped her chin toward the pasteboard sign tacked to the porch balustrade:

WANTED: PURTY SERVENE GIRL. 25 SENTS A DAY PLUSS TIPPS

"What?" Slash said. "You think you're gonna work there?"

"Why not?" Hattie smiled coquettishly at him, flinging her hair out from her neck with the back of one hand. "You think I'm *purty*, don't you?"

"No, no." Slash shook his head, eyeing the run-down-looking place and the two well-worn doxies leaning forward against the second-floor balcony railing, smoking and regarding the newcomers with bland interest. "You can't work there. That's no place for you. You said yourself you hated tobacco smoke."

"Oh, I can put up with it for a day or two. And don't be so protective, Sla . . . er, I mean, *Uncle Jim*." Still smiling, Hattie batted her long, lovely ashes at him, then cut her gaze to Pecos. Her voice acquired a sharp but melodramatic scolding tone. "You neither, *Uncle Melvin*. You two old scalawags drank up all our money in that tumbledown mining cabin of ours. We have nary a dime to our names. I think it's time I take matters into my own hands and try to build us a stake so we can ride down out of the mountains before we get snowed in for the winter. If I left earning a living to you two, we'd starve!"

"You gonna apply for the serving girl job, princess?" asked the short, fat doxie with the jet-black hair, grinning down over the balcony rail at Hattie.

Looking up at her and the redhead, Hattie shaded her eyes with a gloved hand. "I was pondering on it. These two jackasses can't make a living, sure enough, so I thought I'd give it a go."

Pecos gave an injured chuff and said under his breath to Slash, "She don't have to sound *that* convincing, does she?"

"I know what you mean, honey," said the redhead, then scowling at Slash and Pecos. "Men aren't worth the cheap busthead runnin' through their veins these days."

She hacked phlegm from her throat and spat the big plop into the dirt of the street near Slash. To Hattie, she said,

"Come on in and talk to Clifford. He runs the place, what there is of it."

"You just stick to servin', though, honey," instructed the black-haired whore, letting her dark-eyed gaze flick with no little envy across Hattie's young, ripe frame. "Don't you go crowdin' me an Iris. The toughnuts around here would take one look at you an' never throw another dollar in our jars again!"

"Oh, don't worry," Hattie assured them, swinging down from her sorrel's back. "I have no intention of working the line."

"No, she don't," Slash said pointedly to the two doxies. "If we caught her doin' that—me an', uh, Uncle Melvin here—we'd take a switch to her backside so she wouldn't sit down again till Christmas."

"Say, you're handsome!" said the black-haired gal. "Why don't you come on up here an' let me curl your toes for you, handsome!"

"You too, big man," said the redhead to Pecos, beckoning broadly with her arm. "Get up here, an' let's me an' you play some slap 'n' tickle." She dipped her chin and raised a flirtatious brow. "You can tickle me all you want. I don't slap hard at all!"

She and the dark-haired gal had a good, long, cackling laugh that quickly turned into a raucous coughing fit for each. It ended with both hacking more phlegm over the balcony and into the street near Slash and Pecos's horses.

"I do apologize," Hattie told the doxies. "But Uncles Jim an' Melvin have little but lint in their pockets. They can't afford either one of you ladies, and even if they could, they too need to be looking for work. Don't you, Uncles Jim and Melvin?"

Hattie smiled sweetly at them.

Slash and Pecos grumbled.

Hattie tossed her horse's reins up to Slash. "Tend my horse

for me, Uncle Jim. You two behave yourselves, now, you hear?" She started for the saloon's front steps but glanced once more over her shoulder to say, "And make yourselves useful. I'll be checking!"

With that, she lifted the hem of her skirt up above her ankles and mounted the Honeysuckle Saloon's front veranda.

When she'd disappeared inside, Slash turned to Pecos and said, "You know, I think she was really enjoying that."

"Yeah." Pecos snorted. "Maybe you shoulda shot her and let ole Otis Pettypiece live."

They chuckled as they rode off down the street.

CHAPTER 26

Hattie straightened her blouse, tossed her hair behind her shoulders, and stepped through the batwings. She paused to look around the shabby room, with its dirty windows and dusty animal heads mounted on the papered walls above a five-foot-high strip of shabby, bullet-pocked wainscoting.

The horseshoe-shaped bar lay straight ahead, curving into the middle of the room from the left. A wooden stairway flanked the bar, rising to the second story, all the rooms of which faced the first floor from behind a railing that ran along all four of the building's walls.

Despite the dust and bullet holes, the place tried for a Victorian splendor, with its carpeted stairs, papered walls, varnished oak bar, leaded backbar mirror, and the large oil painting of hard-charging wild horses above the piano abutting the wall on the saloon's far side, on the other side of the bar. Instead of sand boxes, brass spittoons stood here and there around the room, though one had been kicked over and not picked up yet, muddy brown liquid oozing from its lip onto the dark brown wooden floor.

There was even a crystal chandelier, an elaborate, expensive trimming for these far-flung parts, plunging down from the second-floor ceiling. Hattie wouldn't have been surprised to see a bird's nest in it.

The Honeysuckle Saloon was nearly deserted, though it must have had a profitable lunch hour, for several tables were still cluttered with dirty plates, beer glasses, and coffee cups. One old man sat at the bar, pensively drinking a beer and smoking a cigarette. He found Hattie's figure in the back-bar mirror, and smiled at her, half-closing his eyes as though enjoying a particularly vivid waking dream.

Three other men were toiling on the far side of the bar, to the right of the piano and a potted palm. *Two* were toiling, rather, installing a new window in that wall, while the third man stood behind them, his back to Hattie, issuing orders in a thick Irish brogue.

"Easy now, Clell. Go easy there, Beau—that window came all the way up from Denver. It'll likely get shot out again on Saturday night, but by god I want it put in right and without so much as a nick!"

The toilers merely grunted and grumbled as they fitted the window, with a stained-glass upper quarter—the stained paintings portraying lounging, naked women—into the frame. The toilers were beefy men in shabby work clothes, a wooden toolbox bristling with tools on the floor near their hobnailed boots.

The third man was short and stocky, a thick, unruly brush of silver-gray hair clumsily brushed to one side of his head. As Hattie walked around the bar, heading toward him, the man glanced toward her, glanced away, then turned back again, his blue eyes flickering with sudden male interest.

"Are you Clifford?" Hattie stopped before him, clenching her hands together in front of her. She was only half-feigning nervousness. She did in fact want the serving-girl job. She knew from experience that from such a position she could find out in a very short time far more about the under-workings of a town than she could if she wandered about the boardwalks with a notebook in hand, interrogating the town's citizens or sitting in cafés and saloons, hoping to eavesdrop on a particularly informative conversation.

"Why, yes . . . yes, I am," Clifford said, smiling unctuously at the pretty Pinkerton, not bothering to restrain the indiscreet forays of his goatish gaze. "What can I help you with, young lady?"

"I wanted to apply for the job you have posted on the porch rail—the serving-girl job."

"The serving-girl job? You? Really?" There went his eyes again. It was almost as though he could see right through her clothes. The man's scrutiny made her skin crawl, but she'd better get used to it. She'd gotten used to it before. She could get used to it again.

"Yes. Aren't . . ."—Hattie closed her hands together, dipped her chin demurely, and made her voice small—"aren't I pretty enough?"

"Oh, I don't know . . ." Clifford used the occasion to give her another thrice-over. He chuckled under his breath, brushed his fist across his nose, and said, "Well . . . it sorta depends on how you look in your uniform."

Hattie just realized that the two window installers had stopped their work to stare at her. The shorter of the two was down on one knee, on one side of the window, while the other one, taller, was on his feet, on the other side of the window, holding a hammer down low by his side. Nails bristled from between his thick, chapped lips as he breathed, his lumpy chest rising and falling heavily.

Clifford realized they were staring at her, too. "You two get back to work. I hired you to install a window, not ogle my prospective help!"

Reluctantly, they returned to their work.

"Uniform?" Hattie asked.

Clifford walked around behind the bar. He leaned down, looked around some shelves, and finally pulled out a flat box from beneath the bar. He set it atop the bar and said, "You run along upstairs and try that on. Let me see you in it. Then I'll know if you're right for the job. My business depends on a servin' girl who can look good in the uniform. I haven't had one in a coon's age—not since the gold boom, what little there was of it, fizzled out before it really got started and half the town, purty girls included, left for the lower climes."

"A uniform, eh?" Hattie hefted the box in both hands. "Sure is light." She laughed a little uneasily.

"You go on upstairs and try it on. You can have Lilac's old room."

"Lilac?"

"My last serving girl. Iris an' Lilly work the line. I call all my girls flower names. You know—so they fit in with 'honeysuckle'?"

"Brilliant."

"Iris an' Lilly don't normally have time to sling drinks. They're professionals, you understand. Big moneymakers." Clifford winked meaningfully at Hattie, and chuckled.

The other two men snorted laughs as they installed the window, casting quick furtive glances over their shoulders at Hattie.

Clifford added, "I like to keep a girl on special for hustlin' drinks out from the bar, an' maybe dancin' to the piano on Saturday nights now an' then. I got a good piano player. That's him at the bar."

Hattie glanced at the old man at the bar, who raised his beer glass to her in salute.

Clifford said, "The girl's gotta look good in the uniform."

"I understand, Mister, uh . . . ?"

"Hicks. Clifford Hicks. You can call me Mister Hicks until we see what you look like in the uniform."

Again, the window installers laughed.

"All right . . . Mister Hicks." Again, Hattie's skin crawled.

"Go on upstairs, now," Clifford said, giving Hattie a gentle shove toward the stairway. "Room number four. You'll see the plate. I'll look you over, and if you don't look too bad, we'll talk turkey."

"Turkey," Hattie said, fingering the light-as-air box in her hands. "All . . . all right. Room four it is. I hope I don't disappoint you, Mister Hicks."

"Me, too, honey," Hicks said. "Hard to find a girl who looks good in the uniform. Damn hard."

Feeling the eyes of all three men on her, hearing them snickering softly, Hattie drifted on up the stairs and into a room off the balcony, opposite the side of the saloon in which the window was being installed. She came out ten minutes later.

Clifford Hicks had been waiting impatiently, pretending to be supervising the two window installers. In reality, he was imagining what was going on behind the closed door of room four on the balcony.

Now, as he heard the door latch click and turned to see Hattie step out of the room, a giant fist tightened around his gut. He stepped heavily out toward the middle of the room, where he could get a better look at the girl in the red-and-black, lace-edged corset and bustier, as well as fishnet stockings and the black stilettos she'd obviously found in Ivy's room.

She stepped up to the railing and looked down at Clifford gazing up at her, his lower jaw hanging, his cheeks turning crimson. "Do I look all right?" Hattie asked him.

Clifford's throat went dry. Sweat beads popped out on his forehead.

Behind him, the two window installers—the shorter one holding up one side of the window, while the taller one tacked the other side into place—both stopped what they were doing to turn around and stare up in open-mouthed fascination.

Behind them, the window lurched, glinting, then slipped out of its frame. The bottom right corner struck the floor with a bang, and the entire pane shattered loudly, glass flying every which way.

Clifford wheeled to stare in silent horror at his precious window.

Hattie chewed her thumbnail. "I'll take that as a yes," she said, and flounced back into the room.

Slash and Pecos took a ride around town, getting the lay of the land, before riding over to the barbershop. They tied their horses outside, then Slash walked up onto the boardwalk and pushed through the door, making the bell jangle loudly.

The little bespectacled barber had been sacked out in one of the two barber chairs, his arms crossed on his chest. Now he jerked his head up with a wailing yell, startled out of a deep sleep. He thumbed his glasses up his nose and eyed the two newcomers as though they were grizzlies busting into his shop for a meal.

"Oh . . . it's you two," he said, relaxing slightly but remaining in his chair, his hand on the arms. The horror left his gaze, but a wariness remained. Glancing at the two strangers' holstered pistols, he appeared to be wondering if he were about to be robbed.

"Just us," Slash said, holding his hands out away from his guns as he stepped into the room. Pecos walked in behind him. "How much for a bath, amigo? Me an' my pard here been rode hard an' put up wet."

The little man climbed out of his chair. He snapped his brocade vest down at the bottom, flattening out the wrinkles, and turned his chin to a chalkboard on which his prices were printed. "Twenty cents per bucket for a bath." He regarded each of the two dusty newcomers critically, adding, "Are you sure you both couldn't do with a *hair trim* and a *shave* in addition to a bath?"

Pecos ran his hand along his jaw. "I think we just been insulted, pard."

"Maybe later," Slash said. "Me, I just wanna a good long soak in a hot bath. But . . . *twenty cents a bucket?*" He scowled at the little man incredulously.

"Boom town prices," the little man said, lifting his chin imperiously and pooching out his lips, which were mantled by a little, carefully trimmed pewter mustache.

"Look around you, pard," Pecos told him, glancing out the window to his right. "I do believe you're livin' in the past."

The little man glanced out the window at the deserted street, then drew his mouth corners down in defeat. He drew a deep, fateful breath, stared at the floor, and said, "All right—ten cents a bucket."

"A nickel," Slash said. "Or we'll go wallow in the stream yonder."

"Oh, for cryin' in the—" The little barber cut himself off sharply. He swung around and disappeared through a rear door. "Right this way!"

He led Slash and Pecos out the rear of the barbershop building, across a ten-foot strip of hardpan, then up four steps and into the bathhouse beyond it. The bathhouse resembled a small, wooden-floored dancehall outfitted with six copper tubs. Pegs and benches lined the walls, as did shelves housing towels. A big range abutted the front wall, and two boilers steamed on the burners. A wooden bucket hung from the mouth of a pump poking up out of the floor near the range.

While the little barber stoked the stove, Slash and Pecos walked over to one of the benches, took off their coats and hats, pegged them, and sat down. Slash kicked out of a boot, glanced at the tubs lined out before him, and said, "Looks like you got a tub for every man remaining in the town, amigo."

He gave a wry chuff.

"Go ahead an' laugh. You're obviously not from around here or you'd feel the sting, as well."

"Nah, just passin' through," Pecos said, pulling off one of his boots with a grunt.

"Trail up here had plenty of traffic on it," Pecos said, trying to make the comment sound offhand as he kicked off his second boot. "I mean, judgin' by the tracks. A fairly good-sized bunch must have passed through here yesterday. Must have been a small rush on your place, eh, Mister, uh . . . ?"

The little man whipped around from the range, his pasty cheeks reddening. "Let me give you two strangers a bit of advice."

"Please do," Slash said. "We could use it."

"Leave here. Soon. Tonight. Tomorrow morning at the latest. Or . . . if you decide to stay, which I wholeheartedly discourage, keep your mouths shut. In other words, don't go around asking questions. Even innocent questions up here in Honeysuckle will get a man killed!"

CHAPTER 27

"Well, that went well," Slash said as he and Pecos filed out of the barbershop after a good long soak in their respective tubs.

"No, it didn't," Pecos said, running a hand through his still-wet hair, then setting his hat on his head. "Didn't go well at all. We didn't learn a damn thing about them gold robbers."

Slash gave him a rueful smile. "I was being ironic."

"You were being what?"

"Iron . . . oh, Jesus, never mind. I sure wish one of these women you're always throwin' in with would teach you how to read."

"Hell, I haven't had me a steady woman, book-learned or not, in a month of . . ."

Slash cut him off with a nudge. "Look there."

"Where?"

"There." Slash jerked his chin toward where the man wearing the town marshal's star sat directly across the street on a loafer's bench fronting the butcher shop and grocery store. As he'd been doing the first time Slash and Pecos had spied the man, he was fanning his face with his hat, though it was getting on in the afternoon and the air was noticeably cooler than before.

Slash had a feeling the movement was a nervous tic.

The town marshal didn't look away when Slash and Pecos stared back at him. He kept his eyes on them, grinning cryptically, as though he knew a deep secret about them but he'd be damned if he was going to share what it was.

"Afternoon," Slash said with a nod, holding up one hand in a genial wave.

The lawman said nothing in response. He made no gesture. He just kept sitting there, smiling behind his rectangular, gold-framed spectacles, using his hat to fan his angular face, framed by thick red muttonchops.

Pecos glanced curiously at Slash. Both men grabbed their reins off the hitchrack fronting the barbershop and swung up into the leather. Slash could see, out of the corner of his eye that the lawman continued to stare at them, that seedy, puzzling grin remaining on his lips.

"What do you suppose he wants?" Pecos said under his breath.

"Hard to know if he don't say."

"Maybe he's mute." Slash glanced over his shoulder at the man, then turned back to Pecos. "Or maybe he's tryin' to spook us."

"He's done that," Pecos said, also glancing over his shoulder at the man.

Trying to ignore the lawman, Slash peered up the street toward the Honeysuckle Saloon and Dance Hall. "What do you say we tend these cayuses, then see how Hattie's getting along?"

"You're worried about her, aren't you?" Pecos asked, grinning.

Slash frowned as though deeply offended. "I ain't one bit worried! Slash . . . er, uh, Jimmy Braddock. Don't *get* worried!" He shifted his gaze back in the direction of the Honeysuckle. "I'm just wonderin' if she's made any more progress in the investigation than we have."

"Well, that wouldn't take much," Pecos said as they booted their horses up toward the livery barn sitting just beyond the barbershop.

As they approached the barn, a tall, stoop-shouldered man with a sunken-jawed, hawk-like face stepped out of the inside shadows, holding a steaming tin cup in one gloved hand. Long, grizzled gray hair hung down from his leather-billed immigrant cap. A tightly rolled quirley drooped from one side of his mouth. He blinked against the sunshine as he stopped between the double open doors to size up his visitors.

He glanced beyond them toward the obliquely grinning lawman, then, returning his gaze to Slash and Pecos, said, "You two ain't from around here."

"Nah, just passin' through," Slash said, swinging down from the leather.

"Nobody just passes through Honeysuckle," the liveryman said, not so vaguely suspicious. "This is the end of the trail." He glanced again, tentatively, maybe a little anxiously, toward the lawman. "A man comes here, he comes here for a reason."

"You want to know ours?" Pecos asked him, looping his shotgun's lanyard over his head and right shoulder, letting the double-gauge dangle down his back. He walked almost confrontationally up to the liveryman, letting his height go to work for him, but smiling affably down at the man, who stood nearly a whole head shorter.

The liveryman, in his sixties, stared at the double-bore cannon poking up from behind Pecos's right shoulder. He scrutinized Pecos himself then, cutting his eyes to Slash, standing to Pecos's right, he shook his head and said, "Nope. No, I don't."

"For some reason, I had a feelin' that's what you was

gonna say," Pecos said. "Here, take our hosses." He handed the man his reins. "They don't need a stall. Your corral will be fine. They'll likely want to stretch and roll and maybe tussle for a while."

Slash handed the hawk-faced man his own reins. "Treat 'em right. An' you can stow our gear in a corner till we come back for it."

The hawk-faced man glanced at the lawman once more, then turned his begrudging look back to Slash and Pecos. "How long you stayin'?"

"Don't know yet," Pecos said.

Slash frowned at the man. "If you suggest we move along, just like the barber over there done, we're gonna start to get our feelin's hurt."

Holding both sets of reins in one hand, his coffee in his other hand, the liveryman said, "It's seventy-three cents a night for the whole nine yards. That includes a rubdown and a bait of oats or parched corn, whichever I got more of." He paused then added commandingly, "I will take your compensation up front."

Slash and Pecos glanced at each other, skeptically.

Slash dug into his pocket for some coins, saying, "What's the matter, mister? You thinkin' we're not gonna be around to pay later?"

"I'm just sayin', I will be compensated now."

Slash and Pecos each stuffed their coins into a pocket of the man's overalls, then pinched their hat brims to him. "Nice talkin' to ya," Pecos said.

The liveryman didn't respond to that. He just stood there, holding both horses' reins in one hand, his coffee in his other hand, staring after Slash and Pecos walking along the street toward the Honeysuckle. Slash glanced back over his shoulder. Just as he'd suspected, the town badge-toter was still giving him and Pecos the woolly eyeball, though that silly grin had faded from his mouth.

"He's still there," Slash said.

"He makes me nervous."

"Everybody I've met so far in this high-up ass-end of nowhere makes me as fidgety as a virgin bride."

Looking around, Slash saw a silhouette in a dusty window on the opposite side of the street. The silhouette quickly jerked away, out of sight. Slash gave a wry chuff. Then he and Pecos mounted the Honeysuckle's front steps, crossed the veranda, and pushed through the batwings.

Like they always did without thinking, Slash stepped to the left, Pecos to the right, blinking as they scanned the shadowy room. One of the few men inside the place, just then sinking into a chair at a table to the right of the horseshoe-shaped bar, said, "Say, Clifford, what happened to that new window you said you had shipped in from Denver?"

A gray-haired man who had been nailing a plank over a window on the bar's far side, stopped pounding and turned, scowling, toward the bar. "The new serving girl."

"The new serving girl broke your window?" came the skeptical reply.

Still scowling toward the bar, the man who'd been hammering the nail into the plank—one of several planks he'd nailed over the window frame before him, Slash saw—said, "In a manner of speakin', she bloody well did, all right." He spoke with a heavy Irish brogue.

Just then Slash saw what the Irish barman, Clifford, had been talking about. He'd been referring to the scantily clad young woman turning away from the bar, holding a tray bearing two beers. Slash blinked as though to clear his vision.

No, his eyesight was fine.

The gorgeous brunette, outfitted in a corset and bustier, with red and black feathers dancing in her piled-up hair, was none other than the pretty Pinkerton her ownself—Operative Number One, or, as she'd been more recently known, Hattie Friendly.

Pecos saw her at the same time. "Holy cow," he grunted, then chuckled. "We came to the right place, after all."

Slash looked up at his partner standing to his right. Pecos was grinning lewdly, his blue eyes flinging bayonets of bawdy passion. Slash elbowed him sharply in the ribs. "Stop ogling her, you reprobate. That's Hattie!"

Pecos jerked a disbelieving look at him. "Huh?"

Slash jerked his head. Pecos turned back to the girl, who was setting a beer down on the table of the man who'd asked Clifford about the window. The man was grinning up at the pretty new serving girl, his pasty cheeks becoming two bright red apples. "Holy cow!" Pecos repeated.

"Yeah."

Slash glanced around the room once more. Only a half-dozen men occupied the place—three at the bar and three at two tables. All six were so distracted by the new serving girl that they hadn't even noticed the two strangers still standing by the batwings.

"Let's have us a seat," Slash said, brushing past Pecos and heading for a table against the front wall to his right.

Hattie had just delivered the other beer to the table at which two men in shabby business suits sat on the bar's other side, under a gigantic snarling grizzly head. As she turned back toward the bar, her eyes found Slash and Pecos, and she grinned.

Slash blushed. He could feel Pecos blush, as well. The heat of embarrassment fairly radiated off the man, as though off a fully stoked woodstove.

Their embarrassment must have infected Hattie, for her cheeks suddenly blossomed like a rose after a silky spring rain. She glanced down at her attire, so meager that Slash silently opined he could have stuffed the whole ensemble into one boot and still have had room for his foot. She swung around and headed back to the bar with her tray.

A small man who appeared to be a half-breed drew a couple of beers from a tap, and when Slash and Pecos had sat down at their table, Hattie brought the beers over atop the tray.

"Since you're both on duty," Hattie said, softly enough for only Slash and Pecos to hear, "I knew you wouldn't want anything stronger than beer."

"Thanks, thanks," Slash said, as she set a beer down in front of him.

"Yeah, uh . . . thanks, darlin'," Pecos said.

"You can look at me, you know."

"What's that?" Slash was running his thumb over a pair of initials carved into the top of the table.

"I said you can look at me. That carving don't look all that interesting, if you ask me, Uncle Jim," she added a little more loudly and fashioning a warm smile, glancing around the room, not wanting to seem overly secretive.

Slash looked up at her. So did Pecos.

"Well?" Hattie said.

"Well, what?" asked Slash.

Hattie held her arms out to each side, the tray in one hand. *"How do I look, Uncle Jim and Uncle Melvin?"*

"Oh!" Slash said, feigning surprise. "Lookee there . . . you're all gussied up in a serving girl's costume! Lookee there, Uncle Melvin—did you notice that?" He elbowed his partner.

"No," Pecos muttered tensely, trying very hard to keep his eyes on the girl's face, though other revealed parts of her attracted his gaze like magnets attracted steel. "I didn't notice that until just now when you mentioned it, Uncle Jim. Lookee, there—why, you're right purty, Miss Hat . . . er, I mean, our precious *niece* Hattie."

Hattie lowered her arms and sucked in a cheek. "You two are embarrassed."

"No, no, we're not," Slash protested.

"Surely you've seen serving girls before . . . in their *uniforms*, as Mister Hicks calls this getup."

"We sure have, darlin'," Pecos said. "But I don't recollect we ever seen one as . . . as . . . as . . ."

"Careful, Uncle Melvin, you nasty scalawag!" Slash raked out at him. "That's our niece you're talkin' to." Looking up at Hattie, trying very hard to keep his eyes on only her eyes, Slash said, "What he means is, uh, we sorta understand now how the window got broke."

He grinned.

Hattie snorted a laugh, tucking her upper lip under her bottom teeth.

She glanced self-consciously around the room. So did Slash and Pecos. They, as did Hattie, noticed that several glances were being cast their way.

Slash had a feeling that he and Pecos were no longer nearly as interesting as they had been before word of the new serving girl had started spreading around town. More men were coming in, their eyes moving right to Hattie. As soon as they saw her, crimson flushes crept onto their unshaven faces, and they elbowed each other and muttered under their breaths, like schoolboys taking notice of the pretty new girl in the class.

"Tread easy, girl," Slash warned her as three men sat down at a nearby table, giving her the brashly roving eyeball. "That uniform there is beginnin' to attract a crowd."

"Don't worry," Hattie said. "I can handle myself quite well. I have my Derringer tucked under my garter belt."

Inwardly, Slash groaned at the imagined image of the little popper snugged up tight against her pretty leg.

"Hope you don't have to use it," Pecos said, glancing around the room as two more men entered the saloon. "Since you only got two bullets an' this place is fillin' up fast."

"I have to get back to work now, Uncle Jim and Uncle Melvin," Hattie said loudly enough for those near their table to hear. "I just wanted to make sure you're behaving yourselves, is all." Lowering her voice again quickly and leaning down toward them, she said, "I've already learned something important. Remember that word that Jupiter Dodge mentioned overhearing when he was in the barn loft and the gold thieves were bedding down in the barn beneath him?"

"Yeah," Slash said, keeping his own voice low, but smiling up at the girl as though they were having a frivolous conversation. " 'Spanish' was the word."

Hattie cast her own somewhat strained smile around the room, then turned back to Slash and Pecos. "Mister Hicks said that weeknights around here were pretty slow. They could get downright tedious, in fact. But on the weekends— Friday an' Saturday nights—the boys from the *Spanish Bit* converged on the town and gave him a walloping business."

"What's the Spanish Bit?" Pecos asked.

"According to Mister Hicks, it's a ranch and gold mine up in the mountains. That's all he said, and I didn't prod him. Didn't want him to get suspicious. Anyway, Friday is three days away. Maybe we'll learn more then. I have to get back to work. You two be careful!"

She hurried back to the bar. All heads in the room swiveled to follow her.

"We ain't the ones who need to be careful," Slash said.

"Yeah," Pecos said. "We wouldn't look near so good in that uniform."

Slash cursed, brushed his fist across his nose, and tipped back his beer, sucking down half in three big swallows.

CHAPTER 28

Pecos took down a good third of his own frothy ale, licked foam from his mustache, and turned to Slash, keeping his voice low, though there was little need, as there were enough men in the saloon now to cover the former cutthroats' conversation. "What do you think about that?"

"Hattie's uniform?" Slash asked. "I think it's, well—"

"The Spanish Bit, you cork-headed fool!"

"Oh, I done already forgot about that," Slash said, chuckling. He couldn't help watching Hattie move about the tables, delivering beer and whiskey to the good dozen men in the place. Hell, every man left in the town must be here. "The Spanish Bit, eh? Well, I reckon we'd better ride out an' look it over, do a little investigative work of our own."

"Yeah, we can't let Operative Number One steal our thunder," Pecos said, fingering his chin whiskers, while also indulging his eyes on the pretty Pink.

"Don't make much sense, though." Slash took another sip of his beer, then revolved the heavy glass absently on the table, in its own wet ring. "Why would a gold mine steal gold?"

"There's a point."

"That old jasper Jupiter Dodge was probably hearing things. Or, hell, anything could have been meant by the word

'Spanish.' It didn't have to be the Spanish Bit. Maybe one of the other riders was Spanish . . . or named Spanish." Slash grimaced and shook his head.

"What else we got to go on?" Pecos said.

"Let's mosey around town tonight, see if we kick anything else up. If not, let's ride out tomorrow in search of this Spanish Bit Ranch and Gold Mine. Shake the tree a little. See if any gold eggs fall out of any hidden nests, though I'm right doubtful."

"I am, too, an' it grieves me."

"Why?"

"By now ole Bleed-Em-So prob'ly thinks we made off with the gold. He probably thinks we're headin' for Mexico."

"Well, if we'd run into a telegraph office somewhere along the trail here, we could have cabled him. But we didn't. I didn't see any lines on the way up here, so there's probably no telegraph here, either. Which means we're on our own. You, me, an' Hattie. We can't worry about what . . ."

Slash let his voice dribble to silence when another man strode through the batwings and into the saloon. Right away, Slash saw the newcomer wasn't a man. She was a young woman dressed like a man, though there was no way any man would wear her man's attire the way she did—in pure female fashion. In addition to a supple, high-breasted female body, she had blue eyes and red-blond hair, which hung straight down from the flat brim of her tan, low-crowned Stetson, the crown of which was trimmed with a snakeskin band.

She wore faded denim trousers, a less faded denim shirt, and a red kerchief tightly knotted around her neck. On her right thigh rode a handsome Bisley revolver in a hand-tooled brown holster. On her left breast was pinned a five-pointed star, similar to the one the big, elderly gent with the red muttonchops had been wearing.

The badge-toting young woman strode straight into the

room like she owned the place, like she expected a crowd to converge on her in admiration. Like a princess braving the mire for a confab with her subjects. The badge-toting princess stopped near the bar, grinning from ear to ear, saucily, and looked over the men bellied up to the mahogany before her, their backs to her.

When none so much as glanced over their shoulders at her, she frowned and loudly cleared her throat. "Pete . . . Norm . . . how you boys doin'?" she asked cheerily, pulling her shoulders back and cocking one soft leather boot out before her and wagging it.

A couple of the men glanced at her in the mirror and merely nodded. Another glanced over his shoulder, gave her a fleeting smile, said, "Oh, hello, Lisa—how's it goin'?"

Before she could respond, he turned his head to stare at what every other man in the room was staring at—all except for Slash and Pecos, that was—which was Hattie.

The badge-toting young lady, Lisa, followed the men's lusty gazes toward the object of their attraction, to where Hattie was delivering a round of beers to several men on the other side of the bar. Lisa studied the comely Pinkerton chatting affably with her customers, and then Lisa's mouth and eyes pinched, and her cheeks acquired an even deeper color than the deep tan they'd had before.

She stood there for nearly a full minute, glaring at Hattie, her chest rising and falling heavily. She turned her head, and her angry blue eyes swept the room quickly. They came to rest on Slash and Pecos, who were staring back at her. She studied both men critically, as though she thought she recognized them from somewhere.

Slash slowly raised his hand to pinch his hat brim to the young, badge-toting lady, and offered a tentative smile. She did not return the acknowledgment. She merely stared, lips pursed, as though trying to quell a building rage inside her. She glanced once more at Hattie, her angry flush in place, then wheeled and pushed back out through the batwings, disappearing as quickly as she'd appeared.

Pecos frowned at Slash. "What do you suppose that was all about?"

Slash shrugged, shook his head. "Heck if I know. Don't look like she cottoned to Hattie overmuch."

"Probably hasn't had all that much competition for the menfolk's stares in this one-hoss town," Pecos said with a chuckle.

Slash finished his beer, set the glass down on the table. "Let's haul our freight, walk around a little, find something to eat."

Pecos finished his own beer and rose from his chair. "I could use a steak."

"Me, too."

They took their time devouring tough but tasty elk steaks and fried potatoes in Alma May's Café, finding Alma May, the spidery little aged gal who ran the place, to be warm, spry, and friendly. She was chatty while she cooked and served the two former cutthroats until Pecos, swabbing the last of the grease from his plate with a baking powder biscuit, cleared his throat and asked, "I wonder if anyone's hirin' out at the gold mine."

Alma May was standing at her counter, filling her corncob pipe from an open tin of Union Leader. She jerked her eyes to Pecos, frowning, and said, "What gold mine?"

"The Spanish Bit," Slash told her, hooking an arm over the back of his chair, regarding her over his shoulder.

"We don't talk about the Spanish Bit around here, understand? It ain't healthy. Now, if you two handsome devils wanna make it to my age, you'll dry yourselves up on that topic an' go back to where you came from."

Before Slash or Pecos could probe her further, she swung around and disappeared through a curtained doorway. Presently, the sound of clattering pots and pans issued from the kitchen, as did the aromatic smoke of Alma May's corncob pipe.

Slash and Pecos shared a look. "We're makin' friends real fast here in Honeysuckle."

Slash finished his coffee and rose from his chair.

They fetched their saddlebags and rifles from the livery barn, then tramped over to the tall, narrow, three-story log hotel. The proprietor was an elderly gent named Dan Syvertson. Was everyone left in town, save the good-looking deputy town marshal, old? Likely, the young had had somewhere else to go when the boom went bust. The older folks did not, so they stayed on. Slash shivered, thinking about the chill of the snowy winters up in these climes.

Old Dan Syvertson remained in his padded rocking chair by a hot fire snapping and crackling in a stone hearth, stroking a large black cat stretched out on his lap. "A dollar a night for the two of you. Full payment up front. Sign the register and you can have, uh . . . room nine. *No!*"

Old Syvertson paused, studying the low timbered ceiling. "Was it room nine?" he asked himself, moving his lips beneath his chalk-white, soup-strainer mustache. His head was bald on top and badly liver-spotted, with a fringe of snowy hair around the sides, covering his ears. "No, no—room ten!" he amended. "Room ten."

He smiled sheepishly. "I was tryin' to remember the one with two beds. Fetch the key yourself from the ring there behind the counter, and don't be shootin' up the place or cavortin' with fallen women, or I'll sic the town law on ya, an' it won't go well for ya. No, sir! Toss your jingle on the counter there. I'll tend to it later, after Felix here has had his beauty sleep an' decides it's time to head out to wreak holy hell on the mouse population."

He chuckled and continued rocking and stroking the sound-asleep cat.

Slash and Pecos tossed their coins onto the counter.

Pecos plucked the key from the ring.

As he and Slash headed for the narrow, halved-log stairs flanking the lobby's front desk, Syvertson said, "Market hunters?"

Slash and Pecos glanced back at the old-timer. He was eyeing their rifles and the big sawed-off shotgun hanging down Pecos's back. "Somethin' like that," Slash said. " 'Night to ya, pops."

He and Pecos climbed the stairs to the second story. Pecos took the lead as they walked down the narrow hall, the floorboards squawking beneath their boots. Their spurs chimed softly. Otherwise, the building was silent.

Slash had a feeling that not only were there no other customers currently enjoying the hotel's accommodations, there likely hadn't been any rooms rented here in some weeks. Syvertson probably kept the place open because he had nowhere else to go, nothing else to do.

The hall was lit by the single window at the hall's far end. As the sun had sunk behind the western ridges over an hour ago, there wasn't much light left in this valley in which the town nestled, which meant the hall was in twilight edging toward deep darkness. Pecos stopped in front of room ten, identified by a small block of wood tacked to the door, with the number 10 burned into it. Balancing his saddlebags on his left shoulder and holding his rifle in his left hand, he fumbled the key into the lock.

Slash stepped up beside him. "Hold on."

Pecos glanced at him. "What?"

"What did you think about that look on old Syvertson's face?"

"Which one?"

"The one when he was trying to remember which room to put us in."

Pecos bunched his lips, shrugged. "So the old-timer had trouble rememberin' which room had two beds. Hell, you have trouble rememberin' which boot goes on which foot even when you ain't three sheets to the wind."

"All right—go ahead."

"Go ahead an' what?"

"Go ahead an' go on in. Throw caution to the wind!"

"Caution to the—?" Pecos scowled at his partner. "What, you think there's trouble on the other side of this door?"

"I reckon we're about to find out. You just go in first. Your big ugly carcass makes a good shield."

"Well, hell, now you're makin' me nervous."

"Go ahead, Mister Smart Mouth. Go on in."

"All right—I just will!" Pecos poked the key in the lock, jerked it angrily to one side. They heard the metallic rasp of the locking bolt being slid out of the frame and then the click as it fit snugly into the door. Pecos shoved the door open wide. "Here I am—goin' in fir—"

He took one step into the room and froze. He cursed softly.

Slash stood behind him, staring over Pecos's left shoulder. He drew a low, whistling breath through taut lips when he saw the silhouetted figure aiming a double-barrel shotgun straight out from his right shoulder.

Her right shoulder, he saw when she took two slow steps straight forward and into the watery, yellow light of a lamp burning on the room's wall in front of her. The deputy town marshal, Lisa, held the shotgun steady in both hands, the flickering light winking off her blue eyes beneath her hat brim and off the badge pinned to the swell of her denim shirt.

Slash could only see part of her face because of the room's dancing shadows, but it was her, all right. The angry eyes and the badge gave her away, as did the signature swells of her denim-clad figure.

"Make one ill-advised move toward any of that arsenal you two cutthroats are carryin'," she said tightly, "an' I'll go to work with this twelve-gauge, an' Old Syvertson will be scrubbin' you both off the walls from now till Christmas!"

CHAPTER 29

"Now, what'd I tell ya, Mister Smart Mouth?" Slash poked Pecos in the back. "I don't know what you call that there, but I call it trouble. Honey, did you say that was a twelve-gauge?"

"I did say it was a twelve-gauge."

"Ain't that funny? That's what my big, stupid friend here carries."

"Shut up."

Slash raised his left hand and the rifle he held in his right hand, keeping the barrel aimed at the ceiling. "All right, I will. I will shut up."

The young woman backed up. "Step in here. Like I said, you try anything . . ."

"Oh, I know," Slash said, following Pecos into the room, the man's broad back and shoulders right in front of him. "That's a twelve-gauge. I know what a twelve-gauge can do, 'cause, like I said, my friend here—"

"I told you to shut up," the young deputy said, her voice as taut as freshly stretched barbed wire, and just as prickly. She stared straight down the double bores at the two men as she pressed her back up against a dresser, which was the room's only furnishing aside from the two small beds covered in bearskins. "Now, close the door."

"What you got in mind, darlin'?" Slash asked.

"Not what you're thinkin'," the girl shot back at him, through gritted teeth. "You two are nearly as old as Old Syvertson, an' he's so old the hills stand up and give him their chairs!"

"Not by a long shot!" Pecos said. She'd finally riled the big man into speech.

"Pretty close."

"Syvertson's old enough to be our father," Slash pointed out, also feeling nettled by the girl's arrogance. It was one thing for a pretty young woman to threaten a man's life with a double-bore shotgun, another altogether to assume he was older than he really was.

Slash closed the door.

"Just wanted to make sure you didn't try to skin out on me," the young deputy said, still aiming down the barrel. "Now—all guns on the bed. Slow. One by one. Any fast moves an' they'll be dumpin' you both out of the same bucket into a single grave."

"You sure got a way with words," Pecos said, dropping his Colt revolving rifle onto the bed to his right.

Slash dropped his own rifle on the same bed. "She paints a right purty picture, don't she?"

When all their guns were on the bed, their bowie knives as well, and their hands were in the air, Pecos said, "Now suppose you tell us what this is all about. We haven't been in town long enough to have broken the law."

"You two old cutthroats have broken plenty of laws," the girl said. She laughed caustically, showing the white ends of her teeth, her blue eyes flat and hard. "I know who you two are. Slash Braddock an' the Pecos River Kid. Pa was pretty damn sure when he seen you ride into town, but after I took a look at you over to the Honeysuckle, I went back over to the office and shuffled through a stack of ancient wanted circulars."

"There she goes insultin' our ages again, Slash," Pecos said, keeping his hands in the air.

"Young folks these days."

"Most folks prob'ly couldn't tell from the likenesses on those old pictures."

"They could tell, all right," Slash said. "We haven't changed all that much."

"But I could tell," the young deputy continued. "I've been a student of your work for a long time. I've read about your depravations and sundry reprehensible high jinks in the *Police Gazette* and the *Rocky Mountain News*. You robbed the Atchison, Topeka and Santa Fe more times than anybody. For five years running, the Butterfield Stage Company put a four-thousand-dollar bounty on your heads. They wanted you shot on sight! You rode with Pistol Pete an' was there when that old scalawag an' reprobate was killed in the Lunatic Mountains. You paralyzed Chief Marshal Luther T. 'Bleed-Em-So' Bledsoe, an'—"

Pecos pointed an angry finger at her. "Pete weren't no scalawag an' reprobate. He was a man to ride the river with, Pete was!"

"And as honest as the day is long!" Slash said. "An' wounding Bledsoe was an accident, though he sure had it comin'."

Without blinking, sliding her bright-eyed, zealous gaze between the two veteran owlhoots, the young deputy continued. "You once rode the border country with 'Cormorant' Jim Clark and Sassy Maldoon and Frank Sanchez until Judge Isaac Parker's deputies ran Clark an' Maldoon down in the Indian Territory an' gave 'em necktie parties in Fort Smith. Tilghman killed Clark in Taos. You killed Wild Wayne Tatum in Cross-Eyed Kate's Parlor House in Bisbee, Arizona—"

"That was a fair fight," Slash pointed out, defensively. "He drew on me first, but he was so drunk he—"

". . . an' they call you Slash 'cause Roscoe Lee Rose caught you cheatin' at stud poker an' tried to cut out your heart."

"I've never cheated at poker a day in my life!"

"Hah!" Pecos said.

She cut her eyes to Pecos. "They say you once sparked the actress Delilah O'Bannon."

"That's true," Pecos pointed out a little sadly. "She broke my heart."

"He sparked her, all right," Slash laughed, "till her husband found them together, drunker than Georgia moonshiners in the storeroom in the White Buffalo Saloon in Cheyenne, an'—"

"That's enough, Slash!" Pecos said.

"He still has buckshot where the sun don't shine due to that reprehensible bit of cuckolding high jinks," Slash told the shotgun-wielding young woman. "It wasn't a broken heart he got out of the deal. It was a mighty sore ass!"

Pecos whipped toward him, gritting his teeth and clenching his fists at his sides. "That does it—I'm haulin' you outside, an' I'm gonna—"

"Pipe down, both of you!" the girl yelled.

Pecos turned back to her, remembering that she was holding a shotgun on them. "Say, uh, darlin'," he said, frowning curiously at her, "what's this all about, anyways? We left trouble behind us, an' we're only just passin' through Honeysuckle. We don't do what we used to do no more. We've settled down."

"Tame as the widow lady's parlor cats," Slash added.

"Tame as the widow lady's parlor cats—my foot!" Deputy Lisa removed one hand from her shotgun, reached behind, plucked a pair of handcuffs from her belt, and tossed them at Pecos, who caught them against his chest. She tossed a second set to Slash, then reestablished her two-handed grip on the barn-blaster. "Put on them bracelets. Make 'em tight. I'm takin' you in. Gonna get you off the streets. Gonna send for a couple of deputy U.S. marshals from Denver so they can haul you down out of the mountains and string you up!"

A deep flush burned in her cheeks. She'd followed the cutthroats' careers, and now, improbably, unexpectedly, she— way out here on the backside of nowhere—was going to be the lawman . . . er, law *woman* . . . to burn them down!

Slash and Pecos shared a glance, silently conferring on whether to tell her about their deal with Chief Marshal Bledsoe. With their eyes, they warned each other to keep quiet. Neither was entirely sure why—maybe an old, habitual suspicion about other folks' true motives—but they decided the information could wait until they knew exactly what the young law woman was really up to.

"Well, Slash, I reckon she's got us," Pecos said, ratcheting the cuffs around his wrists.

Slash winced at the ominous sound of his own cuffs racketing closed. "I reckon she does at that."

"Turn around, open the door, and move out. Don't try anything or I'll blast you, and old Syvertson . . ."

"We know, we know," Slash said, dourly as he fumbled the door open with both cuffed hands, "old Syvertson will be scrubbing us off the walls till May Day."

"You got it."

Slash led the threesome down the hall and then down the stairs. Hearing the boot thumps and spur chimes on the stairs, old Syvertson looked up, the big black cat still sprawled on his lap. The old man's eyes glinted devilishly, and he grinned in kind.

"You got 'em, Lisa. Good on ya! I'm just glad they paid in advance." He chuckled.

"Thank you for cooperating with law and order," Lisa said, prodding the two cutthroats across the hotel's small, shadowy lobby and out the front door. "I'll be back for their gear."

"You keep 'em locked up tight, now," the old man urged.

"I don't want 'em comin' back and wreakin' their savage re-venge on me an' Felix here!"

"Don't worry, Pops—you and Felix can rest easy," Lisa called behind her, as she thumped on down the porch steps behind her two prisoners. "These two cutthroats' days of death an' destruction are over!"

"*Yippee-ky-yaaaa!*" came the old man's gleeful cry behind them, as he stomped his feet on the floor.

Slash and Pecos walked side by side straight down the near-dark street. The only lights were those emanating from the town's two saloons, on opposite sides of the street from each other, and from Alma May's Café. A penetrating chill had descended. Though not a breath of wind moved along the street, Slash could hear the constant roar of the breeze assaulting the high, stony, pine-stippled ridges above and beyond Honeysuckle.

As he moved along the street, approaching the squat jailhouse just ahead now and on his right, he decided to take what little advantage of the situation he could by trying to glean some information from the pretty, young, overzealous lawdog.

"Deputy?" he called to the girl, who remained a safe distance behind him and Pecos.

"Shut up."

"Ah, come on," Slash complained. "I was just wonderin' what it is you could think me an' my depraved partner was hunting here in Honeysuckle. I mean, it don't look like you have a bank or anything like that."

"Yeah," Pecos chimed in. "Not even a Western Union office, as far as I can tell."

"Shut up," came the girl's cold reply, beneath her crunching boots.

Slash glanced at his partner and gave a defeated sigh.

"Nice try, anyway, partner," Pecos said.

"Thanks."

"No talking!" the girl ordered.

"You're a toughnut, ain't ya?" Pecos asked her.

"No talking!"

Pecos leaned toward Slash and whispered, "You really think she'd shoot us for talking?"

Slash glanced back at her walking forthrightly behind them, keeping the scattergun aimed at their backs. Then he returned his gaze to Slash. "Yeah. Yeah, I do."

Slash walked up to the jailhouse's front door and stopped. Pecos stopped behind him. Slash turned to the girl.

"What, you need me to open it for you an' give you a warm welcome, maybe offer you a biscuit and some tea?" she said snidely. "Go on in—it ain't locked, and we don't affect city manners, Pa an' me."

Slash gazed at her. He glanced at the solid stone building behind him, a light showing in the one lone window left in the door. His guts recoiled at the idea of being locked up. For all his years running on the wrong side of the straight and narrow, he'd spent only a handful of days behind bars at any one time.

And he hadn't liked them at all. Even the idea of being locked up in an iron cage turned his blood cold.

He looked at the shotgun in the girl's hands, considered making a play for it. He still had his pearl-gripped Derringer in his right-hand coat pocket. The girl hadn't thought to look for a hideout weapon, her only weakness as far as Slash could tell.

Lisa backed up a step and quirked her mouth corners up in a wry, challenging grin. "Go ahead," she said, reading Slash's mind. "I'd like you to. I'd love to have my name in the *Rocky Mountain News* . . . right beside your death notice."

Pecos arched a warning brow at him. "I think she really would, partner." He gave his head a quick, fateful wag. "She's got the drop on us, all right."

Slash spat angrily into the dust. He doubted he'd have time

to get the Derringer clear of his pocket before she shredded him. He'd save the surprise of the nasty little popper for later.

He flipped the metal door latch and stepped into the small but homey-looking jailhouse office. The man Slash and Pecos had seen before, sitting out in front of the place and then on the porch of the butcher shop/grocery store, was now kicked back in a chair behind a rolltop desk to Slash's left, facing the front wall. The town marshal had his boots propped on the desk. He leaned back in a wooden swivel chair, long arms crossed on his broad chest, snoring raucously, his thick red mustache blowing up with every exhalation.

"Go on," Lisa said, prodding both Slash and Pecos with her shotgun's barrel. "Get in there!"

"Ouch!" Slash protested, stumbling forward.

The old lawman awoke with a startled jerk and an anxious gasp, sitting up in his chair with an angry squawk of the swivel. He reached first for the big, horn-gripped hogleg resting atop the desk, then, realizing a lead swap wasn't imminent, reached for the rectangular spectacles beside the heavy Colt. He placed them on his nose and stretched the bows behind his ears.

"What . . . what in God's name are you up to, Lisa?" he grumbled, peering through the rectangular lenses, his voice thick and phlegmy from what had apparently been a protracted nap.

"Well, I'll be damned," Slash said, standing in the middle of the room, staring at the man in wide-eyed astonishment. "Hey, Pecos—lookee who we got here." A smile spread Slash's lips and glittered in his brown eyes.

"Ah, hell," Pecos said, his own features betraying his shock and recognition. He thrust his arm up and a finger forward. "That there's Red . . . Red . . . Red . . ."

"Ingram," Slash finished for him.

"Damn, Red," Pecos said. "I didn't recognize you from a

distance. I didn't know that was you out there, givin' us the woolly eyeball!"

"Likewise," the tall, red-haired, red-mustached, and red-muttonchopped lawman said, placing both knobby fists on the desk before him and rising stiffly from his chair. "I didn't recognize you two fellas, neither, at first. It was Lisa who done that, though she's never seen you in the flesh like I have. She recognized you from your likenesses sketched on wanted circulars over the years, which she peruses with the frequency and pious zeal of a Baptist preacher flipping through his Bible."

Red Ingram's flinty gaze was on his daughter. "I told you to stay clear of these two scalawags, *Deputy*. What'd you do—wait for me to drift asleep, then waltz into the Honeysuckle to arrest 'em?"

"Not at all," Lisa bragged. "I was waiting in the hotel. Took 'em down easy as pie. Why, I've arrested passed-out drunks who had more teeth to 'em."

Slash and Pecos scowled at the wild young woman indignantly. Then Slash said, "This is your daughter, Red?"

"That she is, that she is, I am sometimes sorry to say," Ingram confessed. "For some dang reason, I saw fit to pin a deputy town marshal's star to her shirt. But only because after the boom went bust, there was nobody else to pin it on." Again, his reproving gaze shot to his daughter. "How many times do you think you can disobey my direct orders before I'll fire you, Lisa?"

"Pa!" the girl said, stomping her foot in exasperation. "I just took down two of the gnarliest criminals in all the western frontier. I arrested Slash Braddock an' the Pecos River Kid!"

"Yeah—you did, did you? Now, what you suppose you're gonna do with 'em?"

"I'm gonna lock 'em up!" Again, Lisa prodded the two cutthroats with her shotgun barrel, jerking her chin toward one of the three cells lining the stone building's rear wall. "Get in there, and be quick about it, or I'll—"

"Yeah, yeah, we know," Pecos said as Slash opened the door of the middle cell. "They'll be scrubbin' us off the walls till the cows come home." He glanced at Red Ingram standing at his desk. "She's got colorful language, anyway, Red. I'll give her that!"

"She comes by her nastiness honestly," Slash added. "I'll give her that, too!"

When Lisa Ingram had turned the big key in the cell door's lock, she swung toward her father, frowning. "What'd he mean by that?"

Red winced and walked over to the potbelly stove standing in the middle of the room. A speckled black coffeepot was steaming atop the stove. Ingram grabbed a tin cup from a nail in a ceiling support post by the stove, and a leather pad, and filled the cup with hot black mud. "Ummm, daughter, I been meanin' to tell you this for some time now, but . . ."

Red seemed to have trouble proceeding.

"Um *what*?" Lisa said, canting her head to one side.

"He was an outlaw before he ever became a lawman," Slash told her.

"For a very short time," Red said.

"But he was a bad one, old Red Ingram was. Until he saw fit to change his ways. Then he was a county sheriff over in Utah. Tangled with us a time or two."

"Almost caught you, too—damn your rancid hides!" Ingram glowered at the two cutthroats peering back at him through the cell's bars. "The only reason I wasn't able to quite run you down was because I, being only a county sheriff in some of the remotest territory anywhere in the country, was badly outmanned. You always seemed to somehow slither over one territorial line after another—gone from sight."

He sipped his coffee, swallowed, then eyed Slash and Pecos again, severely. "If you'd stayed in Utah a little longer, I likely would have turned the key on you at the very least, possibly turned you both toe down, which would have been no worse than what you deserved."

"Not much to rob out thataway," Pecos said. "We was just cooling our heels out in Utah, robbing a few stagecoaches now an' then just to keep from gettin' bored."

"What in the hell are you doing here, Red?" Slash asked the lawman now standing by the cell door, beside his fiery daughter. "You an' this bronco of a daughter of yours."

Slash glanced at the girl again. Now, in the light, he saw that she was a true beauty. Whereas Hattie Friendly was china-doll beautiful, this young woman, roughly Hattie's age, was a wild child of the mountains, with fiery blue eyes and wild hair and obviously the temper of a she-lion with cubs. Her face was oval-shaped, with a pug nose, and a firm jaw along the same lines as her father's. Her hair was sort of a tawny red, and its unkempt condition, hanging down from beneath her Stetson in knots and tangles, flecked with dust and seeds, somehow added to her raw, natural beauty.

She was as wild as the mountains, this girl.

The years obviously hadn't been kind to her father. Slash had noticed that Red walked with a limp. While a big man, he'd been whittled down to bones and sinew, and his face, sandwiched by the thick red muttonchops, looked a little like that of an embalmed Indian—one with eyes the same sky blue as his daughter's, though touched with the cream splotches of cataracts that were likely the result of all his years hunting owlhoots in the burning Utah sun.

CHAPTER 30

"What brings me here to Honeysuckle?" Red Ingram said, peering through the cell bars at Slash and Pecos. "I came here with the others when gold was found in the quartz veins and slab rock lining the creeks up thisaway. I'd had to turn in my badge over in Utah."

He reached down to pat his left knee. "Took a bullet to this leg during a bank robbery. Damn near shattered my knee. A sawbones put it back together again, but I can't ride like I used to, an' even if I could, Lisa here has to help me into the saddle. Damned embarrassin'."

Red sipped his coffee.

"When the boom went bust, the town offered me the badge an' a monthly salary. Figured there wouldn't be much to do except collect taxes an' arrest a drunk now an' then, an', until now . . . when you two old cutthroats rode into town . . . I was right. I hired Lisa because she wanted the job so bad, bein' a student of the law as well as *bad men*, and I needed some way to keep her out of trouble, with all the lowly men in these parts doggin' her heels with their tongues hangin' out."

Lisa flushed and looked away, but a pleased grin twitched

at her mouth corners, as though she was embarrassed by a compliment.

Again, Red sipped his coffee and slid his milky gaze between the two incarcerated cutthroats. "That's what I'm doin' here. Now, suppose you tell me what you two are doin' here."

"An' who's that prissy little miss slingin' drinks in the Honeysuckle?" Lisa asked sharply, flaring her nostrils at the two jailbirds. "She rode in with you. I seen her."

"Daughter?" Red asked, arching a brow at each former cutthroat in turn.

Slash gave a dry chuff. "Does either of us look purty enough to have fathered that little chestnut-haired filly?"

"The mother would have to be one hell of a looker, I'll give you that," Red said.

"You can say that again," Lisa added, with little of her father's good-natured ribbing.

"You have your mother's beauty but little of her charm," Slash told her.

"You never knew my mother."

"No, but your old man's as ugly as a boar hog, and a snake has more charm than you do."

"Admit it—I rattled you," Lisa said with a smug smile.

"Let's get back to the looker in the Honeysuckle," Ingram said with loud impatience, beetling his red brows.

"We just picked her up along the trail," Pecos said. "An orphan child. Her old man . . ." He glanced at Slash. "Didn't she say he was a prospector, Slash?"

"Yeah, yeah, a pick 'n' shoveler. Died from a cave-in. The poor child's mother was a doxie from Leadville. Dead. Now, with the father dead, she had nowhere else to go, so she was heading to Denver but got turned around on the trail. She was wanderin' this way all alone in the big cruel world, so we let her throw in with us . . ."

"For protection from vermin trail thieves."

"Like yourselves," Lisa said. "I'm surprised you didn't rob her blind or worse . . ."

"Well," Slash said, shortly, "she didn't have nothin' to rob, and while we might be vermin trail thieves, our honor is intact as is hers."

"How long that will last, with her workin' amongst your unwashed populace over at the Honeysuckle in little enough cloth to swaddle a newborn baby, I wouldn't want to wager on," Pecos added.

Red Ingram walked up close to the cell, narrowing one suspicious eye and arching the other brow. His coffee cup steamed in his big, knotted right hand. "Now for the big question—what are you two doin' here?"

"Just driftin' through," Pecos said.

"No one drifts through Honeysuckle," the tough, pretty, tangle-haired deputy pointed out.

"We didn't know that," Slash said. "So I reckon we'll be driftin' back the way we came."

"You're here to rob the gold—admit it!" Lisa yelled. "Come out an' admit it, or I'll blast you!"

She stepped back and raised the shotgun in her hands once more, rearing back both heavy hammers with ratcheting clicks.

Slash cast the marshal an imploring look. "Leash your wildcat, Red!"

Red said, "Lisa, galldangit—put that scattergun down before you hurt someone!"

"They're here for the gold, Pa! I'm gonna make 'em admit it!"

"They can't admit it if they're running down the back wall yonder. Now put the gun down, child!" Ingram glanced at Slash and Pecos. "I do apologize for her behavior, fellas. She lost her mother when she was shin-high to a tadpole, so she knows only her father's raggedy ways. I've been softening in my later years, but Lisa here is still hardening up."

"She does need some tempering," Pecos admitted, eyeing the wild child cautiously through the cell bars.

"You might try a finishing school back East," Slash advised.

"I'm gonna finish you right here less'n you admit you're here for the Spanish Bit gold," Lisa threatened, staring down the double-barrel greener at the prisoners.

Slash and Pecos shared a quick, conferring glance, then returned their gaze to the big twin barrels bearing down on them.

"Lisa, give me that." Ingram set his coffee cup down and wrapped his big hands around the shotgun.

"No, Pa!"

"Give it here, dammit, before that cannon goes off an' we got one hell of a mess to clean up!"

Slash and Pecos stepped back from the cell door, flinching, before Red Ingram had finally wrestled the big double-bore out of his daughter's hands without detonating either barrel. Lisa looked up at the old man, face flushed with fury, her hat on the floor, her thick hair lying in tangles down the side of her head and on her shoulders.

"Pa, you ain't gonna get nowhere coddling those two old cutthroats!"

"Don't worry, we'll have 'em on a diet of bread an' water pronto!"

"Now you're just makin' fun!" Lisa shot back at him, rage flashing in her eyes. "You never wanted to arrest 'em in the first place."

Red glanced at Slash and Pecos sheepishly. "Well, hell . . . they got federal bounties on their heads. Let the feds handle 'em. I don't get paid enough to hold two cutthroats as mean an' nasty as Slash Braddock and the Pecos River Kid."

"We'll take that as a compliment," Slash said, dryly. He

didn't want to mention that he and Pecos had both received pardons from none other than the president himself. He wasn't sure why, but something held him back. He'd show those cards only when absolutely necessary.

To his daughter, Red said, "You go make your last rounds now, Lisa. Then head on home to bed. I'll stay here and sleep in my chair, keep an eye on these two curly wolves. Maybe see if I can't pry a little more information out of 'em."

Lisa scooped her hat off the floor and glanced at her father sidelong. "You're not gonna let 'em go—are ya, Pa?"

"Oh, hell, no. Not since you went and arrested 'em. I'll send a rider over to Aspen bright an' early tomorrow morning, have him send a telegram to Denver. I'll have the chief marshal send a couple of deputies for these two raggedy-assed owlhoots. They'll be doin' the midair two-step inside of two weeks." Red placed a hand behind his head, pantomiming a rope, and made violent strangling sounds, sticking out his tongue and puffing out his cheeks.

Lisa smiled joyfully. "You promise?"

Red placed a tender hand on the girl's cheek and beamed down at her. "Would I lie to my purtiest daughter?"

"I'm your only daughter."

"Oh, that's right—I'm so old I forget!" Red laughed. "Run along now, girl. I'll watch 'em tonight. You can watch 'em tomorrow night. You know I sleep better sittin' up in a chair, anyways."

"All right, Poppa." Lisa glanced once more in disdain at the two incarcerated cutthroats, then placed her Greener in the rack by the door, blew her adoring father a kiss with her hand, and left.

"That's quite the deputy you got there, Red," Pecos said, staring at the door through which Lisa had disappeared. The soft thumps of her footsteps dwindled off down the street.

"I'll take that as a compliment," Red said, pouring himself another cup of coffee.

When he'd set the pot back on the stove, he took a sip, then looked at his two prisoners again. "If you ain't here for the Spanish Bit gold, what are you here for?"

"We never even heard of the Spanish Bit until your deputy mentioned it," Slash lied.

"Yeah, what is the Spanish Bit, anyways?" Pecos asked, making the question sound innocent enough, though that was the question burning in both his and Slash's minds.

Red took another sip of his coffee and eyed both prisoners suspiciously. "Gold mine. The first one in the area, and the last one. The only one left. When the poor quality of the gold in this area, not to mention the scarcity of it, drove everyone else out, the Spanish Bit remained. A big mine connected to a big ranch. They send gold out of these mountains once every couple of months. They send it with a whole passel of heavily armed guards. So far . . . no one has been fool enough to make a play for it. Let me warn you fellas that even back in your heyday, the Spanish Bit gold would have been out of your league."

"No point in gettin' nasty, Red," Slash said.

"Hell, we'd like as not have made a play for it back in our prime," Pecos countered, "but seein' as how we don't have a gang anymore, and we're old—leastways, Slash is old—it's probably a might out of our reach. You're right."

Slash turned to the town marshal. "Come on, Red. You know we're not here for the Spanish Bit gold. We're just coolin' our heels, that's all. Why don't you let us go? We're not worth the trouble. I know it'll hurt your daughter's feelin's all to hell—seein' as how she's countin' on seein' the feds play cat's cradle with our necks an' all—but maybe, to make it up to her, you could buy her a pony instead."

All three men had a good laugh at that.

Pecos wiped tears of humor from his eyes and said, "Open the door, Red. It'll be our secret."

"I don't know, boys," Red said, stepping back and studying the floor as though for a course of action. "I'm gonna have to ponder on it. I'll sleep on it an' get back to you in the mornin'. What I should do is exactly what I said—send for the marshals. But seein' as how you're no longer runnin' with your gang, an' you're damn near as old as I am—"

"Hold on, now," Slash said. "I don't think we're that—"

Slash elbowed him hard, cutting him off.

Slash drew a mouth corner down.

". . . and likely not even worth the expense of a trial and a hangin'," Red continued from where Slash had interrupted him, "I'll study on it overnight and get back to you tomorrow."

He yawned and set his empty coffee cup on his desk. "I'll be hanged!" he said, stretching. "It ain't all that late, but I'm sooo tired, I reckon I'm gonna fold my old bones back into this chair and pick up where I left off when you boys an' my daughter so rudely interrupted me."

Pecos yawned. "I think I'm about ready to head that way myself."

He sagged down onto one of the cell's two cots and tossed his hat onto the floor.

"I reckon I might as well, too, then," Slash said. He sat down, kicked out of his boots, lay down on the cot, rested his head on the flat, musty pillow that smelled of too many other men's sweat, and drew the single wool blanket up to his chin.

" 'Night, fellas," Red said, and blew out the lamp.

" 'Night, Red," Pecos said.

"Yeah, g'night, Red." Slash yawned, squirmed around on the unfamiliar cot, getting comfortable, and closed his eyes.

The night was so quiet, even here at the heart of town, that Slash and Pecos both felt themselves slip right off into deep sleep despite the uncertainty of their futures. The night was less than restful, however.

Slash woke up after what he thought wasn't much over an hour of shut-eye to Red's raucous snoring. Slash had shared camp with some loud woodcutters before, but Red had those old roarers beat by double and maybe even three times. The town marshal of Honeysuckle snored so loudly he made the floor shudder. He sounded like a dragon sitting right outside the cell door, getting ramped up to burn another village.

"Jumpin' Jehosophat, Red," Slash yelled, "stuff a sock in your mouth!"

Red stopped snoring long enough for Slash to fall back asleep, only to be awakened not much later by Pecos yelling, "Slash, for godsakes, roll your skinny-assed carcass over! You're snorin' even louder than Red was!"

Slash hadn't been back asleep for more than another half hour before Pecos started bringing the building down with his own snoring. He and Red both yelled at him to turn over. When Pecos hauled his big body over, making the cot creak dangerously, and lay facedown, merciful silence once more fell over the jailhouse.

But not for long.

All night, the three unfettered snorers played round robin, trying to get at least one and sometimes two of the others to wake up and try another position. Slash was almost glad to see the gray wash of dawn in the jailhouse's lone front window. Red Ingram woke himself up with another crow-like snore and lowered his feet to the floor. He rose creakily, snorting and hacking phlegm into the sandbox beside his desk.

"Ah, god," he said. "Ah, god . . ."

He tramped, sort of wobbling on his hips, out away from his desk, his boots drumming on the hard-packed earthen floor. He snagged a key ring off a ceiling support post by the cold woodstove and jabbed a key into the cell door's lock. He twisted the key and swung open the door. He beckoned broadly, still wobbling like a landed sailor after months at sea, and hacked more phlegm from his lungs.

"Out," he croaked, swinging his arm again, as though hazing cattle through a chute, and jerked his chin toward the office's front door. "Out with ya both. Go on—haul your freight!"

"What's goin' on?" Pecos asked. He'd been half-asleep when the door had squawked open. Now he lifted his head from his pillow, blinking.

Slash stomped into his boots and scooped his hat off the floor. "Ain't sure, but I think we're gettin' the bum's rush."

"Out—both of ya!" Red croaked again, blinking his sleepy eyes. "Get out! Out! I ain't a young man. I can't afford another night's sleep like that one. A man my age needs quality shut-eye, by god!"

"All right, all right, Red," Pecos said. "Just let me get my boots on!"

"Out! Out! Out!"

"Hurry, partner," Slash said, "before he changes his mind."

"Out now an' *to hell with both your cutthroat hides*!" Red bellowed.

Stomping into his second boot, Pecos glanced at Slash and said, "I don't think he's gonna change his mind. It looks like he's plumb tired o' the both of us."

"Well, let's pull foot before his wildcat daughter shows up for work," Slash said, hurrying out of the cell and tramping toward the office door. "I for one am right allergic to twelve-gauge buck!"

"Out of here and out of town!" Red yelled as Pecos, setting his hat on his head, hurried to catch up to Slash. "Out of town right now. Before sunrise! Don't dally, an' don't show your faces in Honeysuckle again or you'll be settlin' up with my daughter and her double-bore!"

Tucking his shirttails into his pants, Pecos jogged to catch up to Slash. Falling into step beside the shorter man, he said, "What do you think of that?"

"I think you an' your snorin' wore out your welcome. Mine, too, I guess."

"*My* snorin'?" Pecos laughed without mirth. "Hell, I thought you an' ole Red was gonna bring the house down!"

"Oh, shut up!"

"Why didn't you draw the Derringer? I know you still had it."

"Oh, I would have if it came to that. But first I wanted to hear more about the Spanish Bit. I wanted to hear a little more about Red and his wild-assed daughter, too."

"You think they're legit?"

"Who knows?"

"Well, what're we gonna do now?"

"What can we do?" Slash said. "I reckon we'd best high-tail it out of town unless we want to face Lisa Ingram again an' that twelve-gauge she's so damned fond of."

"But . . . but what about the gold?"

Slash stopped in front of the hotel. "I said we're leavin' town. We're not givin' up on the gold. No—not by a long shot. Let's fetch our gear from room ten—if old Syvertson hasn't already hocked it, that is—an' take a ride deeper into the mountains, see if we can't locate the Spanish Bit Ranch and Gold Mine."

Slash turned to start up the steps of the hotel's front veranda.

Behind him, Pecos said, "You think we're gonna find *stolen* gold at a *gold mine*?"

"I know it don't make sense," Slash said, trying the hotel's front door.

Locked.

He glanced at Pecos and said, "It don't make sense *now*, but I'll be damned if it won't *soon*."

"If we live till *soon*," Pecos grumbled, glancing warily back in the direction of the stone jailhouse. Another thought occurred to him. "What about Hattie?"

"What about her?"

"We can't just leave her in town all alone."

"Ah, hell," Slash said. "That purty little Pink can take care of herself."

Slash rapped loudly on the hotel's front door.

CHAPTER 31

Two hours earlier, Hattie had awakened with a start. At first, she couldn't remember where she was. The room around her, cloaked in the shadows of the predawn darkness, resembled a room in some fragmented dream, like the nonsensical dreams she often had just before waking.

The room was small, barely larger than a broom closet. She could see the flowered wallpaper and the dresser on her left.

She also saw the skimpy outfit lying on top of it, where she'd left it last night after the saloon had closed just after midnight. It all came back to her—the stolen gold, the town, the job, and the Honeysuckle Saloon and Dance Hall.

She also remembered the noise she'd heard in her sleep, which had awakened her. The faint chirp of a floorboard. She peered toward the door standing three feet from the foot of her bed. She looked at the crack between the door and the floor. An eerie blue light shone dimly in the crack. The light was broken by a single dark blob, as though someone were standing there, just outside the door, the person's feet blocking the light.

Hattie could almost feel the man standing there. At the moment, she couldn't hear him, but the prickling of the fine hairs across the back of her neck, and a chill in her belly, told the young Pinkerton detective that a man was there, sure enough.

She thought she could hear him breathing. She thought she could also hear a slight creak in the door, as though the man were pressing his weight against it.

Hattie's belly grew colder.

Her blood quickened through her veins.

"I know you're out there," she said softly, so that only the man in the hall could hear. "Go away, or I'll yell for Mister Hicks!"

The door creaked faintly again. It was joined by a faint snicking sound, like the soft brush of cloth against wood. The man was pressing himself up against the door.

Hattie thought she could even smell him now—a sickly sweet, unwashed man smell.

Her heart thudding, she tossed her covers aside and dropped her feet to the floor. She grabbed a robe off a chair back and pulled it on. She slid her feet into rabbit-skin slippers, then slid her Derringer out from beneath the corset and bustier on the dresser.

Slowly, quietly, she walked to the door. Her heart was really beating now. It beat so hard, rapping against her ribs, that it ached.

She drew a deep breath and pressed an ear to the door. She winced when a floorboard gave a faint chirp beneath her left foot. On the other side of the door, another floorboard squawked. The door creaked as though from the sudden removal of the man's weight.

"Hello?" Hattie said, staring at the door. "You go away, or I'll—"

Quickly, she twisted the key in the lock, then turned the doorknob. She opened the door a crack, half expecting the man to shove the door wide and throw himself on top of her. Ready for such a move, she raised the Derringer in her right hand and pressed her thumb against the hammer, ready to draw it back and fire.

But no one stood before her.

The floor chirped to her left. She whipped her head that way in time to glimpse a man—or a person, anyway—turn the hall corner and head for the stairs.

"Hey!" Hattie rasped, angrily.

The only response was a clipped, high-pitched, mocking chuckle.

Squeezing the Derringer in her right hand, Hattie hurried down the hall to her left. She glanced down the stairs in time to see a man's silhouette turn the corner at the bottom and disappear, boots or shoes thudding softly. There was another soft, mocking chuckle.

Hattie frowned down the carpeted steps, heart no longer racing as fast as before, a deep suspicion tempering her fear. "Who in the . . . ?"

Probably one of her customers from the previous night. Maybe he'd spent the night up here, with either Lilly or Iris. He was maybe still drunk and, knowing which room belonged to Hattie, who had recently become known in these environs as "Rose," had decided to have a little fun. She should probably let it . . . and him . . . go.

But she was a true-blue Pinkerton. Her curiosity would not yield. Maybe that was a good thing. Maybe the man had had more on his mind than merely pulling an impish joke on an attractive saloon girl. And, anyway, who did he think he was, trying to frighten her like that?

Hattie hurried down the stairs, her slippers nearly soundless on the carpeted steps, her robe winging out to both sides, as did her hair, which she'd given only a cursory brushing after retiring to her room. She'd been so tired after all those hours on her feet, and so sore from being pinched and grabbed all night, that she'd fallen right to sleep.

She gained the bottom of the stairs and made the sharp

turn around the newel post on her right. She headed down the short hall toward the saloon's back door, which was open a crack. The man had gone out that way and had not latched the door behind him. She stepped up to it, shoved it open a foot, and stuck her head out.

She looked both ways along the rear of the saloon. She heard another mocking laugh and jerked her head forward to peer straight out ahead of her. The man stood half behind a shed about fifty feet straight out beyond her, peering with one eye back toward her. The half of his mouth that she could see was twisted in a mocking grin.

He pulled his head back behind the shed, and once again he was gone.

Hattie ground her back teeth and bounded forward. As she moved out away from the hotel's rear door, she realized her mistake. She'd let herself get flanked. She heard at least one person, possibly two, move up from behind her. They must have been standing to each side of the hotel, hidden. There was a strained grunt, and as Hattie began to whip around, raising the Derringer, a burlap bag was pulled down over her head and shoulders, slamming her arm down.

The Derringer barked in her right hand, the slug plunking into the ground dangerously close to her feet.

Hattie tried to scream, but someone grabbed her tightly, placing something, maybe a hand, over her mouth. Arms snaked around her, and two men, whom she could hear laughing devilishly, picked her up off the ground and began carrying her quickly—in which direction, she did not know.

She was badly disoriented. Her heart was back racing again in terror. She could barely breathe in the tight sack, and what little air she was able to suck into her lungs was fetid with the pine-tar smell of burlap. She felt as though she were drowning inside the sack, and she fought desperately, kicking, trying to punch her assailants, but to no avail.

One of them held her arms fast against her sides, while the other held her legs.

They carried her maybe a hundred jostling feet, turning sharply once, then stopped and set her brusquely down on something. Whatever they'd set her on, it was all sharp edges and very uncomfortable. Mixed with the smell of the burlap was the verdant, piney aroma of wood. They'd set her on a woodpile.

"Pull the sack off," ordered a low, dull voice that Hattie thought sounded vaguely feminine. "Hurry up, Vernon, dammit!" the speaker added, sounding even more like a female, but a female with a low, hoarse, unpleasant voice.

Vernon pulled the sack off Hattie's head. She raked in a deep breath as her hair fell back down around her shoulders, tumbling against her face. Cool, fresh air pressed against her. She drew it into her lungs and looked around, squinting into the murky, dawn shadows.

Sure enough, she was sitting on a woodpile inside a small shed. Four people stood in a ragged semicircle around her. One was a woman. The other three were men. They wore trail gear and pistols. The woman's stout body was clad in a knee-length wool coat secured with a wide, brown belt to which were attached two holsters housing long-barreled revolvers. She wore high men's riding boots. On her head was a floppy-brimmed felt hat. A chin thong dangled down her lumpy chest.

Hattie thought she might have been in her early thirties, maybe a little older. Her cheeks were fat enough to be smooth, the eyes darkly shadowed beneath her hat brim. Long, tangled, dark-brown hair hung down the woman's shoulders. Her nose was doughy; her eyes were flat and mean as they studied Hattie, the woman's upper lip curled disdainfully.

"Who're you?" she asked.

Hattie spat sharply to one side, to try to rid her mouth of

the awful, cloying smell of moldy burlap. "Took the words right out of my mouth."

The woman stepped forward, bunched her lips, and slapped Hattie hard across her left cheek.

"*Oh!*" Hattie cried, falling onto her right side against the lumpy, sharp-edged chunks of split wood.

The men standing to each side of the rotund woman grinned beneath the brims of their own weather-stained Stetsons.

"Let's try again," the woman said. "Who are you?"

Hattie sat up, caressing her stinging cheek and regarding the woman angrily. "Go to hell!"

The woman bunched her lips again and cocked her arm for an even harder blow.

"Wait!" Hattie cried, raising her left arm up in front of her, shield-like. "The name's Hattie. Hattie Dunbar!" Dunbar was her mother's maiden name.

"Who the hell on God's green earth is Hattie Dunbar?" the woman asked.

"I'm from a cabin east of here," Hattie said, deciding to go with the same story she'd given Clifford Hicks.

"Who're those two old hornswogglers that Red Ingram has locked up in his jail?"

"*What?*" Hattie said, not having to feign surprise.

The mean-eyed woman glanced at the men around her. "Forget it. Let's take her back to the ranch. Daddy'll wanna have a talk with her."

"Wait!" Hattie said. "You've got no right to take me anywhere. I work here—in the Honeysuckle."

"We'll see about that." The fat woman glanced at a man standing to her right.

The man held his hand up. "Look here," he ordered.

Hattie looked at the man's hand. As she did, the woman lifted a block of wood and smashed it against Hattie's right temple.

Hattie crumpled, and everything went as dark as the darkest night until she found herself again with the sack over her head, lying sprawled on what felt like feed sacks. She must have been in a wagon because the sacks were jostling around violently beneath her, while she bounced around on top of them.

Her hands were tied behind her back, and her ankles were tied as well. She couldn't move much or pull the sack from her head, which felt as though someone had driven a stout-bladed knife through it, from just above her left eye to the back of her neck.

It throbbed as though a big, tender heart was now where her brain used to be.

She felt the sun on her body, still clad in her nightgown and robe. She'd lost her slippers, so her feet were bare, and she could feel the warm sun on them as well. It was stifling hot and stinky inside the burlap sack, which pushed in and out as she breathed, sucking air through the coarse fabric.

Grunting, wincing against the ever-present throbbing pain in her head, Hattie sat up, working her head around, trying to finagle the sack off her head.

"Settle down," came the toneless voice of the mean-eyed woman. "Or I'll bull-whip ya!"

"Where are you taking me?" Hattie cried out.

"Shut up or I'll bullwhip ya!"

Hattie recoiled at the notion. She couldn't imagine what a bullwhipping would feel like on top of the braining the mean-eyed woman had given her. She lay back down, gritting her teeth against the wagon's every pitch and sway, crying out in agony when one or two of the wheels slammed hard into a chuckhole.

It was a long ride. Hattie supposed it seemed longer than it really was, given her physical agony, but she knew by the way the sun slid from one side of the wagon to the other that they were on the trail for at least a couple of hours. She could hear the clomping of other shod mounts, probably horses, behind her, and she occasionally heard men talking in a desultory fashion.

The second hour was an exercise in pure, unmitigated misery, and Hattie had to set her jaws and grit her teeth to get through it, though she thought for sure that at any second her tender brain would swell up and explode.

Tears streamed from her eyes, dampening the inside of the sack.

Torture. The ride was pure torture . . .

She grew hopeful when the wagon started to slow.

She blew a slow sigh of relief when it stopped altogether, hoping that it would not start up again after a short pause. Twice the woman had stopped the wagon to rest the mules. Hattie knew that at least two mules were pulling the wagon, because she'd heard them bray a time or two.

"Well, here we are, little girl," said the mean-eyed woman in her low, toneless voice. "Home again, home again, jiggidy-jag!"

Hattie sighed and slumped against the feed sacks.

"Franklin!" the mean-eyed woman called. "We got somebody up at the mine?"

"Kentucky and Giff are pullin' duty at the mine, Gerta," came the response in a male voice from a distance.

"Good," Gerta said. "Fetch Daddy! Tell him we got trouble!" In a lower voice, which Hattie could tell was directed at her, Hattie, the mean-eyed woman said, "But no more trouble than you got, little girl!"

CHAPTER 32

Slash raised his field glasses to his eyes and adjusted the focus.

He was still breathing hard from the climb up the side of the windy ridge that he and Pecos now lay belly down upon, at its crest, and his breathing made his hands shake. He drew a deep breath, silently cursing the thin, high-altitude air, and steadied himself. Bringing the glasses up against his face, he gazed down into the valley below him, to the northwest.

A small ranch headquarters sat in a bowl-shaped clearing roughly five hundred yards from the base of the ridge. It lay at the upper end of the long valley that Slash and Pecos had followed away from Honeysuckle, clinging to a trail that followed the windy ridgeline roughly halfway between the valley bottom and the ridge's bald crest. The trail was the only one out here, and it was deeply carved, though it appeared to have carried more traffic in the past than it had recently.

At one time, it had been traversed by heavy wagons, probably ore wagons, though in more recent months it had seen only horse and light wagon traffic. The deep ruts had been eroded and filled in with grass and rain-washed gravel.

A mile behind where the two former cutthroats now lay belly down on the ridge, the trail had forked, one tine angling north, leading down into the valley. An ancient, wooden sign had identified the descending trail as leading to the SPANISH BIT RANCH.

The other tine had been marked SPANISH BIT MINE. Another, newer sign beside it warned: STAY OUT! TRESPASSERS WILL BE SHOT! This secondary trail, which Slash and Pecos had followed, was fainter than the main trail and had continued following the ridge.

They'd followed this secondary trail leading to the mine because it clung to the high ground, and they'd wanted to find a vantage from which they could get a better lay of the land, which was what they were doing now.

"Can you see anything with them old peepers of yours?" Pecos asked.

"I can see plenty."

"Let me have a look."

"Hold your water."

Slash stared through the glasses, moving them slowly from side to side, up and down, sweeping the ranch headquarters with the single sphere of magnified vision. He brought up the single, two-story log house with a broad front veranda and a long log bunkhouse, a pair of big barns, and several corrals, including a circular stone corral with a snubbing post. That would be the breaking corral.

He perused the small, squat, double-doored building sitting off by itself, to the right of the cabin. That would be the blacksmith shop, though it was hard to tell for sure. Both doors were closed, and no smoke rose from the stone chimney running up one wall, which would be where the bellows was situated. On most working ranches Slash had been on, the blacksmith was working almost around the clock, keeping implements in good repair and all the horses shod.

There were woodpiles, trash piles, privies, and several outlying buildings nearly buried in overgrown willows and other brush. He thought there was a hangdog look to the other buildings, as well. Even the main lodge. Shakes were missing from the roof, and some of the windows were shuttered, as though maybe the glass was gone. Tumbleweeds had blown up to form a bristling rampart against the foundation.

"What is it?" Pecos said.

Slash lowered the glasses. "What's what?"

"You got that look on your face—sorta like the one when you've found out your favorite girl in a parlor house is occupied."

"Oh, shut the hell up an' have a look yourself, eagle eye." Slash shoved the glasses against Pecos's chest.

Chuckling ruefully, Pecos took the binoculars in his gloved hands and raised them to his eyes. While he gave the ranch the twice-over, Slash leaned back against a rock, dug out his makings sack, and rolled a smoke. He knew he shouldn't. He felt a stone-sized chunk of tar in his throat, kicked up by his lungs during his trek up this haystack butte, but he was too old to give up his bad habits.

He scratched a match to life on his thumb, touched the flame to the quirley, and drew the smoke deep into his chest, enjoying the brief exhilaration and the taste of the tobacco.

"Well, what do you think?" he asked Pecos before taking another deep drag off the cigarette.

Pecos lowered the glasses. The skin above his long, broad nose was pinched up. He shrugged. "Well, they don't take real good care of the place. And I don't see no hands . . ."

He let his voice trail off, frowning.

Slash had heard it too—the sound of a wagon clattering in the distance.

Slash grabbed the glasses out of Pecos's hands and, rising up on his knees once more, trained the binoculars on the ranch headquarters again.

"You could say 'please,' you old catamount!"

"Please."

"I mean *before* you grab 'em out of my hand, ya pecker-wood!"

Slash stared down at the yard, into which a wagon was just then clattering, trailed by three horseback riders. "Shut up."

"Don't tell . . ." Again, Pecos let his words trickle to silence, for with his naked eyes, he'd spied the wagon pulling into the yard.

Slash followed the wagon with the field glasses. What he at first thought was a man driving, he now saw was a woman—a stout one in man's clothing, including a long, wool coat. She wore a man's Stetson with a long neck thong and a big pistol holstered on her waist.

Slash had at first thought the ranch was deserted. Now, as the woman drew the wagon to a halt in front of the house and on the far side of a windmill and stock tank, where it was now partially hidden from his vantage, several men walked out of the bunkhouse in a slow, languid way, as though they'd been lying around or maybe playing poker, as one was still holding cards in his hand, while a cigarette drooped from between his lips.

A big man and two other smaller men stepped out of the house, also moving slowly, in a desultory way, as though they'd been doing little more than the men in the bunkhouse. As they all gathered around the wagon, Slash lowered the glasses.

"What's goin' on?" Pecos said.

"See for yourself, Melvin." Slash shoved the glasses at Pecos, who lifted them again to his eyes and peered through them. He hadn't gazed long at the ranch yard before he lowered them and turned to Slash. "Well, at least we know someone's home."

"Yeah, someone's home, all right. Don't know much about 'em, though."

"Did you see what they were carryin' in the back of the wagon?"

Slash shrugged a shoulder. "Looked like feed sacks, maybe dry goods. They must not have been far behind us on the trail." He sat back against a rock, poked his cigarette between his lips, and took a drag. "There's somethin' off about this place, though."

"What's off about it?"

"The buildings look run-down. Here it is the middle of the week, and until a minute ago, no one was out in the yard doin' a damn thing. There's damn few horses in any of those corrals, and, more important, did you see a single cow down there or anywhere down the valley? That's all ranch graze, but I didn't see a single bovine tuggin' at the needlegrass."

"Sure enough, I seen all that," Pecos said, a tad defensively but also sheepishly. He raked his fingers down his cheek and glanced sidelong at Slash. "So . . . what're you thinkin', since you got such a good head on your shoulders."

"I say we ride on up and take a look at the mine. Maybe that's where they're concentrating their efforts. Hell, maybe they're pulling so much gold out of the mountain up there"—he jerked his chin toward a nearly bald hogback peak to the east, which he figured must be where the Spanish Bit Mine lay—"that they sold off all their cattle and they're just runnin' the mine."

"Hmm," Pecos said. "Maybe. But they musta found a different trail for haulin' it out, 'less they ain't haulin' much out anymore. There's been damn little traffic on this trace."

He lifted the glasses again to gaze down into the ranch yard. "Wait," he said.

"What?"

Pecos stared through the glasses, holding them steady in his big hands. He adjusted the focus slightly. "Well, ain't that peculiar?"

"What?" Slash asked again, with more heat this time, sitting up with interest.

"Never mind."

"Never mind *what*?"

"I was just wonderin' what two o' them ranch hands down there was carryin' into the house. I thought it was movin', but when I looked again, I seen it was just a big feed bag."

Slash gave a mocking snort. "Eagle eye."

"Oh, shut up!"

"Come on, eagle eye." Slash field-stripped his smoke, then climbed to his feet. "Let's check out the mine with them eagle eyes of yours. If we don't find that gold soon, there ain't gonna be no place for us to run or hide that ole Bleed-Em-So won't find us."

Pecos started following his partner back down the hill toward where their ground-hitched horses waited. "Quit mockin' me, or I'll kick your scrawny butt!"

Heading northeast, they climbed up and over a steep divide.

At the bottom of the divide, the trail swung to the left and opened onto a windy, rocky bench. Slash figured they were a thousand or so yards up from the ranch, which lay below to the west, on their left. Ahead, at the foot of the hogback hunk of what appeared to be limestone and granite, lay several old log buildings resembling little more than trash out here on this moonscape of rocks and stunted cedars and junipers.

An egg-shaped mine portal, fronted by mounded gray tailings, gaped in the wall of the mountain a good hundred yards above and to the right of the buildings.

A cold wind blew, and clouds were starting to gather, quickly shunted this way and that by a wind that didn't seem to know which direction it wanted to blow, so it tried all four at nearly the same time. Tumbleweeds and grit blew around the rocks. The wind moaned and whistled and made the buildings groan as Slash and Pecos approached, lowering their heads and hat brims against the blowing dust.

They drew rein before the buildings. The hovels appeared to be the remains of a small town, but they were likely part of the old mine compound. Since the place was so remote, it was like a small town of sorts.

There was a saloon, a mercantile, even a restaurant and a barbershop. Bunkhouses and possibly the mine superintendent's office flanked these few business buildings—several two- and three-story log structures with boarded-up windows.

In fact, all of the windows that Slash could see had been boarded over.

Up the hill on his right, he saw no activity whatever around the mine. Several rusted ore cars sat like the derailment of a miniature train outside of the gaping mine portal. The stamping mill, at the foot of the tailings, teetered to one side, like a windmill that had been battered by a stiff wind. The big iron stamping ball lay on the ground, its cable still attached; Slash could see it through the mill's wooden stilts.

Slash and Pecos looked at each other. They silently communicated the same knowledge: no mining had been done here in years.

"What the hell's goin' on?" Pecos asked above the wind as fast-moving clouds slid ghostly shadows around them. Some of the clouds tore on the roofs of the bunkhouses and on the top of the old stamping mill. "A ranch that don't look like it's really a ranch an' a mine that ain't been functional in a coon's age."

"And still a good twenty or thirty men from the Spanish Bit showin' up in Honeysuckle every weekend to stomp with their tails up," Slash added. "Curious. Downright curious as a five-legged cat."

CHAPTER 33

Shaking his head in befuddlement, Slash glanced around at the compound of the Spanish Bit Mine.

His gaze held on a two-story building just ahead and on his left. It had been obscured by a large pile of trash—old brown bottles and rusted airtight tins layered by tumbleweeds likely blown up from the lower valley.

The single word SALOON was stretched across the building's front story in large, badly faded green letters. It was the only building whose windows hadn't been boarded. At least the ones on the lower story. Or, if they'd been boarded, the boards had been removed. Slash thought it might be a reflection of the sunlight off the large main, first-story window, but there appeared to be a lamp burning inside.

"Let's check that place out," he said, jerking his chin toward the saloon.

"If you're thirsty, I got a bottle in my saddlebags," Pecos quipped as he booted his own mount toward one of the two wooden hitchracks fronting the old watering hole.

The two former cutthroats dismounted, tossed their reins over the rack, and stepped up onto the badly rotted boardwalk fronting the saloon. The saloon had a regular wooden door, not batwings. Slash tripped the steel latch and was surprised when the door swung free in its frame.

He arched a brow at Pecos, who swung his shotgun, which hung down his back, around to his chest, gripping the savage gut-shredder in both hands.

"If there's trouble, step aside, pard. You don't wanna catch my buck in your back, though it ain't the least of what you deserve."

Slash stuck his tongue out at him, then slid one of his Colts from its holster and cocked it. He opened the door and strode quickly into the saloon. He stepped to the left, Pecos to the right, both men extending their guns out before them.

They looked around.

There were a half-dozen tables and chairs just ahead of them and a crude bar with plank shelving flanking it beyond the tables and chairs. A lamp burned where it hung from a ceiling support post in the middle of the room. A stairway ran up the right wall, off the right end of the bar. Dust and cobwebs were everywhere, though someone had recently tried to give the place a cursory sweeping. A broom and dustpan stood against the wall to Slash's left. The pan was filled with dust and a mummified rat skeleton.

Slash sniffed. "Cigar smoke," he whispered, puzzled.

"There." Pecos dropped his chin.

Slash followed his gaze to a table ten feet ahead. A half-full whiskey bottle stood on the table. Two hands of cards lay facedown on the table, the bottle between them. A shot glass stood near each of the card hands. One glass was empty, the other a third full.

Near one of the card hands was an ashtray in which a slender, black cigarillo burned. The gray smoke curled lazily upward into the saloon's musty air.

A man's head and upper torso darted up from behind the bar, on the bar's right end. A half a blink later, another man's head and upper torso darted up from behind the bar's left end.

"Down, Slash!" Pecos bellowed.

"I see 'em!"

As Pecos dropped to a knee behind the gamblers' table, Slash dove over a table to his left.

The two men behind the bar snapped rifles to their shoulders, and both of those rifles spoke at nearly the same time, one round pounding into the table behind which Pecos cowered. The slug shattered the half-full shot glass and blew cards in all directions.

The other shooter flung a bullet into the back of the chair behind which Slash just then hit the floor. As the chair flew violently back over his legs, Slash rolled up off his left shoulder and raised his six-shooter toward the man cocking his rifle behind the bar's left side. Just as his opponent aimed down his barrel at Slash, Slash triggered his Colt.

The man's hat went flying back off his head and into the dusty, mostly empty shelves behind him. The man's rifle crashed, the slug flying wide and plunking into the front wall behind Slash.

The man cursed sharply and pulled his head down behind the bar.

Pecos aimed his gut-shredder over the top of the gamblers' table and filled the room with thunder. Buckshot peppered the bar and blasted several empty shelves off the wall behind it, evoking a shrill yell from the rifle-wielding devil on that end of the bar.

"One o' these rannies has a cannon!" the man screamed to his friend, both men hunkered down behind the bar.

"I seen it," his friend said in a high voice pinched with anxiety. "But he's only got one more load!"

"Plenty more in my pocket, friend!" Pecos fired verbally back. "Besides, twelve-gauge buck don't see that spindly bar as no obstacle at all. No, sir—not at all!"

Pecos filled the room with thunder again.

A shrill, agonized scream rose from the bar's right side. It was followed by the heavy thud of a body hitting the floor.

Pecos whooped victoriously as he broke his smoking barnblaster open and plucked the spent shells from the tubes.

The other man, on the bar's left side, jerked his head and rifle over the bar top, but before he could get a shot off at Pecos, Slash triggered his Colt twice. The man cursed and drew his head back down behind the bar, but not before one of Slash's slugs had cut a nasty furrow across the man's left cheek and the other had grazed his shoulder. Slash kept firing, giving Pecos time to reload his cannon, carving gouts of wood out of the bar and keeping the shooter pinned down.

When Slash's pistol clicked on an empty chamber, he holstered it and reached for the other one. He'd only gotten it half-raised before Pecos gave another raucous yell and loosed an ear-rattling thunderclap again, blowing a large, raggededged hole in the front of the bar.

Pecos whooped again, shriller this time, and wreaked havoc with his second barrel.

Another ragged hole was blasted through the front of the bar, two feet to the right of the first one.

"*Oh!*" the man behind the bar cried. "Ah, Jesus—stop! Help! Please! *Help!*"

Slash looked at Pecos through the chalky cloud of powder smoke wafting around them. "You think you got him?"

Pecos shrugged as he broke the coach gun again. "Sounds like it."

"Yeah." Slash heaved himself to his feet, wincing from the bruising he'd taken when he'd hit the floor after throwing himself around like a man half his age. He kicked a chair out of his way in frustration and lifted his head to cast a cautious gaze over the bar. "It sounds like it. But . . ."

The man behind the bar cursed. "Stop! Stop it, now—you hear? You got me! I'm done!"

"You sure about that?" Slash called.

"*Yesss!*" The man's voice broke, and he sucked a breath through gritted teeth.

Pecos clicked his freshly reloaded shotgun closed. "Want me to send another wad through the bar, Slash?"

"*Noooo!*" screeched the man behind the bar. He was breathing hard. It sounded like he was flopping around like a landed fish.

Slash looked at Pecos and held his hand up, palm out. Holding his second Colt in his right hand, he moved quietly around the end of the bar. He jerked his head for a quick look behind the bar, drew it back, just in case the second bushwhacker was playing possum, then took another look.

The man was down, all right. He hadn't been faking his misery. The blast had taken him in his upper left chest. A couple of pellets had struck his narrow, dimpled chin. Blood trickled down his chin and his neck. Wood slivers from the bar were embedded in his cheeks and neck.

He lay parallel to the bar, boots near Pecos, head lying near the lifeless heap of his partner. This man had short black hair and a black mustache. A three- or four-day growth of beard stubble shadowed his lean, angular face. He wore denims, a wool shirt, suspenders, and a deerskin jacket with hammered silver conchos for buttons.

Two guns were holstered on his hips. His Winchester lay on the floor between him and his dead partner.

"What's your name, friend?" Slash asked.

The man stared up at him through glassy, chocolate-brown eyes. He was breathing hard, and he was losing blood fast. "Ken . . . Kentucky Dade."

"What are you doin' here, an' why'd you bushwhack us, Kentucky Dade?"

The man curled a nostril and hardened his jaws. "Go to hell!"

Slash chuckled. "You're halfway there, you bushwhackin' idjit!"

As Pecos walked over to the bar, then hoisted himself onto it, leaning toward the back wall so he could see Kentucky Dade on the floor, Slash walked up to Dade and knelt down beside him.

"I can make your journey to the smoking gates a lot more painful it needs to be, Kentucky." Slash poked the barrel of his Colt into one of the holes carved by Pecos's gut-shredder.

Kentucky Dade howled, lifting his chin and gritting his teeth. "Oh, sweet merciful Jesus . . . *please don't do that*!"

Slash pulled the pistol barrel out of the hole. "What are you doin' here, an' why'd you bushwhack us, Kentucky?"

Pecos looked at the front door, for both he and Slash were aware that if two men were here, others could be on the lurk, as well. Turning back to Kentucky Dade, Pecos said, "Might as well tell us. You're done, Kentucky. Finished. You don't owe no one a damn thing. Why should your pards get to spend all that money when you're as dead as last year's Thanksgiving turkey?"

Dade looked from him to Slash. He licked his trembling lips. "We're here . . . we're here to guard the . . . the . . . gold." He'd said that last word as though it were poison on his tongue.

"How many of you are there?"

"Here?" Dade said. "Just me and Cheshire." He rolled his eyes to indicate his dead poker buddy.

Slash stared grimly down at the dying man. "Where's the rest of you?"

"At the ranch." Dade's voice was growing thick and rheumy, and his breathing was slowing. His eyes were turning glassier as death stole up on him.

"Where's the gold?" Pecos asked.

"At . . . at the mine." Dade winced as a pain spasm racked

him. "Just . . . j-just behind the door." He winced again and
writhed. "Pl . . . please . . . just leave me now to . . . die in
peace."

But he died right there and then. There didn't appear anything peaceful about it. He jerked. His eyes rolled back in
their sockets, his chin lifted, and he stopped moving. A last,
rattling breath rippled through his lips.

Slash looked at Pecos, his own eyes round and bright.
Could Kentucky Dade have been telling the truth? Could it
be that easy? Could the gold really be here, within a few hundred yards?

"I think we'd best get up to the mine, partner," Pecos said
through a big, toothy grin.

"Me, too." Slash hurried out from behind the bar. He holstered the Colt, pulled the other one, and began reloading.
"We'd best take it easy, though. He could be leadin' us into a
trap."

"Ah, hell," Pecos said. "He was dyin'. He knew he was.
He didn't have no reason to lie and let his pards walk away
with all that gold just as he was shakin' hands with ole
Scratch."

"Yeah, well, just the same," Slash said, punching the last
bullet into the sixth chamber, flicking the Colt's loading gate
closed and spinning the wheel. "Let's take 'er easy."

Slash stepped slowly out onto the saloon's boardwalk.
Pecos came out behind him, holding his shotgun straight out
in front of him. Seeing no one around—there was only the
wind and windblown grit and bouncing tumbleweeds and
the clouds tearing on the top of the mountain—Slash stepped
off the boardwalk and slid his rifle from its scabbard.

"Let's walk." He racked a round into his Winchester's action and off-cocked the hammer. "Make us smaller targets
than ridin'."

"You know I don't like to walk no further than the privy,
but I reckon you got a point for a change."

Looking around carefully, they moved out away from the saloon. They crossed what passed for a street, headed around behind the mercantile, which was all boarded up and listing in the wind like a gale-battered ship, and started up the mountain, following a switch-backing trail. Shingles from the dilapidated buildings blew around them, one almost striking Pecos, who cursed and pulled his hat down tighter on his head.

Wind-battered, keeping their heads down, but also looking around cautiously, they climbed the trail. They were huffing and puffing and blinking grit from their eyes by the time they made it around the giant tailing and stood before the portal. A door was framed inside the portal, mounted on square-hewn timbers. It appeared to be a thick door of heavy lumber. A padlock secured it.

Slash cursed.

"Don't get your bloomers in a twist." Pecos grinned and held up the twelve-gauge.

"The others might hear the blast."

"If they didn't hear the blasts in the saloon, I doubt they'll hear this. Especially in this wind."

"All right—if you think your double-aught buck can blast through heavy-gauge steel."

"There you go insulting Mister Richards again." Richards was the company that had manufactured Pecos's beloved shotgun.

"Nothin' personal."

Slash stepped back and poked two fingers in his ears as Pecos raised the double-bore, aiming at the stout steel lock.

The gun roared like an exploding dragon. The lock and the hasp simply disappeared. In their place was a large, round hole in the door.

"Now," Pecos said, grinning proudly. "Don't you feel bad about doubting Mister Richards?"

"Oh, shut up."

Pecos shook his head wearily. "You don't got a grateful bone in your body, do you?"

Slash stuck his hand into the hole, grabbing the door and pulling. The door swung heavily open, and a breath like that of a grizzly bear pushed against Slash. At least, the breath of a bear that had dined on bat guano and mushrooms. There was also the smell of solid rock as well as the lingering cordite stench from the blast.

Slash and Pecos stood staring side by side into the broad hole in the mountain. Timbers framed the chasm, holding the mountain back, preventing cave-ins. The light penetrated only for twenty feet or so.

Slowly, Slash and Pecos walked into the mine, looking around.

They'd started walking just beyond where the light penetrated when Pecos stopped suddenly. "There." He pointed.

Slash squinted into the shadows. "Where?"

Pecos walked forward and dropped to a knee beside two strongboxes sitting side by side at the base of the mine's right wall. Pecos patted one of the boxes and smiled up at Slash. "Right here."

Slash walked forward. He recognized the box that the robbers had stolen out of the freight wagon. "There was no lock on it. There wasn't a lock on either box."

"Open it."

Pecos lifted the hasp and pulled up the lid. "Well, I'll be—" He stopped when a shadow slid over his right shoulder, obscuring the box. "Slash, would you please get out of my light?"

Slash's voice was tense as he said, "I'm not in your light."

Pecos looked over his shoulder, and his heart skipped a beat. Slash had seen it, too. Him, rather. The man walking slowly toward them, silhouetted against the light from the open door behind him.

The man walked a little uncertainly, holding his left arm taut against his right side. He held a rifle straight out from his right hip.

He continued forward, a man-shaped silhouette, until gray light reflected off the mine's chipped and gouged walls shone in his chocolate eyes, pinched with both pain and humor.

Kentucky Dade stopped six feet away from Slash and Pecos. He wheezed out a laugh, seemed to strangle on it for a second, the rifle quivering in his shaky right hand. "You should see the look on your faces!" he choked out, like some slow-dying crow that had somehow found humor in his bitter end.

CHAPTER 34

"What you got there, honey?" yelled a distant male voice.

Hattie, still in the wagon, still with the fetid burlap bag over her head, cocked an ear to listen.

To her right, only a couple feet away, the stout woman, Gerta, shouted, "We got us some trouble all wrapped up in this purty little package out here, Daddy! I think we best confer over it!"

Hattie winced. Gerta's toneless voice was grating as well as predatory. Its loudness also made her throbbing head throb harder.

"Purty little package, eh?" returned the man in the distance. "Well, bring the package on in here, then. Gettin' cold out there, an' I already got me a chill in my old bones!"

In the distance, boots clomped and scraped across wood. In her mind's eye, Hattie saw the man who'd yelled—an older gent, judging by the brittle rasp in his voice—step off a porch and into a house. There was the thud of a door closing behind him.

"Cobb," Gerta said.

Brusquely, big hands grabbed Hattie and pulled her out of the wagon. She gave a groaning start as the man hefted her in his arms, then tossed her up over his shoulder, like she was nothing more than a bag of potatoes.

"Rest of you fellas," said the man carrying Hattie, "off-load the wagon into the supply shed."

"You got it, Cobb," said a man nearby. Hattie could sense—even smell—several men standing around the wagon. She could smell cigarette smoke, hear the plop of chaw being spat into the dirt.

Cobb carried Hattie for what Hattie judged was a hundred feet or so. She gritted her teeth against the swollen heart in her forehead, feeling crusty blood on her cheek, where it had run down from the gash in her temple.

Someone followed her and Cobb. Hattie could hear footsteps, hear someone breathing behind her. It sounded like a woman breathing—Gerta. Cobb clomped up ten or eleven steps to a porch, then gave a grunt and jerked to one side as he opened a door, which groaned on its hinges.

He stepped into a house, which smelled of old cooking and leather and damp wool and the pine smoke of a fire, and swung Hattie down off his shoulder. Hattie's stomach rose into her throat as she dropped several feet onto a hard, wooden surface with a jolt.

"Oh!"

It felt like a table beneath her.

"What we got here?"

A hand grabbed the sack and pulled it off Hattie's head. The hand grabbed some of her hair, too, pulling. "Oww!"

An old man's face pushed up close to Hattie's. He was maybe in his sixties. He had little hair on the top of his head. The horseshoe of lusterless brown hair around the sides of his head hung, long and scraggly and unwashed, nearly to his shoulders.

His face was long and angular. It bore a thin, patchy beard flecked with gray. The old man's eyes were brown and severely slanted. They were mantled by heavy gray brows that slanted over them like furry caterpillars, giving him a vague Satanic look. The eyes themselves beneath those slanted brows were strangely boyish. They were penetrating in their intensity, and they owned a raw intelligence. Possibly a diabolical intelligence, but intelligence just the same.

Those intelligent eyes set in that raw, savage face made the older man appear even more menacing.

The old man—"Daddy," as Gerta had called him—wore a linsey-woolsey tunic under a smoke-stained buckskin vest lined with wool and baggy canvas trousers. The trouser cuffs were stuffed into the high tops of old cavalry boots. He was lean and bony. He wore a bowie knife on one hip, a big ivory-handled pistol on his other hip, positioned for the cross-draw in a soft leather holster on which had been sewn a small Texas flag.

There were only two other people in the room, both flanking Daddy. One was Gerta. The other was a tall, broad-shouldered man with dull eyes and a thick handlebar mustache. That had to be Cobb. Several other men, a half dozen or more, were peering into the house through the two large windows, one on each side of the door, which Gerta had kicked closed.

Leaning forward at the waist, Daddy studied Hattie closely, as though he were trying to peer through her eyes, each one in turn, all the way to her soul. He reached out and touched a finger to the dried blood that had run down the left side of her face.

"That's a nasty goose egg on your forehead there, princess."

Hattie grimaced and pulled her head back from the man's touch.

He quirked a little smile. "Who are you, princess?"

"I don't understand why I'm bein' treated this way," Hattie said in a pinched, terrified voice that she really didn't have to feign. She felt as though she were a rabbit who'd just found herself invited to a rattlesnake party.

How these rattlesnakes had gotten onto her, and why they'd brought her here, she had no idea. She had a feeling she was about to find out.

"You were brought here, princess," Gerta said in her tone-less, menacing voice, "because we reco'nized you in the Honeysuckle last night." She glanced at the old man. "Me an' the boys stopped in for a drink." Turning back to Hattie, she continued with, "We seen you in Tin Cup. You boarded the stage with the preacher. That makes you a Pinkerton, on account of they was all Pinkerton agents who boarded that stage."

Hattie stared at the woman, aghast.

She vaguely remembered seeing Gerta and the other three men who'd brought Hattie here in the saloon last night. She hadn't served them. They'd been standing at the bar. She'd had no reason to pay them much attention. Now, as she studied Gerta and the old man in turn, she tried to feign innocence, but she knew that her eyes were likely expressing only shock and deep dismay.

How had they found her out? If they knew about her, did they know about Slash and Pecos, then, as well?

The question must have been in Hattie's eyes.

Gerta answered it for her. "It don't take all that much money to turn a Pinkerton agent."

"Who . . . ?" Hattie found herself asking on a thin exhalation.

"The preacher," said Cobb. He grinned, showing tobacco-rimmed teeth. His eyes glittered like a snake's mesmerizing a cottontail.

"Glen Howell?" That was the tall field agent from Denver whom Hattie had been partnered with. She'd been assured that Howell was as pure as the day was long. "But . . . but . . . you killed him, too!"

"He shouldn'ta gone trustin' no stage robbers!" Gerta said with mock castigation. "I reckon the gold we promised him clouded his judgment." She threw her head back and cackled loudly at the ceiling.

Daddy turned to Cobb and then to Gerta. "You sure she's a Pink? She sure don't look like a Pink."

Gerta said, smiling, "Well, Daddy, I doubt you've ever seen a Pink before in your whole life—now, have you? Admit it!"

"No, no," Daddy allowed, "I reckon I haven't. U.S. marshals an' Texas Rangers aplenty, but never a Pinkerton." He turned back to Hattie. "I didn't know they had 'em this purty, though."

He reached out and slid a thick tangle of hair back from Hattie's cheek, and whistled. "She sure is purty! Just like Christmas mornin'." He turned to frown over his shoulder at Gerta. "Why'd you bring her here? Why didn't you just kill her? I don't wanna have nothin' to do with killin' this girl. I've done enough killin' in my years on the ole owlhoot trail, but I never could kill a woman. Leastways, not such a purty one. Look at them button eyes! I'd just as soon you took care of it before you got here, honey."

"Hell, if she didn't die in the stage, she must have nine lives. Or so thick a hide that a forty-five round can't pierce it. I peppered that coach—I sure did." Gerta grimaced, perplexed. "How did you survive that, little girl?"

Hattie said nothing. She just sat there at the end of the long, timber eating table, glaring her hatred at Gerta. She remembered the *rat-tat-tat* of the savage gun, the bullets blasting through the panels of the coach, as though the Concord had been no more substantial than a matchbox. She remembered hearing the screams of the other Pinkerton agents beneath the shrill screams she heard spewing from her own throat.

She remembered the blood. All the blood, flying everywhere . . .

Gerta looked at Daddy. "We were informed in Honeysuckle that she rode in with two old gents. I mean, not as old as you, Daddy, but older'n Cobb, anyways."

"Two older gents, eh?" Daddy was still leaning forward, raking Hattie up and down and sideways with his weirdly scrutinizing gaze, but his words were directed at Gerta. "Who are they? *Where* are they? You kill 'em?"

"Ingram had 'em locked up in his jail, but he let 'em go last night. I don't know why. He didn't seem to know why, either. Old-timer's disease, I guess. According to old Anders at the livery barn, they split town." Gerta stepped up beside Daddy and cast her angry scowl at Hattie. "Who were they—the men you rode to town with? More Pinkertons?"

Hattie shook her head. "No. Just two old fellas I threw in with along the trail."

"You a whore?" Daddy asked Hattie with a lascivious grin.

Cobb smiled.

"No, I'm not a whore," Hattie indignantly declared, closing her arms on her chest. "We were just friends. I was riding alone, so I threw in with them, that's all. They were good to me."

She spat that last sentence out like an incrimination against her captors.

"Any sign of Hogue and the others in town?" Daddy asked Gerta.

"Nope." Gerta popped her lips as she spoke the single word, brandishing it, shaking her head, keeping her insinuating gaze on Hattie.

Daddy worked his lips as he turned to Hattie again. "You kill Hogue, Drew Handy, Wild Pete, an' the two Injuns?"

"Who're they?" Hattie asked, feigning ignorance. The

men Daddy had named were likely the ones the two former cutthroats had killed in the dugout saloon, on their way to Honeysuckle. The men Gerta, Cobb, and the rest of the gang had left behind to clean their trail of possible trackers.

They hadn't done such a good job, though, Hattie proudly, silently declared to herself. Slash and Pecos had taken them down hard.

"You didn't kill Hogue, Drew Handy, Wild Pete, an' the two Injuns," Gerta told Hattie. "At least, not alone."

"I told you—I don't know who you're talking about."

Daddy swept his right hand up quickly, drawing it back behind his shoulder. He started to swing it forward toward Hattie. Hattie jerked her head back and to one side, her hair tumbling over her face. As Daddy's hand started flying toward Hattie, he grabbed it with his left as though to hold it back.

"Ohhh, you . . . *ohhhh*!" Daddy bellowed, grinding his right fist against his left hand. "I don't wanna have to hurt you, girl, but I will. I will—yes, sir—less'n I get some honest answers from you!"

"Don't!" Hattie cried. "Stop! Leave me alone. I was only doing my job!"

It was finally Cobb's turn to speak. Making his jaws and eyes hard, he stepped forward and said, "Who killed Hogue, Drew Handy, Wild Pete, an' the two Injuns?"

Hattie leaned back, her hair obscuring her face, and closed her eyes. She was trying to calm herself down while preparing for the worst. The very worst.

Whatever these killers did to her, she would not tell them about Slash and Pecos. She didn't know where her two partners were. She had no idea why they'd ended up in the jail in Honeysuckle last night. All she could do was guess that they'd gotten themselves into trouble in the town's other watering hole and had found themselves in the hoosegow.

Not so strange for two former cutthroats, she supposed.

Where they were now, she had no idea. They were, however, her only chance. Having seen how well they'd handled themselves against the five gang members in the dugout saloon, they were her pretty *good* chance— if they knew where she was.

Which they likely didn't since she didn't know where *they* were.

She probably didn't have much time left, anyway. Judging by the anger she saw in the three sets of eyes glaring at her, here where she sat, wrists and ankles tied, at the end of the table, her goose was likely cooked.

Panic threatened to overwhelm her. She drew a slow, deep breath, trying to hold it at bay. She remembered her Pinkerton training. Handle every situation, even the bad situations, the way you eat an apple—one bite at a time. Keep your mind clear and moving logically toward solving the problem at hand.

"You heard Cobb," Gerta said loudly, puffing up her big lumpy chest with anger. "Who killed our men?" She grabbed Hattie's chin and squeezed it painfully. "The two old fellas you rode into Honeysuckle with?"

"Who else?" Cobb said tightly. "Sure wasn't her. Not all five, anyways."

"*Who?*" Gerta said, squeezing Hattie's chin until tears streamed down the young Pink's eyes.

Hattie squeezed her eyes closed and kept her mouth shut. She wouldn't give these killers the benefit of knowing one more thing. Even if it got her killed.

"Who else?" Daddy said. He shoved Gerta's hand away from Hattie's chin. "Can't you see you're hurtin' the girl? Looks like you already done hurt her enough, the poor child."

"Poor child?" Gerta laughed at the old man. "Oh, Daddy— you an' your big heart. She's a Pink! And she knows who those two older men are, and *where* they are, an' I'm gonna get it out of her if I have to cut her toes an' fingers off to do it!"

"Now, now, now," Daddy said, placing his hands on Gerta's shoulders. "You just calm down, honey. You'll do nothing of the kind. Yes, I do believe this girl knows who them fellas are, an' where they are. But now that we got her"—he canted his head toward Hattie—"I got me a feelin' we'll know where they are soon enough. Because they'll be here . . . lookin' fer her."

"You think they'll track her here?"

"I got a feelin' they're here already, honey-child. Here . . . or at the mine."

"Yes," Gerta said, nodding, her cheeks drawn and pale. "The mine . . ."

Daddy turned to Cobb. "Who we got up at the mine?"

"Kentucky Dade and Giff Cheshire."

"Good men," Daddy said, "but they might need help. Take a half-dozen more up there. Keep the rest here. Tell 'em to stay on their toes. Tell 'em to be ready for trouble." He narrowed one eye and gave a coyote grin. "Have one of 'em man the Gatlin' gun in the barn."

"You got it, Mister Greenleaf," Cobb said, and hurried out of the house.

"You think they'll come here, Daddy?" Gerta asked the old man.

Daddy turned to Hattie. "Yes, I do." He gave the young Pink's chin an affectionate squeeze and smiled knowingly. "Yes, I do, indeed."

CHAPTER 35

"What's the matter?" asked Kentucky Dade, laughing. "You two look like you just seen a ghost!"

Pecos rose slowly, slowly raising his hands palms out.

"I'll be damned," Slash said, also raising his hands and staring nervously at the Winchester Dade was aiming in both shaking hands.

"Did you like my performance?"

"I gotta admit—it was purty damn good," allowed Pecos.

"Yeah, yeah," Slash said. "You, uh . . . you must've growed up in some traveling theater outfit. You sure did look dead to me."

"Nah," Dade said, his voice raspy and pinched with the pain of the dozen or so widely scattered buckshot pellets in his chest and neck. Blood bibbed his shirt. He must have lost a whole quart on the climb from the saloon to the mine. "I feel like I got a good two, three minutes left. I'm gonna put 'em to good use!"

"Why don't you set that rifle down so we can talk about this?"

"About what?" Dade said. "You stealin' my gold? *Our* gold—Mister Greenleaf's and all the rest of the boys and Gerta's."

"Mister Greenleaf?" Slash looked at Pecos.

Pecos narrowed his eyes, studying the name for a few seconds, then looking in surprise at Dade. "*John* Greenleaf?"

"That'd be the one."

"Damn," Pecos said to Slash. "I thought he was dead."

"I thought he died in the Texas state pen," Slash added.

The notorious Texas outlaw John Greenleaf had been running off his leash way back before the War Between the States. He'd paused to fight on the side of the Confederacy, and when he returned to Texas to find that carpetbaggers had moved in, buying up ranches for back taxes, he took right up where he'd left off—robbing stagecoaches and banks and then trains, and also killing willy-nilly, like a rabid wolf, since the war had inspired in him a great desire for further bloodshed.

Slash and Pecos had run into the notorious Greenleaf—a queer and dangerous sort of fellow, as Slash remembered—and part of his old gang in Mexico a time or two. They'd played poker together, visited the senoritas together, though they'd otherwise stayed clear of the unpredictable old rapscallion, who was known to kill men for petty grievances and sundry imagined reasons.

Nigh on twenty years ago, the Texas Rangers had caught up with Greenleaf, who must have been in his forties even then. They'd killed most of his gang, wounded Greenleaf himself, and thrown him in the state pen, where Slash and Pecos had both assumed, apparently incorrectly, that he'd died.

What had distinguished the old thief and killer was that he'd raised a child—a girl, if Slash remembered correctly—on the outlaw trail. The girl had been storied for her ugliness, dangerousness, as well as a queer and mercurial nature that she'd come by honestly, given who her father was. She'd spent some time in prison, as well, but not nearly as much as old Greenleaf had.

"Downright surprising to hear that old thief's name again," Slash opined. "After all these years . . ."

"I can't believe he ain't dead," Pecos said.

"He probably thinks you two old goats are dead, too."

Slash and Pecos shared an offended scowl, then gazed curiously at the man holding the quivering long gun on them.

"I know who you two are," Dade said, still giving a coyote grin. "Slash Braddock an' the Pecos River Kid. Before my very eyes!" He chuckled with glee. "Took you killin' me to recognize you, I reckon. The infamous Snake River Marauders!" He coughed up some blood, spat it to one side, and shook his head as if to clear it. "Reckon I should be honored."

"Or," Slash suggested, "you could just put the rifle down and we could swap big windies . . ."

"No time. I'm dyin' . . . you kilt me . . . an' I'm takin' you two green-fanged devils along with me to powwow with Saint Pete."

Slash said, "Don't expect us to put in a good word for you."

Dade grinned down the Winchester's barrel, drawing a breath, trying to steady his shaking hands. "Which one of you wants it first?"

"He does," Slash and Pecos said at the same time, canting their heads toward each other.

The rifle thundered.

Slash and Pecos jerked with starts.

They blinked in hang-jawed shock. Slash looked down at himself. Not seeing any bullet holes, he started to turn toward Pecos, who'd started to turn toward him at the same time.

Kentucky Dade made a strangling sound.

They turned toward him. He wore a shocked look. The rifle was sagging in his arms. Fresh blood—fresher than the stuff Pecos had spilled—welled from the blood-red bib of his shirt front.

Dade opened his mouth as though to speak, but then the rifle dropped from his hands to the mine floor. His knees buckled, and then he crumpled atop the rifle.

Slash stared toward where a new figure was silhouetted against the gray light of the open mine door. The figure walked slowly toward him and Pecos. The figure had a rifle in its hands, aimed straight out from the person's right hip. Batwing chaps flapped against the person's legs, and spurs rang softly, echoing off the mine's stone walls.

As the newcomer approached, fifteen feet away and closing slowly, Slash saw the long blond hair hanging from the man's tan Stetson to jostle down Lisa Ingram's shoulders. Wearing a plaid wool coat, she stopped ten feet away from Slash and Pecos and the outlaw she'd just polished off.

Slash lowered his hands, chuckling and shaking his head. "Boy, that was some nice timin', sweetheart."

"I couldn't agree more!" Pecos said, also chuckling his relief.

Lisa Ingram gritted her teeth and squeezed her carbine in both her gloved hands. "I ain't neither one of you old cutthroats' sweetheart. Now, get your hands back up before I gut-shoot you both and leave you howlin'!"

"What?" Pecos said.

"Get 'em up!"

"Ah, come on, sweetheart," Slash said. "We came up here to—"

"I know what you came up here for. You came up here to steal the stolen gold." Lisa loudly cocked the carbine again. The spent shell casing clattered to the stone floor, where it rolled, making a tinny warble. "Get 'em up, or, like I said, you're wolf bait!"

"Easy," Slash said, raising his hands again, shoulder high. "Just take it easy. We didn't come here to steal no stolen gold. We came here to retrieve it for them it rightly belongs to."

"Hey," Pecos said, also raising his hands. "How'd you know it was stolen, anyways?"

"I know all about what goes on up here," Lisa said, her jaws still hard, gray light from the entrance reflecting off her flinty eyes. "Leastways, I've had my suspicions. Pa forbade me from ridin' up here. He said the mine an' the ranch were out of our jurisdiction, and, besides, there's dangerous secrets out this way.

"Well, I've always been right curious about dangerous secrets. And I've been right curious about the Spanish Bit for the past two years, when the ranch changed hands, and suddenly the mine was supposedly open again after it had been shut down for the previous three years."

"You've been up here before, then?" Slash asked.

"Yes."

"You knew it was a ghost."

"I knew."

"Did you tell your pa?" Pecos asked.

Lisa shook her head. "I tried. He didn't want to hear nothin' about the Spanish Bit. You see, folks around Honeysuckle who get curious about the Spanish Bit—the ranch or the mine—end up in shallow graves, pushin' up daisies somewhere around these mountains. I reckon I learned over the years to keep my mouth shut and to mind my own business, though it chafed me raw to do so. But when you two old cutthroats showed up . . ."

"You got curious again," Slash said.

"That's right." Lisa gave a stiff smile. "I got curious an' ambitious."

Pecos frowned. "How do you mean?"

"I got ambitious to make a name for myself." Lisa's smile broadened. "I may not be able to bring down the Spanish Bit, but I can take down the two famous Snake River Marauders still runnin' off their leashes."

"Get your name in all the papers, eh?" Slash said.

Lisa's smile grew smug. She gave a slow, arrogant blink.

"But you wouldn't be makin' Chief Marshal Henry T. Bledsoe very happy," Pecos told her.

"Bleed-Em-So?" Lisa stitched her brows and canted her head to one side. "Don't be silly. Everyone knows he's carryin' Slash's bullet in his back."

"What everyone don't know—only a special few," Slash said, "is that we ride for ole Bleed-Em-So now ourselves."

"Pshaw!"

"That's right," Pecos said. "Like Slash done tried to explain, we ain't here to *steal* this gold. We're here to *retrieve* it. On Bledsoe's orders."

"Leastways, now we have to retrieve it"—Slash cast his partner an ironic glance—"since it got stole out from under us."

"Yeah, well . . . ," Pecos said through a sigh.

"Hah!" Lisa laughed without mirth. "You expect me to believe—"

She cut her question off with a squeal as Slash bounded forward, swinging his left arm up against the underside of the girl's rifle. She triggered a round into the low ceiling. Inside the stone sarcophagus, the report sounded like a cannon blast.

Ears ringing, Slash wrapped his hand around the barrel and jerked the carbine out of her grip. At the same time, Pecos bolted forward and grabbed the girl's Schofield revolver from the holster thonged on her shapely right thigh.

Recoiling from the sudden, obviously unexpected attack, the deputy town marshal of Honeysuckle tripped over her own spurs and hit the mine floor on her butt.

Glaring up at the ex-cutthroats, she cursed them roundly, hurling miniature sabers from her angry eyes.

"I didn't know that about your bloodline," Pecos quipped to Slash. "If I had, I might not have been so quick to ride with you, partner."

"Yeah, well," Slash said, stepping back and working the carbine's cocking lever, ejecting all the cartridges from the breech, "she don't know the half of it . . . unfortunately."

He leaned the empty carbine against the mine wall. "I'm just gonna set this here, honey. If you go reloadin' it, I'm gonna tan your behind."

"I ain't your honey and get your mouth off my behind!"

"Yeah, Slash," Pecos said with a chuckle, "get your mouth off the girl's behind." He held the pistol out to her. "Here. Don't reload it, or you'll feel my hand on your behind, too. It won't feel half as good as Slash's."

Sitting on her rump on the mine floor, legs bent before her, Lisa looked uncertainly from Slash to Pecos, then back again. "You don't expect me to believe you're not gonna kill me . . ."

"Nah," Slash said. "We ain't in the business of killin' purty deputy town marshals."

"Yeah," Pecos added. "Our reputations are bad enough without addin' savage killers of purty deputy town marshals to the list." He turned to Slash. "Well, partner, we came for one strongbox of gold. Now we got two. We gonna take both back to Denver?"

"Why not? You can bet the other one's stolen, too." Slash went to the strongboxes and dropped to a knee. He lifted the lid from the one that had been stolen out of his and Pecos's wagon. He whistled, shook his head, feeling the old burn of gold-lust again. "We can't very well just leave it here, can we?"

He lifted the unlocked lid from the other one and frowned down at the gold ingots stacked inside. Even in the dim light, the gold shone, as beautiful and radiant as the most beautiful woman in the world . . .

"Say . . . ," Slash said, frowning down at the bars.

"What is it?"

He picked up one of the ingots, scrutinized it, and turned to Pecos. He brushed his right thumb across the figure of a

Spanish bit stamped into its center. The words SPANISH BIT, HONEYSUCKLE COL. TERR. were also stamped into the face of the ingot. "Look there."

Pecos dropped to a knee to study the gold, then turned his puzzled gaze to Slash. "I don't get it. There ain't no gold comin' out of this mine."

Slash chewed the inside of his cheek, pondering. "You know what they're doin'?"

"Pray tell."

"They're stealin' the gold and haulin' it here to melt it down and stamp it with the Spanish Bit's old brand. Then they probably take new bars to the railhead and on to the U.S. Mint in Frisco."

"I'll be damned!" Pecos raked the back of his knuckles across the nub of his chin. "That's why they don't want it to get out that the mine's closed, only a ghost. They want everyone to believe they're minin' their own gold, takin' their own gold to Frisco, when it's really *stolen* gold they're sellin' to the Mint." Pecos whistled. "We sure have uncovered one hell of a criminal enterprise here, pard!"

"What about Greenleaf and his killers?" Slash said. "We gonna bring them back to Denver, too? Along with the gold?"

Pecos pondered the question. Lisa was still sitting on her butt on the mine floor, staring dubiously up at the two ex-cutthroats, as though she was having trouble believing she wasn't dead yet. That the notorious cutthroats hadn't fed her a pill she couldn't digest.

"Prob'ly too many for us to handle by ourselves," Pecos said finally. "Maybe we'd best get *our* gold back to Denver and have ole Bleed-Em-So invite more marshals to the party up here."

"Maybe you're ri—"

Lisa cut Slash off with: "They have the saloon girl." She'd

said it almost casually, as though she were noting the time of day.

Slash and Pecos jerked shocked looks at her. "*What?*" they asked in unison.

"They rode out of town with her early this mornin'. I was fetchin' my horse from the livery barn, to track you two, when I seen 'em go by. They had a sack over her head, and they had her in the back of the wagon, but it was her, all right. She was whimpering like she was hurt. I recognized her by that cute little form of hers that had all the men in the saloon last night ready to gnaw on their own boots."

Slash lurched to his feet and regaled the girl with a look. "They took Hattie, and you didn't do anything to stop 'em?"

Lisa gave a coy shrug. "What could I do against all o' them? Gerta was there. No one messes with Gerta." Lisa feigned a yawn, patting her fingers against her lips. "Besides . . . Poppa wouldn't like me interferin' in Spanish Bit business."

"Hatties's a Pinkerton!" Pecos told Lisa, also rising.

"Is she, now? Hmm. Well, I reckon she got her purty little rump into a real fix, didn't she? Maybe she'll bat her eyes, and they'll let her go."

Slash and Pecos shared a worried look. "I thought I seen that feed sack move. Down at the ranch. That was Hattie!"

Slash glanced at the two strongboxes. "We'll leave the gold for now, fetch it after we've got Hattie back from them curly wolves."

Slash and Pecos hurried back toward the mine entrance. They both cursed when they saw snow coming down, swirled by the wind—big, heavy, wet flakes. Some of it was sticking to the ground. As they started down the trail away from the mine, Lisa yelled, "Hey, wait for me! I'm the one wearin' the badge here!" Catching up to them, she said, "What're you gonna do? Greenleaf has a good twenty, thirty men riding for him."

"If that's counting the five we turned toe down back along the trail, then it's twenty or thirty minus five," Slash said.

They dropped onto the level ground, Lisa having to run at times to keep pace, holding her Winchester on her shoulder. They tramped through a break between the old mercantile and another dilapidated building and started across the street toward where Slash and Pecos's mounts, and a strawberry roan, which must be Lisa's, stood tied to the hitchrack, their tails blowing in the swirling wind, the wet snow gathering on their saddles.

Walking to Slash's right, Pecos stopped. "Oh-oh."

"What is—?"

Before Slash could finish the question, he saw what Pecos had seen—six or seven horseback riders trotting toward them from the north, following a trail that must lead up from the valley directly to the west, where the ranch lay. They all wore yellow slickers, and the wind was nipping at their hats, the wet snow sticking to their hat brims and crowns.

One man rode out in front of the others. He was tall and dark, with a thick mustache drooping down both sides of his broad mouth.

Apparently just then seeing Slash, Pecos, and Lisa Ingram, he drew back on his cream's reins. The others abruptly halted their horses around him. They stared at Slash, Pecos, and Lisa, who stared back at them a full five seconds before Pecos said tightly, "What do you say, Slash?"

Slash brought his Winchester down from his shoulder, pumping a round into the chamber, and dropped to a knee. "*I say let's do-si-do!*"

CHAPTER 36

As Slash raised his rifle, the lead rider bellowed, "Get 'em!" and rammed his spurs into his cream's loins. The horse whinnied and lunged into a turf-chewing gallop as the rider raised his own carbine straight out in his right hand.

"Take him, pard," Slash yelled. "I got the one behind him!"

The first man's carbine cracked beneath the howling wind.

Pecos, who'd shrugged his twelve-gauge off his shoulder, took the cannon in both hands and tripped one of its two triggers. The first man screamed as the buckshot tore into him, turning him into a big yellow bird in his yellow rain slicker as he flew straight back out of his saddle, flapping arms and legs that served poorly as wings.

He hit the ground on his butt and rolled, his hat flying off in the wind.

The horse shot straight up the street past Slash and Pecos and Lisa, laying its ears back and whinnying shrilly.

Slash drew a bead on the second rider galloping toward him. The Winchester barked, and the second rider cursed sharply as he dropped his own rifle. He fell back and sideways down his horse's right hip. Only his head and shoulders hit the street.

His right boot had gotten caught in his stirrup, and he

screamed again in agony as the horse dragged him straight off up the street on the heels of the fleeing cream. The scuffed snow slush behind him was blood-painted pink.

Slash pumped another cartridge into his Winchester's breech but held fire. Having seen what had happened to their two partners, the other five riders were holding back and quickly dismounting the sidestepping horses. Slash drew a bead on one, but the man was bouncing around too much, and the slug sailed over him and plunked into the street beyond him.

As the others scrambled for cover, they triggered their own rifles. Slugs sliced the air around Slash, Pecos, and Lisa, plunking into the two buildings behind them. Pecos discharged the second barrel of his sawed-off, but the double-ought buck merely tore into the wood of a building corner as his target leaped around and behind it.

"Ow!" Lisa cried.

As he worked his rifle's cocking lever, Slash glanced toward the girl on his right, between him and Pecos. She'd fallen back on her butt, this time clutching her bloody upper left arm. Her Winchester dangled in her right hand. Slash saw what had happened. Forgetting that Slash had emptied her carbine, she'd been trying in vain to return fire, and one of the killers' slugs had ripped into her.

"Thanks for emptying my guns, damn you!" she screeched at Slash, pain in her eyes.

Slash took his Winchester in his left hand and, crouching low, scrambled over to her. "Cover me, Pecos! I'm gonna take the deputy to cover!"

"All right, but hurry up—I'm low on ammo!" Pecos said, shoving his double-gauge back behind his shoulder and clawing his big Russian .44 from the holster on his right thigh.

As he returned fire on the five outlaws, who were now shooting from cover on both sides of the broad street, Slash grabbed Lisa's right hand and drew her up over his shoulder.

"Ow!" the girl cried. "I ain't a sack of potatoes!"

"No, you're too loud for potatoes!" Slash shambled off toward the saloon as bullets buzzed around his head and thudded into the street with angry whines. All three horses—his, Pecos's buckskin, and Lisa's roan—had wisely jerked their reins free of the hitchrack fronting the saloon and run off in the direction of the two dead men's fleeing mounts, away from the lead storm.

"My rifle!" Lisa shouted. She'd left her carbine in the street.

"I only got two hands, darlin'!" Slash was carrying his own Winchester in his right hand while holding the girl on his left shoulder.

"I ain't your darlin', cutthroat!"

"Well, okay, then . . . your loss . . ." Breathless, gritting his teeth against the five killers' onslaught of flying lead, Slash pushed through the door that he and Pecos had left standing half open and deposited the girl on the saloon floor, leaning her back against the wall, under a badly faded oil painting of an Indian on a horse with hungry-looking wolves surrounding him.

Pecos triggered his last shot from the boardwalk, then ducked into the saloon as well. He closed the door against the killers' lead, but he hadn't even gotten it latched before two bullets plunked through the front window and ground themselves into a table.

Pecos dropped to a knee between the door and the now-broken window and broke his shotgun to commence reloading. "How bad she hit?" he called to Pecos.

Slash was inspecting the girl's upper left arm, holding it in both of his hands. "I've cut myself worse shaving."

"I didn't say it was serious," Lisa said defensively, studying the blood dribbling from the thin furrow that the bullet had cut across the outside of her arm. "I just said I was hit."

Slash drew a handkerchief from his coat pocket, wrapped it around the girl's arm, and tied it. He winced as another bullet smashed through the window and into the wall about three feet from the oil painting, over Slash and the girl's head. He looked again at Lisa. "You'll be okay till a sawbones can look at it."

He frowned at her. She was as white as a sheet as she continued staring at her arm. "What's the matter? It can't hurt that bad."

"Nothin'."

"What is it?" He was thumbing fresh cartridges through his Winchester's loading gate.

"It's just . . . I . . . I get all whoozy when . . . I see my own blood . . ." Lisa sagged back against the wall, her chest rising and falling sharply. "I'll be okay in a minute."

"She okay?" Pecos asked as a bullet slammed into the door to his left, causing it to lurch in its frame.

Slash chuckled. "She's fine as frog hair. She just ain't *quite* as tough as she lets on." He winked at the girl, who was hardening her jaws against her own anxiety, trying fiercely to compose herself.

"You both go to hell!" she raged.

"There ya go, darlin'," Slash patted her chap-clad right leg. "You'll be just fine! For now, anyways," he added grimly, casting a glance out the window. "I can't guarantee beyond that!"

Staying low, he scuttled over to the front window as more bullets smashed through it to screech through the saloon and slam into walls or tables or chairs. He dropped to a knee to the right of the broken front window and pressed his shoulder against the wall, pumping a fresh round into his Winchester's action.

Outside, someone shouted. Another man shouted as though in reply. Then the shooting out there picked up. A veritable fusillade of lead came hurling through the mostly broken-out front window, breaking out what was left of the glass and hammering the bar and the back wall at the rear of the room.

"Get low, Deputy!" Slash shouted.

Lisa rolled down to her right shoulder and lay taut against the floor, holding that arm over her head as broken glass peppered her.

"What the hell's goin' on?" Slash yelled above the din at Pecos.

Also crouching low against the wall on the window's far side, Pecos yelled, "If I had to venture a guess, I'd say they mean business!"

"I think one or two are giving another one cover!"

"You think?"

Edging a careful glance around the window frame, Slash spied a blur of fast movement out on the boardwalk fronting the saloon, to his left.

"Pecos, the door!" he bellowed.

Right on cue, the door burst open, and a big man heaved himself through the opening, turning toward Pecos and Slash, gritting his teeth and raising the rifle in his hands. Slash started to bring up his own Winchester, but not before Pecos, who'd swung toward the door, tripped both triggers of his appropriately nicknamed gut-shredder.

Ka-boooomm!

The whole building leaped as the rifleman was hurled off his feet and straight back against the wall behind him, his violent meeting with the wall sounding almost as loud as Pecos's twelve-gauge.

Dropping his rifle, what was left of the intruder sagged straight down to the floor. He looked at what little was left of his chest and belly, through the bloody threads of his rain slicker. He gave a weary sigh and, extending his legs straight out before him, slid sideways along the wall to pile up on his left shoulder, already as dead as a post.

"I'll be damned if you didn't call that one right!" Pecos bellowed at Slash.

Slash glanced out the window into the snowy dimness of

the approaching evening, noting that the gunfire out there had suddenly stopped—a dirge of silence of sorts for the fallen intruder. "I usually do."

"Just 'cause I don't have time to argue the point don't mean I concede it," Pecos muttered, already plucking the smoking wads out of the coach gun's tubes.

Slash snaked his Winchester through the window's bottom right corner. He could see the two men on the other side of the street—the two who must have been covering for the dead man now leaking his life out in front of the door.

One crouched behind a rain barrel. The other was hunkered down behind a pile of moldering gray food crates. Pecos could see only brief glimpses of both men's hat crowns and mostly concealed bodies, but he could hear them conferring in low tones between wind gusts.

The one crouching behind the rain barrel, to the left of the other one, suddenly snaked his rifle over the top of the barrel, aiming toward the saloon. Slash planted a bead on him quickly and squeezed the Winchester's trigger.

The man flinched as flames lapped from his own rifle. He jerked back violently then, switching his rifle to his left hand, scrambled to his feet, turning and hurrying toward a corner of the mercantile behind him.

Slash drew his head back behind the window frame, for he'd seen the other man, hunkered down behind the crates, drawing a bead on him. That bullet sawed through the glassless window to thud ominously into the saloon's rear wall.

Slash glanced out the window to see the man he'd wounded start around the mercantile's left front corner. Again, Slash drew another hasty bead and fired. The bullet drilled through the fleeing killer's left ear, spewing blood out the other side of his head. The man staggered sideways as though badly drunk, widening his legs as he fought desperately to get his boots beneath him.

He was out of luck. He was already dead. His brain just

hadn't told his feet yet. It did in the following seconds, though, for Slash saw the man drop in the trash-strewn lot beside the mercantile as he, Slash, turned his attention to the man hunkered behind the crates.

At the same time, Pecos fired his Russian .44 at the man, out the window to Slash's left. Both bullets merely chewed wood from the crates as the man himself retreated back into the break between the two buildings beside him.

Slash jerked with a start when he became aware of a presence beside him, just off his left shoulder. "Jesus, Mary, an' Joseph, darlin'—you gave me a start!"

Holding her Bisley .44 barrel up in her right hand, Lisa peered outside and then at the man slumped at the base of the opposite wall, just inside the open door through which snowflakes swirled to melt on the blood spilled there. "You two old scalawags still got some wood in your firebox," she observed.

She glanced at Slash. He thought for a few seconds there she was actually going to smile.

"There's a spark or two," Slash allowed. "You ready to go to work?"

"What do you mean?"

"You and Pecos keep an eye on the window here. Shoot at anything that moves—'ceptin' me, of course." He gave a dark snort. "I'm gonna head out the back and see if I can get around the other two, try to get 'em in a whipsaw."

Slash moved to the back of the room, keeping to the left wall. When he got to the back, he crouched, in case anyone shot into the building from the front, and pushed through a door nearly directly behind the bar. Through the door was a small storage area—gray, dingy in the weak light coming through a small rear window, and empty save for the scuttling of a mouse or a rat.

He made for the back door, unlatched it, cracked it, and looked around carefully. Seeing no one in the near vicinity, he stepped through the door and closed it behind him. The snow was still falling—large but widely scattered flakes. It changed suddenly from near dusk to a sudden sunrise, and the clouds parted, vivid lemon rays angling down from a break in the otherwise purple sky.

Weird weather, but not all that weird, really, for the high country.

The sun disappeared as quickly as it had shone itself, then reappeared again in another break in the clouds, directly over the mountain to the west, where the mine lay.

Slash moved along the rear of the saloon to the north. At the far end, he stopped and edged a cautious peek around the corner toward the front. There was a ten-yard, trash-littered gap, soggy with wet snow, between the saloon and the next building beyond.

The gap was empty. Slash was about to cross it to the next building when a rifle began barking in the distance. The shots sounded as though they were coming from the area fronting the saloon.

Another gun—a pistol—began answering the first reports. That was probably Lisa shooting out of the saloon's front window. There were the rocketing thunderclaps, one after another, of Pecos's gut-shredder, and Slash knew the two surviving killers—or at least one of them—were making another assault.

Pecos and Lisa were holding him off.

Slash waited till the sun disappeared again, purple cloud shadows swirling around him, then ran across the gap to the rear of the next building—a small, box-like building that had likely been a "hog pen," or a doxie's crib in which to entertain her clients. The miners had likely given her plenty of business, way out here.

Slash continued to the crib's far end. He cast another glance around the corner, then jerked his head back behind the crib again, his heart thudding.

A man was walking along the side of the crib, heading toward Slash. Slash didn't think he'd seen him, for when Slash had looked along the crib, the man had had his head turned to peer back over his shoulder toward the front. He'd had two pistols in his hands, and he'd been holding them barrel up, hammers cocked.

Slash set his rifle down against the crib. He drew the Colt from his left hip, quietly clicked the hammer back. He raised the barrel, drew a deep breath.

He was about to step around the corner of the crib, to confront the man trying to steal up on him, but then he stopped, blinked as he reconsidered the move. He dropped to a knee. He removed his hat. He tossed the hat high in the air and snaked his gun around the corner while tilting his head to aim down the barrel.

He was glad he'd changed strategy.

His opponent had stopped six feet away. He was waiting for Slash. He'd either heard him or glimpsed him. But he was waiting, all right. Now, having seen the hat and expecting Slash's head to be where it would have been if he hadn't taken a knee, the man stretched his lips back from his teeth and triggered both his pistols straight out from his shoulders.

From close range, the .45s sounded nearly as loud as Pecos's sawed-off.

The stabbing flames, as well as the bullets, caromed over Slash's head.

Instantly, the killer saw his mistake. He glanced at Slash's hat, just then landing on a snowy sage tuft. The man's jubilant snarl turned in a flash to deep chagrin and bright-eyed horror. He dropped his lower jaw and lowered his terror-stricken eyes to Slash, grinning up at him, aiming down the barrel of his own cocked .44.

The killer, a medium-tall man with a chaw-stained yellow mustache and chin whiskers, cocked his guns again and tried to jerk them down.

Before he could do that, much less squeeze a trigger, he was dropping to his knees outside the pearly gates and beseeching ole St. Pete for hallowed passage, which likely wouldn't come. In fact, even as Slash lowered his smoking Colt and watched the killer hit the slushy ground on his back, blood geysering from the dead-center of his chest, Slash thought he could hear ole Pete's hysterical laughter up there amidst the golden clouds.

A rifle cracked in the distance.

It was followed by the thunder of Pecos's cannon.

A man screamed. Slash hurried through the gap toward the main street. He spied movement on his right—a man running toward him, but on the other side of the street. His hat was off, and his oilskin flapped wildly as he ran, stumbling, dropping to a knee and then running again, only to stumble and fall.

A tall figure, murky in the jostling purple shadows, moved toward the fallen man. The fallen man bellowed an angry curse, then, twisting around to face the man walking toward him, clawed a pistol from a holster on his hip.

The tall figure stopped about ten feet from the fallen man. The shotgun in Pecos's hands thundered, blossoming orange flames.

The head of the fallen man slammed back against the ground. He moved his arms and legs, like a bug on a pin, and then his head rolled to one side and the rest of him lay still.

Pecos looked up toward Slash. The tall ex-cutthroat broke his shotgun and began plucking out the spent shells. A gust of snow-laden wind blew clouds over him, and he disappeared in the stormy, high-mountain murk.

CHAPTER 37

"There you go, little girl," Gerta said, slamming a tin plate down on the table before Hattie. "A plate of beans for you. Now that Daddy and I have eaten, you can eat, too. *You* eat last. After *we've* dined. Consider it a privilege you don't deserve!"

Gerta was crouched over Hattie, the fat woman's mannish face only six inches from Hattie's. Gerta had the flat, menacing eyes of a wild dog.

"Th-thank you," Hattie said, cowering from the explosive woman's anger.

Gerta kept her head close to Hattie's, staring at her as though she wanted to shove her hand down her throat, rip out her beating heart, and eat it right there before her helpless, trussed-up prey.

Hattie stared down at the steaming plate. There weren't many beans on it, and no bread to go with it.

That was just fine. Hattie wasn't one bit hungry. She hated the fear she felt toward this animal-like woman glaring down at her from six inches away, but there it was.

"I suppose," Gerta said, spitting the words out like prune pits, "you think I should untie your hands so you can eat!"

Hattie swallowed. "I guess I don't see how I could eat otherwise."

"Well, I sure as hell am not going to feed you like a baby—now, am I?" Gerta slammed her pudgy fist down on the table beside Hattie, making the plate leap.

Hattie leaped in her chair, startled and terrified. "No . . . no, I don't suppose you would do that, Gerta."

"You're right—I wouldn't!"

Gerta stepped away to grab a skinning knife off the table, from the far end, near the dry sink, where she'd cut ham to cook with the beans. Her own plate as well as Daddy's plate remained on the table. There were also the remains of a grainy loaf of bread and some cheese.

A hurricane lamp hung over the table by a rope attached to a nail in a rafter. The table was lit in a watery, bleached-out light, leaving the rest of the kitchen and the large house beyond it in deep, mysterious darkness. Hattie could hear Daddy and several men talking outside in the yard, not far from the front door, which was closed now against the high-mountain chill.

Hattie sensed the men's and Gerta's nervousness about the men they'd sent up to the mine. Hattie shared the same apprehension. Not for the Spanish Bit men, of course, but for Slash and Pecos. Were they up there? Had they run into the Spanish Bit riders?

Were they still alive?

Hattie was more than a little apprehensive about her own fate as well. Her ankles were tied tightly together beneath her hide-bottom chair. Her wrists were just as snugly tied behind her back. She felt like a lamb trussed up for butchering. As if her predicament wasn't bad enough, Gerta acted as though she couldn't wait to kill her and would do so in a heartbeat if Hattie merely looked at her wrong.

Gerta moved back toward Hattie with the skinning knife. She stepped around behind Hattie, standing behind the young

Pinkerton for several seconds. Hattie's skin crawled. She could hear Gerta breathing back there; she could see the woman's shadow angling back over her left shoulder. But she couldn't see the woman herself.

Hattie gritted her teeth, felt her stomach tighten, wondering if the skinning knife was about to be stuck in her back.

"What's the matter?" Gerta asked in her dull, toneless voice. "Scared?"

Hattie didn't say anything.

"Huh?" Gerta asked, louder, even more belligerently. "You *scared*?"

"Yes, yes, Gerta, I'm scared. Of course, I'm scared."

"Good," Gerta said, sounding delighted but still angry. "You should be scared!"

Hattie felt Gerta saw through the ropes binding her hands behind her back. She squeezed her eyes shut in dread. She was sure the woman was going to cut her, to make her pay for some perceived slight.

She was surprised when her hands came free without a nick. Gerta stepped up beside her and slammed the knife into the table, where it quivered wildly before dwindling to stillness.

"There you go. Eat your beans." Gerta moved around the table and picked up the old Spencer rifle she'd leaned against a ceiling support post, within easy reach of the chair she'd been sitting in when she and the man called Greenleaf, or "Daddy," had eaten supper. "I'm gonna go outside an' confer with Daddy."

Hattie saw her eyes flick toward the knife embedded in the center of the table, within Hattie's reach. Gerta's mouth corners betrayed a fleeting humor, challenging Hattie to pull the knife out of the table. The woman opened the door and clomped out. Daddy had just come up on the porch.

"Any sign of the men?" Gerta asked him.

"Not yet, honey."

"Soon, though—don't you think, Daddy?"

"If they're going to ride back tonight, I'd think they'd be back soon, honey. But there's a chance they dealt with what they had to deal with up there, and they decided to spend the night. I saw clouds up there on the mountain. Likely snow on the trail, and that's a dangerous trail down over them rocks."

"You don't suppose we have to worry they'd run off with the gold—do you, Daddy?" Gerta asked.

"No, no. Our men are loyal. We pay them well, give them plenty of time to sow their wild oats in Mexico and California. Besides"—Daddy chuckled—"they know our reputations well enough to know that if they ever tried such a thing, we'd stalk them to the ends of the earth to get our reckoning."

Gerta laughed her weird, snickering, snorting laugh. "Ain't that the truth, Daddy?"

The door opened suddenly, and Daddy ducked through it. Hattie jerked with a start. She'd been sitting in her chair, staring at the beans on her plate, not eating, listening to the conversation out on the porch. Now she felt vaguely sheepish as she sat there, not having touched her supper.

"Hey, now—that won't do, Gerta," Daddy admonished his daughter, pointing at the knife embedded in the table. "That simply won't do! What're you tryin' to do—get that poor girl killed? Leavin' such a temptation as that, an' her hands untied!"

Daddy stomped over to the table, pulled the knife out of the heavy oak plank, and threw it onto a shelf. Swinging back toward Gerta, he scowled at her, brow-beating her. She stood to Hattie's left, off the end of the table, pooching her lips out guiltily.

Finally, Daddy chuckled, shook his head. "You're up to your old, crazy tricks again—aren't you, honey? Always got badness on your mind. Poison mean you are, deep down."

"Just like you, Daddy, I reckon." Gerta smiled, her full, pale cheeks reddening with pride.

"I reckon so, I reckon so." Daddy chuckled.

"What're we gonna do with her, Daddy? Once the trouble up there on the mountain's been taken care of."

"Well, then, I reckon we won't need her anymore."

Gerta's breathing seemed to quicken. Her eyes glittered as she stared at Daddy, her lips spreading another delighted smile. She looked like a snake with the prospect of a rabbit supper making its rattles quake.

"Too bad." Daddy came over and stared down at Hattie. He slid her hair back from her cheek, appraised her with his dull, dark-brown gaze, which was impossible to read.

Hattie was glad it was. She had a feeling the evil she might see behind those eyes, lying raw as freshly ground beef inside the man's cold soul, would turn her inside out with fear. Gerta wore her evil on her sleeve. Daddy's was tucked away inside him, concealed and disguised maybe even to himself, which would likely make its manifestation all the more surprising and horrifying.

These were bad people. Hattie had known bad people before, back in Chicago, where she'd been plying her Pinkerton skills before being sent out here on this job running down the gold thieves. But now she realized she really hadn't known what bad was. At least, she hadn't known before she'd met Daddy and Gerta.

Now she was getting a nice big double dose of the knowledge. She hoped she'd live to use it.

"Yes, too bad," Daddy said again with a weary sigh, letting Hattie's hair flop back against her cheek. He looked at Gerta and said with a devilish, faintly mocking edge, "Such a pretty, pretty girl. Have you ever seen a *young* woman more *beautiful*, honey?"

Gerta's cheeks flushed again, this time with raw hatred. Her eyes narrowed at Hattie as she said, "Oh, I don't think she's all that purty, Daddy. At least, she ain't gonna be nearly so purty when I'm finished with her!"

She rose up and down on the toes of her stovepipe boots.

Daddy chuckled, bemused by his daughter, in whom he obviously saw so much of himself. He stretched, yawned, and pulled his baggy canvas trousers up his broad, bony hips. "I'm tired. The men are gonna stay up, keepin' an eye out for possible trouble." He glanced at Hattie. "In case there are any more Pinkerton agents lurking around this end of the valley. Me, I'm old an' tired. I'm gonna hit the old mattress sack."

"I'll stay awake, too, Daddy," Gerta said. She walked around to the other side of the table and plopped down in the chair across from Hattie. She scowled over the table at the young Pinkerton and said, "I'm gonna stay awake all night long, keeping careful watch on the Pink here."

"Don't kill her, honey," Daddy admonished. "Not until I say you can. Hear?"

"Don't I always do as you say, Daddy?"

Daddy chuckled, walked over, bent down, and pressed his lips to Gerta's greasy head. He squeezed her shoulder, looked at Hattie, gave her a lewd wink that put ice in her blood, then swung around to the stairs and climbed up into the second story.

Gerta leaned back in her chair and rested her rifle across her lap. "Go ahead an' eat," she ordered. "We don't let food go to waste around here, little girl!"

Hattie choked the beans down.

She didn't see that she had a choice. Anyway, she needed sustenance. It would likely be a long night and an even longer day tomorrow. Or maybe not all that long. If Slash and Pecos were dead, Hattie would likely soon follow the old cutthroats to her own unmarked grave.

Still, she needed to eat. Anxiety had used up her energy, and she needed to replace it, in case she needed it again.

She was glad she did eat the beans. It turned out she

needed the energy, after all. Gerta didn't stay awake long. In fact, after only about a half hour of sitting in the chair across from Hattie, glaring at her stonily, Gerta's eyes grew heavy. Soon her chin was sagging to her chest, and she was snoring. She sat like that, waking briefly from time to time, but mostly sitting there with her head sagging or wobbling around on her shoulders, snoring almost as loudly as Slash and Pecos had snored in camp.

While Gerta slept, Hattie worked on the ropes binding her wrists. She worked on them off and on all night long, taking short breaks to rest. Gerta had tied the ropes tightly around Hattie's wrists, but Hattie worked on them, moving her hands around steadily, trying to loosen the knots, which she did by increments so small as to be almost unnoticeable during any given hour.

By dawn, she was exhausted from her efforts. Her wrists were raw and bloody, and they burned. She had, however, loosened the ropes enough to make her hopeful that, if the snoring Gerta, and Daddy, also snoring in the second story, would keep on snoring for another hour, she might be able to free herself and make her escape. She doubted she could make it through the barrier of toughnuts on patrol around the ranch, whom she'd heard milling in the yard from time to time all night, but she had no choice but to try.

Hattie Friendly was not one to give up, even when the odds were piled high against her.

She gave a rare curse, however, when, about a half hour later, Daddy stopped snoring in the room above her. The old man grunted and mumbled to himself. Hattie heard the creaking of a bed and the chirp of a floorboard as the old man rose and then the pounding as he stomped into his boots.

Gerta heard the pounding in the ceiling and snapped her own head up with a loud, "*Wha . . . ?*" She jerked up her rifle, squeezing it in her hands and glaring suspiciously across the table at Hattie. "Wha . . . what are you up to, little girl?"

Daddy came thundering down the stairs. "Horses . . ."

"What's goin' on, Daddy?" Gerta asked, looking around anxiously.

Hattie looked around, too, as she heard hooves thudding and men shouting.

"Sounds like we're under attack!" Daddy gained the bottom of the stairs and pulled an old-model Winchester rifle off two pegs in the kitchen's front wall, then, pumping a round into the breech, walked over to the window to the right of the door. Gerta rose and hurried to the window and stood gazing out into the yard with her father.

Beyond them, Hattie saw several horses just then ride into the yard, galloping around from behind the house, on the right side. Hattie couldn't tell how many horses there were—maybe a half-dozen or so. None appeared to be carrying riders.

No. That wasn't right, she saw as she turned her head this way and that to see around Daddy and Gerta standing in the window before her. The horses were carrying riders, all right. Only the riders were tied belly down across their saddles. They were wrapped in yellow oilskins that only partly concealed them. Their heads and arms flopped down the near sides of the saddles, fingers nearly brushing the ground.

The yellow rain slickers were thickly spotted with blood. In fact, some looked more red than yellow.

"What do you think, Daddy?" Gerta asked softly.

"I think . . . I think that don't look too good, honey." Daddy placed a comforting hand on Gerta's broad back and said, "You stay here with our hostage. I'm gonna go out and see what in God's name is goin' on."

"Be careful, Daddy," Gerta urged as the old man opened the door, stepped out onto the porch, and drew the door closed behind him.

Staring out into the yard, where the seven horses had stopped near the front of the house, the Spanish Bit men milling around them cautiously, talking anxiously amongst themselves, Gerta turned her head to cast Hattie a threatening glare over her shoulder.

When she turned her head back toward the window, Hattie let a satisfied little half-smile tug at her mouth.

Hattie saw Daddy step over to the porch rail and stare down into the yard at the horses and the dead men tied across their saddles. The Spanish Bit outlaws had formed a ragged semicircle to one side of the horses. Holding his rifle in front of him, high across his chest, Daddy told one of the men to stop standing around ogling the dead men and to check them out.

One of the men—a big, fat-bellied man with long, curly red hair and a thick, curly red beard—stepped up to a chestnut horse. With his gloved left hand, he drew up the head of the dead man before him, by its hair, and crouched to stare into the slack-jawed face.

Hattie saw two open eyes staring in death at the red-bearded man.

The red-bearded man turned to Daddy and said, "Cobb."

Daddy cursed.

The red-bearded man walked over to another dead man, drew the man's head up by its hair and said, "Henshaw."

Again, Daddy cursed.

The red-bearded man walked over to the next dead man and pulled the man's head up by its long, silver-blond hair. The red-bearded man froze as the man whose head he'd just pulled up formed an angry scowl and said, "Ow—stop pullin' my hair, you heedless son of a three-legged coot!"

Hattie's eyes widened in shock as she saw the dead man pull a short but savage-looking shotgun down from his right shoulder, from beneath the rain slicker, and shove it toward the red-bearded man's man fat belly. The red-bearded man only stared down at the double-bore cannon in hang-jawed shock, apparently unable, as was Hattie, to wrap his mind around a dead man wielding a shotgun.

The shotgun roared like near thunder, and the fat, red-bearded man went flying straight back into two other men as though he'd been lassoed from behind. Then Hattie's mind went blank from shock for a second or two—a second or two during which all hell broke loose.

CHAPTER 38

Ten minutes earlier, Slash had removed his hat and edged a look around the side of a lumber pile, ancient and moldering, toward the back of the Spanish Bit barn.

A man stood out there smoking a cigarette. He was a little hard to see, as it wasn't quite dawn, but a little light was filtering into the valley now—enough to temper the darkness so Slash could see with some detail a few feet around him. He could smell the smoke from the man's cigarette.

The smell made Slash want one, though of course he wouldn't be taking the time to hammer another nail in his coffin anytime soon. He had some big fish to fry, many a man to kill . . .

The man keeping watch was maybe ten feet from Slash, who hadn't expected him to be out there. He'd figured on only one man being in the barn, manning the Gatling gun in the loft, but he'd been wrong. The man in the loft had been smart enough to post a man outside the rear of the barn to watch his flank.

Last night, during their long, wet night together in the saloon up at the mine compound, Lisa had filled Slash and Pecos in on what she knew about the Spanish Bit headquarters, where Hattie was being held. If they hadn't killed her by now, that was. Slash didn't think they had. They'd assume she wasn't the only one on their trail, and they'd want to use her for leverage.

What Lisa had told Slash and Pecos about had included the Gatling gun. She'd spied it both times she'd ridden down as close to the ranch as she'd dared come and risk being seen. Knowing now what she knew about the ranch and the mine—that they were both merely cover for a very lucrative gold-stealing operation—she was sure the outlaws had the machine gun manned in the loft all the time.

It was damn sure being manned now, Slash thought, or this man wouldn't be out here. The killers sensed trouble was coming. They'd *know* trouble was coming in a few minutes, when the horses hauling the seven dead men would gallop into the yard.

Slash and Pecos had captured the dead men's horses last night. Very early this morning, they'd tied the dead men over their saddles, wrapped in their rain slickers. They'd tied all the dead men over the horses except one. Pecos had taken that man's place. At this very moment, Pecos and Lisa were likely driving the horses down from the mountain toward the ranch.

Again, Slash edged a glance around the lumber pile. The man was still out there, smoking a quirley and humming to himself a little nervously. He was tall and thin, with long, brown hair under a shabby black opera hat. He wore spectacles with one dark lens, likely a bum eye. A Henry rifle rested on his right shoulder. He was smoking the quirley and sort of prancing around just outside the half-open barn door, nervous and chilly and tired after the long, cold night's vigil trying to stay awake.

Slash knew how the man felt. He himself had it worse.

After circling around to the north of the ranch, he'd tied his horse in a shallow wash and crawled practically half a mile to the lumber pile here on the ranch yard's north edge. The ground was frosty and damp, so he himself was frosty and damp; he resisted the urge to shiver.

Slash regarded the smoking picket once more, sizing up the situation. His hand strayed to the big bowie knife sheathed on the right side of his cartridge belt. Time to see if his aim was as good as it used to be. Back in his younger days, he'd obsessively practiced throwing the big knife, killing time in outlaw camp or just needing something to do between jobs, between carouses and parlor girls.

Now, however, having become a respectable businessman, he hadn't practiced with the bowie in some time.

He saw no other plan here than the bowie, however. He needed to dispatch the picket as quietly as possible. He was about to find out how rusty he was . . .

Slash slid the knife from its sheath. He looked at the smoking picket again. The man had just turned to press his back against the barn wall as he stared straight out from the barn to the north. The track of his gaze was maybe fifteen feet to Slash's right. Slash needed him to turn directly at Slash, to help ensure a sound bowie strike.

Gripping the bowie in his gloved right hand, Slash gave a low whistle.

Frowning, the man pushed away from the barn and turned toward Slash, letting the quirley drop from between his fingers and bringing the Henry down from his shoulder. Slash flung the bowie from behind his own right shoulder, watched it turn end over end in the air, forming an arc. As it began its descent, it turned end over end once more before the pointed tip embedded itself with a crunching thud in the picket's upper right chest.

A miss! Slash had been aiming for the heart!

He'd likely only punctured the man's lung . . .

The man stumbled backward against the barn with a heavy

thud. He dropped the rifle and grunted and flung his left hand toward the bowie's handle. At the same time, he looked around with pain-bright eyes. He saw Slash running toward him.

Sliding down the barn wall, he opened his mouth to yell but only loosed a gurgling grunt before Slash silenced him forever with a decisive blow from his Winchester's brass-plated butt.

Slash watched the man sag to the ground and roll onto a shoulder, eyes rolling back in his head. Slash drew a breath, held it, looking around, half-expecting someone to have heard the commotion and come running.

"Hey, Bishop," a man called from somewhere above Slash, from inside the barn, "what the hell you doin' down there? Rasslin' a rabid barn cat?"

Slash's heart thudded. He could feel the throb in his temples. Had he just gotten himself killed—and likely his partner, not to mention Lisa Ingram and Hattie Friendly?

"Hey, get your butt up here, will you?" said the man in the barn loft. "I gotta pee like a Prussian plow horse!"

"Okay, okay!" Slash said, brushing a fist across his mouth to disguise his voice.

He reached down to wrap his right hand around the bowie's handle. He placed his left foot against the man's arm and pulled the blade free with a wet sucking, grinding sound.

"Hurry up, dammit—quit playin' with yourself down there!"

"Comin'!" Slash gave the bowie's blade a cursory cleaning on his victim's coat. Sheathing the knife, he stepped into the barn and peered around, frowning into the heavy shadows.

Where was the ladder to the loft?

He looked around quickly, striding down the barn's main alley, breathless with anxiety.

"What the hell are you doin', Bishop?" yelled the man in the loft. "I told you, I'm about to bust my seams up here!"

Rungs, rungs. Slash was looking for wooden ladder rungs . . .

There!

Quickly, he ran to the outside wall. He climbed quickly with one hand, holding his rifle in his other hand. He poked his head above the loft floor and peered toward the front of the loft. The Gatling gunner was perched on a milking stool before the Gatling gun, the brass canister aimed down into the yard through the open loft doors.

The gunner twisted around to look back toward Slash. "Jesus—about time!" He rose from the stool, pulled his pants up higher on his lean hips.

He was in the late twenties, with a thick shock of sandy blond hair curving down over his left eyebrow. He also wore a heavy, quilted elk-hide coat against the chill. Doffing his hat and brushing a hand quickly back through his hair, he began walking toward Slash across the loft. The only hay up here was some musty, leftover old stuff strewn across the floor.

Slash was still on the ladder, his hips level with the loft floor. He set his rifle on the floor to his right and quickly slid the bowie from its sheath.

The man walking toward him stopped abruptly.

He blinked. Slash could barely see his face in the loft's darkness. The man was silhouetted against the two, big open doors that were filled with the milky light of the fast-approaching dawn. Outside, birds were chirping.

Hooves thudded—a handful of horses coming fast.

The man had heard the horses right after he'd seen that the man in the loft with him was not who he'd thought he was. He turned his head to his left, listening as the horses entered the yard and set the Spanish Bit men to yelling exclamations.

He whipped his head back toward Slash, his right hand reaching for the revolver holstered on his right hip, on the outside of his coat. Slash threw the bowie. It flashed in the pearl light as it tumbled through the air.

Whoo-whoo-whoo-whoo . . .

The point of the blade hit its intended target with a resolute thump.

The man stopped abruptly and looked down at the bowie's hide-wrapped handle protruding from his chest. "Oh," he said on a heavy sigh.

Outside the horses had stopped. That meant that Pecos was going to need Slash at the Gatling gun within a minute . . .

Slash stood facing the Gatling gunner, who swiped his hand toward the revolver once more. Missing it, he reached for it again. This time he wrapped his hand around the gun's walnut grips.

"No, no, no, no," Slash said, heart racing. Keeping his voice low, he said, "You're dead. *Fall!*"

He started to bring his rifle up but knew he couldn't use it without alerting the men in the yard, now likely circling the horses and Pecos, that something was up.

Slash cursed and strode quickly to the man with the knife in his chest. The man was slowly sliding his revolver from its holster. Slash couldn't believe what he was seeing. The man before him, fifteen feet away, had a foot-length blade in his chest, likely in his heart, and he was still trying with what appeared some success to draw his revolver!

Slash stopped before the man, just as the man's shaking hand and shaking gun cleared leather. Slash grabbed the gun, over the man's own hand. Slash couldn't believe the strength remaining in the shaking hand. The man himself grimaced at Slash, gurgling between his lips, from which blood was dribbling down from both mouth corners. He fumbled for Slash with his other hand but was having trouble keeping it raised.

"For cryin' in the queen's ale, bucko," Slash said through gritted teeth, trying to wrestle the pistol out of the man's hand, "you're dead!"

Finally, the gun came free. Slash tossed it away and started to raise his rifle to bean the Gatling gunner with the Winchester's butt, but then the man leaned toward him. Gritting his teeth, he wrapped his hands around Slash's neck, grinding his thumbs into Slash's throat. His eyes were flat, and his face was already going pale—Slash could see that in the growing dawn light filtering into the loft—but he still had a hell of a death grip!

Slash hadn't been prepared for the attack from a dead man. Or a man nearly dead, anyway. He stumbled backward, tripped over his spurs, and fell to the loft floor on his back.

His half-dead assailant fell on top of him, blood still oozing from his mouth and dribbling up around the blade in his chest. He ground his thumbs once more into Slash's throat. Unable to work the man's hands free of his neck, Slash wrapped his hands around the blade handle painfully grinding into his own chest, just beneath his breastbone.

Gritting his teeth, he twisted the handle and thus the knife embedded in his assailant's chest.

The man's grip loosened. His head jerked, his eyes widened in horror as he stared straight down into Slash's own eyes. Slash twisted the blade again, working it around, hearing the soft grinding in the man's own brisket as the razor-edged steel shredded the man's ticker.

"Oh," the man said through a weary groan, whispering. "Oh . . . oh . . . oh . . ."

The light faded from his eyes. His hands fell to both sides of Slash's neck. His head sagged toward Slash's head. Keeping his hands on the bowie's handle, Slash pushed the man over to one side and onto his back.

"Damn," Slash said, breathless, heavily gaining his feet. "Doesn't *anything* ever go as planned?"

Outside, voices sounded. They seemed louder now.

Slash's heart hiccupped.

Pecos!

He ran over to the Gatling gun and stared over the canister

into the yard just as one of the men gathered around the dead men's horses blew straight back off his feet, taking two other men to the ground with him. The first, cannon-like blast was followed quickly by a second blast. Another man was hurled up and back with a shrill cry, slamming another man to the ground before he himself hit the ground and rolled wildly, ass over teakettle.

As all seven of the horses gathered down there began leaping wildly, as did the men around the horses, jerking back in shock, then whipping up their guns, Slash saw one of the "bodies" drop from a bucking horse. Pecos hit the ground and rolled, his sawed-off, double-barrel shotgun gripped in his left hand, while his right hand grabbed for the big Russian thonged low on his right thigh.

Slash swiveled the Gatling's barrel, taking aim at the men congregated in the yard below, and wrapped his right hand around the wooden handle of the crank.

He shouted, "Get your head down, Pecos, you big ugly galoot!"

Slash turned the crank, and the Gatling gun began caterwauling, spewing flames and fire.

CHAPTER 39

The echo of Pecos's second twelve-gauge blast hadn't stopped rocketing around the ranch yard, and the second man nearly cut in two by the double-ought hadn't stopped rolling on the ground, before Pecos kicked himself free of his horse's back as well as the yellow rain slicker he'd shrouded himself in.

He hit the ground and rolled, feeling a lightning bolt of pain in his shoulder. Dropping his shotgun, he clawed his Russian from the holster on his right thigh. He looked up through the dust wafting around him, noting with a rippling chill that one of the hooves of the horse he'd just kicked free of missed smashing to pulp his left temple by the width of a cat's whisker.

With another chill, he saw several rifles being leveled on him by the yelling, wide-eyed Spanish Bit men around him.

One snapped off a shot, which, since the shooter himself was moving and Pecos was also still moving, missed its target by a good foot, pluming dirt to Pecos's left. At the same time that Pecos brought up the cocked Russian and shot the shooter just above the man's square, brass cartridge belt, Pecos heard a familiar voice shout something, though the only words he could make out above the cacophony around him were "big ga-loot!"

Grinding his molars in anger but knowing what was coming, he threw himself belly down to the ground and hooked his right arm over his head, while the left one, on fire with pain, hung limp at his side.

The signature *rat-tat-tat* belching of a Gatling gun filled the air, drowning out all the other sounds—the men's shouts and the fleeing horses' screams—and made the ground beneath Pecos shudder like a giant beast trembling fearfully. Around him, the men's shouts turned to screams, and he felt warm, wet liquid splash him as Slash and the Gatling gun went to work, giving the savage, murdering gold robbers a taste of their own medicine . . .

Giving them no time to pray.

Inside the cabin, Gerta stared in silent shock out the window to the right of the door, as the second blast resounded outside and a second man went hurtling back off his feet, blood flying in all directions around him.

Still sitting in the hide-bottom chair at the table, Hattie stared in silent shock, as well, vaguely aware of her lower jaw dropping as she saw the "dead man," who'd just killed two of the gold robbers and knocked at least three more to the ground, tumble off the side of his suddenly pitching horse and roll. His head came up, long silver-blond hair flying, to show the flushed face of the Pecos River Kid.

At the same time, a thundering clatter rose from somewhere on the north side of the ranch yard. The horses galloped away in all directions, leaving the men who'd been standing around them open to the 45-caliber bullets being sprayed by what could only be a Gatling gun—for Hattie would remember the distinctive caterwauling roar of such a weapon on her deathbed.

Gerta gasped, her thickly rounded shoulders drawing back

as her lungs filled with air. Hattie gasped, as well, as she stared out from behind Gerta and the Spanish Bit men performing a bizarre death dance, each man dancing to the beat of the 45-caliber rounds plunging into him, ripping and tearing, causing blood to spew and the men's screams to rise above even the thunderous roar of the savage machine gun.

"Daddy!" Gerta cried as her father, who'd gone running down the porch steps into the yard, raising his rifle to return fire, was punched sideways and down as at least one bullet tore into him.

"Daddy!" Gerta cried again, louder, pounding the palms of her hands against the window.

Seething, her fleshy face mottled red and white, she turned toward where she'd leaned her rifle against a post. She pumped a cartridge into the Spencer's action and started toward the door.

Hattie leaped up out of her chair. Over the past several minutes, she'd made more progress on the ropes binding her wrists. She'd gotten six or seven inches of slack between them. Now she launched herself off her bound feet at Gerta. She looped her wrists over Gerta's head and drew the seven-inch length of rope back against the woman's fat neck. With her ankles still being bound, she couldn't find much purchase for her feet.

She fell backward against the table and brought Gerta back with her, pulling back harder and harder against the woman's throat.

Gerta strangled and fought, dropping the Spencer to the floor. Spitting and snarling like a trapped wildcat, she flung her hands up toward Hattie's wrists. Hattie drew them back even farther, feeling the rope, slick with the blood from her own cut wrists, slice into Gerta's neck. Hattie leaned farther back over the table, gritting her teeth, her heart racing as she continued to choke the life out of Gerta's soft, fleshy body.

Gerta gave up on trying to loosen Hattie's grip and began

flailing her fists toward Hattie's head, trying to punch her. Hattie leaned far back against the table, drawing farther and farther back on the rope, just out of Gerta's desperate reach.

Gradually, Gerta stopped punching. Just as gradually, Hattie felt the taut muscles in Gerta's body slacken. For another full minute, as the Gatling gun continued wailing outside but in shorter, intermittent bursts, Gerta continued making strangling sounds. Then the sounds died, her hands dropped to her sides, and her big body fell slack against Hattie.

Hattie removed her bound wrists from around Gerta's neck.

Gerta sagged to the floor at Hattie's feet.

The cabin door flew open. Hattie looked in horror at Daddy stumbling through the doorway, his chest matted in blood, holding his old Winchester rifle low in his right hand. He stopped when he saw his daughter piled up on the floor.

"No!" Daddy cried, staring down in bright-eyed shock at the dead Gerta. He raised his enraged gaze to Hattie and yelled again, "*Noooo!*"

At the same time, straightening, he raised the rifle in his hands. He cocked a round into the action and aimed down the barrel at Hattie's head. Hattie turned away from the certain bullet. She squeezed her eyes closed.

The rifle belched loudly, the report rocketing around inside the kitchen.

Hattie jerked with a start. She opened her eyes, frowning, wondering why she didn't feel anything except her heart racing like a bronco stallion in her chest.

Daddy stood before her, blinking rapidly, the rifle sagging in his arms. The front of his head had been blown out by a bullet fired from behind him. His knees buckled, and he dropped straight down to the floor to land in a bloody heap next to his daughter.

Just beyond where he'd been standing, out on the porch, stood a blue-eyed young blond woman dressed in men's range clothes, including a tan Stetson and batwing chaps that fit snug against her slender but rounded hips. Her face was boyishly tanned but pretty, her eyes cold and unyielding.

She held a smoking Bisley revolver straight out in her right hand, gray smoke curling from the barrel. A five-pointed silver star winked on the left breast of her wool plaid coat. She looked half wild.

Slowly, she lowered the pistol.

It was then that Hattie realized that the Gatling gun had fallen silent. Beyond the blonde with the silver star, the Spanish Bit men lay in bloody heaps around where the seven horses had been standing less than two minutes ago.

The blonde stared at Hattie. Hattie stared uncertainly back at her.

The blonde looked Hattie up and down, then curled one half of her upper lip in sneering disdain. She turned around and stepped back out onto the porch. In the yard beyond her, the Pecos River Kid lay amongst the dead Spanish Bit riders. He was howling like a wounded coyote.

Quickly, Hattie slipped a knife from a sheath on Daddy's belt and crouched to saw through the ropes binding her ankles. When she'd sawed through the rope still binding her wrists, she ran outside to where the pretty blonde stood crouching over the Pecos River Kid, who flopped against the ground like a landed fish.

"Pecos, what is it?" Hattie cried, dropping to a knee beside the man. "Are you *hit*?"

Before Pecos could respond, Slash came running out of the barn, holding his hat in one hand, his rifle in the other hand. "What happened, partner?" he shouted, running faster. "Did I hit you? I told you to keep your head down, ya big fool!"

Slash stopped near Pecos, breathless. Leaning forward, hands on his knees to catch his breath, he said, "Where ya hit? You're a bloody mess, partner!"

Pecos was writhing, holding his left arm down by his side, like an injured wing. "My sh-sh-*shoulder!*"

"What?" Slash said, dropping to a knee to regard the man's shoulder.

"Dis . . . dislocated the cussed thing when . . . when I d-dropped from the hoss!"

Slash stared curiously down at his partner's arm. It was one of the few parts of the big man's body that *wasn't* bloody.

"I ain't hit!" Pecos bellowed. "My shoulder, fer godsakes! It came out of its cussed socket!"

Slash saw the bulge in the big man's left shoulder, just behind the seam in his coat. He waved to Lisa and Hattie. "Step back, ladies. Time for Doctor Slash to go to work." He grabbed Pecos's hand.

"No, no, you don't, you devil!" Pecos bellowed.

"Stop your cussed caterwauling!"

"Leave me be! Oh, god, it hurts!"

"Oh, come on." Slash took a firm hold of Pecos's left hand and placed his right boot on the man's side. "You're makin' a damn fool out of yourself in front of these ladies. I'm right ashamed of you, you big *Nancy-boy!*"

"Don't you *daaarrrre!*"

Before Pecos had gotten "dare" out of his mouth, Slash gave Pecos's hand a hard tug.

There was a grinding, crunching sound as the bone slid back into its socket.

Pecos jerked as though he'd been struck by lightning. He opened his mouth, drew a breath, and flopped back against the ground, where he lay staring intently up at the sky, round-eyed, as though he were watching something both horrible and amazing. He moved his legs a little, but he'd otherwise stopped writhing.

Slash stood over him, frowning down at his partner's face.

"I do believe I ain't never seen a man turn so completely white."

Something plunked into the ground just off Slash's right boot, between him and where Hattie stood, staring down in concern at the big cutthroat. A rifle's sharp crack reached Slash's ears a half-second later, echoing. Both Hattie and Lisa wheeled, gasping.

Slash reached for the rifle he'd handed to Hattie, but a man's voice kept him from raising it. "Don't do it, Slash!"

Slash stared toward where a man was just then riding out from behind the house. It was Red Ingram, coming around the house's southern front corner. Ingram rode a big dun and was trailing two beefy pack mules. Cream tarpaulins were wrapped around whatever the mules were carrying on their wooden pack frames.

Slash had a pretty good idea what they were carrying, all right . . .

"Pa!" Lisa yelled. She'd started to pull her Bisley; now she left it in its holster, on her right thigh, but kept her hand around the handle. "I don't . . . I don't understand."

"Drop the rifle, Slash!" Red ordered.

"Pa!" Lisa yelled. "What . . . what . . . ?"

"Fetch your horse, daughter."

"*What? Why . . . ?*"

"He's got the gold," Slash said.

Pecos was sitting up now, leaning back on one elbow. He was still a little green around the gills, but he was more concerned about Red Ingram now than he was about his shoulder. "Red . . ." Pecos shook his head slowly. "Red . . . what the hell . . . ?"

"Shut up, Pecos. Slash, throw down that rifle." Ingram looked at his daughter, flushing with impatience. "Fetch your hoss! We're ridin' out of here!"

"The leg must be feelin' better," Slash taunted him. "Leastways, it ain't so hard to climb into the saddle with a busted knee when you've got a coupla hundred thousand dollars in pure gold to fetch."

Lisa looked at the mules. Her eyes returned to her father. "Is . . . is that the gold on them mules, Pa?"

"Yep." Ingram's voice was grim. He kept his eyes on Slash and Pecos. "It's the gold, all right."

"You were workin' for Greenleaf, weren't you?" Slash kept his own hard gaze on Ingram, keeping his rifle in his hand. "You let him know when folks came around, asking about the gold mine . . . the ranch. The *ghost mine* and the *ghost ranch*. You helped him keep the secret, helped him spread the word around town that no one better get too curious about why no miners ever showed up in Honeysuckle. Only ranch hands. Still, gold went out every couple of months. Without any miners or any other sign of mining. You kept the secret. Greenleaf must have been payin' you for that. You'd have been in the best position of anyone in town."

"Yeah . . . yeah," Lisa said, catching on. "Just riders coming through Honeysuckle now and then. Riders with pack mules . . . just like those you're leadin', Pa." Her gold-blond brows beetled over her probing blue eyes. "You were workin' for Greenleaf and his daughter . . . keepin' his secrets, keepin' anyone from riding out to the ranch or the mine to look around. That's why you forbid me from ridin' out here, forbid me from askin' questions about it."

"I was only tryin' to keep you alive, daughter."

"Pa . . . Pa . . ." Lisa still couldn't wrap her mind around it. "Were you takin' *blood money? You?*"

"Why the hell not? I'm an old man. I have a daughter to finish raisin'. The town's all but dead. Where am I gonna get another job after the city council gives me my time an' sends me on my way? I still got a daughter to raise. Look at you,

Lisa. You're as wild as the coyotes! I need to get you out of here. Take you somewhere civilized. Finish raisin' you up.

"You're a beautiful girl. You need better manners. You need to dress nice. Like a woman, not a *man*! You need a good husband. You ain't gonna find none o' that out here. Now!" Ingram glanced at the mules behind him and smiled giddily. "Now . . . hell, we can go to San Francisco an' live high on the hog!"

"Pa, you've gone mad. I'm not goin' anywhere with you an' that gold. How did you get it anyway? How did you know . . . ?"

"I rode out lookin' for you. Got worried about you when you never showed up back in town yesterday. I rode to the mine. Figured you'd followed these two old rapscallions . . . out to the mine . . ."

"You knew we'd head out here." Pecos was grinning shrewdly at the man. "That's why you turned us loose. You opened that cell door so we could ride out here, an' then Greenleaf's men would take care of us . . ." He cut a quick, conferring glance at Slash.

Ingram chuckled. "That's right, Pecos. That's right. I figured I wouldn't have to kill you. Greenleaf would do that. But now . . ." He glanced around at all the dead men lying around them. "Now . . . I reckon I do." He returned his gaze to his daughter. "I found the dead men up on the mountain. I found the gold. Near made my ticker stop, seein' all that color sittin' right there, just inside the cave, no lock on the door. Free an' easy! Ripe for the takin'! So I hurried back to town. Fetched them mules back to the mine, an' . . ."

"So, you weren't too worried about your daughter, then, were you, Red?" Slash accused him sourly.

"Lisa can take care o' herself," Ingram barked. "I knew that! It's for her I went to the trouble. So . . . I wrestled the gold onto them mules . . . me an' my bad knee . . . first the empty boxes . . . then one ingot at a time."

"How'd you know we'd take care of Greenleaf?" Slash asked.

"Oh, I never figured you would. I figured you'd distract him long enough for me to get the gold and hide it till I could find Lisa and high-tail it out of these mountains."

Slash gave a dubious snort. "We did you a hell of a favor."

Red looked around at the dead men, grinning. "Thanks, fellas."

"You had a long night," Pecos observed.

"Shut up, Pecos! Stop lookin' at me like I'm crazy!"

"You're crazy, all right, Pa," Lisa said sadly, slowly shaking her head. "You're crazier'n a tree full of owls . . . if you think I'm gonna help you steal that gold. If you think I'm gonna take part in any of your crazy plan."

She stared at her father in disbelief. "Do you really think I'm gonna stand by and let you kill Slash an' Pecos"—she cut a quick, fleeting glance at Hattie—"an' her, even . . . and then just climb up on my horse and ride out of here with you and your blood money? You really think we're gonna live happily ever after . . . in San Francisco . . . *together*? On *stolen blood money, Pa*!"

Ingram studied her, his own brows furled curiously, his eyes nearly hidden below them, behind his rectangular, gold-framed spectacles that glittered now as the sun swept up and over the eastern ridge where the mine lay. The morning light washed into the valley like liquid gold.

Songbirds piped, oblivious to the carnage here, the sadness.

"Daughter . . . daughter," Ingram said, his voice thick and breaking subtly, "I . . . I did this for *you*! I want you to have a better life, see? I want us *both* to have a better life, Lisa!"

Lisa just stared at him, her face pale beneath her tan. "Pa . . . ," she said, "oh, Pa . . ."

Slowly, she moved toward him.

Ingram looked at Slash. He looked at Hattie, and then he

switched his gaze to Pecos. Tears washed over his eyes, behind his glasses. They began to roll down his cheeks.

He loosed a phlegmy sob as he lowered his gaze to his saddle horn. "Lisa, dammit, we never had a damn thing!" He pounded the horn with his fist. "All I done all my life ... leastways, fer most of it ... was chase outlaws for pennies and pisswater! They always had the good life, those cutthroats, did!"

He cast a quick, accusing glance at Slash and Pecos.

"Me ... *us*," Red continued, "we always lived in hovels, scrambling to make a livin'. Look at the kind of life I've given my purty daughter! She runs around these mountains with a gun on her leg and her hair uncombed, like a child raised by wolves!"

"Pa ..." Lisa stopped beside Ingram's horse, on the left side, and extended her hands to her father. "All I ever wanted was a good, peaceable life with you, Pa. Livin' life the right way ... with you ... a lawman I was proud of. That's all I wanted. That's all I still want."

Red lifted his chin and bellowed out a sob. "Ah, *hell*!" He drew a breath, then leaned forward, swung his right leg over his horse's rear. As he stepped down to the ground, his left knee buckled, and he flopped down on his butt.

Lisa fell to a knee beside him. "Pa! Oh, Pa!"

Slash stepped forward to help, but Pecos, still on the ground, grabbed his right pant leg and shook his head. Slash looked at Red and Lisa. They were huddled together now, Lisa's arm around the old man's neck. They were sobbing quietly together. They didn't need any help right now from Slash or anyone else.

"I'm sorry, darlin'," Red said through his tears. "I'm truly sorry. What a damn fool I am!"

"It's okay, Pa," Lisa said. "We'll make it right. We'll make everything right!"

Slash had a feeling they would, at that.

He turned to Hattie, who stood gazing sadly down at the old lawman and his daughter/deputy. "How are you doin', darlin'?" Slash took Hattie's hands in his own, looked at her skinned and bloody wrists, and sucked a sharp breath.

"I'm fine. A little sore is all."

Slash glanced behind her, saw the two bodies piled up in the house, just inside the front door. "Oh, jeepers," he said, looking down at her again with concern.

"I'm fine, Slash." Hattie cut her gaze between them, her eyes welling with tears of relief. "I sure am glad to see you two old cutthroats, though—I'll tell you that!"

Pecos whistled his surprise. "Who'da thought?"

Hattie kissed Slash right square on the mouth, then wrapped her arms around his waist and pressed her left cheek taut against his chest. Flushing, Slash glanced at Pecos, who arched an ironic brow at him.

Slash shrugged, flushing, then pressed his cheek to the head of the girl in his arms.

EPILOGUE

"Don't really hurt all that bad," Pecos said, three weeks later as they rode into Fort Collins aboard their big Pittsburg freighter.

The wagon clattered emptily behind the two mules the ex-cutthroats had found not far from where they'd left the wagon east of Tin Cup. The mules had gotten a little wild over the month they'd been on their own in the Sawatch Range, so it had taken Slash and Pecos a while to run them down. Once they had, the rangy beasts had taken quickly again to the hames and harnesses, the straps and buckles, not to mention to their feed sacks filled with parched corn.

"What don't hurt that bad?" Slash asked, rocking with the freighter's pitch and sway. "Your shoulder?"

"No, my heart. It don't really hurt all that bad—you know, from turnin' all that gold over to ole Bleed-Em-So at Union Station."

"Oh, that. Well . . ."

Pecos glanced at Slash sitting beside him in the driver's seat, steering the team through the town's midday traffic under a glaring Colorado sun. "Does yours?"

Slash snorted a caustic laugh. "To tell you the truth, I got one hell of a chill, watchin' them Pinkertons and Wells Fargo detectives load that gold into the express car. I was as cold as a Dakota winter, but I was sweatin' like a butcher in the dog days of a Missouri summer!"

They'd taken their leave of Miss Hattie Friendly in Denver, as well. But, with them doing what they did for the chief marshal, and Hattie working for the Denver Pinkertons, they had a feeling they'd see the lovely young Pink again soon.

"Yeah," Pecos allowed, shrugging a guilty shoulder and turning his head forward to stare over the mules' twitching ears. "I gotta admit—I did feel so sick there for a few minutes, I thought I was gonna lose my lunch."

He laughed and spat over the side of the wagon.

"You know what was worth it, though?"

"What's that?"

"The look on ole Bleed-Em-So's face when he seen us ride up to Union Station with both them strongboxes in the bed of our wagon. He turned as white as you did after I jerked your shoulder back in place."

Pecos laughed again. "You know—I really do think he was halfways hopin' we'd cut an' run with it!"

"That old devil is just waitin' for us to mess up on one of his jobs, so he can either turn the key on us once an' for all or kick us out with a cold shovel."

"Or hang us."

"Throw us our own necktie party."

"He can't stand it that we're walkin' the straight an' narrow!"

They had a good laugh over that.

After their laughter had dwindled, Slash glanced at Pecos uneasily, and said, "How long do you think we can hold out?"

Pecos frowned at him. "Huh?"

"You know—how long you think we can keep resisting temptation? He's gonna keep makin' it harder an' harder on us—you know that, don't you? The jobs are gonna keep getting' tougher an' tougher, too. You can bet the ranch on that. One way or another, that old devil is gonna have his revenge."

Pecos raked a thumbnail down his cheek, scowling as he pondered the thought.

But then, as Slash turned the wagon into the freight yard, Pecos thumbed his hat back off his forehead and smiled. "Say, now . . . look at that."

"Look at what?"

"That. *Them.* Lookee there, Slash. I do believe we got us a pair of lovely women waitin' for us. Don't that beat all?"

Slash drew back on the mules' reins, slowing the wagon to a stop. He stared straight ahead toward the freight yard office. Jaycee Breckenridge's sleek chaise buggy sat at an angle before it, her handsome cream gelding standing in the traces.

Jaycee herself sat in a chair on the office's small front porch, beyond the wagon. Beside her sat Myra Thompson. They each held a saucer and a teacup on their laps, but now, seeing Slash and Pecos sitting in the big freight wagon just inside the yard, Myra rose smiling from her chair, taking her cup and saucer in one hand and pointing with the other hand and saying something to Jay.

Yesterday, Slash had sent Myra a telegram from Denver, informing her that they were safe and sound, and that they'd be home by noon the following day. Myra must have told Jay. Now, here both women were—waiting for the two cutthroats on the freight office porch.

Slash stared at Jaycee, still sitting in her chair. Jay's gaze met Slash's. She wore a copper-colored silk and taffeta gown trimmed with white lace. The gown matched the thick tresses of copper red hair tumbling down from a spruce green picture hat trimmed with an ostrich plume. Jay wore long, stylish, spruce green gloves, and she held a beaded reticule on her lap, beside her teacup.

Jay stared across the yard at Slash, her expression serious, vaguely curious, as though, even from this distance, she was trying to plumb the man's soul with her eyes.

Slash stared back at her, feeling his heart quicken and his lips shape a slow smile.

Jay smiled, then, too, and rose from her chair.

Myra set her teacup and saucer down on the porch rail and came down the steps, holding the hem of her wool skirt above her black, high-heeled boots. She stepped out around Jay's horse and stopped, staring toward Slash and Pecos, shading her eyes from the noon sun with her hand.

She beckoned broadly and cocked her head to one side, her own brown-eyed gaze glued to Pecos. "Well?" she called. "What're you two cutthroats waiting for? You have a couple of ladies waiting for you over here!"

Pecos turned to Slash. "Yeah, Slash—what are we old cutthroats waitin' for?"

Slash drew a deep breath, felt his heart flutter a little, nervously. He released the breath slowly. "I don't know about you, partner," he said, "but this devil ain't old. In fact, I feel younger'n I've felt in years!"

Slash shook the ribbons over the mules' backs and rattled on into the yard.